Jeffery Deaver was born outside of Chicago in 1950. After receiving a Bachelor of Journalism degree from the University of Missouri, Deaver worked as a magazine writer, then enrolled at Fordham Law School. After graduation he decided to practice law for a time, and worked for several years as an attorney for a large Wall Street firm.

The author of twenty novels, Deaver has been nominated for four Edgar Awards from the Mystery Writers of America, an Anthony award, and is a three-time recipient of the Ellery Queen Reader's Award for Best Short Story of the Year. In 2001 he won the W. H. Smith Thumping Good Read Award for his Lincoln Rhyme novel *The Empty Chair*, and in 2004 was awarded the Crime Writers Association of Great Britain's Ian Fleming Steel Dagger Award for *Garden Of Beasts*. Translated into 25 languages, his novels have appeared on a number of bestseller lists around the world.

Visit the author's website at:
www.jefferydeaver.com

THE TWELFTH CARD

Geneva Settle is working on her research project into her slave ancestor Charles Singleton when she is suddenly the target of a professional assassin. A man who will kill anyone in his way unless top criminalist Lincoln Rhyme can piece together the deadly puzzle . . . Trapped inside a paralysed body, Rhyme's brilliant mind is channelled through his partner, policewoman Amelia Sachs. Rhyme and Sachs find that the only way to stop the killer is to discover the secret Charles Singleton took to his grave over 140 years ago — a secret that threatens to destroy the future of human rights itself . . .

Books by Jeffery Deaver
Published by The House of Ulverscroft:

THE DEVIL'S TEARDROP
GARDEN OF BEASTS

LINCOLN RHYME SERIES:
THE STONE MONKEY
THE EMPTY CHAIR
THE VANISHED MAN

JEFFERY DEAVER

THE TWELFTH CARD

Complete and Unabridged

CHARNWOOD
Leicester

First published in the
United States of America

First published in Great Britain in 2005 by
Hodder and Stoughton, London

First Charnwood Edition
published 2006
by arrangement with
Hodder and Stoughton
a division of Hodder Headline, London

The moral right of the author has been asserted

British Library CIP Data

Deaver, Jeffery
    The twelfth card.—Large print ed.—
    Charnwood library series
    1. Rhyme, Lincoln (Fictitious character)—Fiction
    2. Sachs, Amelia (Fictitious character)—Fiction
    3. Forensic pathologists—Fiction 4. Quadriplegics
    —Fiction 5. Suspense fiction 6. Large type books
    I. Title
    813.5′4 [F]

    ISBN 1–84617–230–6

Published by
F. A. Thorpe (Publishing)
Anstey, Leicestershire

Set by Words & Graphics Ltd.
Anstey, Leicestershire
Printed and bound in Great Britain by
T. J. International Ltd., Padstow, Cornwall

This book is printed on acid-free paper

To the memory of Christopher Reeve,
a lesson in courage, a symbol of hope.

'Some people are your relatives but others are your ancestors, and you choose the ones you want to have as ancestors. You create yourself out of those values.'

— Ralph Ellison

I

THE THREE-FIFTHS MAN

Tuesday, October 9

1

His face wet with sweat and with tears, the man runs for freedom, he runs for his life.

'There! There he goes!'

The former slave does not know exactly where the voice comes from. Behind him? To the right or left? From atop one of the decrepit tenements lining the filthy cobblestoned streets here?

Amid July air hot and thick as liquid paraffin, the lean man leaps over a pile of horse dung. The street sweepers don't come here, to this part of the city. Charles Singleton pauses beside a pallet stacked high with barrels, trying to catch his breath.

A crack of a pistol. The bullet goes wide. The sharp report of the gun takes him back instantly to the war: the impossible, mad hours as he stood his ground in a dusty blue uniform, steadying a heavy musket, facing men wearing dusty gray, aiming their own weapons his way.

Running faster now. The men fire again. These bullets also miss.

'Somebody stop him! Five dollars' gold if you catch him.'

But the few people out on the streets this early — mostly Irish ragpickers and laborers trooping to work with hods or picks on their shoulders — have no inclination to stop the Negro, who has fierce eyes and large muscles and such frightening determination. As for the reward, the shouted offer came from a city constable, which means there's no coin behind the promise.

At the Twenty-third Street paintworks, Charles veers west. He slips on the slick cobblestones and falls hard. A mounted policeman rounds the corner and, raising his nightstick, bears down on the fallen man. And then —

And? the girl thought.

And?

What happened to him?

Sixteen-year-old Geneva Settle twisted the knob on the microfiche reader again but it would move no farther; she'd come to the last page on this carriage. She lifted out the metal rectangle containing the lead article in the July 23, 1868, edition of *Coloreds' Weekly Illustrated*. Riffling through the other frames in the dusty box, she worried that the remaining pages of the article were missing and she'd never find out what happened to her ancestor Charles Singleton. She'd learned that historical archives regarding black history were often incomplete, if not forever misplaced.

Where was the rest of the story?

Ah . . . Finally she found it and mounted the carriage carefully into the battered gray reader, moving the knob impatiently to locate the continuation of the story of Charles's flight.

Geneva's lush imagination — and years of immersing herself in books — had given her the wherewithal to embellish the bare-bones magazine account of the former slave's pursuit through the hot, foul streets of nineteenth-century New York. She almost felt she was back

4

there, rather than where she really was at the moment: nearly 140 years later in the deserted fifth-floor library of the Museum of African-American Culture and History on Fifty-fifth Street in Midtown Manhattan.

As she twisted the dial, the pages streamed past on the grainy screen. Geneva found the rest of the article, which was headlined:

SHAME

THE ACCOUNT OF A FREEDMAN'S CRIME

CHARLES SINGLETON, A VETERAN OF THE WAR BETWEEN THE STATES, BETRAYS THE CAUSE OF OUR PEOPLE IN A NOTORIOUS INCIDENT

A picture accompanying the article showed twenty-eight-year-old Charles Singleton in his Civil War uniform. He was tall, his hands were large and the tight fit of the uniform on his chest and arms suggested powerful muscles. Lips broad, cheekbones high, head round, skin quite dark.

Staring at the unsmiling face, the calm, piercing eyes, the girl believed there was a resemblance between them — she had the head and face of her ancestor, the roundness of his features, the rich shade of his skin. Not a bit of the Singleton physique, though. Geneva Settle was skinny as a grade-school boy, as the Delano Project girls loved to point out.

5

She began to read once more, but a noise intruded.

A click in the room. A door latch? Then she heard footsteps. They paused. Another step. Finally silence. She glanced behind her, saw nobody.

She felt a chill, but told herself not to be freaked. It was just bad memories that put her on edge: the Delano girls whaling on her in the school yard behind Langston Hughes High, and that time Tonya Brown and her crew from the St. Nicholas Houses dragged her into an alley then pounded her so bad that she lost a back tooth. Boys groped, boys dissed, boys put you down. But it was the girls who made you bleed.

Get her down, cut her, cut the bitch . . .

More footsteps. Another pause.

Silence.

The nature of this place didn't help. Dim, musty, quiet. And there was no one else here, not at eight-fifteen on a Tuesday morning. The museum wasn't open yet — tourists were still asleep or having their breakfasts — but the library opened at eight. Geneva had been waiting here when they unlocked the doors, she'd been so eager to read the article. She now sat in a cubicle at the end of a large exhibit hall, where faceless mannequins wore nineteenth-century costumes and the walls were filled with paintings of men in bizarre hats, women in bonnets and horses with wack, skinny legs.

Another footstep. Then another pause.

Should she leave? Go hang with Dr. Barry, the librarian, until this creepy dude left?

6

And then the other visitor laughed.

Not a weird laugh, a fun laugh.

And he said, 'Okay. I'll call you later.'

A snap of a cell phone folding up. *That's* why he'd been pausing, just listening to the person on the other end of the line.

Told you not to worry, girl. People aren't dangerous when they laugh. They aren't dangerous when they say friendly things on cell phones. He'd been walking slowly because that's what people do when they're talking — even though what kind of rude claimer'd make a phone call in a library? Geneva turned back to the microfiche screen, wondering, You get away, Charles? Man, I hope so.

Yet he regained his footing and, rather than own up to his mischief, as a courageous man would do, continued his cowardly flight.

So much for objective reporting, she thought angrily.

For a time he evaded his pursuers. But escape was merely temporary. A Negro tradesman on a porch saw the freedman and implored him to stop, in the name of justice, asserting that he had heard of Mr. Singleton's crime and reproaching him for bringing dishonor upon all colored people throughout the nation. The citizen, one Walker Loakes, thereupon flung a brick at Mr. Singleton with the intent of knocking him down. However,

Charles dodges the heavy stone and turns to the man, shouting, 'I am innocent. I did not do what the police say!'

Geneva's imagination had taken over and,

7

inspired by the text, was writing the story once again.

But Loakes ignores the freedman's protests and runs into the street, calling to the police that the fugitive is headed for the docks.

His heart torn, his thoughts clinging to the image of Violet and their son, Joshua, the former slave continues his desperate run for freedom.

Sprinting, sprinting . . .

Behind him comes the gallop of mounted police. Ahead of him, other horsemen appear, led by a helmeted police officer brandishing a pistol. 'Halt, halt where you are, Charles Singleton! I am Detective Captain William Simms. I've been searching for you for two days.'

The freedman does as ordered. His broad shoulders slump, strong arms at his sides, chest heaving as he sucks in the humid, rancid air beside the Hudson River. Nearby is the tow boat office, and up and down the river he sees the spindles of sailing ship masts, hundreds of them, taunting him with their promise of freedom. He leans, gasping, against the large Swiftsure Express Company sign. Charles stares at the approaching officer as the clop, clop, clop of his horse's hooves resonate loudly on the cobblestones.

'Charles Singleton, you are under arrest for burglary. You will surrender to us or we will subdue you. Either way you will end up in shackles. Pick the first and you will suffer no pain. Pick the second, you will end up bloody. The choice is yours.'

'I have been accused of a crime I did not commit!'

'I repeat: Surrender or die. Those are your only choices.'

'No, sir, I have one other,' Charles shouts. He resumes his flight — toward the dock.

'Stop or we will shoot!' Detective Simms calls.

But the freedman bounds over the railing of the pier like a horse taking a picket in a charge. He seems to hang in the air for a moment then cartwheels thirty feet into the murky waters of the Hudson River, muttering some words, perhaps a plea to Jesus, perhaps a declaration of love for his wife and child, though whatever they might be none of his pursuers can hear.

★   ★   ★

Fifty feet from the microfiche reader forty-one-year-old Thompson Boyd moved closer to the girl.

He pulled the stocking cap over his face, adjusted the eyeholes and opened the cylinder of his pistol to make sure it wasn't jammed. He'd checked it earlier but, in this job, you could never be too certain. He put the gun into his pocket and pulled the billy club out of a slit cut into his dark raincoat.

He was in the stacks of books in the costume exhibit hall, which separated him from the microfiche-reader tables. His latex-gloved fingers pressed his eyes, which had been stinging particularly sharply this morning. He blinked from the pain.

9

He looked around again, making sure the room was in fact deserted.

No guards were here, none downstairs either. No security cameras or sign-in sheets. All good. But there were some logistical problems. The big room was deathly quiet, and Thompson couldn't hide his approach to the girl. She'd know someone was in the room with her and might become edgy and alert.

So after he'd stepped inside this wing of the library and locked the door behind him, he'd laughed, a chuckle. Thompson Boyd had stopped laughing years ago. But he was also a craftsman who understood the power of humor — and how to use it to your advantage in this line of work. A laugh — coupled with a farewell pleasantry and a closing cell phone — would put her at ease, he reckoned.

This ploy seemed to work. He looked quickly around the long row of shelves and saw the girl, staring at the microfiche screen. Her hands, at her sides, seemed to clench and unclench nervously at what she was reading.

He started forward.

Then stopped. The girl was pushing away from the table. He heard her chair slide on the linoleum. She was walking somewhere. Leaving? No. He heard the sound of the drinking fountain and her gulping some water. Then he heard her pulling books off the shelf and stacking them up on the microfiche table. Another pause and she returned to the stacks once again, gathering more books. The thud as she set them down. Finally he heard the screech of her chair as she sat once more. Then silence.

Thompson looked again. She was back in her chair, reading one of the dozen books piled in front of her.

With the bag containing the condoms, razor knife and duct tape in his left hand, the club in his right, he started toward her again.

Coming up behind her now, twenty feet, fifteen, holding his breath.

Ten feet. Even if she bolted now, he could lunge forward and get her — break a knee or stun her with a blow to the head.

Eight feet, five . . .

He paused and silently set the rape pack on a shelf. He took the club in both hands. He stepped closer, lifting the varnished oak rod.

Still absorbed in the words, she read intently, oblivious to the fact that her attacker was an arm's length behind her. Thompson swung the club downward with all his strength toward the top of the girl's stocking cap.

Crack . . .

A painful vibration stung his hands as the baton struck her head with a hollow snap.

But something was wrong. The sound, the feel were off. What was going on?

Thompson Boyd leapt back as the body fell to the floor.

And tumbled into pieces.

The torso of the mannequin fell one way. The head another. Thompson stared for a moment. He glanced to his side and saw a ball gown draped over the bottom half of the same mannequin — part of a display on women's clothing in Reconstruction America.

No . . .

Somehow, she'd tipped to the fact that he was a threat. She'd then collected some books from the shelves as a cover for standing up and taking apart a mannequin. She'd dressed the upper part of it in her own sweatshirt and stocking cap then propped it on the chair.

But where was she?

The slap of racing feet answered the question. Thompson Boyd heard her sprinting for the fire door. The man slipped the billy club into his coat, pulled out his gun and started after her.

2

Geneva Settle was running.

Running to escape. Like her ancestor Charles Singleton.

Gasping. Like Charles.

But she was sure she had none of the dignity her ancestor displayed in his flight from the police 140 years ago. Geneva sobbed and screamed for help and stumbled hard into a wall in the frenzy of panic, scraping the back of her hand.

There she go, there she go, the skinny little boy-girl . . . Get her!

The thought of the elevator terrified her, being trapped. So she chose the fire stairs. Slamming into the door at full speed, she stunned herself, a burst of yellow light in her vision, but the girl kept right on going. She leapt from the landing down to the fourth floor, tugging on the knob. But these were security doors and didn't open from the stairwell. She'd have to use the door on the ground floor.

She continued down the stairs, gasping for breath. Why? What was he after? she wondered.

Skinny little Oreo bitch got no time fo' girls like us . . .

The gun . . . That's what'd made her suspicious. Geneva Settle was no gangsta girl, but you couldn't be a student at Langston Hughes High School in the heart of Harlem without having seen at least a few guns in your life. When she'd heard a distinctive click — very different from the cell phone closing — she wondered if the laughing man was just fronting, here for trouble. So she'd stood casually, gotten a drink of water, ready to bolt. But she'd peeked through the stacks and spotted the ski mask. She realized there was no way to get past him to the door unless she kept him focused on the microfiche table. She'd stacked up some books noisily then stripped a nearby mannequin, dressed it in her hat and sweatshirt and rested it on the chair in front of the microfiche machine. Then she'd waited until he approached and, when he had, she'd slipped around him.

Bust her up, bust the bitch up . . .

Geneva now stumbled down another flight.

The tap of footsteps above her. Jesus Lord, he *was* following! He'd slipped into the stairwell after her and was now only one landing away. Half running, half stumbling, cradling her scraped hand, she raced down the stairs as his footsteps grew closer.

Near the ground floor she leapt four steps to the concrete. Her legs went out from underneath her and she slammed into the rough wall. Wincing at the pain, the teenager climbed to her feet, hearing his footsteps, seeing his shadow on the walls.

Geneva looked at the fire door. She gasped at the chain wrapped around the bar.

No, no, no . . . The chain was illegal, sure. But that didn't mean the people who ran the museum wouldn't use one to keep thieves out.

14

Or maybe this man had wrapped it around the bar himself, thinking she might escape this way. Here she was, trapped in a dim concrete pit. But did it actually seal the door?

Only one way to find out. Go, girl!

Geneva pushed off and crashed into the bar.

The door swung open.

Oh, thank —

Suddenly a huge noise filled her ears, pain searing her soul. She screamed. Had she been shot in the head? But she realized it was the door alarm, wailing as shrilly as Keesh's infant cousins. Then she was in the alley, slamming the door behind her, looking for the best way to go, right, left . . .

Get her down, cut her, cut the bitch . . .

She opted for right and staggered into Fifty-fifth Street, slipping into a crowd of people on their way to work, drawing glances of concern from some, wariness from others. Most ignored the girl with the troubled face. Then, from behind her, she heard the howl of the fire alarm grow louder as her attacker shoved the door open. Would he flee, or come after her?

Geneva ran up the street toward Keesh, who stood on the curb, holding a Greek deli coffee carton and trying to light a cigarette in the wind. Her mocha-skinned classmate — with precise purple makeup and a cascade of blonde extensions — was the same age as Geneva, but a head taller and round and taut as a drum, round where she ought to be, with her big boobs and ghetto hips, and then some. The girl had waited on the street, not having any interest in a

15

museum — or any building, for that matter, with a no-smoking policy.

'Gen!' Her friend tossed the coffee cup into the street and ran forward. 'S'up, girl? You all buggin'.'

'This man . . .' Geneva gasped, felt the nausea churn through her. 'This guy inside, he attacked me.'

'Shit, no!' Lakeesha looked around. 'Where he at?'

'I don't know. He was behind me.'

'Chill, girl. You gonna be okay. Let's get outa here. Come on, run!' The big girl — who cut every other P.E. class and had smoked for two years — started to jog as best she could, gasping, arms bouncing at her sides.

But they got only half a block away before Geneva slowed. Then she stopped. 'Hold up, girl.'

'Whatchu doing, Gen?'

The panic was gone. It'd been replaced by another feeling.

'Come on, girl,' Keesh said, breathless. 'Move yo' ass.'

Geneva Settle, though, had made up her mind. Anger was what had taken the place of her fear. She thought: He's goddamn not getting away with it. She turned around, glanced up and down the street. Finally she saw what she was looking for, near the mouth of the alley she'd just escaped from. She started back in that direction.

★ ★ ★

A block away from the African-American museum Thompson Boyd stopped trotting through the crowd of rush-hour commuters. Thompson was a medium man. In every sense. Medium-shade brown hair, medium weight, medium height, mediumly handsome, mediumly strong. (In prison he'd been known as 'Average Joe.') People tended to see right through him.

But a man running through Midtown draws attention unless he's heading for a bus, cab or train station. And so he slowed to a casual pace. Soon, he was lost in the crowd, nobody paying him any mind.

While the light at Sixth Avenue and Fifty-third remained red, he debated. Thompson made his decision. He slipped off his raincoat and slung it over his arm, making sure, though, that his weapons were accessible. He turned around and started back toward the museum.

Thompson Boyd was a craftsman who did everything by the book, and it might seem that what he was doing now — returning to the scene of an attack that had just gone bad — was not a wise idea, since undoubtedly the police would be there soon.

But he'd learned that it was times like this, with cops everywhere, that people were lulled into carelessness. You could often get much closer to them than you otherwise might. The medium man now strolled casually through the crowds in the direction of the museum, just another commuter, an Average Joe on his way to work.

It's nothing less than a miracle.

Somewhere in the brain or the body a stimulus, either mental or physical, occurs — I want to pick up the glass, I have to drop the pan that's burning my fingers. The stimulus creates a nerve impulse, flowing along the membranes of neurons throughout the body. The impulse isn't, as most people think, electricity itself; it's a wave created when the surface of the neurons shifts briefly from a positive charge to a negative. The strength of this impulse never varies — it either exists or it doesn't — and it's fast, 250 m.p.h.

This impulse arrives at its destination — muscles, glands and organs, which then respond, keeping our hearts beating, our lungs pumping, our bodies dancing, our hands planting flowers and writing love letters and piloting spacecraft.

A miracle.

Unless something goes wrong. Unless you're, say, the head of a crime scene unit, searching a murder scene in a subway construction site, and a beam tumbles onto your neck and shatters it at the fourth cervical vertebra — four bones down from the base of the skull. As happened to Lincoln Rhyme some years ago.

When something like that occurs, then all bets are off.

Even if the blow doesn't sever the spinal cord outright, blood floods the area and pressure builds and crushes or starves the neurons. Compounding the destruction, as the neurons

18

die they release — for some unknown reason — a toxic amino acid, which kills even more. Ultimately, if the patient survives, scar tissue fills the space around the nerves like dirt in a grave — an appropriate metaphor because, unlike neurons in the rest of the body, those in the brain and spinal cord do not regenerate. Once dead, they're numb forever.

After such a 'catastrophic incident,' as the men and women of medicine so delicately put it, some patients — the lucky ones — find that the neurons controlling vital organs like lungs and heart continue to function, and they survive.

Or maybe they're the *unlucky* ones.

Because some would rather their heart stopped cold early on, saving them from the infections and bedsores and contractures and spasms. Saving them too from attacks of autonomic dysreflexia, which can lead to a stroke. Saving them from the eerie, wandering phantom pain, which feels just the same as the genuine article but whose searing aches can't be numbed by aspirin or morphine.

Not to mention an utterly changed life: the physical therapists and the aides and the ventilator and the catheters and the adult diapers, the dependency . . . and the depression, of course.

Some people in these circumstances just give up and seek out death. Suicide is always an option, though not an easy one. (Try killing yourself if all you can move is your head.)

But others fight back.

'Had enough?' the slim young man in slacks,

19

white shirt and a burgundy floral tie asked Rhyme.

'No,' responded his boss in a voice breathless from the exercise. 'I want to keep going.' Rhyme was strapped atop a complicated stationary bicycle, in one of the spare bedrooms on the second floor of his Central Park West town house.

'I think you've done enough,' Thom, his aide, said. 'It's been over an hour. Your heart rate's pretty high.'

'This is like bicycling up the Matterhorn,' Rhyme gasped. 'I'm Lance Armstrong.'

'The Matterhorn's not part of the Tour de France. It's a mountain. You can climb it, but you can't bike it.'

'Thank you for the ESPN trivia, Thom. I wasn't being literal. How far have I gone?'

'Twenty-two miles.'

'Let's do another eighteen.'

'I don't think so. Five.'

'Eight,' Rhyme bargained.

The handsome young aide lifted an acquiescing eyebrow. 'Okay.'

Rhyme had wanted eight anyway. He was elated. He lived to win.

The cycling continued. His muscles powered the bicycle, yes, but there was one huge difference between this activity and how you'd pedal a stationary bike at Gold's Gym. The stimulus that sent the impulse along the neurons came not from Rhyme's brain but from a computer, via electrodes connected to his leg muscles. The device was known as an FES ergometer bike. Functional electrical stimulation uses a computer, wires and electrodes to mimic the nervous system and send tiny jolts of electricity into muscles, making them behave exactly the same as if the brain were in charge.

FES isn't much used for day-to-day activity, like walking or using utensils. Its real benefit is in therapy, improving the health of badly disabled patients.

Rhyme had been inspired to start the exercises because of a man he much admired, the late actor Christopher Reeve, who'd suffered an even more severe trauma than Rhyme's in a horseback-riding accident. Through willpower and unflagging physical effort — and surprising much of the traditional medical community — Reeve had recovered some motor ability and sensation in places where he'd had none. After years of debating whether or not to have risky experimental surgery on his spinal cord, Rhyme had finally opted for an exercise regimen similar to Reeve's.

The actor's untimely death had inspired Rhyme to put even more energy than before into an exercise plan, and Thom had tracked down one of the East Coast's best spinal cord injury doctors, Robert Sherman. The M.D. had put together a program for him, which included the ergometer, aquatherapy and the locomotor treadmill — a large contraption, fitted with robotic legs, also under computer control. This system, in effect, 'walked' Rhyme.

All this therapy had produced results. His heart and lungs were stronger. His bone density was that of a nondisabled man of his age. Muscle mass had increased. He was nearly in the same shape as when he'd run Investigation Resources at the NYPD, which oversaw the Crime Scene Unit. Back then he'd walk miles every day, sometimes even running scenes himself — a rarity for a captain — and prowl the streets of the city to collect samples of rocks or dirt or concrete or soot to catalog in his forensic databases.

Because of Sherman's exercises Rhyme had fewer pressure sores from the hours and hours his body remained in contact with the chair or bed. His bowel and bladder functions were improved and he'd had far fewer urinary tract infections. And he'd had only one episode of autonomic dysreflexia since he'd started the regimen.

Of course another question remained: Would the months of grueling exercise do something to actually *fix* his condition, not just beef up the muscles and bone? A simple test of motor and sensory functions would tell him instantly. But that required a visit to a hospital and Rhyme never seemed to find the time to do it.

'You can't take an hour off?' Thom would ask.

'An hour? An hour? When in recent memory does a trip to the hospital take an hour? Where would that particular hospital be, Thom? Neverland? Oz?'

But Dr. Sherman had finally pestered Rhyme into agreeing to undergo the test. In half an hour he and Thom would be leaving for New York Hospital to get the final word on his progress.

At the moment, though, Lincoln Rhyme was thinking not of that, but of the bicycle race he was presently engaged in — which *was* on the Matterhorn, thank you very much. And he happened to be beating Lance Armstrong.

When he was finished Thom removed him from the bicycle, bathed then dressed him in a white shirt and dark slacks. A sitting transfer into his wheelchair and Rhyme drove to the tiny elevator. He went downstairs, where red-haired Amelia Sachs sat in the lab, a former living room, marking evidence from one of the NYPD cases that Rhyme was consulting on.

With his one working digit — the left ring finger — on the touch-pad controller, Rhyme deftly maneuvered the bright red Storm Arrow wheelchair through the lab to a spot next to her. She leaned over and kissed him on the mouth. He kissed her back, pressing his lips against hers hard. They remained like this for a moment, Rhyme enjoying the heat of her proximity, the sweet, floral smell of soap, the tease of her hair against his cheek.

'How far'd you get today?' she asked.

'I could be in northern Westchester by now — if I hadn't been pulled over.' A dark glance at Thom. The aide winked at Sachs. Water off a duck.

Tall, willowy Sachs was wearing a navy blue pantsuit with one of the black or navy blouses that she usually wore since she'd been promoted to detective. (A tactical handbook for officers warned: *Wearing a contrasting shirt or blouse presents a clearer target at the chest area.*) The outfit was functional and frumpy, a far cry from what she'd worn on the job before she became a cop; Sachs had been a fashion model for a few years. The jacket bulged slightly at the hip, where her Glock automatic pistol rode, and the slacks were men's; she needed a rear wallet pocket — the only place she felt comfortable stashing her illegal, but often useful, switchblade knife. And, as always, she was wearing sensible, padded-sole shoes. Walking was painful for Amelia Sachs, thanks to arthritis.

'When do we leave?' she asked Rhyme.

'For the hospital? Oh, you don't have to come. Better to stay here and get the evidence logged in.'

'It's almost logged. Anyway, it's not a question of having to come. I *want* to.'

He muttered, 'Circus. It's becoming a circus. I *knew* it would.' He tried to lob a blameful look at Thom but the aide was elsewhere.

The doorbell rang. Thom stepped into the hall and returned a moment later, trailed by Lon Sellitto. 'Hey, everybody.' The lieutenant, squat and wearing his typically rumpled suit, nodded cheerfully. Rhyme wondered what his good mood was due to. Maybe something to do with a recent arrest or the NYPD budget for new officers or maybe only that he'd lost a few pounds. The detective's weight was a yo-yo and he complained about it regularly. Given his own situation, Lincoln Rhyme didn't have any patience when somebody groused about physical imperfections like too much girth or too little hair.

But today it seemed that the detective's enthusiastic spirit was work related. He waved several documents in the air. 'They upheld the conviction.'

'Ah,' Rhyme said. 'The shoe case?'

'Yep.'

Rhyme was pleased, of course, though hardly surprised. Why would he be? *He'd* put together the bulk of the case against the murderer; there was no way the conviction would have collapsed.

It had been an interesting one: Two Balkan diplomats had been murdered on Roosevelt Island — the curious strip of residential land in the middle of the East River — and their right shoes stolen. As often happened when faced with tough cases, the NYPD hired Rhyme on as a consulting criminalist — the au courant jargon for forensic scientist — to help in the investigation.

Amelia Sachs had run the scene, and the evidence had been gathered and analyzed. But the clues had not led them in any obvious directions, and the police were left to conclude that the murders had somehow been inspired by European politics. The case remained open but quiescent for some time — until an FBI memo went around the NYPD about a briefcase abandoned at JFK airport. The case contained articles about global positioning systems, two dozen electronic circuits and a man's right shoe. The heel had been hollowed out and inside was a computer chip. Rhyme had wondered if it was one of the Roosevelt Island shoes and, sure enough, it was. Other clues in the briefcase led

25

back to the murder scene as well.

Spy stuff . . . shades of Robert Ludlum. Theories began to circulate immediately and the FBI and the State Department went into overdrive. A man from Langley showed up too, the first time Rhyme could remember the CIA taking an interest in one of his cases.

The criminalist still laughed at the disappointment of the global-conspiracy-loving Feds, when, a week after finding the shoe, Detective Amelia Sachs led a tactical team in a take-down of a businessman from Paramus, New Jersey, a gruff fellow who had at best a *USA Today* grasp of foreign politics.

Rhyme had proven through moisture and chemical analysis of the composite heel material that the hollowing-out had occurred weeks *after* the men had been killed. He found too that the computer chip had been purchased from PC Warehouse, and that the GPS information not only wasn't secret, it had been downloaded from websites that were a year or two out of date.

A staged crime scene, Rhyme had concluded. And went on to trace stone dust in the briefcase to a kitchen and bathroom countertop company in Jersey. A fast look at the phone records of the owner and credit card receipts led to the conclusion that the man's wife was sleeping with one of the diplomats. Her husband had found out about the liaison and, along with a Tony Soprano wannabe who worked for him in the slab yard, killed her lover and the man's unfortunate associate on Roosevelt Island, then staged the evidence to make the crime seem politically motivated.

'An *affair*, yes, though not a diplomatic one,' Rhyme had offered dramatically at the conclusion of his testimony in court. '*Undercover* action, yes, though not espionage.'

'Objection,' the weary defense lawyer had said.

'Sustained.' Though the judge couldn't keep from laughing.

The jury took forty-two minutes to convict the businessman. The lawyers had, of course, appealed — they always do — but, as Sellitto had just revealed, the appellate court upheld the conviction.

Thom said, 'Say, let's celebrate the victory with a ride to the hospital. You ready?'

'Don't push it,' Rhyme grumbled.

It was at that moment that Sellitto's pager went off. He looked at the screen, frowned and then pulled his cell phone off his belt and made a call.

'Sellitto here. What's up? . . . ' The big man nodded slowly, his hand absently kneading his belly roll. He'd been trying Atkins lately. Eating a lot of steaks and eggs had apparently not had much effect. 'She's all right? . . . And the perp? . . . Yeah . . . That's not good. Hold on.' He looked up. 'A ten twenty-four call just came in. That African-American museum on Five-five? The vic was a young girl. Teenager. Attempted rape.'

Amelia Sachs winced at this news, exuding sympathy. Rhyme had a different reaction; his mind automatically wondered: How many crime scenes were there? Did the perp chase her and

27

possibly drop evidence? Did they grapple, exchanging trace? Did he take public transportation to and from the scene? Or was a car involved?

Another thought crossed his mind as well, one that he had no intention of sharing, however.

'Injuries?' Sachs asked.

'Scraped hand is all. She got away and found a uniform on patrol nearby. He checked it out but the beast was gone by then . . . So, can you guys run the scene?'

Sachs looked at Rhyme. 'I know what you're going to say: that we're busy.'

The entire NYPD was feeling a crunch. Many officers had been pulled off regular detail and assigned to anti-terrorism duty, which was particularly hectic lately; the FBI had gotten several anonymous reports about possible bombings of Israeli targets in the area. (The reassignments reminded Rhyme of Sachs's stories her grandfather would tell about life in prewar Germany. Grandpa Sachs's father-in-law had been a criminal police detective in Berlin and was constantly losing his personnel to the national government whenever a crisis arose.) Because of the diverted resources, Rhyme was busier than he'd been in months. He and Sachs were presently running two white-collar fraud investigations, one armed robbery and a cold-case murder from three years ago.

'Yep, really busy,' Rhyme summarized.

'Either rains or it pours,' Sellitto said. He frowned. 'I don't quite get that expression.'

'Believe that's 'Never rains but it pours.' A

statement of irony.' Rhyme cocked his head. 'Love to help. I mean it. But we've got all those other cases. And, look at the time, I have an appointment now. At the hospital.'

'Come on, Linc,' Sellitto said. 'Nothing else you're working on's like this — the vic's a kid. That's one bad actor, going after teenagers. Take him off the street and who knows how many girls we'll save. You know the city — doesn't matter what else is going on. Some beast starts going after kids, the brass'll give you whatever you need to nail him.'

'But that'd make it *five* cases,' Rhyme said petulantly. He let the silence build up. Then, reluctantly, he asked, 'How old is she?'

'Sixteen, for Christ's sake. Come on, Linc.'

A sigh. He finally said, 'Oh, all right. I'll do it.'

'You will?' Sellitto asked, surprised.

'Everybody thinks I'm disagreeable,' Rhyme scoffed, rolling his eyes. 'Everybody thinks I'm the wet blanket — there's another cliché for you, Lon. I was just pointing out that we have to consider priorities. But I think you're right. This's more important.'

It was the aide who asked, 'Your helpful nature have anything to do with the fact you'll have to postpone your hospital visit?'

'Of course not. I didn't even think about *that*. But now you mention it, I guess we better cancel. Good idea, Thom.'

'It *isn't* my idea — you engineered it.'

True, he was thinking. But he now asked indignantly, 'Me? You make it sound like *I've* been attacking people in Midtown.'

29

'You know what I mean,' Thom said. 'You can have the test and be back before Amelia's through with the crime scene.'

'There might be delays at the hospital. Why do I even say 'might'? Always are.'

Sachs said, 'I'll call Dr. Sherman and reschedule.'

'Cancel, sure. But don't reschedule. We have no idea how long this could take. The perp might be an organized offender.'

'I'll reschedule,' she said.

'Let's plan on two, three weeks.'

'I'll see when he's available,' Sachs said firmly.

But Lincoln Rhyme could be as stubborn as his partner. 'We'll worry about that later. Now, we've got a rapist out there. Who knows what he's up to at the moment? Probably targeting somebody else. Thom, call Mel Cooper and get him in here. Let's move. Every minute we delay is a gift to the perp. Hey, how's *that* expression, Lon? The genesis of a cliché — and you were there.'

3

Instinct.

Portables — beat cops — develop a sixth sense for knowing when somebody's concealing a gun. Veterans on the force'll tell you it's really nothing more than the way the suspect carries himself — less a matter of a pistol's heaviness in pounds than the weight of consequences of having it close to you. The power it gives you.

The risk of getting caught too. Carrying an unlicensed weapon in New York comes with a Cracker Jack prize: an automatic stint in jail. You carry concealed, you do time. Simple as that.

No, Amelia Sachs couldn't say exactly how she understood it, but she knew that the man leaning against a wall across the street from the Museum of African-American Culture and History was armed. Smoking a cigarette, arms crossed, he gazed at the police line, the flashing lights, the officers.

As she approached the scene Sachs was greeted by a blond NYPD uniform — so young he had to be a rookie. He said, 'Hi, there. I was the first officer. I — '

Sachs smiled and whispered, 'Don't look at me. Keep your eyes on that garbage pile up the street.'

The rookie looked at her, blinked. 'Sorry?'

'Garbage,' she repeated in a harsh whisper. 'Not me.'

'Sorry, Detective,' said the young man, who sported a trim haircut and a nameplate on his chest that read R. *Pulaski*. The tag had not a single ding or scratch on it.

Sachs pointed to the trash. 'Shrug.'

He shrugged.

'Come on with me. Keep watching it.'

'Is there — ?'

'Smile.'

'I — '

'How many cops does it take to change a lightbulb?' Sachs asked.

'I don't know,' he said. 'How many?'

'I don't know either. It's not a joke. But laugh like I just told you a great punch line.'

He laughed. A little nervous. But it was a laugh.

'Keep watching it.'

'The trash?'

Sachs unbuttoned her suit jacket. 'Now we're not laughing. We're concerned about the garbage.'

'Why — ?'

'Ahead.'

'Right. I'm not laughing. I'm looking at the trash.'

'Good.'

The man with the gun kept lounging against a building. He was in his forties, solid, with razor-cut hair. She now saw the bulge at his hip, which told her it was a long pistol, probably a revolver, since it seemed to swell out where the cylinder would be. 'Here's the situation,' she said softly to the rookie. 'Man on our two

32

o'clock. He's carrying.'

Bless him, the rookie — with spiky little-boy hair as shiny beige as caramel — kept looking at the garbage. 'The perp? You think it's the perp in the assault?'

'Don't know. Don't care. I care about the fact that he's carrying.'

'What do we do?'

'Keep on going. We pass him, watching the garbage. Decide we're not interested. Head back toward the scene. You slow up and ask me if I want coffee. I say yes. You go around to his right. He'll keep his eyes on me.'

'Why will he watch you?'

Refreshing naiveté. 'He just will. You double back. Get close to him. Make a little noise, clear your throat or something. He'll turn. Then I'll come up behind him.'

'Sure, I've got it . . . Should I, you know, draw down on him?'

'No. Just let him know you're there and stand behind him.'

'What if he pulls his gun?'

'*Then* you draw down on him.'

'What if he starts to shoot?'

'I don't think he will.'

'But if he does?'

'*Then* you shoot him. What's your first name?'

'Ronald. Ron.'

'How long you out?'

'Three weeks.'

'You'll do fine. Let's go.'

They walked to the garbage pile, concerned. But then they decided it was no threat and started back. Pulaski stopped suddenly. 'Hey, how 'bout some coffee, Detective?'

Overacting — he'd never be a guest on *Inside the Actor's Studio* — but all things considered it was a credible performance. 'Sure, thanks.'

He doubled back then paused. Shouted: 'How do you like it?'

'Uhm, sugar,' she said.

'How many sugars?'

Jesus Lord . . . She said, 'One.'

'Got it. Hey, you want a Danish too?'

Okay, cool it, her eyes told him. 'Just coffee's fine.' She turned toward the crime scene, sensing the man with the gun study her long red hair, tied in a ponytail. He glanced at her chest, then her butt.

Why will he watch you?

He just will.

Sachs continued toward the museum. She glanced in a window across the street, checking out the reflection. When the smoker's eyes swiveled back toward Pulaski she turned quickly and approached, jacket pulled aside like a gunfighter's dust coat so she could get her Glock out fast if she needed to.

'Sir,' she said firmly. 'Please keep your hands where I can see them.'

'Do as the lady says.' Pulaski stood on the other side of the guy, hand near his weapon.

The man glanced at Sachs. 'That was pretty smooth, Officer.'

'Just don't move those hands. Are you carrying a weapon?'

'Yeah,' the man replied, 'and it's bigger than

34

what I used to carry in the Three Five.'

The numbers referred to a precinct house. He was a former cop.

Probably.

'Working security?'

'That's right.'

'Let me see your ticket. With your left hand, you don't mind. Keep your right where it is.'

He pulled out his wallet and handed it to her. His carry permit and security guard's license were in order. Still, she called it in and checked out the guy. He was legit. 'Thanks.' Sachs relaxed, handing him back the papers.

'Not a problem, Detective. You got yourself some scene here, looks like.' Nodding toward the squad cars blocking the street in front of the museum.

'We'll see.' Noncommittal.

The guard put the wallet away. 'I was Patrol for twelve years. Retired on a medical and was going stir crazy.' He nodded at the building behind him. 'You'll see a couple other guys carrying round here. This's one of the biggest jewelry operations in the city. It's an annex for the American Jewelry Exchange in the diamond district. We get a couple million bucks' worth of stones from Amsterdam and Jerusalem every day.'

She glanced at the building. Didn't look very imposing, just like any other office building.

He laughed. 'I thought it'd be a piece of cake, this job, but I work as hard here as when I was on a beat. Well, good luck with the scene. Wish I could help, but I got here after the excitement.'

He turned to the rookie and said, 'Hey, kid.' He nodded toward Sachs. 'On the job, in front of people, you don't call her 'lady.' She's 'Detective.''

The rookie looked at him uneasily but she could see he got the message — one that Sachs herself had been going to deliver when they were out of earshot.

'Sorry,' Pulaski said to her.

'You didn't know. Now you do.'

Which could be the motto of police training everywhere.

They turned to go. The guard called, 'Oh, hey, rookie?'

Pulaski turned.

'You forgot the coffee.' Grinned.

At the entrance to the museum Lon Sellitto was surveying the street and talking to a sergeant. The big detective looked at the kid's name tag and asked, 'Pulaski, you were first officer?'

'Yes, sir.'

'What'sa story?'

The kid cleared his throat and pointed to an alley. 'I was positioned across the street, roughly there, on routine patrol. At about oh-eight-thirty the victim, an African-American female, sixteen years of age, approached me and reported that — '

'You can just tell it in your own words,' Sachs said.

'Sure. Okay. What it was, I was standing right about there and this girl comes up to me, all upset. Her name's Geneva Settle, junior in high school. She was working on a term paper or something on the fifth floor.' Pointing to the museum. 'And this guy attacks her. White, six feet, wearing a ski mask. Was going to rape her.'

'You know that how?' Sellitto asked.

'I found his rape pack upstairs.'

'You looked in it?' Sachs asked, frowning.

'With a pen. That's all. I didn't touch it.'

'Good. Go on.'

'The girl gets away, comes down the fire stairs and into the alley. He's after her, but he turns the other way.'

'Anybody see what happened to him?' Sellitto asked.

'No, sir.'

He looked over the street. 'You set up the press perimeter?'

'Yes, sir.'

'Well, it's fifty feet too close. Get 'em the hell away. Press're like leeches. Remember that.'

'Sure, Detective.'

You didn't know. Now you do.

He hurried off and started moving the line back.

'Where's the girl?' Sachs asked.

The sergeant, a solid Hispanic man with thick, graying hair, said, 'An officer took her and her friend to Midtown North. They're calling her parents.' Sharp autumn sunlight reflected off his many gold decorations. 'After they get in touch with them, somebody was going to take 'em to Captain Rhyme's place to interview her.' He laughed. 'She's a smart one. Know what she did?'

'What?'

'She had an idea there might be some trouble, so she dressed up this mannequin in her sweatshirt and hat. The perp went after that. Bought her time to get away.'

Sachs laughed. 'And she's only sixteen? Smart.'

Sellitto said to her, 'You run the scene. I'm going to get a canvass going.' He wandered up the sidewalk to a cluster of officers — one uniform and two Anti-Crime cops in dress-down plain clothes — and sent them around the crowd and into nearby stores and office buildings to check for witnesses. He rounded up a separate team to interview each of the half dozen pushcart vendors here, some selling coffee and doughnuts at the moment, others setting up for lunches of hot dogs, pretzels, gyros and falafel pita-bread sandwiches.

A honk sounded and she turned. The CS bus had arrived from the Crime Scene Unit HQ in Queens.

'Hey, Detective,' the driver said, getting out.

Sachs nodded a greeting to him and his partner. She knew the young men from prior cases. She pulled off her jacket and weapon, dressed in white Tyvek overalls, which minimized contamination of the scene. She then strapped her Glock back on her hip, thinking of Rhyme's constant admonition to his CS crews: Search well but watch your back.

'Give me a hand with the bags?' she asked, hefting one of the metal suitcases containing basic evidence-collection and -transport equipment.

'You bet.' A CSU tech grabbed two of the other cases.

She pulled on a hands-free headset and plugged it into her Handi-Talkie just as Ron Pulaski returned from his press push-back duty. He led Sachs and the Crime Scene officers into the building. They got off the elevator on the fifth floor and walked to the right, to double doors below a sign that said, *Booker T. Washington Room.*

'That's the scene in there.'

Sachs and the techs opened the suitcases, started removing equipment. Pulaski continued, 'I'm pretty sure he came through these doors. The only other exit is the fire stairwell and you can't enter from the outside, and it wasn't jimmied. So, he comes through this door, locks it and then goes after the girl. She escaped through the fire door.'

'Who unlocked the front one for you?' Sachs asked.

'Guy named Don Barry, head librarian.'

'He go in with you?'

'No.'

'Where is he now?'

'His office — third floor. I wondered if maybe it was an inside job, you know? So I asked him for a list of all his white male employees and where they were when she was attacked.'

'Good.' Sachs had been planning to do the same.

'He said he'd bring the list down to us as soon as he was done.'

'Now, tell me what I'll find inside.'

'The girl was at the microfiche reader. It's around the corner to the right. You'll see it easy.' Pulaski pointed to the end of a large room filled with tall rows of bookshelves, beyond which was an open area where Sachs could see mannequins dressed in period clothing, paintings, cases of antique jewelry, purses, shoes, accessories — your typical dusty museum displays, the sort of stuff you look at while you're really wondering what restaurant to eat at after you've had enough culture.

'What's security like around here?' Sachs was looking for surveillance cameras on the ceiling.

'Zip. No cameras. No guards, no sign-in sheets. You just walk in.'

'Never easy, is it?'

'No, ma' . . . No, Detective.'

She thought about telling him that 'ma'am' was okay, not like 'lady,' but didn't know how to explain the distinction. 'One question. Did you close the fire door downstairs?'

'No, I left it just the way I found it. Open.'

'So the scene could be hot.'

'Hot?'

'The perp could've come back.'

'I . . .'

'You didn't do anything wrong, Pulaski. I just want to know.'

'Well, I guess he could've, yeah.'

'All right, you stay in the doorway here. I want you to listen.'

'For what?'

'Well, the guy shooting at me, for instance. But probably better if you heard footsteps or

40

somebody racking a shotgun first.'

'Watch your back, you're saying?'

She winked. And started forward to the scene.

* * *

So, she's Crime Scene, thought Thompson Boyd, watching the woman walk back and forth in the library, studying the floor, looking for fingerprints and clues and whatever it was they looked for. He wasn't concerned about what she might find. He'd been careful, as always.

Thompson was standing in the sixth-floor window of the building across Fifty-fifth Street from the museum. After the girl got away, he'd circled around two blocks and made his way into this building, then climbed the stairs to the hallway from which he was now looking over the street.

He'd had a second chance to kill the girl a few minutes ago; she'd been on the street for a moment, talking to officers, in front of the museum. But there were way too many police around for him to shoot her and get away. Still he'd been able to take a picture of her with the camera in his mobile phone before she and her friend had been hustled off to a squad car, which sped west. Besides, Thompson still had more to do here, and so he'd taken up this vantage point.

From his prison days Thompson knew a lot about law enforcers. He could easily spot the lazy ones, the scared ones, the ones who were stupid and gullible. He could also spot the talented cops, the smart ones, the ones who were a threat.

Like the woman he was looking at right now.

As he put drops in his perpetually troubled eyes, Thompson found himself curious about her. As she searched the scene she had this concentration in her eyes, looking sort of devout, the same look Thompson's mother sometimes used to get in church.

She disappeared from view but, whistling softly, Thompson kept his eyes on the window. Finally the woman in white returned to view. He noted the precision with which she did everything, the careful way she walked, her delicate touch as she picked up and examined things so as not to hurt the evidence. Another man might've been turned on by her beauty, her figure; even through the jumpsuit, it was easy to imagine what her body was like. But those thoughts, like usual, were far from his mind. Still, he believed he sensed some small enjoyment inside him as he watched her at work.

Something from his past came back to him . . . He frowned, looking at her walking back and forth, back and forth . . . Yes, that was it. The pattern reminded him of the sidewinder rattlesnakes his father would point out when they were hunting together or going for walks in the Texas sand near the family trailer, outside Amarillo.

Look at them, son. Look. Ain't they

something? But don't you get too close. They'll kill you in a kiss.

He leaned against the wall and continued to study the woman in white, moving back and forth, back and forth.

4

'How does it look, Sachs?'

'Good,' she replied to Rhyme, via their radio connection.

She was just finishing walking the grid — the word referring to a method of searching a crime scene: examining it the way you'd mow a lawn, walking from one end of the site to the other then returning, slightly to the side. And then doing the same once more, but the second time walking perpendicular to the first search. Looking up and down too, floor to ceiling. This way, no inch or angle was left unseen. There are a number of ways to search crime scenes but Rhyme always insisted on this one.

''Good' means what?' he asked testily. Rhyme didn't like generalizations, or what he called 'soft' assessments.

'He forgot the rape pack,' she replied. Since the Motorola link between Rhyme and Sachs was mostly a means to bring his surrogate presence to crime scenes, they usually dispensed with the NYPD conventions of radio protocol, like ending each transmission with a *K*

'Did he now? Might be as good as his wallet for ID'ing him. What's he got in his?'

'Little weird, Rhyme. It's got the typical duct tape, box cutter, condoms. But there's also a tarot card. Picture of this guy hanging from a scaffold.'

44

'Wonder if he's a genuine sicko, or just a copycat?' Rhyme mused. Over the years many killers had left tarot cards and other occult memorabilia at crime scenes — the most notable recent case being the Washington, D.C., snipers of several years earlier.

Sachs continued, 'The good news is that he kept everything in a nice slick plastic bag.'

'Excellent.' While perps might think to wear gloves at the crime scene itself, they often forgot about prints on the items they carried with them to commit that crime. A discarded condom wrapper had convicted many a rapist who'd otherwise been compulsive about not leaving his prints or bodily fluids at a scene. In this case, even if the killer thought to clean off the tape, knife and condoms, it was possible that he'd forgotten to wipe the bag.

She now placed the pack in a paper evidence bag — paper was generally better than plastic for preserving evidence — and set it aside. 'He left it on a bookshelf near where the girl was sitting. I'm checking for latents.' She dusted the shelves with fluorescent powder, donned orange goggles and shone an alternative light source on the area. ALS lamps reveal markings like blood, semen and fingerprints that are otherwise invisible. Playing the light up and down, she transmitted, 'No prints. But I can see he's wearing latex gloves.'

'Ah, that's good. For two reasons.' Rhyme's voice had a professorial tone. He was testing her.

Two? she wondered. One came immediately to mind: If they were able to recover the glove they

45

could lift a print from *inside* the fingers (something else perps often forgot). But the second?

She asked him.

'Obvious. It means he's probably got a record, so when we *do* find a print, AFIS'll tell us who he is.' State-based automated fingerprint identification systems and the FBI's Integrated AFIS were computer databases that could provide print matches in minutes, as opposed to days or even weeks with manual examinations.

'Sure,' Sachs said, troubled that she'd blown the quiz.

'What else rates the assessment 'good'?'

'They waxed the floor last night.'

'And the attack happened early this morning. So you've got a good canvas for his footprints.'

'Yep. There're some distinct ones here.' Kneeling, she took an electrostatic image of the print of the man's tread marks. She was sure they were his; she could clearly see the trail where he'd walked up to Geneva's table, adjusted his stance to get a good grip on the club to strike her and then chased her down the hall. She'd also compared the prints with those of the only other man who'd been here this morning: those of Ron Pulaski, whose mirror-shined issue shoes left a very different impression.

She explained about the girl's using the mannequin to distract the killer and escape. He chuckled at her ingenuity. She added, 'Rhyme, he hit her — well, the mannequin — really hard. A blunt object. So hard he cracked the plastic through her stocking cap. Then he must've been mad she fooled him. He smashed the microfiche reader too.'

'Blunt object,' Rhyme repeated. 'Can you lift an impression?'

When he was head of the Crime Scene Unit at the NYPD, before his accident, Rhyme had compiled a number of database files to help identify evidence and impressions found at scenes. The blunt object file contained hundreds of pictures of impact marks left on skin and inanimate surfaces by various types of objects — from tire irons to human bones to ice. But after carefully examining both the mannequin and the smashed microfiche reader, Sachs said, 'No, Rhyme. I don't see any. The cap Geneva put on the mannequin — '

'Geneva?'

'That's her name.'

'Oh. Go on.'

She was momentarily irritated — as she often was — that he hadn't expressed any interest in knowing anything about the girl or her state of mind. It often troubled her that Rhyme was so detached about the crime and the victims. This, he said, was how a criminalist needed to be. You didn't want pilots so awed by a beautiful sunset or so terrified of a thunderstorm that they flew into a mountain, the same was true with cops. She saw his point but to Amelia Sachs victims were human beings, and crimes were not scientific exercises; they were horrific events. Especially when the victim was a sixteen-year-old girl.

She continued, 'The cap she put on the

47

mannequin dispersed the force of the blow. And the microfiche reader's shattered too.'

Rhyme said, 'Well, bring back some of the pieces of what he hit. There might be some transfer there.'

'Sure.'

There were some voices in the background at Rhyme's. He said in an odd, troubled tone, 'Finish up and get back here soon, Sachs.'

'I'm almost done,' she told him. 'I'm going to walk the grid at the escape route . . . Rhyme, what's the matter?'

Silence. When he spoke next he sounded even more bothered. 'I have to go, Sachs. It seems I have some visitors.'

'Who — ?'

But he'd already disconnected.

★   ★   ★

The woman in white, the pro, had disappeared from the window of the library.

But Thompson Boyd wasn't interested in her anymore. From his perch sixty feet above the street he was now watching an older cop, walking toward some witnesses. The man was middle-aged, heavy and in a God-wrinkled suit. Thompson knew this sort of officer too. He wasn't brilliant but he'd be like the bulldog he resembled. There was nothing that would stop him from getting to the heart of a case.

When the fat cop nodded toward another man, a tall black man in a brown suit, walking out of the museum, Thompson left his vantage

48

point and hurried downstairs. Pausing at the ground floor, he took his pistol out of his pocket and checked it to make sure nothing had become lodged in the barrel or cylinder. He wondered if it had been this — the sound of opening and closing the cylinder in the library — that had alerted the girl that he was a threat.

Now, even though nobody seemed to be nearby, he checked the pistol absolutely silently.

Learn from your mistakes.

By the book.

The gun was in order. Hiding it under his coat, Thompson walked down the dim stairway and exited through the far lobby, on Fifty-sixth Street, then stepped into an alley that took him back toward the museum.

There was no one guarding the entrance to the other end of the alley at Fifty-fifth. Undetected, Thompson eased up to a battered green Dumpster, stinking of rotting food. He looked into the street. It had been reopened to traffic but several dozen people from offices and shops nearby remained on the sidewalks, hoping for a look at something exciting to tell their office-mates and families about. Most of the police had left. The woman in white — the kissing snake — was still upstairs. Outside were two squad cars and a Crime Scene Unit van, as well as three uniformed cops, two plain-clothes ones and that fat, rumpled detective.

Thompson gripped the gun firmly. Shooting was a very ineffective way to kill someone. But sometimes, like now, there was no option. If you

49

had to shoot, procedures dictated you aimed for the heart. Never the head. The skull was solid enough to deflect a bullet in many circumstances, and the cranium was also relatively small and hard to hit.

Always the chest.

Thompson's keen, blue eyes looked over the heavy cop in the wrinkled suit, as he glanced at a piece of paper.

Calm as dead wood, Thompson rested the gun on his left forearm, aimed carefully with a steady hand. He fired four fast shots.

The first one hit the thigh of a woman standing on the sidewalk.

The others struck his intended victim just where he'd aimed. The three tiny dots appeared in the center of his chest; they'd become three rosettes of blood by the time the body hit the ground.

★   ★   ★

Two girls stood in front of him and, though their physiques were totally opposite, it was the difference in their eyes that Lincoln Rhyme noticed first.

The heavy one — dressed in gaudy clothes and shiny jewelry, her fingernails long and orange — had eyes that danced like skittish insects. Unable to look at Rhyme, or anything else, for more than a second, she made a dizzying visual circuit of his lab: the scientific instruments, the beakers, chemicals, the computers and monitors, wires everywhere. At Rhyme's legs and his wheelchair, of course. She chewed gum loudly.

The other girl, short, skinny and boyish, had a stillness about her. She gazed at Lincoln Rhyme steadily. One fast glance at the wheelchair, then back to him. The lab didn't interest her.

'This's Geneva Settle,' explained the calm patrolwoman, Jennifer Robinson, nodding at the slim girl, the one with the unwavering eyes. Robinson was a friend of Amelia Sachs, who'd arranged for her to drive the girls here from the Midtown North house.

'And this's her friend,' Robinson continued, 'Lakeesha Scott. Lose the gum, Lakeesha.'

The girl gave a beleaguered look but stuffed the wad somewhere in her large purse, without bothering to wrap it.

The patrolwoman said, 'She and Geneva went to the museum together this morning.'

'Only I didn't see nothing,' Lakeesha said preemptively. Was the big girl nervous because of the attack, he wondered, or was she uncomfortable because Rhyme was a crip? Both probably.

Geneva was dressed in a gray T-shirt and black baggy pants and running shoes, which Rhyme guessed was the fashion among high school students nowadays. Sellitto had said the girl was sixteen but she looked younger. While Lakeesha's hair was done in a mass of thin gold and black braids, tied so taut that her scalp showed, Geneva's was cropped short.

'I told the girls who you are, Captain,' Robinson explained, using the title that was some years out of date. 'And that you're going to

51

ask them some questions about what happened. Geneva wants to get back to her school but I said she'd have to wait.'

'I have some tests,' Geneva said.

Lakeesha tsked a sound through her white teeth.

Robinson continued, 'Geneva's parents are out of the country. But they're getting the next flight back. Her uncle's been staying with her while they've been away.'

'Where are they?' Rhyme asked. 'Your parents?'

'My father's teaching a symposium at Oxford.'

'He's a professor?'

She nodded. 'Literature. At Hunter.'

Rhyme chided himself for being surprised that a young girl from Harlem would have intellectual, globe-trotting parents. He was angry for stereotyping but mostly piqued that he'd made a flawed deduction. True, she was decked out like a gangsta but he might've guessed she had academic roots; she'd been attacked during an early-morning visit to a library, not hanging out on the street corner or watching TV before school.

Lakeesha fished a package of cigarettes out of her purse.

Rhyme began, 'There's no — '

Thom walked through the doorway. ' — smoking in here.' He lifted the pack away from the girl and stuffed it back into her bag. Unfazed that two teenagers had suddenly materialized on his watch, Thom smiled. 'Soft drinks?'

'You got coffee?' Lakeesha asked.

'I do, yes.' Thom glanced at Jennifer Robinson and Rhyme, who shook their heads.

'I like it strong,' the big girl announced.

'Do you?' Thom asked. 'So do I.' To Geneva: 'Anything for you?'

The girl shook her head.

Rhyme glanced longingly at the bottle of scotch sitting on a shelf nearby. Thom noticed and laughed. The aide disappeared. To Rhyme's distress, Patrolwoman Robinson said, 'I've got to get back to the house, sir.'

'Ah, you do?' Rhyme asked, dismayed. 'You sure you couldn't stay a little longer?'

'Can't, sir. But you need anything else, just gimme a call.'

How about a babysitter?

Rhyme didn't believe in fate but, if he had, he would have noted a deft jab here: he'd taken on the case to avoid the test at the hospital and now was being paid back for the deception by suffering through an immensely awkward half hour or so in the company of two high school girls. Young people were not his forte.

'So long, Captain.' Robinson walked out the door.

He muttered, 'Yeah.'

Thom returned a few minutes later with a tray. He poured a cup of coffee for Lakeesha and handed Geneva a mug, which, Rhyme smelled, contained hot chocolate.

'I took a guess you'd like something anyway,' the aide said. 'You don't want it, you can leave it.'

'No, that's fine. Thanks.' Geneva stared at the

hot surface. Took a sip, another, lowered the cup and gazed at the floor. Took several more sips.

'You're all right?' Rhyme asked.

Geneva nodded.

'I am too,' Lakeesha said.

'He attacked both of you?' Rhyme asked.

'Naw, not me.' Lakeesha looked him over. 'You like that actor broke his neck?' She slurped her coffee, added more sugar. Slurped again.

'That's right.'

'An' you can't move nothin'?'

'Not much.'

'Damn.'

'Keesh,' Geneva whispered. 'Chill, girl.'

'Just, you know, damn.'

Silence again. Only eight minutes had passed since they'd arrived. It seemed like hours. What should he do? Have Thom run out and buy a board game?

There were, of course, questions that had to be asked. But Rhyme was reluctant to do so himself. Interviewing and interrogation were skills he didn't possess. When he was on the force he'd questioned suspects maybe a dozen times, and had never had one of those oh-Jesus moments when the grillee broke down and confessed. Sachs, on the other hand, was a natural at the art. She warned rookies that you could blow an entire case with a single wrong word. She called it 'contaminating the mind,' the counterpart to Rhyme's number-one sin: contaminating a crime scene.

Lakeesha asked, 'How you move round in that chair?'

'Shhh,' Geneva warned.

'I only askin'.'

'Well, don't.'

'Ain't no harm in *asking* nothin'.'

Lakeesha had lost her skittishness completely now. Rhyme decided she was actually pretty savvy. She acts uneasy at first, making it seem like she's naive, vulnerable, that you have the advantage, but all the while she's sizing things up. Once she's got a handle on the situation, she knows whether or not to trot out the bluster.

In fact, Rhyme was thankful for something to make conversation about. He explained about the ECU, the environmental control unit, how the touch pad under his left ring finger could direct the movement and speed of the wheelchair.

'One finger?' Keesha glanced at one of her orange nails. 'That all you can move?'

'That's right. Other than my head and shoulders.'

'Mr. Rhyme,' Geneva said, looking at a red Swatch, which sat large and obvious on her thin wrist, 'about those tests? The first one's in a couple of hours. How long'll this be?'

'School?' Rhyme asked, surprised. 'Oh, you can stay home today, I'm sure. After what happened, your teachers'll understand.'

'Well, I don't really *want* to stay home. I need to take the tests.'

'Yo, yo, girl, time out. Here the man say you can take a pass, all one hundred percent phat, and you sayin' no. Come on. That wack.'

Geneva looked up into her friend's eyes. 'And

55

you're taking your tests too. You're not skipping.'

'It ain't skippin', you got a pass,' the big girl pointed out with flawless logic.

Rhyme's phone rang and he was grateful for the interruption.

'Command, answer phone,' he said into the hands-free microphone.

'Def!' Lakeesha said, lifting her eyebrows. 'Look at that, Gen. I want one of them.'

Eyes narrowing, Geneva whispered something to her friend, who rolled her eyes and slurped more coffee.

'Rhyme,' Sachs's voice said.

'They're here, Sachs,' Rhyme said in a brittle voice. 'Geneva and her friend. And I'm hoping you're — '

'Rhyme,' she repeated. It was a particular tone. Something was wrong.

'What is it?'

'The scene was hot, after all.'

'He was *there*?'

'Yep. Never left. Or doubled back.'

'Are you okay?'

'Yeah. It wasn't me he was after.'

'What happened?'

'Got up close, into an alley. Fired four shots. He wounded a bystander . . . and he killed a witness. His name was Don Barry. He was in charge of the library at the museum. He took three rounds in the heart. Died instantly.'

'You're sure the shooter's the same?'

'Yep. The shoe prints I found from his shooting position match the ones in the library. Lon was just starting to interview him. He was

56

standing right in front of him when it happened.'

'He get a look at the doer?'

'Nope. Nobody did. He was hiding behind a Dumpster. Couple of the uniforms on the scene went to work on the woman to save her. She had a major bleeder. He got away in the crowd. Just disappeared.'

'Somebody take care of the details?'

Calling the next of kin. *Details.*

'Lon was going to make the calls but he had phone problems or something. There was a sergeant on the scene. He did it.'

'All right, Sachs, come on back with what you've found . . . Command, disconnect.' He looked up and found the two girls staring at him.

He explained, 'It looks like the man who attacked you didn't leave, after all. Or he came back. He killed the head librarian and — '

'Mr. Barry?' A gasp from Geneva Settle. She stopped moving, simply froze.

'That's right.'

'Shit,' Lakeesha whispered. She closed her eyes and shivered.

A moment later Geneva's mouth tightened and she looked down. She set the cocoa on a table. 'No, no . . . '

'I'm sorry,' Rhyme said. 'Was he a friend of yours?'

She shook her head. 'Not really. He was just helping me with my paper.' Geneva sat forward in her chair. 'But it doesn't matter if he was a friend or not. He's dead — that's so terrible.' She whispered angrily, 'Why? Why did he do it?'

'He was a witness, I'd guess. He could identify

the man who attacked you.'

'So he's dead because of me.'

Rhyme muttered some words to her, no, how could it be her fault? She didn't plan on being attacked. It was just bad luck for Barry. Wrong time, wrong place.

But the reassurance had no effect on the girl. Her face grew taut, her eyes cold. Rhyme didn't have a clue what to do next. It wasn't enough that he had to endure the presence of teenagers — now he had to comfort them, get their minds off this tragedy. He wheeled closer to the girls and pushed his patience to its limit by making small talk.

5

An endless twenty minutes later, Sachs and Sellitto arrived at Rhyme's, accompanied by a young, blond patrol officer named Pulaski.

Sellitto explained that he'd requisitioned the kid to cart the evidence back to Rhyme's and help with the investigation. Clearly a rookie, he had 'eager' written on his smooth forehead. He'd obviously been briefed about the criminalist's disability; he was overly oblivious to the fact that the man was paralyzed. Rhyme hated these fake reactions. He infinitely preferred Lakeesha's brashness.

Just, you know, damn . . .

The two detectives greeted the girls. Pulaski looked them over sympathetically and asked in a kid-friendly voice how they were doing. Rhyme noted a nicked wedding ring on his finger and deduced a high school marriage; only having children of your own could produce this kind of look.

Lakeesha answered, 'Messed up is what I be. Buggin' . . . Some asshole tryin' to bust up my girlfriend. Whatta you think?'

Geneva said she was doing all right.

'I understand you're staying with a relative?' Sachs asked.

'My uncle. He's living at our place till my folks get back from London.'

Rhyme happened to look at Lon Sellitto.

59

Something was wrong. He'd changed dramatically in the past two hours. The boisterous mood had vanished. His eyes were spooked and he was fidgety. Rhyme noticed too that his fingers repeatedly touched a particular spot on his cheek. He'd rubbed it red.

'Get dinged by some lead?' Rhyme asked, recalling that the detective had been right next to the librarian when the perp had shot him. Maybe Sellitto had been hit by a bullet fragment or bit of stone if a slug had passed through Barry and struck a building.

'What?' Then Sellitto realized he'd been rubbing his skin and dropped his hand. He said in a soft voice, so the girls couldn't hear, 'I was pretty close to the vic. Got spattered by some blood. That's all. Nothing.'

But a moment later he absently started the rubbing again.

The gesture reminded Rhyme of Sachs, who had the habit of scratching her scalp and worrying her nails. The compulsion came and went, linked somehow to her drive, her ambition, the indefinable churning inside most cops. Police officers hurt themselves in a hundred different ways. The harm ranged from the minor inflictions of Sachs's, to destroying marriages and children's spirits with harsh words, to closing your lips around the tangy barrel of your service pistol. He'd never seen it in Lon Sellitto, though.

Geneva asked Sachs, 'There was no mistake?'

'Mistake?'

'About Dr. Barry.'

60

'I'm sorry, no. He's dead.'

The girl was motionless. Rhyme could feel her sorrow.

Anger too. Her eyes were black dots of fury. Then she looked at her watch, said to Rhyme, 'Those tests I mentioned?'

'Well, let's just get some questions out of the way and then we'll see. Sachs?'

With the evidence now set out on the examining table and chain of custody cards completed, Sachs pulled up a chair beside Rhyme and interviewed the girls. She asked Geneva exactly what had happened. The girl explained she'd been looking up an article in an old magazine when somebody came into the library. She'd heard hesitant footsteps. Then a laugh. The voice of a man ending a conversation and the snap of a closing cell phone.

The girl squinted. 'Hey, you know, maybe what you could do is check out all the mobile companies in town. See who was on the phone then.'

Rhyme gave a laugh. 'That's a good thought. But at any given moment in Manhattan there're about fifty thousand cell phone calls in progress. Besides, I doubt he was really on the phone.'

'He was frontin'? How you know that?' Lakeesha asked, furtively slipping two sticks of gum into her mouth.

'I don't *know* it. I suspect it. Like the laughing. He was probably doing it to make Geneva drop her guard. You tend not to notice people on cell phones. And you rarely think of them as being a threat.'

61

Geneva was nodding. 'Yeah. I was kinda freaked when he first came into the library. But when I heard him on the phone, well, I thought it's rude to be talking on a phone in a library but I wasn't scared anymore.'

'What happened then?' Sachs asked.

She explained that she'd heard a second click — she thought it sounded like a gun — and saw a man in a ski mask. She then told how she'd dismantled the mannequin and dressed it in her own clothes.

'That phat,' Lakeesha offered proudly. 'My sista here, she smart.'

She sure is, Rhyme thought.

'I hid in the stacks till he walked to the microfiche reader then I ran for the fire door.'

'You didn't see anything else about him?' Sachs asked.

'No.'

'What color was the mask?'

'Dark. I don't know exactly.'

'Other clothes?'

'I didn't see anything else really. Not that I remember. I was pretty freaked.'

'I'm sure you were,' Sachs said. 'When you were hiding in the stacks, were you looking in his direction? So you'd know when to run?'

Geneva frowned for a moment. 'Well, yeah, that's right, I was looking. I forgot about that. I watched through the bottom shelves so I could run when he got close to my chair.'

'So maybe you saw a little more of him then.'

'Oh, you know, I did. I think he had brown

62

shoes. Yeah, brown. Sort of a lighter shade, not dark brown.'

'Good. And what about his pants?'

'Dark, I'm pretty sure. But that's all I could see, just the cuffs.'

'You smell anything?'

'No ... Wait. Maybe I *did*. You know, something sweet, like flowers.'

'And then?'

'He came up to the chair and I heard this crack and then another couple of sounds. Something breaking.'

'The microfiche reader,' Sachs said. 'He smashed it.'

'By then I was running as fast as I could. To the fire door. I went down the stairs and when I got to the street I found Keesh and we were going to run. But I was thinking maybe he was going to hurt somebody else. So I turned around and' — she looked at Pulaski — 'we saw you.'

Sachs asked Lakeesha, 'Did you see the attacker?'

'Nothin'. I was just chillin' and then Gen come up, runnin' all fast and buggin' an' ever'thing, you know what I'm sayin'? I didn't see nothin'.'

Rhyme asked Sellitto, 'The doer killed Barry because he was a witness — what'd *he* see?'

'He said he didn't see anything. He gave me the names of the museum's white, male employees in case it was one of them. There're two but they checked out. One was taking his daughter to school at the time, the other was in the main office, people around him.'

63

'So, an opportunistic perp,' Sachs mused. 'Saw her go inside and went after her.'

'A museum?' Rhyme asked. 'Odd choice.'

Sellitto asked both girls, 'Did you see anyone following you today?'

Lakeesha said, 'We come down on the C train durin' rush hour. Eighth Avenue line . . . be all crowded and nasty. Couldn't see nobody weird. You?'

Geneva shook her head.

'How 'bout recently? Anybody hassling you? Hitting on you?'

Neither of them could think of anybody who'd seemed to be a threat. Embarrassed, Geneva said, 'Not exactly a lot of stalkers coming round after me. They'd be looking for a little more booty, you know. Blingier.'

'Blingier?'

'Girl mean flashy,' translated Lakeesha, who obviously typified both booty and bling. She frowned and glanced at Geneva. 'Why you gotta go there, girl? Don't be talkin' trash 'bout yo'self.'

Sachs looked at Rhyme, who was frowning. 'What're you thinking?'

'Something's not right. Let's go over the evidence while Geneva's here. There might be some things that she can help explain.'

The girl shook her head. 'That test?' She held up her watch.

'This won't take long,' Rhyme said.

Geneva looked at her friend. 'You can just make it to study period.'

'I'ma stay with you. I can't be sittin' for all

64

them hours in class worryin' 'bout you and ever'thing.'

Geneva gave a wry laugh. 'No way, girl.' She asked Rhyme, 'You don't need her, do you?'

He glanced at Sachs, who shook her head. Sellitto jotted down her address and phone number. 'We'll call you if we have any more questions.'

'Take a pass, girl,' she said. 'Just kick it an' stay home.'

'I'll see you at school,' Geneva said firmly. 'You'll be there?' Then lifted an eyebrow. 'Word?'

Two loud snaps of gum. A sigh. 'Word.' At the door the girl paused and turned back, said to Rhyme, 'Yo, mister, how long fo' you get outa that chair?'

No one said anything to fill the awkward moment. Awkward to everyone, Rhyme supposed, but himself.

'It'll probably be a long time,' he said to her.

'Man, that suck.'

'Yeah,' Rhyme said. 'Sometimes it does.'

She headed into the hall, toward the front door. They heard, 'Damn, watch it, dude.' The outer door slammed.

Mel Cooper entered the room, looking back at the spot where he'd nearly been run down by a teenager who outweighed him by fifty pounds. 'Okay,' he said to no one. 'I'm not going to ask.' He pulled off his green windbreaker and nodded a greeting to everyone.

The slim, balding man had been working as a forensic scientist for an upstate New York police department some years ago when he'd politely but insistently told Rhyme, then head of NYPD forensics, that one of his analyses was wrong. Rhyme had far more respect for people who pointed out mistakes than for sycophants — provided, of course, they were correct, which Cooper had been. Rhyme had immediately started a campaign to get the man to New York City, a challenge at which he ultimately succeeded.

Cooper was a born scientist but even more important he was a born *forensic* scientist, which is very different. It's often thought that 'forensic' refers to crime scene work, but in fact the word means any aspect of debating issues in courts of law. To be a successful criminalist you have to translate raw facts into a form that'll be useful to the prosecutor. It's not enough, for instance, to simply determine the presence of nux vomica plant materials at a suspected crime scene — many of which are used for such innocuous medical purposes as treating ear inflammations. A true forensic scientist like Mel Cooper would know instantly that those same materials produce the deadly alkaloid poison strychnine.

Cooper had the trappings of a computer-game nerd — he lived with his mother, still wore madras shirts with chinos and had a Woody Allen physique. But looks were deceiving. Cooper's longtime girlfriend was a tall, gorgeous blonde. Together they would sail in unison across ballroom floors in dance competitions, in which they were often top champions. Recently they'd taken up skeet shooting and winemaking (to which Cooper was meticulously applying principles of chemistry and physics).

Rhyme briefed him on the case and they turned to the evidence. Rhyme said, 'Let's look at the pack.'

Donning latex gloves, Cooper glanced at Sachs, who pointed out the paper bag containing the rape pack. He opened it over a large piece of newsprint — to catch bits of ambient trace — and extracted the bag. It was a thin plastic sack. No store logo was printed on it, only a large yellow smiley face. The tech now opened the bag, then paused. He said, 'I smell something . . . ' A deep inhalation. 'Flowery. What is that?' Cooper carried the bag to Rhyme and he smelled it. There was something familiar about the fragrance, but he couldn't decide what. 'Geneva?'

'Yes?'

'Is that what you smelled back in the library?'

She sniffed. 'Yeah, that's it.'

Sachs said, 'Jasmine. I think it's jasmine.'

'On the chart,' Rhyme announced.

'What chart?' Cooper asked, looking around.

In each of his cases, Rhyme made whiteboard charts of evidence found at crime scenes and profiles of the perps. 'Start one,' he ordered. 'And we need to call him something. Somebody give me a name.'

No one had any inspiration.

Rhyme said, 'No time to be creative. October ninth today, right? Ten/nine. So he'll be Unsub one-oh-nine. Thom! We need your elegant handwriting.'

'No need to butter up,' the aide said as he stepped into the room with another coffeepot.

'Unsub one-oh-nine. Evidence and profile charts. He's a white male. Height?'

Geneva said, 'I don't know. Everybody's tall to me. Six feet, I'd guess.'

'You seem observant. We'll go with that. Weight?'

'Not too big or small.' She fell quiet for a moment, troubled. 'About Dr. Barry's weight.'

Sellitto said, 'Make it one eighty. Age?'

'I don't know. I couldn't see his face.'

'Voice?'

'I didn't pay any attention. Average, I guess.'

Rhyme continued, 'And light brown shoes, dark slacks, dark ski mask. A pack in a bag that smells of jasmine. He smells of it too. Soap or lotion maybe.'

'Pack?' Thom asked. 'What do you mean?'

'Rape pack,' Geneva said. A glance at Rhyme. 'You don't need to sugarcoat anything for me. If that's what you were doing.'

'Fair enough.' Rhyme nodded at her. 'Let's keep going.' He noticed Sachs's face turn dark as she watched Cooper pick up the bag.

'What's wrong?'

'The smiley face. On a rape pack bag. What kind of sick asshole'd do that?'

He was perplexed by her anger. 'You realize that it's *good* news he used that, don't you, Sachs?'

'Good news?'

'It limits the number of stores we have to search for. Not as easy as a bag with an individuated logo on it but better than unprinted plastic.'

'I suppose,' she said, grimacing. 'But still.'

Wearing latex gloves, Mel Cooper looked through the bag. He took out the tarot card first. It showed a man hanging upside down by his foot from a scaffold. Beams of light radiated from his head. His face was oddly passive. He didn't seem to be in pain. Above him was the Roman numeral for twelve, XII.

'Mean anything, to you?' Rhyme asked Geneva.

She shook her head.

Cooper mused, 'Some kind of ritual or cult thing?'

Sachs said, 'Got a thought.' She pulled out her cell phone, placed a call. Rhyme deduced that the person she'd spoken to would be arriving soon. 'I called a specialist — about the card.'

'Good.'

Cooper examined the card for prints and found none. Nor was any helpful trace revealed.

'What else was in the bag?' Rhyme asked.

'Okay,' the tech replied, 'we've got a brand-new roll of duct tape, a box cutter, Trojan condoms. Nothing traceable. And . . . bingo!' Cooper held up a little slip of paper. 'A receipt.'

Rhyme wheeled closer and looked it over. There was no store name; the slip had been printed by an adding machine. The ink was faded.

'Won't tell us very much,' Pulaski said then seemed to think he shouldn't be talking.

What was *he* doing here? Rhyme wondered.

69

Oh, that's right. Helping Sellitto.

'Sorry to differ,' Rhyme said stridently. 'Tells us a lot. He bought all the items in the pack at one store — you can compare the receipt to the price tags — well, along with something else he bought for five ninety-five that wasn't in the bag. Maybe the tarot deck. So we've got a store that sells duct tape, box cutters and condoms. Got to be a variety store or variety drugstore. We know it's not a chain because there's no logo on the bag or receipt. And it's low-budget since it only has cash drawers, not computerized registers. Not to mention the cheap prices. And the sales tax tells us that the store is in . . . ' He squinted as he compared the subtotal on the receipt with the amount of tax. 'Goddamnit, who knows math? What's the percentage?'

Cooper said, 'I've got a calculator.'

Geneva glanced at the receipt. 'Eight point six two five.'

'How'd you do that?' Sachs asked.

'I just kind of can,' she said.

Rhyme repeated, 'Eight point six two five. That's the combined New York state and city sales tax. Puts the store in one of the five boroughs.' A glance at Pulaski. 'So, Patrolman, still think it's not very revealing?'

'Got it, sir.'

'I'm decommissioned. Sir isn't necessary. All right. Print everything and let's see what we can find.'

'Me?' the rookie asked uncertainly.

'No. Them.'

Cooper and Sachs used a variety of techniques

to raise prints on the evidence: fluorescent powder, Ardrox spray and superglue fumes on slick surfaces, iodine vapor and ninhydrin on porous, some of which raised prints by themselves, while others displayed the results under an alternative light source.

Looking up at the team through his large orange goggles, the tech reported, 'Prints on the receipt, prints on the merchandise. They're all the same. Only, the thing is, they're small, too small to be from a six-foot-tall man. A petite woman or a teenage girl, the clerk's, I'd say. I see smudges too. I'd guess the unsub wiped his own off.'

While it was difficult to remove all the oils and residue left by human fingers, prints could be obliterated easily by a brief rubbing.

'Run what you've got through IAFIS.'

Cooper lifted copies of the prints and scanned them. Ten minutes later the FBI's integrated automated fingerprint identification system had verified that the prints did not belong to anyone on file in the major databases, city, state and federal. Cooper also sent them to some of the local databases that weren't linked to the FBI's system.

'Shoes,' Rhyme announced.

Sachs produced the electrostatic print. The tread marks were worn, so the shoes were old.

'Size eleven,' Cooper announced.

There was a loose correlation between foot size and bone structure and height, though it was tenuous as circumstantial evidence in court. Still, the size suggested that Geneva had probably been right in her assessment that the man was around six feet tall.

'What about a brand?'

Cooper ran the image through the department's shoe-tread database and came up with a match. 'Bass-brand shoes, walkers. At least three years old. They discontinued this model that year.'

Rhyme said, 'The tread wear tells us he has a slightly turned out right foot, but no noticeable limp and no serious bunions, ingrown nails or other *malades des pieds.*'

'I didn't know you spoke French, Lincoln,' Cooper said.

Only to the extent it helped an investigation. This particular phrase had come about when he was running the missing-right-shoes case and had spoken on a number of occasions to a French cop.

'What's the trace situation?'

Cooper was poring over the evidence collection bags containing the tiny particles that had adhered to Sachs's trace collector, which was a sticky roller, like the kind for removing lint and pet hair. Rollers had replaced DustBuster vacuum cleaners as the collector of choice for fiber, hair and dry residue.

Wearing the magnifiers again, the tech used fine tweezers to pick up materials. He prepared a slide and placed it under the microscope, then adjusted the magnification and focus. Simultaneously, the image popped up on several flat-screen computer monitors around the room. Rhyme turned his chair and examined the images closely. He could see flecks that appeared to be bits of dust, several fibers, white puffy objects, and what looked like tiny amber shells shed by insects — exoskeletons. When Cooper moved the stage of the scope, some small balls of spongy, off-white fibrous material were visible.

'Where did this come from?'

Sachs looked over the tag. 'Two sources: the floor near the table where Geneva was sitting and beside the Dumpster where he was standing when he shot Barry.'

Trace evidence in a public place was often useless because there were so many chances for strangers unconnected to the crime to shed material. But similar trace being found in *two* separate locations where the perp had been suggested strongly that it had been left by him.

'Thank you, Lord,' Rhyme muttered, 'for thy wisdom in creating deep-tread shoes.'

Sachs and Thom glanced at each other.

'Wondering about my good mood?' Rhyme asked, continuing to stare at the screen. 'Was that the reason for the sidelong look? I *can* be cheerful sometimes, you know.'

'Blue moon,' the aide muttered.

'Cliché alert, Lon. You catch that one? Now, back to the trace. We know he shed it. What *is* it? And can it lead us to his den?'

Forensic scientists confront a pyramid-shaped task in analyzing evidence. The initial — and usually easiest — job is to *identify* a substance (finding that a brown stain, for instance, is blood and whether it's human or animal, or that a piece of lead is a bullet fragment).

The second task is to *classify* that sample, that is, put it in a subcategory (like determining that the blood is O positive, that the bullet that shed the fragment was a .38). Learning that evidence falls into a particular class may have some value to police and prosecutors if the suspect can be linked to evidence in a similar class — his shirt has a type-O-positive bloodstain on it, he owns a .38 — though that connection isn't conclusive.

The final task, and the ultimate goal of all forensic scientists, is to *individuate* the evidence — unquestionably link this particular bit of evidence to a single location or human being (the DNA from the blood on the suspect's shirt matches that of the victim, the bullet has a unique mark that could be made only by his gun).

The team was now low on this forensic pyramid. The strands, for instance, were fibers of some sort, they knew. But more than a thousand different fibers were made in the United States annually and over seven thousand different types of pigments were used to color them. Still, the team could narrow down the field. Cooper's analysis revealed that the fibers shed by the killer were plant based — rather than animal or mineral — and they were thick.

'I'm betting it's cotton rope,' Rhyme suggested.

Cooper nodded as he read through a database of vegetable-based fibers. 'Yep, that's it. Generic, though. No manufacturer.'

One fiber contained no pigments but the other had a staining agent of some kind. It was brown and Cooper thought the stain might be blood. A test with the phenolphthalein presumptive blood test revealed that it was.

'His?' Sellitto wondered.

'Who knows?' Cooper responded, continuing to examine the sample. 'But it's definitely human. With the compression and fractured ends, I'd speculate the rope's a garrotte. We've seen that before. It could be this was the intended murder weapon.'

His blunt object would be simply to subdue his victim, rather than to kill her (it's hard, messy work beating someone to death). He also had the gun, but that would be too loud to use if you wanted to keep the murder quiet in order to escape. A garrotte made sense.

Geneva sighed. 'Mr. Rhyme? My test.'

'Test?'

'At school.'

'Oh, sure. Just a minute . . . I want to know what kind of bug that exoskeleton's from,' Rhyme continued.

'Officer,' Sachs said to Pulaski.

'Yes, m' . . . Detective?'

'How 'bout you help us out here?'

'Sure thing.'

Cooper printed out a color image of the bit of exoskeleton and handed it to the rookie. Sachs sat him down in front of one of the computers and typed in commands to get into the department's insect database — the NYPD was one of the few police departments in the world that had not only an extensive library of insect information but a forensic entomologist on staff.

75

After a brief pause the screen began to fill with thumbnail images of insect parts.

'Man, there're a lot of them. You know, I've never actually done this before.' He squinted as the files flipped past.

Sachs stifled a smile. 'Not exactly like *CSI*, is it?' she asked. 'Just scroll through slowly and look for something you think matches. 'Slow' is the key word.'

Rhyme said, 'More mistakes in forensic analysis occur because technicians rush than because of any other cause.'

'I didn't know that.'

Sachs said, 'And now you do.'

6

'GC those white blobs there,' Rhyme ordered. 'What the hell are they?'

Mel Cooper lifted several samples off the tape and ran them through the gas chromatograph/ mass spectrometer, the workhorse instrument in all forensic labs. It separates unknown trace into its component parts and then identifies them. The results would take fifteen minutes or so, and while they waited for the analysis Cooper pieced together the bullet the emergency room doctor had removed from the leg of the woman whom the killer had shot. Sachs had reported the gun had to be a revolver, not an automatic, since there were no brass cartridges ejected at the scene of the shooting outside the museum.

'Oh, these're nasty,' Cooper said softly, examining the fragments with a pair of tweezers. 'The gun's small, a .22. But they're magnum rounds.'

'Good,' Rhyme said. He was pleased because the powerful magnum version of the rimfire 22-caliber bullet was rare ammunition and therefore would be easier to trace. The fact that the gun was a revolver made it rarer still. Which meant they should be able to find the manufacturer easily.

Sachs, who was a competitive pistol shooter, didn't even need to look it up. 'North American Arms is the only one I know of. Their Black

Widow model maybe, but I'd guess the Mini-Master. It's got a four-inch barrel. That's more accurate and he grouped those shots real tight.'

Rhyme asked the tech, who was poring over the examination board, 'What'd you mean by nasty?'

'Take a look.'

Rhyme, Sachs and Sellitto moved forward. Cooper was pushing around bits of blood-stained metal with the tweezers. 'Looks like he made them himself.'

'Explosive rounds?'

'No, almost as bad. Maybe worse. The outer shell of the bullet's thin lead. Inside, the slug was filled with these.'

There were a half dozen tiny needles, about three-eighths of an inch long. Upon impact, the bullet would shatter and the pins would tumble in a V pattern throughout the body. Though the slugs were small they'd do far more damage than regular rounds. They weren't designed to stop an attacker; their purpose was solely to destroy internal tissue. And without the numbing effect of a large-caliber slug's impact, these shells would result in agonizing wounds.

Lon Sellitto shook his head, eyes fixed on the needles, and scratched the invisible stain on his face, probably thinking how close he'd come to being hit with one of these slugs. 'Jesus,' he muttered. His voice broke and he cleared his throat, laughed to cover it up and walked away from the table.

Curiously, the lieutenant's reaction was more

troubled than the girl's. Geneva didn't seem to pay much attention to the details of her attacker's gruesome rounds. She glanced again at her watch and slouched impatiently.

Cooper scanned the largest pieces of the bullet and ran the information about the slugs through IBIS, the Integrated Ballistics Identification System, which nearly a thousand police departments around the country subscribe to, as well as the FBI's DRUGFIRE system. These huge databases can match a slug, fragments or brass casing to bullets or weapons on file. A gun found on a suspect today, for instance, can quickly be matched to a bullet recovered from a victim five years ago.

The results on these slugs, though, came back negative. The needles themselves appeared to have been broken off the end of sewing needles, the sort you could buy anywhere. Untraceable.

'Never easy, is it?' Cooper muttered. At Rhyme's direction, he also searched for registered owners of Mini-Masters, and the smaller Black Widows, in .22 magnum, and came back with nearly a thousand owners, none of whom had criminal records. Stores aren't required by law to keep records of who buys ammunition and therefore they never did. For the time being, the weapon was a dead end.

'Pulaski?' Rhyme shouted. 'What's with the bug?'

'The exoskeleton — is that what you called it? That's what you mean, sir?'

'Right, right, right. What *about* it?'

'No matches yet. What exactly *is* an exoskeleton?'

Rhyme didn't answer. He glanced at the screen and saw that the young man was only a small way into the Hemiptera order of insects. He had a long way to go. 'Keep at it.'

The GC/MS computer beeped; it had completed its analysis of the white blobs. On the screen was a peak-and-valley chart, below which was a block of text.

Cooper leaned forward and said, 'We've got curcumin, demethoxycurcumin, bis-demethoxy-curcumin, volatile oil, amino acids, lysine and tryptophan, theronine and isoleucine, chloride, various other trace proteins and large proportion of starches, oils, triglycerides, sodium, polysaccharides . . . Never seen that combination.'

The GC/MS was miraculous in isolating and identifying substances, but not necessarily so great in telling you what they added up to. Rhyme was often able to deduce common substances, like gasoline or explosives, just from a list of their ingredients. But these were new to him. He cocked his head and began to categorize those substances in the list that, as a scientist, he knew would logically be found together and which would not. 'The curcumin, its compounds and the polysaccharides obviously fit together.'

'Obviously,' was the wry response of Amelia Sachs, who used to ditch science class in high school to go drag racing.

'We'll call that Substance One. Then the amino acids, other proteins, starches and triglycerides — they're often found together, too. We'll call them Substance Two. The chloride — '

'Poison, right?' asked Pulaski.

' — and sodium,' muttered Rhyme, 'are most likely salt.' A glance at the rookie. 'Dangerous only in the case of people with high blood pressure. Or if you're a garden slug.'

The kid turned back to the insect database.

'So — with the amino acids and starches and oils — I'm thinking Substance Two is a food, salty food. Go online, Mel, and find out what the hell curcumin is in.'

Cooper did. 'You're right. It's a vegetable dye used in food products. Usually found in connection with those other items in Substance One. Volatile oils too.'

'What sort of food products?'

'Hundreds of them.'

'How 'bout some for-instances.'

Cooper began to read from a lengthy list. But Rhyme interrupted. 'Hold on. Is popcorn on the list?'

'Let's see . . . yeah, it is.'

Rhyme turned and called to Pulaski, 'You can stop.'

'Stop?'

'It's not an exoskeleton. It's a shell from a popcorn kernel. Salt and oil and popcorn. Should've figured that one out up front, damnit.' It was a cheerful expletive nonetheless. 'On the chart, Thom. Our boy likes junk food.'

'Should I write that?'

'Of course not. He could hate popcorn. Maybe he works in a popcorn factory or movie

81

theater. Just add 'popcorn.' ' Rhyme looked at the chart. 'Now let's find out about that other trace. The off-white stuff.'

Cooper ran another GC/MS test. The results indicated that it was sucrose and uric acid.

'The acid's concentrated,' the tech said. 'The sugar's pure — no other foodstuffs — and the crystalline structure's unique. I've never seen it milled like that.'

Rhyme was troubled by this news. 'Send it to the FBI's bomb people.'

'Bomb?' Sellitto asked.

Rhyme said, 'Haven't been reading my book, hmmm?'

'No,' the big detective shot back. 'I've been busy catching bad guys.'

'Touché. But it'd be helpful to at least take a look at the headings from time to time. As in 'Homemade Explosive Devices.' Sugar's often an ingredient. Mix it with sodium nitrate and you've got a smoke bomb. With permanganate, it's a low explosive — which can still do a lot of damage if you pack it into a pipe. I'm not sure how the uric acid figures but the Bureau's got the best database in the world. They'll tell us.'

The FBI's lab is available to handle evidence analysis for state and local law enforcers, at no charge, provided that the requesting agency agrees to two things: to accept the FBI's results as final and to show them to the defendant's lawyer. Because of the Bureau's generosity — and its talent — the agents are inundated with requests for assistance; they run more than 700,000 analyses a year.

Even New York's finest would stand in line like everyone else to get this bit of sugar analyzed. But Lincoln Rhyme had an in — Fred Dellray, a special agent in the FBI's Manhattan office, often worked with Rhyme and Sellitto and he carried a lot of weight in the Bureau. Equally important was the fact that Rhyme had helped the FBI set up its PERT system — the Physical Evidence Response Team. Sellitto called Dellray, who was presently on the task force checking out those reports of potential terrorist bombings in New York. Dellray got on the horn to FBI HQ in Washington, D.C., and within minutes a technician had been recruited to help on the Unsub 109 case. Cooper sent him the results of the analyses and compressed digital images of the substance via secure email.

No more than ten minutes passed before the phone rang.

'Command, answer,' Rhyme snapped into his voice recognition control system.

'Detective Rhyme, please.'

'This's Rhyme.'

'I'm Examiner Phillips down on Ninth Street.' Washington's Ninth Street, he meant. FBI headquarters.

'What do you have for us?' Rhyme asked briskly.

'And thanks for calling back so fast,' Sachs said quickly. She sometimes had to run interference for Rhyme's bluntness.

'No worries, ma'am. Well, I was thinking it was pretty odd, what you sent down. So I sent it to Materials Analysis. That did the trick. We've got a ninety-seven percent certainty as to the substance.'

How dangerous was the explosive? Rhyme wondered. He said, 'Go ahead. What is it?'

'Cotton candy.'

That wasn't a street name he knew. But there were a number of new-generation explosives that had detonation rates of thirty thousand feet per second, ten times the speed of a bullet. Was this one of those? He asked, 'What're its properties?'

A pause. 'It tastes good.'

'What's that?'

'It's sweet. It tastes good.'

Rhyme asked, 'You mean it's *real* cotton candy, like you'd find at a fair?'

'Yeah, what'd you think I meant?'

'Never mind.' Sighing, the criminalist asked, 'And the uric acid was from his shoe when he stepped in some dog pee on the sidewalk?'

'Can't say *where* he stepped on it,' the examiner said, displaying the precision the Bureau was known for. 'But the sample *does* test positive for canine urine.'

He thanked the man and disconnected. He turned to the team. 'Popcorn and cotton candy on his shoes at the same time?' Rhyme mused. 'Where'd that put him?'

'Ball game?'

'The New York teams haven't played at home lately. I'm thinking maybe our unsub walked through a neighborhood where there'd been a fair or carnival in the past day or so.' He asked Geneva, 'Did you go to any fairs recently? Could he have seen you there?'

84

'Me? No. I don't really go to fairs.'

Rhyme said to Pulaski, 'Since you're off bug detail, Patrolman, call whoever you need to and find out every permit that's been issued for a fair, carnival, festival, religious feast, whatever.'

'I'm on it,' the rookie said.

'What else do we have?' Rhyme asked.

'Flakes from the carriage of the microfiche reader, where he hit it with the blunt object.'

'Flakes?'

'Bits of varnish, I'd guess, from whatever he used.'

'Okay, run them through Maryland.'

The FBI had a huge database of current and past paint samples, located in one of its Maryland facilities. This was mostly used for matching paint evidence to cars. But there were hundreds of samples of varnish as well. After another call from Dellray, Cooper sent the GC/MS composition analysis and other data on the lacquer flakes off to the Bureau. Within a few minutes the phone rang, and this FBI examiner reported that the varnish matched a product sold exclusively to manufacturers of martial arts equipment, like nunchakus and security batons. He added the discouraging news that the substance contained no manufacturer's markers and was sold in large quantities — meaning it was virtually untraceable.

'Okay, we've got a rapist with a nunchaku, funky bullets, a bloody rope . . . man is a walking nightmare.'

The doorbell rang and a moment later Thom ushered in a woman in her twenties, his arm around her shoulders.

'Look who's here,' the aide announced.

The slim woman had spiky purple hair and a pretty face. Her stretch pants and sweater revealed an athletic body — actually, a *performer's* body, Rhyme knew.

'Kara,' Rhyme said. 'Good to see you again. I deduce *you're* the specialist Sachs called.'

'Hi.' The young woman hugged Sachs, greeted the others and closed her hands around Rhyme's. Sachs introduced her to Geneva, who looked her over with a reserved face.

Kara (it was a stage name; she wouldn't reveal her real one) was an illusionist and performance artist who had helped Rhyme and Sachs as a consultant in a recent murder case, where a killer used his skills as a magician and sleight-of-hand artist to get close to victims, murder them and get away.

She lived in Greenwich Village, but had been visiting her mother in a care facility uptown when Sachs had called, she explained. They spent a few moments catching up — Kara was putting together a one-woman show for the Performance Warehouse in Soho, and was dating an acrobat — then Rhyme said, 'We need some expertise.'

'You bet,' the young woman said. 'Whatever I can do.'

Sachs explained about the case. She frowned and whispered, 'I'm sorry,' to Geneva when she heard about the attempted rape.

The student just shrugged.

'He had this with him,' Cooper said, holding

up The Hanged Man tarot card from the rape pack.

'We thought you could tell us something about it.'

Kara had explained to Rhyme and Sachs that the world of magic was divided into two camps, those who were entertainers, who made no claim to having supernatural skills, and those who asserted they had occult powers. Kara had no patience for the latter — she was solely a performer — but because of her experience working in magic stores for rent and food money she knew something about fortune-telling.

She explained, 'Okay, tarot's an old method of divining that goes back to ancient Egypt. The tarot deck of cards're divided into the minor arcana — they correspond to the fifty-two-card playing deck — and the major arcana, zero through twenty-one. They sort of represent a journey through life. The Hanged Man's the twelfth card in the major arcana.' She shook her head. 'But something doesn't make sense.'

'What's that?' Sellitto asked, subtly rubbing his skin.

'It's not a bad card at all. Look at the picture.'

'He *does* look pretty peaceful,' Sachs said, 'considering he's hanging upside down.'

'The figure in the picture's based on the Norse god Odin. He hung upside down for nine days on a search for inner knowledge. You get this card in a reading, it means you're about to start a quest for spiritual enlightenment.' She nodded at a computer. 'You mind?'

Cooper waved her to it. She typed a Google

search and a few seconds later found a website. 'How do I print this out?'

Sachs helped her, and a moment later a sheet rolled out of the laser printer. Cooper taped it up on the evidence board. 'That's the meaning,' she said.

The Hanged Man does not refer to someone being punished. Its appearance in a reading indicates spiritual searching leading to a decision, a transition, a change of direction. The card often foretells a surrendering to experience, ending a struggle, accepting what is. When this card appears in your reading you must listen to your inner self, even if that message seems to be contrary to logic.

Kara said, 'It has nothing to do with violence or death. It's about being spiritually suspended and waiting.' She shook her head. 'It's not the kind of thing a killer would leave — if he knew anything at all about tarot cards. If he'd wanted to leave something destructive, it would've been The Tower or one of the cards from the sword suit in the minor arcana. Those're bad news.'

'So he picked it only because it looked scary,' Rhyme summarized. And because he planned to garrotte, or 'hang,' Geneva.

'That's what I'd guess.'

'That's helpful,' Rhyme said.

Sachs too thanked her.

'I should get back. Have to rehearse.' Kara

shook Geneva's hand. 'Hope things work out okay for you.'

'Thanks.'

Kara walked to the door. She stopped and looked at Geneva. 'You like illusion and magic shows?'

'I don't get out too much,' the girl said. 'Pretty busy in school.'

'Well, I'm doing a show in three weeks. If you're interested, all the details are on the ticket.'

'The . . . ?'

'Ticket.'

'I don't have a ticket.'

'Yes, you do,' Kara said. 'It's in your purse. Oh, and the flower with it? Consider it a good luck charm.'

She left, and they heard the door close.

'What's she talking about?' Geneva asked, looking down at her purse, which was closed.

Sachs laughed. 'Open it up.'

She unzipped the top and blinked in surprise. Sitting just inside was a ticket to one of Kara's performances. Next to it was a pressed violet. 'How did she do that?' Geneva whispered.

'We've never quite been able to catch her,' Rhyme said. 'All we know is, she's pretty damn good.'

'Man, I'll say.' The student held up the dried purple flower.

The criminalist's eyes slipped to the tarot card, as Cooper taped it to the evidence board, next to its meaning. 'So, it *seems* like the sort of thing a killer would leave in an occult assault. But he didn't have a clue what it was. He picked

89

it for effect. So that means . . . ' But his voice faded as he stared at the rest of the evidence chart. 'Jesus.'

The others looked at him.

'What?' Cooper asked.

'We've got it all wrong.'

Taking a break from rubbing his face, Sellitto asked, 'Whatta you mean?'

'Look at the prints on what was in the rape pack. He wiped his own off, right?'

'Yeah,' Cooper confirmed.

'But there *are* prints,' the criminalist offered. 'And they're probably the clerk's, since they're the same that're on the receipt.'

'Right.' Sellitto shrugged. 'So?'

'So he wiped his prints *before* he got to the cash register. While he was in the store.' Silence in the room. Irritated that nobody caught on, the criminalist continued, 'Because he *wanted* the clerk's prints on everything.'

Sachs understood. 'He *meant* to leave the rape pack behind. So we'd find it.'

Pulaski was nodding. 'Otherwise, he'd just have wiped everything after he got it home.'

'Ex-actly,' Rhyme said with a hint of triumph in his voice. 'I think it was staged evidence. To make us *think* it was a rape, with some kind of occult overtones. Okay, okay . . . Let's step back.' Rhyme was amused at Pulaski's uneasy glance at Rhyme's legs when the criminalist used the expression. 'An attacker tracks down Geneva in a public museum. Not the typical setting for sexual assault. Then he hits her — well, the mannequin — hard enough to kill her, if not knock her out for hours. If that's the case then what's he need the box cutter and duct tape for? And he leaves a tarot card he thinks is scary but is really just about spiritual searching? No, it wasn't an attempted rape at all.'

'What's he up to then?' Sellitto asked.

'That's what we damn well better find out.' Rhyme thought for a moment then asked, 'And you said that Dr. Barry didn't see anything?'

'That's what he told me,' Sellitto replied.

'But the unsub still comes back and kills him.' Rhyme frowned. 'And Mr. One-oh-nine broke up the microfiche reader. He's a pro, but tantrums're very *un*-pro. His vic's getting away — he's not going to waste time thumpin' on things because he's having a bad morning.' Rhyme asked the girl, 'You said you were reading some old newspaper?'

'Magazine,' she corrected.

'On the microfiche reader?'

'Right.'

'Those?' Rhyme nodded at a large plastic evidence bag containing a box of microfiche trays that Sachs had brought back from the library. Two slots, carriages one and three, were empty.

Geneva looked at the box. She nodded. 'Yeah. Those were the ones that had the article I was reading, the missing ones.'

'Did you get the one that was in the reader?'

Sachs replied, 'There wasn't one. He must've taken it with him.'

'And smashed the machine so we wouldn't notice that the tray was gone. Oh, this is getting

91

interesting. What was he up to? What the hell was his motive?'

Sellitto laughed. 'I thought you didn't care about motive. Only evidence.'

'You need to draw the distinction, Lon, between using motive to *prove* a case in court — which is speculation at best — and using motive to lead you to the evidence, which conclusively convicts a perp: A man kills his business partner with a gun that we trace to *his* garage loaded with bullets *he* bought per a receipt with *his* fingerprints on it. In that case who cares if he killed the partner because he thinks a talking dog told him to or because the guy was sleeping with his wife? The *evidence* makes the case.

'But what if there *are* no bullets, gun, receipt or tire tracks? Then a perfectly valid question is *why* was the vic killed? Answering that can point us toward the evidence that *will* convict him. Sorry for the lecture,' he added with no apology in his voice.

'Good mood gone, is it?' Thom asked.

Rhyme grumbled, 'I'm missing something here and I don't like it.'

Geneva was frowning. Rhyme noticed and asked, 'What?'

'Well, I was thinking . . . Dr. Barry said that somebody else was interested in the same issue of that magazine that I was. He wanted to read it, but Dr. Barry told him he'd have to wait until I was through with it.'

'Did he say who?'

'No.'

Rhyme considered this. 'So let's speculate: The librarian tells this *somebody* that you're interested in the magazine. The unsub wants to steal it and he wants to kill you because you've read it or *will* read it.' The criminalist wasn't convinced this was the situation, of course. But one of the things that made him so successful was his willingness to consider bold, sometimes farfetched theories. 'And he took the one article you were reading, right?'

The girl nodded.

'It was like he knew exactly what to look for . . . What was it about?'

'Nothing important. Just this ancestor of mine. My teacher's into all this *Roots* stuff and we had to write about somebody in our past.'

'Who was he, this ancestor?'

'My great-great-great-whatever, a freed slave. I went to the museum last week and found out there was an article about him in this issue of *Coloreds' Weekly Illustrated.* They didn't have it in the library but Mr. Barry said he'd get the microfiche from storage. It just came in.'

'What was the story about specifically?' Rhyme persisted.

She hesitated then said impatiently, 'Charles Singleton, my ancestor, was a slave in Virginia. His master had this change of heart and he freed all of his slaves. And because Charles and his wife had been with the family for so long and had taught their children to read and write, their master gave them a farm in New York state. Charles was a soldier in the Civil War. He came back home afterwards and in eighteen sixty-eight he got accused of stealing some money from a black educational fund. *That*'s all the article in the magazine was about. I'd just gotten to the part where he jumped into the river to escape from the police when that man showed up.'

Rhyme noted that she spoke well but held on to her words tightly, as if they were squirming puppies trying to escape. With educated parents on one side and homegirl friends like Lakeesha on the other, it was only natural that the girl suffered from some linguistic multiple personality.

'So you don't know what happened to him?' Sachs asked.

Geneva shook her head.

'I think we have to assume that the unsub had some interest in what you were researching. Who knew what the topic of your paper was? Your teacher, I assume.'

'No, I never told him specifically. I don't think I told anybody but Lakeesha. She might've mentioned it to somebody but I doubt it. Assignments don't take up a lot of her attention, you know what I'm saying? Not even her own. Last week I went to this law office in Harlem to see if they had any old records about crimes in the eighteen hundreds but I didn't tell the lawyer there very much. Of course, Dr. Barry would've known.'

'And he would've mentioned it to that other person who was interested in the magazine too,' Rhyme pointed out. 'Now, just for the sake of argument, let's assume there's something in that article that the unsub doesn't want known

— maybe about your ancestor, maybe something else entirely.' A glance at Sachs. 'Anybody still at the scene?'

'A portable.'

'Have 'em canvass the employees. See if Barry mentioned that somebody was interested in that old magazine. Have them go through his desk too.' Rhyme had another thought. 'And I want his phone records for the past month.'

Sellitto shook his head. 'Linc, really . . . this's sounding pretty thin, don't you think? We're talking, what? The eighteen hundreds? This isn't a cold case. It's a *frozen* one.'

'A pro who staged a scene, nearly killed one person, and did kill another — right in front of a half dozen cops — just to steal that article? That's not thin, Lon. That's got searchlights all over it.'

The big cop shrugged and called the precinct to relay the order to the cop still on duty at the crime scene and then called Warrants to have them issue a phone record subpoena on the museum's and Barry's personal phones.

Rhyme looked over the slim girl and decided that he had no choice; he had to deliver the tough news. 'You know what all this might mean, don't you?'

A pause, though he could see in Sachs's troubled glance at Geneva that the policewoman at least knew exactly what it meant. It was she who said to the girl, 'Lincoln's saying that it's likely that he's probably still after you.'

'That's wack,' Geneva Settle offered, shaking her head.

95

After a pause, Rhyme replied solemnly, 'I'm afraid it's anything but.'

★　★　★

Sitting at the Internet access station in a quick-copy shop in downtown Manhattan, Thompson Boyd was reading through the local TV station website, which updated news every few minutes.

The headline of the article he read was: MUSEUM OFFICIAL MURDERED; WITNESS IN ASSAULT ON STUDENT.

Whistling, almost silently, he examined the accompanying picture, which showed the library director he'd just killed talking to a uniformed policeman on the street in front of the museum. The caption read, *Dr. Donald Barry speaks with police shortly before he was shot to death.*

Because of her age, Geneva Settle wasn't identified by name, though she was described as a high school student living in Harlem. Thompson was grateful for that information; he hadn't known which borough of the city she lived in. He hooked his phone to the USB port on the computer and transferred the picture he'd taken of the girl. This he then uploaded to an anonymous email account.

He logged off, paid for his time — in cash, of course — and strolled along lower Broadway, in the heart of the financial district. He bought a coffee from a vendor, drank half of it, then slipped the microfiche plates he'd stolen into the cup, replaced the lid and dropped them into a trash basket.

He paused at a phone kiosk, looked around and saw no one was paying him any attention. He dialed a number. There was no outgoing message from the voice mail service, only a beep. 'Me. Problem with the Settle situation. I need you to find out where she goes to school or where she lives. She's a high school student in Harlem. That's all I know. I've sent a picture of her to your account . . . Oh, one thing — if you get a chance to take care of her yourself, there's another fifty thousand in it for you. Give me a call when you get this message. We'll talk about it.' Thompson recited the number of the phone where he stood then hung up. He stepped back, crossed his arms and waited, whistling softly. He'd gotten through only three bars of Stevie Wonder's 'You Are the Sunshine of My Life' before the phone started to ring.

7

The criminalist looked at Sellitto. 'Where's Roland?'

'Bell? He delivered somebody into witness protection upstate but he should be back by now. Think we should give him a call?'

'Yes,' Rhyme said.

Sellitto called the detective's mobile phone and, from the conversation, Rhyme deduced that Bell would leave Police Plaza immediately and head uptown.

Rhyme noticed Geneva's frown. 'Detective Bell's just going to look out for you. Like a bodyguard. Until we get everything sorted out . . . Now, do you have any idea what Charles was accused of stealing?'

'The article said gold or money or something.'

'Missing gold. Ah, that's interesting. Greed — one of your better motives.'

'Would your uncle know anything about it?' Sachs asked her.

'My uncle? Oh, no, he's my mother's brother. Charles was from my father's side of the family. And Dad just knew a few things. My great-aunt gave me a few letters of Charles's. But she didn't know anything more about him.'

'Where are they? Those letters?' Rhyme asked.

'I have one with me.' She fished in her purse and pulled it out. 'And the others're at home. My aunt thought she might have some more boxes of Charles's things but she wasn't sure where they were.' Geneva fell silent as the brows in her dark, round face furrowed and she said to Sachs, 'One thing? If it's helpful?'

'Go ahead,' Sachs said.

'I remember from one of the letters. Charles talked about this secret he had.'

'Secret?' Sachs asked.

'Yeah, he said it bothered him not to be able to reveal the truth. But there'd be a disaster, a tragedy, if he did. Something like that.'

'Maybe it was the theft he was talking about,' Rhyme said.

Geneva stiffened. 'I don't think he did it. I think he was framed.'

'Why?' Rhyme asked.

A shrug. 'Read the letter.' The girl started to hand it to Rhyme, then caught herself and gave it to Mel Cooper, unapologetic about the faux pas.

The tech placed it in an optical reader and a moment later the elegantly scripted words from the nineteenth century were scrolling across flatscreen monitors from the twenty-first.

Mrs. Violet Singleton
In care of
Mr. & Mrs. William Dodd
Essex Farm Road
Harrisburg, Pennsylvania
July 14, 1863

My dearest Violet:
News has surely reached you of the terrible events in New York of late. I can now report

that peace has returned, but the cost was great.

The climate here has been incendiary, with hundreds of thousands of less fortunate citizens still reeling from the economic panic of several years ago — Mr. Greeley's Tribune reported that unconscionable stock speculation and imprudent lending had led to the 'bursting bubbles' of the world's financial markets.

In this atmosphere, it took merely a small spark to ignite the recent rioting: the order to draft men into the Federal army, which was acknowledged by many to be necessary in our fight against the Rebels, owing to the enemy's surprising strength and resilience. Still, the opposition to the draft was sturdier, and more deadly, than any had anticipated. And we — Coloreds, abolitionists and Republicans, — became the target of their hate, as much as the conscription provost and his men, if not more so.

Rioters, largely Irishmen, swept through the city, attacking any Colored they might see, sacking houses and places of work. I had by happenstance been in the company of two teachers and the director of the Colored Children's Orphanage when a mob attacked the building and set it aflame! Why, more than 200 children were inside! With God's help, we were able to lead the little ones to safety at a nearby police station, but the rioters would have killed us all if they had had their way.

Fighting continued throughout the day. That evening the lynchings began. After one Negro was hanged, his body was set on fire, and the rioters danced around it in drunken revels. I was aghast!

I have now fled to our farm up north and will henceforth keep my attention fixed on my mission of educating children in our school, working the orchard and furthering, however I can, the cause of freedom of our people.

My dearest wife, in the aftermath of these terrible events, life to me seems precarious and fleeting, and — if you are inclined to the journey, — it is my desire that you and our son now join me. I am enclosing herewith tickets for you both, and ten dollars for expenses. I will meet your train in New Jersey and we will take a boat up the river to our farm. You can assist me in teaching, and Joshua can continue his studies and help us and James in the cider mill and shop. Should anyone ask your business and destination, respond as do I: say only that we are caretakers of the farm, tending it for Master Trilling in his absence. Seeing the hatred in the eyes of the rioters has brought home to me the fact that nowhere is safe, and even in our idyllic locale, arson, theft and pillaging might very likely ensue, should it be learned that the owners of the farm are Negroes.

I have come from a place where I was held in captivity and considered to be merely a three-fifths man. I had hoped that moving

North would change this. But, alas, that is not yet the case. The tragic events of the past few days tell me that you and I and those of our kind are not yet treated as whole men and women, and our battle to achieve wholeness in the eyes of others must continue with unflagging determination.

My warmest regards to your sister and William, as well as their children, of course. Tell Joshua I am proud of his achievement in the subject of geography.

I live for the day, now soon, I pray, when I will see you and our son once again.

Yours in love,
Charles

Geneva took the letter off the optical scanner. She looked up and said, 'The Civil War Draft Riots of 1863. Worst civil disturbance in U.S. history.'

'He doesn't say anything about his secret,' Rhyme pointed out.

'That's in one of the letters I have at home. I was showing you this so you'd know he wasn't a thief.'

Rhyme frowned. 'But the theft was, what, five years *after* he wrote that? Why do you think that means he's not guilty?'

'My point,' Geneva said, 'is that he doesn't *sound* like a thief, does he? Not somebody who's going to steal from an education trust for former slaves.'

Rhyme said simply, 'That's not proof.'

'I think it is.' The girl looked over the letter

again, smoothed it with her hand.

'What's that three-fifths-man thing?' Sellitto asked.

Rhyme recalled something from American history. But unless information was relevant to his career as a criminalist, he discarded it as useless clutter. He shook his head.

Geneva explained, 'Before the Civil War, slaves were counted as three-fifths of a person for the purpose of representation in Congress. It wasn't an evil Confederate conspiracy, like you'd think; the *North* came up with that rule. They didn't want slaves counted at all, because that would give the South more representatives in Congress and the electoral college. The South wanted them counted as full people. The three-fifths rule was a compromise.'

'They were counted for representation,' Thom pointed out, 'but they still couldn't vote.'

'Oh, of course not,' Geneva said.

'Just like women, by the way,' Sachs added.

The social history of America wasn't of any interest to Rhyme at the moment. 'I'd like to see the other letters. And I want to find another copy of that magazine, *Coloreds' Weekly Illustrated*. What issue?'

'July twenty-third, 1868,' Geneva said. 'But I've had a tough time finding it.'

'I'll do my best,' Mel Cooper said. And Rhyme heard the railroad track clatter of his fingers on the keyboard.

Geneva was looking at her battered Swatch. 'I really — '

'Hey, y'all,' a man's voice called from the

103

doorway. Wearing a brown tweed sports coat, blue shirt and jeans, Detective Roland Bell walked into the lab. A law enforcer in his native North Carolina, Bell had moved to New York a few years ago for personal reasons. He had a flop of brown hair, gentle eyes and was so easygoing that his urban co-workers sometimes felt a stab of impatience working with him, though Rhyme suspected the reason he sometimes moved slowly wasn't Southern heritage at all but his meticulous nature, owing to the importance of his job within the NYPD. Bell's specialty was protecting witnesses and other potential victims. His operation wasn't an official unit in the NYPD but it still had a name: 'SWAT.' This wasn't the traditional weapons and tactics acronym, though; it was short for 'Saving the Witness's Ass Team.'

'Roland, this is Geneva Settle.'

'Hey there, miss,' he drawled and shook her hand.

'I don't need a bodyguard,' she said firmly.

'Don't you worry — I won't get in your way,' Bell said. 'You got my word of honor on that. I'll stay as outa sight as a tick in tall grass.' A glance at Sellitto. 'Now what're we up against here?'

The heavyset detective ran through the details of the case and what they knew so far. Bell didn't frown or shake his head but Rhyme could see his eyes go still, which signaled his concern. But when Sellitto was done, Bell put on his down-home face again and asked Geneva a number of questions about herself and her family to give him an idea of how to set up the protection detail. She answered hesitatingly, as if she begrudged the effort.

Finally Bell was finished and Geneva said impatiently, 'I really have to go. Could somebody drive me home? I'll get Charles's letters for you. But then I have to go to school.'

'Detective Bell'll take you home,' Rhyme said then added with a laugh, 'but about school, I thought we'd agreed you'd take the day off. Take a makeup.'

'No,' she said firmly. 'I *didn't* agree to that. You said, 'Let's just get some questions out of the way and then we'll see.' '

Not many people quoted Lincoln Rhyme's words back at him. He grumbled, 'Whatever I said, I think you'll *have* to stay home, now that we know the perp may still be after you. It's just not safe.'

'Mr. Rhyme, I need to take those tests. Makeups at my school — they sometimes don't get scheduled, test books get lost, you don't get credit.' Geneva was angrily gripping an empty belt loop on her jeans. She was so skinny. He wondered if her parents were health freaks, keeping her on a diet of organic granola and tofu. It seemed that a lot of professors leaned in that direction.

'I'll call the school right now,' Sachs said. 'We'll tell them there's been an incident and — '

'I think I really want to go,' Geneva said softly, eyes looking steadily into Rhyme's. 'Now.'

'Just stay at home for a day or two until we find out more. Or,' Rhyme added with a laugh, 'until we nail his ass.'

It was supposed to be light, to win her over by talking teenage. But he regretted the words instantly. He hadn't been real with her — solely because she was young. It was like the people who came to visit him and were overly loud and jokey because he was a quad. They pissed him off.

Just like she was pissed at him now.

She said, 'I'd really appreciate a ride, if you don't mind. Or I'll take the train. But I have to leave *now*, if you want those letters.'

Irritated to have to be fighting this battle, Rhyme said with finality, 'I'll have to say no.'

'Can I borrow your phone?'

'Why's that?' he asked.

'There's a man I want to call.'

'A man?'

'He's the lawyer I mentioned. Wesley Goades. He used to work for the biggest insurance company in the country, and now he runs a legal clinic in Harlem.'

'And you want to call him?' Sellitto asked. 'Why?'

'Because I want to ask him if you can keep me from going to school.'

Rhyme scoffed. 'It's for your own good.'

'That's sort of for me to decide, isn't it?'

'Your parents or your uncle.'

'They're not the ones who have to graduate from eleventh grade next spring.'

Sachs chuckled. Rhyme shot her a dark look.

'Just for a day or two, miss,' Bell said.

Geneva ignored him and continued, 'Mr. Goades got John David Colson released from

Sing-Sing after he'd been in prison for ten years for a murder he didn't commit. And he's sued New York, I mean, the state itself, two or three times. He won every trial. And he just did a Supreme Court case. About homeless rights.'

'Won that one too, did he?' Rhyme asked wryly.

'He usually wins. In fact, I don't think he's ever lost.'

'This's crazy,' Sellitto muttered, absently brushing at a dot of blood on his jacket. He muttered, 'You're a kid — '

Wrong thing to say.

Geneva glared at him and snapped, 'You're not going to let me make a phone call? Don't prisoners get to do that, even?'

The big detective sighed. He gestured toward the phone.

She walked to it, looked in her address book and punched in a number.

'Wesley Goades,' Rhyme said.

Geneva cocked her head as the call was connected. She said to Rhyme, 'He went to Harvard. Oh, and he sued the army too. Gay rights, I think.'

She spoke into the phone. 'Mr. Goades, please . . . Could you tell him Geneva Settle called? I was a witness to a crime, and I'm being held by the police.' She gave the address of Rhyme's town house then added, 'It's against my will and — '

Rhyme glanced at Sellitto, who rolled his eyes and said, 'All right.'

107

'Hold on,' Geneva said into the phone. Then turned to the big detective, who towered over her. 'I can go to school?'

'For the test. That's all.'

'There are two of them.'

'All right. Both goddamn tests,' Sellitto muttered. To Bell, he said, 'Stay with her.'

'Like a flat-coated retriever, y'all got that right.'

Into the phone Geneva said, 'Tell Mr. Goades never mind. We've got it worked out.' She hung up.

Rhyme said, 'But first I want those letters.'

'Deal.' She slung her book bag over her shoulder.

'You,' Sellitto barked to Pulaski, 'go with 'em.'

'Yes, sir.'

After Bell, Geneva and the rookie had left, Sachs looked at the door and laughed. 'Now, that's one spitfire.'

'Wesley Goades.' Rhyme smiled. 'I think she was making him up. Probably called time and temperature.'

He nodded toward the evidence board. 'Let's get going on all of this. Mel, you take over street-fair detail. And I want the facts and profile of what we've got so far sent to VICAP and NCIC. I want all the libraries and schools in town polled to see if this guy who talked to Barry also called them and asked about Singleton or that *Coloreds' Weekly* magazine. Oh, and find out who makes smiley-face bags.'

'Tall order,' Cooper called.

'Hey, guess what? *Life's* a tall order

108

sometimes. Then send a sample of the blood on the rope to CODIS.'

'I thought you didn't think it was a sex crime.' CODIS was a database that contained the DNA of known sex offenders.

'The operative words are 'I think,' Mel. Not 'I know to a fucking certainty.' '

'So much for the mood,' Thom said.

'One other thing . . . ' He wheeled closer and examined the pictures of the librarian's body and the diagram of the shooting crime scene, which Sachs had drawn. 'The woman was how far from the vic?' Rhyme asked Sellitto.

'Who, the bystander? I'd guess fifteen feet to the side.'

'Who was hit first?'

'She was.'

'And the shots were grouped tight? The ones that hit the librarian?'

'Real tight. Inches apart. He knows how to shoot.'

Rhyme muttered, 'It wasn't a miss, the woman. He shot her on purpose.'

'What?'

The criminalist asked the best pistol shot in the room, 'Sachs, when you're rapid-firing, what's the one shot that's bound to be the most accurate?'

'The first. You're not fighting recoil.'

Rhyme said, 'He wounded her intentionally — aimed for a major blood vessel — to draw off as many officers as he could and give him a chance to get away.'

Cooper muttered, 'Jesus.'

'Tell Bell. And Bo Haumann and his people at Emergency Services. Let 'em know that's the kind of perp we're dealing with — one who's more than happy to target innocents.'

II

THE GRAFFITI KING

8

The big man walked down the Harlem sidewalk, thinking about the phone conversation he'd had an hour ago. It'd made him happy, made him nervous, made him cautious. But mostly he was thinking: Maybe, at last, things are looking up.

Well, he deserved a boost, just *something* to help him get over.

Jax hadn't had much luck lately. Sure, he'd been glad to get out of the system. But the two months since his release from prison had been coal hard: lonely and without a single lick of anything by way of righteous fortune falling into his lap. But today was different. The phone call about Geneva Settle could change his life forever.

He was walking along upper Fifth Avenue, heading toward St. Ambrose Park, a cigarette in the corner of his mouth. Enjoying the cold fall air, enjoying the sun. Enjoying the fact that people round here gave him a wide berth. Some of it was his unsmiling face. Some of it the prison tat. The limp too. (Though, truth be told, his wasn't any hard-ass, playa limp, wasn't a gimme-respect gangsta limp, it was an oh-fuck-I-been-shot limp. But nobody here knew that.)

Jax wore what he always wore: jeans and a tattered combat jacket and clunky leather work shoes nearly worn through. In his pocket he carried a good-size wad of benjamins, mostly twenties, as well as a horn-handled knife, a pack of cigarettes and on a single chain a single key to his small apartment on 136th Street. Its two rooms featured one bed, one table, two chairs, a second-hand computer and grocery-store two-for-one cookware. It was only a notch better than his recent residence in the New York State Department of Corrections.

He paused and looked around.

There he was, the skinny dude with dusty-brown skin — a man who could've been thirty-five or sixty. He leaned against an unsteady chain-link fence around this park in the heart of Harlem. The sun flared off the wet lip of a malt or wine bottle half-hidden in the yellow grass behind him.

'S'up, man?' Jax asked, lighting another cigarette as he strode up and stopped.

A blink from the skinny guy. He looked at the pack Jax offered. He wasn't sure what this was about but he took a cigarette anyway. He put it in his pocket.

Jax continued, 'You Ralph?'

'Who you?'

'Friend of DeLisle Marshall. Was on S block with him.'

'Lisle?' The skinny guy relaxed. Some. He looked away from the man who could break him in half and surveyed the world from his chain-link perch. 'Lisle out?'

Jax laughed. 'Lisle put four rounds into some sad motherfucker's head. There'll be a nigger in the White House 'fore Lisle gets out.'

'They *do* parole dudes,' Ralph said, his indignation unsuccessfully masking the fact he'd been caught testing Jax. 'So what Lisle say?'

'Sends his word. Told me to look you up. He'll speak for me.'

'Speak for you, speak for you. Okay. Tell me, what his tat look like?' Skinny little Ralph with a skinny little goatee was recovering some of his bravado. It was testing time again.

'Which one?' Jax responded. 'The rose or the blade? And I understand he's got another one near his dick. But I never got close enough to see it.'

Ralph nodded, unsmiling. 'What yo' name?'

'Jackson. Alonzo Jackson. But I go by Jax.' The tag had a righteous reputation attached to it. He wondered if Ralph had heard about him. But apparently not — no raised eyebrows. This pissed Jax off. 'You want to check me out with DeLisle, go right ahead, man, only don't use my name over the phone, you know what I'm saying? Just tell him the Graffiti King came by to have a confab with you.'

'Graffiti King,' Ralph repeated, clearly wondering what *that* was about. Did it mean Jax spread motherfuckers' blood around like spray paint? 'Okay. Maybe I check. Depending. So you out.'

'I'm out.'

'What was you in fo'?'

'AR and weapons.' Then he added with a lowered voice, 'They went after me for a twenty-five, twenty-five attempt. That got knocked down to assault.' A shorthand reference to the Penal Code provision for murder, Section 125.25.

'An' now you a free man. That phat.'

Jax thought this was funny — here's sad-ass Ralph nervous and all when Jax comes along with a cigarette and a s'up, man. But then starts relaxing when he finds out that he did hard time for armed robbery, illegal weapons possession and attempted murder, spraying blood like paint.

Harlem. Didn't you just fucking love it?

Inside, just before he'd been released, he'd tapped DeLisle Marshall for some help and the brother had told him to hook up with Ralph. Lisle had explained why the little skel was a good man to know. 'That man hang out *ever'*where. Like he be ownin' the streets. Know ever'thing. Or can find it out.'

Now, the blood-painting Graffiti King sucked hard on the cigarette and got right down to it. 'Need you to set me up, man,' Jax said in a soft voice.

'Yeah? Whatchu need?'

Which meant both whatchu need and what'm I going to make from it?

Fair enough.

A glance around. They were alone except for pigeons and two short, fine-looking Dominican girls striding past. Despite the cold they wore skimpy tops and tight shorts on their round, knock-me-down bodies. 'Ay, papi,' one called to Jax with a smile and kept going. The girls crossed the street and turned east into their turf. Fifth Avenue had been the dividing line between black and Spanish Harlem — *el barrio* — for years.

116

Once you were east of Fifth, that was the Other Side. Could still be down, could still be phat, but it wasn't the same Harlem.

Jax watched them disappear. 'Damn.' He'd been in prison a long time.

'Word,' Ralph said. He adjusted how he was leaning and crossed his arms like some Egyptian prince.

Jax waited a minute and bent down, whispered into the pharaoh's ear, 'I need a piece.'

'You fresh, man,' Ralph said after a moment. 'Yo' ass get caught with a piece, they violate you back in a minute. And you *still* gotta do a annual in Rikers fo' the gun. Why you wanta take a chance like that?'

Jax asked patiently, 'Can you do it or not?'

The scrawny dude adjusted the angle of his lean and looked up at Jax. 'I think we phat, man. But I ain't sure I know where to find anything fo' you. A piece, I'm saying.'

'Then I ain't sure I know who to give this to.' He pulled out a roll of benjamins, peeled off some twenties, held them out to Ralph. Being real careful, of course. One black man slipping another some money on the streets of Harlem could raise a cop's eyebrow, even if the guy was just tithing to a minister from the nearby Baptist Ascension Pentecostal Church.

But the only eyebrow going up was Ralph's as he pocketed the bills and looked at the rest of the roll. 'You got yourself some tall paper there.'

'Word. And you've got yourself some of it now. And a chance for more. Happy day.' He put the wad away.

Ralph grunted. 'What kinda piece?'

'Small. Something I can hide easy, you know what I'm saying?'

'Cost you five.'

'Cost me two, I could do it.'

'Cold?' Ralph asked.

As if Jax would want a gun with a registration number still stamped on the frame. 'Whatta you think?'

'Then fuck two,' said the little Egyptian. He was ballsier now; you don't kill people who can get you something you need.

'Three,' Jax offered.

'I could do three and hemi.'

Jax debated. He made a fist and tapped Ralph's with it. Another look around. 'Now, I need something else. You got connections at the schools?'

'Some. What schools you talkin' 'bout? I ain't know nothin' 'bout Queens or BK or the Bronx. Only here in the hood.'

Jax scoffed to himself, thinking, 'hood,' shit. He'd grown up in Harlem and never lived anywhere else on earth except for army barracks and prisons. You could call the place a 'neighborhood,' if you had to, but it wasn't 'the hood.' In L.A., in Newark, they had hoods. In parts of BK too. But Harlem was a different universe, and Jax was pissed at Ralph for using the word, though he supposed the man wasn't disrespecting the place; he probably just watched a lot of bad TV.

Jax said, 'Just here.'

'I can ask round.' He was sounding a little

118

uneasy — not surprising, considering that an ex-con with a 25-25 arrest was interested in both a gun and a high school. Jax slipped him another forty. That seemed to ease the little man's conscience considerably.

'Okay, tell me what I supposed to be lookin' fo'?'

Jax pulled a sheet of paper out of his combat jacket packet. It was a story he'd downloaded from the online edition of the New York *Daily News*. He handed the article, labeled *Breaking News Update*, to Ralph.

Jax tapped the paper with a thick finger. 'I need to find the girl. That they're talking about.'

Ralph read the article under the headline, MUSEUM OFFICIAL SHOT TO DEATH IN MIDTOWN. He looked up. 'It don't say nothin' 'bout her, where she live, 'bout her school, nothin'. Don't even say what the fuck her name be.'

'Her name's Geneva Settle. As for everything else' — Jax nodded at the little man's pocket where the money had disappeared — 'that's what I'm paying *you* the benjamins for.'

'Why you want to find her?' asked Ralph, staring at the article.

Jax paused for a minute then leaned close to the man's dusty ear. 'Sometimes people ask questions, look around, and they find out more shit than they really ought to be knowing.'

Ralph started to ask something else but then must've figured that, even though Jax *might've* been talking about something the *girl* had done, the Graffiti King of blood could also mean that Ralph himself was being too fucking nosy.

119

'Gimme a hour or two.' He gave Jax his phone number. The little pharaoh pushed off from the chain link, retrieved his bottle of malt liquor from the grass and started down the street.

★ ★ ★

Roland Bell eased his unmarked Crown Vic through central Harlem, a mix of residential and commercial buildings. The chains — Pathmark, Duane Reade, Popeyes, McDonald's — existed side by side with the mom-and-pop outfits where you could cash checks, pay your bills and buy human-hair wigs and extensions or African arts or liquor or furniture. Many of the older buildings were run down and more than a few were boarded up or sealed with metal shutters covered with graffiti. Off the busier streets, ruined appliances awaited scavengers, trash was banked against buildings and gutters, and both weeds and impromptu gardens filled vacant lots. Graffitied billboards advertised acts at the Apollo and some other big uptown venues, while hundreds of handbills covered walls and plywood, hawking the acts of little-known MCs, DJs and comedians. Young men hung tight in clusters and some watched the squad car behind Bell's with a mix of caution and disdain and, occasionally, raw contempt.

But as Bell, Geneva and Pulaski continued west, the ambiance changed. The deserted buildings were being torn down or renovated; posters in front of the job sites showed what sort of idyllic town houses would soon replace the old ones. Geneva's block, not far from steep, rocky Morningside Park and Columbia University, was beautiful and tree-lined, with clean sidewalks. The rows of old buildings were in good repair. The cars may have sported Clubs on the steering wheels but the vehicles the steel bars protected included Lexuses and Beemers.

Geneva pointed out a spotless four-story brownstone, decorated with carved façades, the ironwork glistening black in the late-morning sun. 'That's my place.'

Bell pulled his car two doors past it, double-parked.

'Uhm, Detective,' Ron Pulaski said, 'I think she meant the one back there.'

'I know,' he said. 'One thing I'm partial to is not advertising where the people we're looking after live.'

The rookie nodded, as if memorizing this fact. So young, Bell thought. So much to learn.

'We'll be inside for a few minutes. Keep an eye out.'

'Yes, sir. What for exactly?'

The detective hardly had time to educate the man in the finer points of bodyguard detail; his presence alone would be enough of a deterrent for this brief errand. 'Bad guys,' he said.

The squad car that had accompanied them here pulled to a stop where Bell pointed, in front of the Crown Vic. The officer inside would speed back to Rhyme's with the letters he wanted. Another car arrived a moment later, an unmarked Chevy. It contained two officers from Bell's SWAT witness protection team, who would remain in and around the town house. After learning that the unsub would target bystanders simply as a diversion, Bell had ordered some reinforcements. The team officers he'd picked for this assignment were Luis Martinez, a quiet, solid detective, and Barbe Lynch, a sharp, young plainclothes officer, who was new to protection detail but gifted with an intuitive radar for sensing threats.

The Carolinian now lifted his lean frame out of the car and looked around, buttoning his sports coat to hide the two pistols he wore on his hips. Bell had been a good small-town cop and he was a good big-city investigator but was truly in his element when it came to protecting witnesses. It was a talent, like the way he could sniff out game in the fields where he'd hunted growing up. Instinct. What he sensed was more than the obvious — like spotting flashes off telescopic sights or hearing the click of pistol receivers or noticing somebody checking out your witness in the reflection of a storefront window. He could tell when a man was walking with a purpose when by all logic he had none. Or when an apparently innocent bad parking job had placed a car in the perfect position to let a killer escape without having to saw the wheel back and forth. He'd see a configuration of building and street and window and think: Now, that's where a man would hide to do some harm.

But at the moment he noted no threat and ushered Geneva Settle out of the car and inside the town house, motioning Martinez and Lynch to follow. He introduced Geneva to them, then

122

the two officers returned outside to check the surrounding area. The girl unlocked the inside security door and they went in and climbed to the second floor, accompanied by the uniformed officer.

'Uncle Bill,' she called, rapping on the door. 'It's me.'

A heavyset man in his fifties with a dusting of birthmarks on his cheek opened the door. He smiled and nodded at Bell. 'Nice to meet you. Name's William.'

The detective identified himself and they shook hands.

'Honey, you all right? Terrible what happen to you.'

'I'm fine. Only the police are going to hang around for a while. They're thinking that guy who attacked me might try again.'

The man's round face wrinkled with concern. 'Damn.' Then he gestured toward the TV. 'You made the news, girl.'

'They mention her by name?' Bell asked, frowning, troubled at this news.

'No. 'Causa her age. And no pictures neither.'

'Well, that's something . . . ' Freedom of the press was all very well and good but there were times when Roland Bell wouldn't mind a certain amount of censorship — when it came to revealing witnesses' identities and addresses. 'Now, y'all wait in the hall. I want to check out the inside.'

'Yes, sir.'

Bell stepped into the apartment and looked it over. The front door was secured by two deadbolts and a steel police lock rod. The front windows looked out on the town houses across the street. He pulled the shades down. The side windows opened onto an alley and the building across the way. The facing wall, though, was solid brick and there were no windows that presented a vantage point for a sniper. Still, he closed the windows and locked them, then pulled the blinds shut.

The place was large — there were two doors to the hallway, one in the front, at the living room, and a second in the back, off a laundry room. He made sure the locks were secured and returned to the hallway. 'Okay,' he called. Geneva and her uncle returned. 'It's looking pretty good. Just keep the doors and windows locked and the blinds drawn.'

'Yes, sir,' the man said. 'I be sure to do that.'

'I'll get the letters,' Geneva said. She disappeared toward the bedrooms.

Now that Bell had examined the place for security, he looked at the room as a living space. It struck him as cold. Spotless white furniture, leather and linen, all covered with plastic protectors. Tons of books, African and Caribbean sculptures and paintings, a china cabinet filled with what seemed like expensive dishes and wineglasses. African masks. Very little that was sentimental, personal. Hardly any pictures of family.

Bell's own house was chockablock with snaps of kin — especially his two boys, as well as all their cousins back in North Carolina. Also a few pictures of his late wife, but out of deference to

124

his new belle — Lucy Kerr, who was a sheriff down in the Tarheel State — there were none of his wife and Bell together, only of mother and sons. (Lucy, who was herself well represented on his walls, had seen the pictures of the late Mrs. Bell and her children and announced she respected him for keeping those up. And one thing about Lucy: She meant what she said.)

Bell asked Geneva's uncle if he'd seen anybody he hadn't recognized around the town house lately.

'No, sir. Not a soul.'

'When will her parents be back?'

'I couldn't say, sir. Was Geneva talked to 'em.'

Five minutes later the girl returned. She handed Bell an envelope containing two yellow, crisp pieces of paper. 'Here they are.' She hesitated. 'Be careful with them. I don't have copies.'

'Oh, you don't know Mr. Rhyme, miss. He treats evidence like it was the holy grail.'

'I'll be back after school,' Geneva said to her uncle. Then to Bell, 'I'm ready to go.'

'Listen up, girl,' the man said. 'I want you t'be polite, the way I told you. You say 'sir' when you talking to the police.'

She looked at her uncle and said evenly, 'Don't you remember what my father said? That people have to earn the right to be called 'sir'? That's what I believe.'

The uncle laughed. 'That's my niece fo' you. Got a mind of her own. Why we love her. Give yo' uncle a hug, girl.'

Embarrassed, like Bell's sons when he'd put

his arm around them in public, the girl stiffly tolerated the embrace.

In the hallway Bell handed the uniformed officer the letters. 'Get these over to Lincoln's town house ASAP.'

'Yes, sir.'

After he'd left, Bell called Martinez and Lynch on his radio. They reported that the street was clear. He hurried the girl downstairs and into the Crown Vic. Pulaski trotted up and jumped in after them.

As he started the engine Bell glanced at her. 'Oh, say, miss, when you got a minute, how 'bout you look in that knapsack of yours and pick me out a book you won't be needing today.'

'Book?'

'Like a schoolbook.'

She found one. 'Social studies? It's kind of boring.'

'Oh, it's not for reading. It's for pretending to be a substitute teacher.'

She nodded. 'Fronting you're a teacher. Hey, that's def.'

'I thought so too. Now, you wanta slip that seat belt on? It'd be much appreciated. You too, rookie.'

9

Unsub 109 might or might not have been a sex offender but in any event his DNA sequence wasn't in the CODIS file.

The negative result was typical of the absence of leads in the case, Rhyme reflected with frustration. They'd received the rest of the bullet fragments, recovered from Dr. Barry's body by the medical examiner, but they were even more badly shattered than the one removed from the woman bystander and were of no better use in an IBIS or DRUGFIRE check than the earlier pieces.

They'd also heard from several people at the African-American museum. Dr. Barry hadn't mentioned to any employees that another patron was interested in the 1868 *Coloreds' Weekly Illustrated*. Nor had the museum phone records revealed anything; all calls went into a main switchboard and were directed to extensions, with no details kept. The incoming and outgoing calls on his cell phone offered no leads either.

Cooper told them what he'd learned from the owner of Trenton Plastics, one of the country's largest makers of plastic shopping bags. The tech related the history of the smiley-face icon, as told to him by the company's owner. 'They think the face was originally printed on buttons by a subsidiary of State Mutual Insurance in the sixties to boost company morale and as a promotional gimmick. In the seventies, two brothers drew a face like it with the slogan *Be happy*. Sort of an alternative to the peace symbol. By then it was being printed on fifty million items every year by dozens of companies.'

'The point of this pop culture lecture?' Rhyme murmured.

'That even if it's copyrighted, which no one seems to know, there are dozens of companies making smiley-face bags. And it'd be impossible to trace.'

Dead end . . .

Of the dozens of museums and libraries that Cooper, Sachs and Sellitto had queried, two reported that a man had called in the past several weeks asking about an issue of *Coloreds' Weekly Illustrated* from July 1868. This was encouraging because it supported Rhyme's theory that the magazine might be the reason Geneva was attacked. But neither of the institutions had the issue and no one could remember the name of the caller — if he'd even given it to them. Nobody else seemed to have a copy of the magazine for them to look at. The Museum of African-American Journalism in New Haven reported that they had had a full set on microfiche but it had disappeared.

Rhyme was scowling at this news when a computer chimed and Cooper announced, 'We've got a response from VICAP.'

He hit a button and sent the email to all the monitors in Rhyme's lab. Sellitto and Sachs huddled around one, Rhyme looked at his own flatscreen. It was a secure email from a detective in the crime scene lab in Queens.

Detective Cooper:
Per your request we ran the crime profile you provided through both VICAP and HITS, and have two matches.

Incident One: Homicide in Amarillo, Texas. Case No. 3451-01 (Texas Rangers): Five years ago, sixty-seven-year-old Charles T. Tucker, a retired state worker, was found dead behind a strip mall near his home. He had been struck in the back of the head with a blunt object, presumably to subdue him, then lynched. A cotton-fiber rope with a slipknot was placed around his neck and thrown over a tree limb then pulled tight by the assailant. Scratch marks at the neck indicated victim was conscious for some minutes before death occurred.

Elements of similarity with Unsub 109 case:

- Victim was subdued with a single blow to the back of the head.
- Suspect was wearing size-11 walking shoes, most likely Bass brand. Uneven wear on right one, suggesting outturned foot.
- Cotton-fiber rope with bloodstains was murder weapon; fibers similar to those found at present scene.
- Motive was staged. The murder appeared to have been ritualistic. Candles were set on the ground at his feet and a pentacle was drawn in the dirt.

129

But investigation into the victim's life and profiling of the offense led investigators to conclude that this evidence was planted to lead the police off. No other motive was established.

- No fingerprints were recovered; suspect wore latex gloves.

Status: Active.

'What's the next case?' Rhyme asked.
Cooper scrolled down.

Incident Two: Homicide in Cleveland, Ohio. Case 2002-34554F (Ohio State Police): Three years ago, a forty-five-year-old businessman, Gregory Tallis, was found dead in his apartment, shot to death.

Elements of similarity with Unsub 109 case:

- Victim was subdued with blows to the back of the head with a blunt object.
- Shoe prints of suspect identical to Bass-brand walking shoes, with outward-pointing right foot.
- Cause of death was three gunshots to the heart. Small caliber, probably .22 or .25, similar to present case.
- No relevant fingerprints were recovered; suspect wore latex gloves.
- Victim's pants were removed and a bottle inserted into his rectum, with apparent intent to suggest he was the victim of a homosexual rape. The Ohio State Police profiler concluded that the scene was staged. The victim was scheduled to

130

testify in a forthcoming organized crime trial. Bank records indicate that the defendant withdrew fifty thousand in cash one week prior to the killing. However, the money could not be traced. Authorities presume that this was the fee paid to a hired killer to murder Tallis.

Status: Open but inactive due to misplaced evidence.

Misplaced evidence, Rhyme thought . . . Jesus. He looked over the screen. 'Staging evidence to set up a phoney motive — and another fake ritualistic assault.' He nodded at The Hanged Man tarot card. 'Subduing with the club, then strangulation or shooting, latex gloves, the Bass shoes, the right foot . . . Sure, it could be our boy. And it looks like he's hired gun. If so, we've probably got two perps: the unsub and whoever hired him. All right, I want everything Texas and Ohio have on both those cases.'

Cooper made some calls. He learned that the Texas authorities would check the file and get back to them as soon as possible. In Ohio, though, a detective confirmed that the file was among those for dozens of cold cases misplaced in a move to a new facility two years ago. They'd look for it. 'But,' the man added, 'don't hold your breath.' Rhyme grimaced at this news and told Cooper to urge them to track it down if at all possible.

A moment later Cooper's cell phone rang and he took the call. 'Hello? . . . Go ahead.' He took some notes, thanked the caller then hung up.

131

'That was Traffic. They finally tracked down outstanding permits for carnivals or fairs big enough to close streets in the past few days. Two in Queens — one neighborhood association and one Greek fraternal order. A Columbus Day festival in Brooklyn and another one in Little Italy. That was the big one. Mulberry Street.'

'We should get some teams out to all four neighborhoods,' Rhyme said. 'Canvass all the discount variety store and drugstores that use smiley-face bags, that sell condoms, duct tape *and* box cutters and use a cheap cash register or adding machine. Give the teams a description of the unsub and see if any clerks can remember him.'

Rhyme was watching Sellitto stare at a small dark dot on his suit coat sleeve. Another bloodstain from the shooting that morning, he assumed. The big detective didn't move. Since he was the senior cop here, he was the one to call ESU and Patrol and arrange for the search teams. It seemed that he hadn't heard the criminalist, though.

Rhyme glanced at Sachs, who nodded and called downtown to arrange for the officers to set up the teams. When she hung up, she noticed Rhyme was staring at the evidence board, frowning. 'What's wrong?'

He didn't answer right away, mulling over what exactly *was* wrong. Then he realized. Fish out of water . . .

'Think we need some help here.'

One of the most difficult problems criminalists face is not knowing their territory. A crime scene analyst is only as good as his knowledge of the area suspects inhabit — the geology, sociology, history, pop culture, employment . . . everything.

Lincoln Rhyme was thinking how little he knew about the world that Geneva Settle lived in: Harlem. Oh, he'd read the stats, of course: The majority of the population were an equal mix of African black (both long-time and recent immigrants) and black and nonblack Hispanic (mostly Puerto Rican, Dominican, Salvadoran and Mexican) followed by white and some Asian. There was poverty and there were gangs and drugs and violence — largely centered around the projects — but much of the neighborhood was generally safe, far better than many parts of Brooklyn, the Bronx or Newark. Harlem had more churches, mosques, community organizations and concerned-parents groups than any other neighborhood in the city. The place had been a mecca for black civil rights, and for black and Hispanic culture and art. It was now the center of a new movement: for fiscal equality. There were dozens of economic redevelopment projects currently under way and investors of all races and nationalities were speeding to sink money into Harlem, taking particular advantage of the hot real estate market.

But these were *New York Times* facts, NYPD facts. They didn't help Rhyme one bit in his understanding of why a professional killer wanted to murder a teenage girl from this neighborhood. His search for Unsub 109 was severely hampered by this limitation. He ordered his phone to make a call, and the software obediently connected him to a number at the FBI's office downtown.

'Dellray here.'

'Fred, it's Lincoln. I need some help again.'

'My friendly fella down in the District help you out?'

'Yep, sure did. Maryland too.'

'Glad to hear it. Hold on. Lemme shoo somebody on outa here.'

Rhyme had been to Dellray's office several times. The tall, lanky black agent's digs in the federal building were filled with books of literature and esoteric philosophy, as well as coatracks of the various clothes he'd wear while working undercover, though he didn't do much fieldwork anymore. Ironically, it was on those costume racks that you'd find FBI Brooks Brothers suits and white shirts and striped ties. Dellray's regular dress was — to put it kindly — bizarre. Jogging outfits and sweats with sports jackets, and he favored green, blue and yellow for his suits. At least he avoided hats, which could make him look like a pimp out of a seventies blaxploitation film.

The agent returned to the phone and Rhyme asked, 'How's the bomb thing going?'

'Another anonymous call this morning, about the Israeli consulate. Just like last week. Only my snitches — even the golden boys — can't tell me one solid little thing. Pisses me off. Anyways, what else you got cookin'?'

'The case is taking us to Harlem. You work it much?'

'I stroll through the place some. But I'm no encyclopedia. BK born and bred.'

'BK?'

'Brooklyn, originally the Village of Breuckelen, brought to us courtesy of the Dutch West India Company in the 1640s. First official city in the state of New York, if you care. Home of Walt Whitman. But you ain't spending a quarter to talk trivia.'

'Can you get away and do a little scrounging on the streets?'

'I'll fitcha in. But I can't promise I'll be much help.'

'Well, Fred, you've got one advantage over me, as far as blending in Uptown.'

'Right, right, right — my ass ain't sitting in any bright red wheelchair.'

'Make that *two* advantages,' replied Rhyme, whose complexion was as pale as the rookie Pulaski's blond hair.

⋆ ⋆ ⋆

Charles Singleton's other letters arrived from Geneva's.

They hadn't been stored very well over the years and were faded and fragile. Mel Cooper carefully mounted them between two thin sheets of acrylic, after chemically treating the creases to make sure the paper didn't crack.

Sellitto walked over to Cooper. 'Whatta we got?'

The tech focused the optical scanner on the first letter, hit a button. The image appeared on

135

several of the computer monitors throughout the room.

My most darling Violet:

I have but a moment to set down a few words to you in the heat and calm of this early Sunday morning. Our regiment, the 31st New York, has come such a long way since we were unseasoned recruits assembling on Hart's Island. Indeed, we now are engaged in the momentous task of pursuing Gen. Robert E. Lee himself, whose army has been in retreat after its defeat at Petersburg, Virginia, on April 2.

He has now taken a stand with his thirty-thousand troops, in the heart of the Confederacy, and it has fallen to our regiment, among others, to hold the line to the west, when he attempts to escape, which surely he must, for both General Grant and General Sherman are bearing down upon him with superior numbers.

The moment now is the quiet before the storm and we are assembled on a large farm. Bare-foot slaves stand about, watching us, wearing Negro cottons. Some of them say nothing, but regard us blankly. Others cheer mightily.

Not long ago our commander rode up to us, dismounted and told of the battle plan for the day. He then spoke — from memory, — words from Mr. Frederick Douglass, words that I recall to be these: 'Once let the black man get upon his person the letters,

'U.S.,' an eagle on his buttons, a musket on his shoulder and bullets in his pockets, and no one on earth can deny that he has earned the right to citizenship in the United States.'

He then saluted us and said it was his privilege to have served with us in this God-sanctioned campaign to reunite our nation.

A hu-rah went up from the 31st the likes of which I have never heard.

And now, darling, I hear drums in the distance and the crack of the four- and eight-pounders, signaling the beginning of battle. Should these be the last words I am able to impart to you from this side of the River of Jordan, know that I love you and our son beyond words' telling. Hold fast to our farm, keep to our fabrication of being caretakers of the land, not owners, and deflect all offers to sell. I wish the land to pass intact to our son and his issue; professions and trades ebb and flow, the financial markets are fickle, but the earth is God's great constant — and our farm will ultimately bring to our family respectability in the eyes of those who do not respect us now. It will be our children's salvation, and that of the generations that will follow. Now, my dear, I must once again take up my rifle and do as God has bid, to secure our freedom and preserve our sacred country.

Yours in eternal love,
Charles
April 9, 1865,
Appomattox, Virginia

Sachs looked up. 'Phew. That's a cliffhanger.'

'Not really,' Thom said.

'What do you mean?'

'Well, we *know* they held the line.'

'How?'

'Because April ninth's the day the South surrendered.'

'Not really concerned about History 101 here,' Rhyme said. 'I want to know about this secret.'

'That's in this one,' Cooper said, scanning the second letter. He mounted it on the scanner.

My dearest Violet:

I miss you, my dear, and our young Joshua too. I am heartened by the news that your sister has weathered well the illness following the birth of your nephew and thankful to our Lord Jesus Christ that you were present to see her through this difficult time. However, I think it best that you remain in Harrisburg for the time-being. These are critical times and more perilous, I feel, than what transpired during the War of Secession.

So much has happened in the month you have been away. How my life has changed from simple farmer and school teacher to my present situation! I am engaged in matters that are difficult and dangerous and — dare I say, — vital for the sake of our people.

Tonight, my colleagues and I meet again at Gallows Heights, which has taken on the aspects of a castle under siege. The days seem endless, the travel exhausting. My life consists of arduous hours and coming and going under cover of darkness, and avoiding too those who would do us harm, for they are many — and not just former Rebels; many in the North are hostile to our cause as well. I receive frequent threats, some veiled, some explicit.

Another night-mare awakened me early this morning. I don't recall the images that plagued my sleep, but after I awoke, I could not return to my slumbers. I lay awake till dawn, thinking how difficult it is to bear this secret within me. I so desire to share it with the world, but I know I cannot. I have no doubt the consequences of its revelation would be tragic.

Forgive my somber tone. I miss you and our son, and I am terribly weary. Tomorrow may see a rebirth of hope. I pray that such is the case.

> Yours in loving
> affection, Charles
> May 3, 1867

'Well,' Rhyme mused, 'he *talks* about the secret. But what *is* it? Must have something to do with those meetings in Gallows Heights. 'Sake of our people.' Civil rights or politics. He mentioned that in his first letter too . . . What the hell *is* Gallows Heights?'

His eyes went to the tarot card of The Hanged Man, suspended from a gallows by his foot.

'I'll look it up,' Cooper said and went online. A moment later he said, 'It was a neighborhood in nineteenth-century Manhattan, Upper West Side, centered around Bloomingdale Road and Eightieth Street. Bloomingdale became the Boulevard and then Broadway.' He glanced up with a raised eyebrow. 'Not far from here.'

'Gallows with an apostrophe?'

'No apostrophe. At least in the hits I found.'

'Anything else about it?'

Cooper looked over the historical society website. 'A couple things. A map from 1872.' He swung the monitor toward Rhyme, who looked it over, noting that the neighborhood encompassed a large area. There were some big estates owned by old-family New York magnates and financiers as well as hundreds of smaller apartments and homes.

'Hey, look, Lincoln,' Cooper said, touching part of the map near Central Park. 'That's your place. Where we are now. It was a swamp back then.'

'Interesting,' Rhyme muttered sarcastically.

'The only other reference is a *Times* story last month about the rededication of a new archive at the Sanford Foundation — that's the old mansion on Eighty-first.'

Rhyme recalled a big Victorian building next to the Sanford Hotel — a Gothic, spooky apartment that resembled the nearby Dakota, where John Lennon had been killed.

Cooper continued, 'The head of the foundation, William Ashberry, gave a speech at the ceremony. He mentioned how much the Upper West Side has changed in the years since it was known as Gallows Heights. But that's all. Nothing specific.'

Too many unconnected dots, Rhyme reflected. It was then that Cooper's computer binged, signaling an incoming email. The tech read it and glanced at the team. 'Listen to this. It's about *Coloreds' Weekly Illustrated*. The curator of Booker T. Washington College down in Philly just sent me this. The library had the only complete collection of the magazine in the country. And — '

' 'Had'?' Rhyme snapped. 'Fucking 'had'?'

'Last week, a fire destroyed the room where it was stored.'

'What'd the arson report say?' Sachs asked.

'Wasn't considered arson. It looks like a lightbulb broke, ignited some papers. Nobody was hurt.'

'Bullshit it wasn't arson. Somebody started it. So, does the curator have any other suggestions where we can find — ?'

'I was *about* to continue.'

'Well, *continue*!'

'The school has a policy of scanning everything in their archives and storing them in Adobe .pdf files.'

'Are we approaching good news, Mel? Or are you just flirting?'

Cooper punched more buttons. He gestured toward the screen. 'Voilà — July twenty-third, 1868, *Coloreds' Weekly Illustrated*.'

'You don't say. Well, read to us, Mel. First of all: Did Mr. Singleton drown in the Hudson, or not?'

Cooper typed and a moment later shoved his

glasses onto the bridge of his nose, leaned forward and said, 'Here we go. The headline is 'Shame, the Account of a Freedman's Crime. Charles Singleton, a Veteran of the War Between the States, Betrays the Cause of Our People in a Notorious Incident.' '

Continuing with the text, he read, ' 'On Tuesday, July fourteenth, a warrant for the arrest of one Charles Singleton, a freedman who was a veteran of the War of Secession, was issued by the New York criminal court, on charges that he feloniously stole a large sum of gold and other monies from the National Education Trust for Freedmen's Assistance on Twenty-third Street in Manhattan, New York.

' 'Mr. Singleton eluded a drag-net by officers throughout the City and was thought to have escaped, possibly to Pennsylvania, where his wife's sister and her family lived.

' 'However, early on the morning of Thursday, the sixteenth, he was noticed by a police constable as he was making his way toward the Hudson river docks.

' 'The constable sounded the alarm and Mr. Singleton took flight. The police officer gave chase.

' 'The pursuit was soon joined by dozens of other law enforcers and Irish rag pickers and workers, doing their civic duty to apprehend the felon (and encouraged by the promise of five dollars in gold to stop the villain). The attempted route of escape was through the warren of disreputable shanties close by the River.

' 'At the Twenty-third Street paint works,

142

Mr. Singleton stumbled. A mounted officer approached and it appeared he would be ensnared. Yet he regained his footing and, rather than own up to his mischief, as a courageous man would do, continued his cowardly flight.

"'For a time he evaded his pursuers. But his escape was merely temporary. A Negro tradesman on a porch saw the freedman and implored him to stop, in the name of justice, asserting that he had heard of Mr. Singleton's crime and recriminating him for bringing dishonor upon all colored people throughout the nation. The citizen, one Walker Loakes, thereupon flung a brick at Mr. Singleton with the intent of knocking him down. However, Mr. Singleton avoided the missile and, proclaiming his innocence, continued to flee.

"'The freedman was strong of body from working an apple orchard, and ran as fast as greased lightning. But Mr. Loakes informed the constabulary of the freedman's presence and, at the piers near Twenty-eighth Street, near the tow boat office, his path was confounded by another contingent of diligent police. There he paused, exhausted, clinging to the Swiftsure Express Company sign. He was urged to surrender by the man who had led his pursuit for the past two days, Detective Captain William P. Simms, who leveled his pistol at the thief.

"'Yet, either seeking a desperate means of escape, or convinced that his evil deeds had caught up with him and wishing to end his life, Mr. Singleton, by most accounts, hesitated for but a moment then leapt into the River, calling out words that none could hear.''

Rhyme interrupted, 'That's as far as Geneva got before she was attacked. Forget the Civil War, Sachs. *This* is the cliffhanger. Keep going.'

''He disappeared from view under the waves and witnesses were sure he had perished. Three constables commandeered a skiff from a nearby dock and rowed along the piers to ascertain the Negro's fate.

''They at last found him, half conscious from the fall, clutching a piece of driftwood to his breast and, with a pathos that many suggested was calculated, calling for his wife and son.''

'At least he survived,' Sachs said. 'Geneva'll be glad about that.'

''He was tended to by a surgeon, taken away and bound over for trial, which was held on Tuesday last. In court it was proven that he stole the unimaginable sum of greenbacks and gold coin worth thirty thousand dollars.''

'That's what I was thinking,' Rhyme said. 'That the motive here's missing loot. Value today?'

Cooper minimized the window containing the article about Charles Singleton and did a web search, jotting numbers on a pad. He looked up from his calculations. 'It'd be worth close to eight hundred thousand.'

Rhyme grunted. ' 'Unimaginable.' All right. Keep going.'

Cooper continued, ' 'A porter across the street from the Freedmen's Trust saw Mr. Singleton gain entry into the office by the back door and leave twenty minutes later, carrying two large

144

satchels. When the manager of the Trust arrived soon after, summoned by the police, it was discovered that the Trust's Exeter Strongbow safe had been broken open with a hammer and crowbar, identical to those owned by the defendant, which were later located in proximity to the building.

''Further, evidence was presented that Mr. Singleton had ingratiated himself, at a number of meetings in the Gallows Heights neighborhood of the city, with such luminaries as the Hons. Charles Sumner, Thaddeus Stevens and Frederick Douglass, and his son Lewis Douglass, on the pretense of assisting those noble men in the furtherance of the rights of our people before Congress.''

'Ah, the meetings Charles referred to in his letter. They *were* about civil rights. And those must be the colleagues he mentioned. Pretty heavy hitters, sounds like. What else?'

''His motive in assisting these famed personages, according to the able prosecutor, was not, however, to assist the cause of Negroes but to gain knowledge of the Trust and other repositories he might plunder.''

'Was *that* the secret?' Sachs wondered.

''At his trial Mr. Singleton remained silent regarding these charges, except to make a general disclaimer and to say that he loved his wife and son.

''Captain Simms was able to recover most of the ill-gotten gains. It is speculated that the Negro secreted the remaining several thousand in a hiding place and refused to divulge its whereabouts. None of it was ever found, excepting a hundred dollars in gold coin discovered on Mr. Singleton's person when he was apprehended.''

'There goes the buried treasure theory,' Rhyme muttered. 'Too bad. I liked it.'

''The accused was convicted expeditiously. Upon sentencing, the judge exhorted the freedman to return the rest of the purloined funds, whose location he nonetheless refused to disclose, clinging still to his claim of innocence, and asserting the coin found on his person had been placed in his belongings after his apprehesion. Accordingly, the judge in his wisdom ordered that the felon's possessions be confiscated and sold to make such restitution as could be had, and the criminal himself was sentenced to five years' imprisonment.''

Cooper looked up. 'That's it.'

'Why would somebody resort to murder just to keep the story under wraps?' Sachs asked.

'Yep, the big question . . . ' Rhyme gazed at the ceiling. 'So what do we know about Charles? He was a teacher and a Civil War veteran. He owned and worked a farm upstate. He was arrested and convicted for theft. He had a secret that would have tragic consequences if it was known. He went to hush-hush meetings in Gallows Heights. He was involved in the civil rights movement and hobnobbed with some of the big politicians and civil rights workers of the day.'

Rhyme wheeled close to the computer screen, looking over the article. He could see no

146

connection between the events then and the Unsub 109 case.

Sellitto's phone rang. He listened for a moment. His eyebrow lifted. 'Okay, thanks.' He disconnected and looked at Rhyme. 'Bingo.'

'What's 'bingo'?' Rhyme asked.

Sellitto said, 'A canvass team in Little Italy — a half block from where they had the Columbus Day fair — just found a discount store on Mulberry Street. The clerk remembered a middle-aged white guy who bought everything in the unsub's rape pack a few days ago. She remembered him because of the hat.'

'He wore a hat?'

'No, he bought a hat. A stocking cap. Only why she remembered him was because when he tried it on he pulled it down over his face. She saw him in a security mirror. She thought he was going to rob her. But then he took it off and put it in the basket with everything else and just paid and left.'

The missing $5.95 item on the receipt probably. Trying it on to make sure it would work as a mask. 'It's probably also what he rubbed his own prints off with. Does she know his name?'

'No. But she can describe him pretty good.'

Sachs said, 'We'll do a composite and hit the streets.' Grabbing her purse, she was at the door before she realized the big detective wasn't with her. She stopped. Looked back. 'Lon, you coming?'

Sellitto didn't seem to hear. She repeated the question and the detective blinked. He lowered his hand from his reddened cheek. And grinned. 'Sorry. You bet. Let's go nail this bastard.'

AFRICAN-AMERICAN MUSEUM SCENE

- Rape pack:
  - Tarot card, twelfth card in deck, The Hanged Man, meaning spiritual searching.
  - Smiley-face bag.
    - Too generic to trace.
  - Box cutter.
  - Trojan condoms.
  - Duct tape.
  - Jasmine scent.
  - Unknown item bought for $5.95. Probably a stocking cap.
  - Receipt, indicating store was in New York City, discount variety store or drugstore.
  - Most likely purchased in a store on Mulberry Street, Little Italy. Unsub identified by clerk.

- Fingerprints:
  - Unsub wore latex or vinyl gloves.
  - Prints on items in rape pack belonged to person with small hands, no IAFIS hits. Possibly clerk's.

- Trace:
  - Cotton rope fibers, some with traces of human blood. Garrotte?
    - No manufacturer.
    - Sent to CODIS.
      - No DNA match in CODIS.
  - Popcorn and cotton candy with traces of canine urine.
    - Connection with carnival or street fair? Checking with Traffic about recent permits. Officers presently canvassing street fairs, per info from Traffic.
      - Confirm festival was in Little Italy.

- Weapons:
  - Billy club or martial arts weapon.
  - Pistol is a North American Arms .22 rimfire magnum, Black Widow or Mini-Master.
  - Makes own bullets, bored-out slugs filled

with needles. No match in IBIS or DRUGFIRE.

- Motive:
  - Uncertain. Rape was probably staged.
  - True motive may have been to steal microfiche containing July 23, 1868, issue of *Coloreds' Weekly Illustrated* magazine and kill G. Settle because of her interest in an article for reasons unknown. Article was about her ancestor Charles Singleton (see accompanying chart).
- Librarian victim reported that someone else wished to see article.
  - Requesting librarian's phone records to verify this.
    - No leads.
  - Requesting information from employees as to other person wishing to see story.
    - No leads.
- Searching for copy of article.
  - Several sources report man requested same article. No leads to identity. Most issues missing or destroyed. One located. (See accompanying chart.)
- Conclusion: G. Settle possibly still at risk.
- Profile of incident sent to VICAP and NCIC.
  - Murder in Amarillo, TX, five years ago. Similar M.O. — staged crime scene (apparently ritual killing, but real motive unknown).
  - Murder in Ohio, three years ago. Similar M.O. — staged crime scene (apparently sexual assault, but real motive probably hired killing). Files missing.

PROFILE OF UNSUB 109

- White male.
- 6 feet tall, 180 lbs.
- Average voice.
- Used cell phone to get close to victim.
- Wears three-year-old, or older, size-11 Bass walkers, light brown. Right foot slightly outturned.
- Additional jasmine scent.
- Dark pants.
- Ski mask, dark.
- Will target innocents to

help in killing victims and escaping.

- Most likely is a for-hire killer.

PROFILE OF PERSON HIRING UNSUB 109

- No information at this time.

PROFILE OF CHARLES SINGLETON

- Former slave, ancestor of G. Settle. Married, one son. Given orchard in New York state by master. Worked as teacher, as well. Instrumental in early civil rights movement.
- Charles allegedly committed theft in 1868, the subject of the article in stolen microfiche.
- Reportedly had a secret that could bear on case. Worried that tragedy would result if his secret was revealed.
- Attended meetings in Gallows Heights neighborhood of New York.
- Involved in some risky activities?

- The crime, as reported in *Coloreds' Weekly Illustrated*:

- Charles arrested by Det. William Simms for stealing large sum from Freedmen's Trust in NY. Broke into the trust's safe, witnesses saw him leave shortly after. His tools were found nearby. Most money was recovered. He was sentenced to five years in prison. No information about him after sentencing. Believed to have used his connections with early civil rights leaders to gain access to the trust.

- Charles's correspondence:
  - Letter 1, to wife: Re: Draft Riots in 1863, great anti-black sentiment throughout NY state, lynchings, arson. Risk to property owned by blacks.
  - Letter 2, to wife: Charles at Battle of Appomattox at end of Civil War.
  - Letter 3, to wife: Involved in civil rights movement. Threatened for this work. Troubled by his secret.

150

10

In the 1920s the New Negro Movement, later called the Harlem Renaissance, erupted in New York City.

It involved an astonishing group of thinkers, artists, musicians and — mostly — writers who approached their art by looking at black life not from the viewpoint of white America but from their own perspective. This groundbreaking movement included men and women like the intellectuals Marcus Garvey and W. E. B. DuBois, writers like Zora Neale Hurston, Claude McKay and Countee Cullen, painters like William H. Johnson and John T. Biggers, and, of course, the musicians who provided the timeless sound track to it all, people like Duke Ellington, Josephine Baker, W. C. Handy, Eubie Blake.

In such a pantheon of brilliance, it was hard for any single artist's voice to stand out, but if anyone's did, it would perhaps be that of poet and novelist Langston Hughes, whose voice and message were typified by his simple words: *What happens to a dream deferred?/Does it dry up like a raisin in the sun? . . . Or does it explode?*

Many memorials to Hughes exist throughout the country, but certainly one of the biggest and most dynamic, and probably the one he'd have been most proud of, was an old, redbrick, four-story building in Harlem, located near

Lennox Terrace on 135th Street.

Like all city schools, Langston Hughes High had its problems. It was continually overcrowded and underfunded and struggled desperately to get and retain good teachers — and to keep students in class as well. It suffered from low graduation rates, violence in the halls, drugs, gangs, teen pregnancy and truancy. Still, the school had produced graduates who'd gone on to become lawyers, successful businessmen and -women, doctors, scientists, writers, dancers and musicians, politicians, professors. It had winning varsity teams, dozens of scholastic societies and arts clubs.

But for Geneva Settle, Langston Hughes High was more than these stats. It was the hub of her salvation, an island of comfort. As she saw the dirty brick walls come into view now, the fear and anxiety that had swarmed around her since the terrible incident at the museum that morning diminished considerably.

Detective Bell parked his car and, after he'd looked around for threats, they climbed out. He nodded toward a street corner and said to that young officer, Mr. Pulaski, 'You wait out here.'

'Yes, sir.'

Geneva added to the detective, 'You can wait here too, you want.'

He chuckled. 'I'll just come hang out with you for a bit, you don't mind. Well, okay, I can see you *do* mind. But I think I'll come along anyway.' He buttoned his jacket to hide his guns. 'Nobody'll pay me any mind.' He held up the social studies book.

Not answering, Geneva grimaced and they proceeded to the school. At the metal detector the girl showed her ID and Detective Bell subtly flashed his wallet and was let around the side of the device. It was just before fifth period, which started at 11:37, and the halls were crowded, kids milling around, heading for the cafeteria or out to the school yard or onto the street for fast food. There was joking, dissing, flirting, making out. A fight or two. Chaos reigned.

'It's my lunch period,' she called over the din. 'I'll go to the cafeteria and study. It's this way.'

Three of her friends came up fast, Ramona, Challette, Janet. They fell into step beside her. They were smart girls, like her. Pleasant, never caused any trouble, on scholarship tracks. Yet — or maybe because of this — they weren't particularly tight; none of them really just hung out. They'd go home after class, practice Suzuki violin or piano, volunteer for literacy groups or work on the spelling bee or Westinghouse science competitions, and, of course, study. Academics meant solitude. (Part of Geneva actually envied the school's other cliques, like the gangsta girls, the blingstas, the jock-girls and the Angela Davis activist sistas.) But now these three were fluttering around her like best homegirls, huddling close, peppering her with questions. Did he touch you? You see his dick? Was he hard? D'you see the guy got capped? How close were you?

They'd all heard — from kids who came in late, or kids cutting class and watching TV. Even though the stories hadn't mentioned Geneva by name, everybody knew she was at the center of the incident, thanks probably to Keesh.

Marella — a track star and fellow junior — walked by, saying, 'What up, girlfriend? You down?'

'Yeah, I'm cool.'

The tall classmate squinted at Detective Bell and asked her, 'Why's a cop carrying yo' book, Gen?'

'Ask him.'

The policeman laughed uneasily.

Fronting you're a teacher. Hey, that's def . . .

Keesha Scott, clustered with her sister and some of her blingsta homegirls, gave Geneva a theatrical double-take. 'Girl, you wack bitch,' she shouted. 'Somebody give you a pass, you *take* a pass. Coulda kicked back, watched the soaps.' Grinned, nodded at the lunchroom. 'Catch you later.'

Some of the students weren't as kind. Halfway to the lunchroom, she heard a boy's voice, 'Yo, yo, it the Fox News bitch with the cracker over there. She still alive?'

'Thought somebody clip that 'ho.'

'Fuck, that debbie be too skinny to hit with anything but a breakdown.'

Raucous laughter erupted.

Detective Bell whirled around but the young men who'd called out those words disappeared in a sea of sweats and sports jerseys, baggy jeans and cargo pants and bare heads — hats being forbidden in the halls of Langston Hughes.

'It's okay,' Geneva said, her jaw set, looking down. 'Some of them, they don't like it when

154

you take school seriously, you know. Raising the curve.' She'd been student of the month a number of times and had a perfect attendance award for both of her prior years here. She was regularly on the principal's honor roll, with her 98 percent average, and had been inducted into the National Honor Society at the formal ceremony last spring. 'Doesn't matter.'

Even the vicious insult of 'blondie' or 'debbie' — a black girl aspiring to be white — didn't get to her. Since to some extent it was true.

At the lunchroom door a large, attractive black woman in a purple dress, with a board of education ID around her neck, came up to Mr. Bell. She identified herself as Mrs. Barton, a counselor. She'd heard about the incident and wanted to know if Geneva was all right and if she wanted to talk with somebody in her department about it.

Oh, man, a counselor, the girl thought, her spirits dipping. Don't need this shit now. 'No,' she said. 'I'm fine.'

'You sure? We could do a session this afternoon.'

'Really. I'm down. It's cool.'

'I should call your parents.'

'They're away.'

'You're not alone, are you?' The woman frowned.

'I'm staying with my uncle.'

'And we're looking out for her,' the detective said. Geneva noticed the woman didn't even ask to see his ID, it was so obvious he was a cop.

'When'll they be back, your folks?'

'They're on their way. They were overseas.'

'You didn't really need to come to school today.'

'I've got two tests. I don't want to miss them.'

The woman gave a faint laugh and said to Mr. Bell, 'I never took school as seriously as this. Probably should have.' A glance at the girl. 'Are you sure you don't want to go home?'

'I spent a lot of time studying for those tests,' she muttered. 'I really want to take them.'

'All right. But after that I think you should go home and stay there for a few days. We'll get your assignments to you.' Mrs. Barton stormed off to break up a pushing match between two boys.

When she was gone, the officer asked, 'You have a problem with her?'

'It's just, counselors . . . They're always in your business, you know?'

He looked like, no, he didn't know, but why should he? This wasn't *his* world.

They started up the hall toward the cafeteria. As they entered the noisy place, she nodded toward the short alcove leading to the girls' restroom. 'Is it okay if I go in there?'

'Sure. Just hold on a minute.'

He motioned to a woman teacher and whispered something to her, explaining the situation, Geneva assumed. The woman nodded and stepped inside the bathroom. Came out a moment later. 'It's empty.'

Mr. Bell stationed himself outside the door. 'I'll make sure only students get in.'

Geneva stepped inside, thankful for the

156

moment or two of peace, to be away from the staring eyes. Away from the edginess of knowing that somebody wanted to hurt her. Earlier, she'd been angry. Earlier she'd been defiant. But now the reality was starting to lap at her heart and left her scared and confused.

She came out of the stall and washed her hands and face. Another girl had come in and was putting on her makeup. A senior, Geneva believed. Tall, fine-looking, with her eyebrows artistically plucked and bangs hotcombed to perfection. The girl gave her the up and down — not because of the news story, though. She was taking inventory. You saw it all the time here, every minute of the day, checking out the competition: What was a girl wearing, how many piercings, real gold or plate, too much glitter, were her braids phat or coming loose, was she draped or wearing a simple hoop or two, are those real extensions or fake? Was she covering up being pregnant?

Geneva, who spent her money on books, not clothes and makeup, always came in low in the ratings.

Not that what God had created helped much. She had to take a deep breath to fill her bra, which she usually didn't even bother to wear. She was that 'egg-yolk-titty bitch' to the Delano Project girls, and she'd been called 'him' or 'he' dozens of times in the last year. (It hurt the worst when somebody'd really mistake her for a boy, not when they were dissing.) Then there was her hair: dense and wiry as steel wool. She didn't have the time to train locs or tie rows. Braids and

157

extensions took forever and even though Keesh would do them for free they actually made her look younger, like she was a little kid dressed up by her moms.

There she go, there she go, the skinny little boy-girl . . . Get her down . . .

The senior next to her at the washbasins turned back to the mirror. She was pretty and broad, her sexy bra straps and thong line evident, hair in a long straightened sweep, her smooth cheeks faintly maroon. Her shoes were red as candy apples. She was everything that Geneva Settle was not.

It was then that the door swung open and Geneva's heart froze.

In walked Jonette Monroe, another senior. Not much taller than Geneva, though broader, bustier, with solid shoulders and cut muscles. Tats on both arms. A long, mocha-shaded face. And eyes that were ice cold — they now squinted in recognition at Geneva, who looked away immediately.

Jonette was trouble. A gangsta girl. Rumors were she was dealing — could get you anything you wanted, meth, crack, smack. And if you didn't come up with the benjamins, she'd whale on you herself — or on your best friend or even your moms — till you stood up to the debt. Twice already this year, she'd been dragged off by the cops, even kicked one in the balls.

Geneva now kept her eyes down, thinking: Detective Bell'd have no way of knowing how dangerous Jonette was when he let her inside.

158

Her hands and face still wet, Geneva started for the door.

'Yo, yo, girl,' Jonette said to her, looking her up and down with a cold glance. 'Yeah, you, Martha Stewart. Don' you be goin' nowhere.'

'I — '

'Shutup.' She glanced at the other girl, the one with the purple cheeks. 'An' you, get the fuck out.'

The senior had fifty pounds and three inches of height on Jonette but the girl stopped preening and slowly gathered up her makeup. She tried to save a bit of dignity, saying, 'Don't go layin' no attitude on me, girl.'

Jonette didn't say a word. She took one step forward; the girl snatched up her purse and fled through the doorway. A lip liner fell to the floor. Jonette picked it up and slipped the tube into her pocket. Geneva started to leave again but Jonette held her hand up and motioned her to the back of the restroom. When Geneva stood, frozen, Jonette grabbed her by the arm and shoved open the doors of the stalls to make sure they were alone.

'Whatta you want?' Geneva whispered, both defiant and terrified.

Jonette snapped, 'Shut yo' mouth.'

Shit, she thought, furious. Mr. Rhyme was right! That terrible man from the library *was* still after her. He'd somehow found out her school and hired Jonette to finish the job. Why the hell *had* she come to school today? Scream, Geneva told herself.

And she did.

Or started to.

Jonette could see it coming and in a flash was behind her, clamping her hand over Geneva's mouth, stifling the sound. 'Quiet!' Her other hand gripped the girl around the waist and pulled her into the far corner of the room. Geneva grabbed her hand and arm and tugged, but she was no match for Jonette. She stared at the girl's bleeding-cross tat on her forearm and whimpered, 'Please . . . '

Jonette rummaged for something in her purse or pocket. What? Geneva wondered in a panic. There was a flash of metal. A knife or gun? What'd they have metal detectors for if it was so goddamn easy to get a weapon into the school?

Geneva squealed, twisting violently.

Then the gang girl's hand swung forward.

No, no . . .

And Geneva found herself looking at a silver police department badge.

'You gonna be quiet, girl?' Jonette asked, exasperated.

'I — '

'Quiet?'

A nod.

Jonette said, 'I don't want anybody outside to hear anything . . . Now, you down?'

Geneva nodded again and Jonette released her.

'You're — '

'A cop, yeah.'

Geneva scrabbled away and pressed against the wall, breathing deeply, as Jonette walked to the door, opened it a crack. She whispered something and Detective Bell stepped inside and locked the door.

'So, you two met,' he said.

'Sort of,' Geneva said. 'She really *is* a cop?'

The detective explained, 'All the schools have undercover officers. They're usually women, pretending to be juniors or seniors. Or, what'd you say? 'Fronting.''

'Why didn't you just *tell* me?' Geneva snapped.

Jonette glanced at the stalls. 'I didn't know we were alone. Sorry to be wack. But I couldn't say anything that'd blow my cover.' The police-woman looked Geneva over, shook her head. 'Shame this had to happen to *you*. You're one of the good ones. I never spent any worry on you.'

'A cop,' Geneva whispered in disbelief.

Jonette laughed in a high, girlish voice. 'I'm the *man*, yep.'

'You're so down,' Geneva said. 'I never guessed.'

Mr. Bell said, 'You remember when they busted those seniors who smuggled some guns into the school a few weeks ago?'

Geneva nodded. 'A pipe bomb too, or something.'

'It was going to be another Columbine, right here,' the man said in his lazy drawl. 'Jonette's the one heard about it and stopped the whole thing.'

'Had to keep my cover so I couldn't take 'em down myself,' she said as if she regretted not being able to bust up the kids personally. 'Now, as long as you're going to be in school, which I

161

think is pretty wack, but that's a different story, long as you're here, I'll keep an eye on you. You see anything makes you uneasy, give me a sign.'

'Gang sign?'

Jonette laughed. 'You'd be a claimer in any gang, Gen, nothing personal. You go throwing me a flag, I think everybody'd know something was up. Better you just scratch your ear. How's that?'

'Sure.'

'Then I'll come over and mess you up some. Give you some shit. Get you out of wherever you are. You cool with that? I won't hurt you. Maybe just push you round a little.'

'Sure, good . . . Listen, thanks for doing this. And I won't say anything about you.'

'I knew that 'fore I told you,' Jonette said. Then she looked at the officer. 'You wanta do it now?'

'You bet.'

Then the pleasant, soft-spoken policeman got a dark look on his face and shouted, 'What the hell're you doing in here?'

Screeching: 'Get yo' motherfuckin' hands off me, asshole!' Jonette had slipped into character again.

The detective took her by the arm and shoved her out the door. She stumbled into the wall.

'Fuck you, I'ma sue yo' fucking ass for abuse or some shit.' The girl rubbed her arm. 'You can't touch me. That a crime, motherfucker!' She stormed off down the hall. After a pause Detective Bell and Geneva stepped into the cafeteria proper.

'Good actress,' Geneva whispered.

'One of the best,' the policeman said.

'She kind of blew *your* cover.'

He handed her back the social studies book, grinned. 'Wasn't exactly working.'

Geneva sat down at a table in the corner and pulled a language arts book out of her knapsack.

Detective Bell asked, 'Aren't you eating?'

'No.'

'Did your uncle give you your lunch money?'

'I'm not really hungry.'

'Forgot, didn't he? All respect, he's not a man who's ever been a father. I can tell. I'll rustle you up something.'

'No, really — '

'Truth is, I'm hungrier than a farmer at sundown. And I haven't had any high school turkey tetrazzini in years. Gonna get me some of that. No trouble to get a second plate. You like milk?'

She debated. 'Sure. I'll pay you back.'

'We'll put it on the city.'

He stepped into the line. Geneva had just turned back to her textbook when she saw a boy look her way and wave. She glanced behind her to see whom he was gesturing at. There was no one else. She gave a faint gasp, realizing that he was indicating her.

Kevin Cheaney was pushing away from the table where he and his homies sat and started loping toward her. Oh, my God! Was he really coming this way? . . . Kevin, a Will Smith look-alike. Perfect lips, perfecter body. The boy who could make a basketball defy gravity, could move like he was a break-dancer competing in a B-Boy Summit show. Kevin was a coal institution at all the jams.

In line, Detective Bell stiffened and started forward but Geneva shook her head that everything was fine.

Which it was. Better than fine. Totally def.

Kevin was destined for Connecticut or Duke on scholarship. Maybe an athletic one — he'd been captain of the team that won last year's PSAL basketball championship. But he could make it on grades too. He didn't have the same love of books and school that Geneva did, maybe, but he was still in the top 5 percent of the class. They knew each other casually — they shared math class this semester and would also find themselves together in the hall or in the school yard from time to time — coincidentally, Geneva told herself. But, okay, fact was that she usually gravitated to where he was standing or sitting.

Most of the down kids ignored or dissed her; Kevin, though, actually said hi from time to time. He'd ask her a question about a math or history assignment, or just pause and talk for a few minutes.

He wasn't asking her out, of course — that'd *never* happen — but he treated her like a human being.

He'd even walked her home from Langston Hughes one day last spring.

A beautiful, clear day she could still picture as if she had a DVD of it.

April 21.

Normally Kevin would hang with the svelte model wannabees, or the brash girls — the blingstas. (He even flirted with Lakeesha some, which infuriated Geneva, who endured the raging jealousy with a gritty, carefree smile.)

So what was he about now?

'Yo, girl, you down?' he asked, frowning and dropping into a battered chrome chair next to her, stretching out his long legs.

'Yeah.' She swallowed, tongue-tied. Her mind was blank.

He said, 'I heard 'bout what happened. Man, that was some mad shit, somebody trying to yoke and choke you. I was fretting.'

'Yeah?'

'Word.'

'It was just weird.'

'Long as you okay, that's cool, then.'

She felt a wave of heat wash over her face. Kevin was actually saying this to *her*?

'Why don't you just roll on back at home?' he asked. 'Whatcha doing here?'

'Language arts test. Then our math test.'

He laughed. 'Damn. You down for school, after all that shit?'

'Yeah. Can't miss those tests.'

'And you cool with math?'

It was just calc. No big deal. 'Yeah, I've got it covered. You know, nothing too heavy.'

'Straight up. Anyway. Just wanted to say, lotta people round here give you shit, I know that. And you take it quiet. But they wouldn't've gone and came in today, way you did. All rolled together, they ain't worth half of you. You got spine, girl.'

Breathless from the compliment, Geneva just looked down and shrugged.

'So, now I see what you really about, you and me, girl, we gotta hang more. But you're never 'round.'

'Just, you know, school an' shit.' Watch it, she warned herself. You don't have to talk his talk.

Kevin joked, 'Naw, girl, that ain't it. I know what's what. You dealin' crank over in BK.'

'I — ' Nearly an 'ain't.' She refused to let it escape. She gave him a self-conscious smile, looked down at the scuffed floor. 'I don't deal in Brooklyn. Only Queens. They got more benjamins, you know.' Lame, lame, lame, girl. Oh, you are pathetic. Her palms bled sweat.

But Kevin laughed hard. Then he shook his head. 'Naw — I know why I got confused. Musta been yo' *moms* selling crank in BK.'

This seemed like an insult, but it was actually an invitation. Kevin was asking her to play the dozens. That's how the old folks referred to it. Now you called it 'snapping,' trading 'snaps' — insults. Part of a long tradition of black poetry and storytelling contests, snapping was verbal combat, trading barbs. Serious snappers'd perform onstage, though most snapping took place in living rooms and school yards and pizza parlors and bars and clubs and on front steps and was about as sad as what Kevin had just offered as his initial volley, like 'Yo' mama so stupid, she asks for price checks at the dollar store.' 'Yo' sister so ugly, she

166

couldn't get laid if she was a brick.'

But today, here, the point had nothing to do with being witty. Because playing the dozens was traditionally men against men or women against women. When a male offered to play with a female, it meant only one thing: flirt.

Geneva, thinking, How weird is this? It took getting attacked to make people respect her. Her father always said that the best can come out of the worst.

Well, go ahead, girl; play back. The game was ridiculously juvenile, silly, but she knew how to snap; she and Keesh and Keesh's sister'd go on for an hour straight. *Yo' mama so fat her blood type is Ragu. Yo' Chevy so old they stole the Club and left the car* . . . .But, her heart beating fiercely, Geneva now simply grinned and sweated silently. She tried desperately to think of something to say.

But this was Kevin Cheaney himself. Even if she could work up the courage to fire off a snap about his mother her mind was frozen.

She looked at her watch, then down at her language arts book. Sweet Jesus, you wack girl, she raged at herself. Say something!

But not a single syllable trickled from her mouth. She knew Kevin was about to give her that look she knew so well, that I-ain't-got-time-t'waste-on-wack-bitches look, and walk off. But, no, it seemed he thought that she just wasn't in the mood to play, probably still freaked from the morning's events, and that was all right with him. He just said, 'I'm serious, Gen, you're about more'n just DJs and braids and bling.

What it is, you're smart. Nice to talk with somebody smart. My boys' — he nodded toward his posse's table — 'they're not exactly rocket scientists, you know what I'm saying?'

A flash in her mind. Go for it, girl. 'Yeah,' she said, 'some of 'em're so dumb, if they spoke their minds, they'd be speechless.'

'Def, girl! Straight up.' Laughing, he tapped his fist to hers, and an electric jolt shot through her body. She struggled not to grin; it was way bad form to smile at your own snap.

Then, through the exhilaration of the moment, she was thinking how right he was, how rarely it happens, just talking with somebody smart, somebody who could listen, somebody who cared what you had to say.

Kevin lifted an eyebrow at Detective Bell, who was paying for the food, and said, 'I know that dude fronting he's a teacher is five-0.'

She whispered, 'Man does sorta have 'Cop' written on his forehead.'

'That's word,' Kevin said, laughing. 'I know he's stepping up for you and all and that's cool. But I just wanta say I'ma watch yo' back too. And my boys. We see anything wack, we'll let him know.'

She was touched by this.

But then troubled. What if Kevin or one of his friends got hurt by that terrible man from the library? She was still sick with sorrow that Dr. Barry had been killed because of her, that the woman on the sidewalk had been wounded. She had a horrible premonition: Kevin laid out in the Williams Funeral Home parlor, like so many other Harlem boys, shot down on the street.

'You don't have to do that,' she said, unsmiling.

'I know I don't,' he said. 'I *want* to. Nobody's gonna hurt you. That's word. Okay, I'ma hang with my boys now. Catch you later? 'Fore math class?'

Heart thudding, she stammered, 'Sure.'

He tapped her fist again and walked off. Watching him, she felt feverish, hands shaking at the exchange. Please, she thought, don't let anything happen to him . . .

'Miss?'

She looked up, blinked.

Detective Bell was setting down a tray. The food smelled so fine . . . She was even hungrier than she'd thought. She stared at the steaming plate.

'You know him?' the policeman asked.

'Yeah, he's down. We're in class together. Known him for years.'

'You look a little addled, miss.'

'Well . . . I don't know. Maybe I am. Yeah.'

'But it doesn't have anything to do with what happened at the museum, right?' he asked with a smile.

She looked away, feeling heat across her face.

'Now,' the detective said, setting the steaming plate in front of her. 'Chow down. Nothing like turkey tetrazzini to soothe a troubled soul. You know, I might just ask 'em for the recipe.'

11

These'd do just fine.

Thompson Boyd looked down at his purchases in the basket, then started for the checkout counter. He just loved hardware stores. He wondered why that might be. Maybe because his father used to take him every Saturday to an Ace Hardware outside of Amarillo to stock up on what the man needed for his workshop in the shed outside their trailer.

Or maybe it was because in most hardware stores, like here, all the tools were clean and organized, the paint and glues and tapes were all ordered logically and easy to find.

Everything arranged by the book.

Thompson liked the smell too, sort of a pungent fertilizer/oil/solvent smell that was impossible to describe, but one that everyone who'd ever been in an old hardware store would recognize instantly.

The killer was pretty handy. This was something he'd picked up from his dad, who, even though he spent all day with tools, working on oil pipelines, derricks and the bobbing, dinosaur-head pumps, would still spend lots of time patiently teaching his son how to work with — and respect — tools, how to measure, how to draw plans. Thompson spent hours learning how to fix what was broken and how to turn wood and metal and plastic into things that hadn't existed. Together they'd work on the truck or the trailer, fix the fence, make furniture, build a present for his mom or aunt — a rolling pin or cigarette box or butcher block table. 'Big or small,' his father taught, 'you put the same amount of skill into what you're doing, son. One's not better or harder than the other. It's only a question of where you put the decimal point.'

His father was a good teacher and he was proud of what his son built. When Hart Boyd died he had with him a shoeshine kit the boy had made, and a wooden key chain in the shape of an Indian head with the wood-burned letters 'Dad' on it.

It was fortunate, as it turned out, that Thompson learned these skills because that's what the business of death is all about. Mechanics and chemistry. No different from carpentry or painting or car repair.

Where you put the decimal point.

Standing at the checkout stand, he paid — cash, of course — and thanked the clerk. He took the shopping bag in his gloved hands. He started out the door, paused and looked at a small electric lawn mower, green and yellow. It was perfectly clean, polished, an emerald jewel of a device. It had a curious appeal to him. Why? he wondered. Well, since he'd been thinking of his father it occurred to him that the machine reminded him of times he'd mow the tiny yard behind his parents' trailer, Sunday morning, then go inside to watch the game with his dad while his mother baked.

He remembered the sweet smell of the leaded gas exhaust, remembered the gunshot-sounding crack when the blade hit a stone and flung it into the air, the numbness in his hands from the vibration of the grips.

Numb, the way you'd feel as you lay dying from a sidewinder snakebite, he assumed.

He realized that the clerk was speaking to him.

'What?' Thompson asked.

'Make you a good deal,' the clerk said, nodding at the mower.

'No thanks.'

Stepping outside, he wondered why he'd spaced out — what had so appealed to him about the mower, why he wanted it so much. Then he had the troubling idea that it wasn't the family memory at all. Maybe it was because the machine was really a small guillotine, a very efficient way to kill.

Maybe that was it.

Didn't like that thought. But there it was.

Numb . . .

Whistling faintly, a song from his youth, Thompson started up the street, carrying the shopping bag in one hand and, in the other, his briefcase, containing his gun and billy club and a few other tools of the trade.

He continued up the street, into Little Italy, where the crews were cleaning up after the street fair yesterday. He grew cautious, observing several police cars. Two officers were talking to a Korean fruit stand owner and his wife. He wondered what that was about. Then he continued on to a pay phone. He checked his voice mail once more, but there were no messages yet about Geneva's whereabouts. That wasn't a concern. His contact knew Harlem pretty good, and it'd only be a matter of time until Thompson found out where the girl went to school and where she lived. Besides, he could use the free time. He had another job, one that he'd been planning for even longer than Geneva Settle's death, and one that was just as important as that job.

More important, really.

And funny, now that he thought about it — this one also involved children.

★   ★   ★

'Yeah?' Jax said into his cell phone.

'Ralph.'

'S'up, dog?' Jax wondered if the skinny little pharaoh was leaning against something at the moment. 'You get the word from our friend?' Meaning the character reference DeLisle Marshall.

'Yeah.'

'And the Graffiti King's cool?' Jax asked.

'Yeah.'

'Good. So where are we on all this?'

'Okay, I found what you want, man. It's — '

'Don't say anything.' Cell phones were the devil's own invention when it came to incriminating evidence. He gave the man an intersection on 116th Street. 'Ten minutes.'

Jax disconnected and started up the street, as two ladies in their long overcoats, wearing

173

elaborate church hats and clutching well-worn Bibles, detoured out of his way. He ignored their uneasy looks.

Smoking, walking steady with his gunshot-not-gangsta limp, Jax inhaled the air, high on being home. Harlem . . . looking around him at stores, restaurants and street vendors. You could buy anything here: West African woven cloth — kente and Malinke — and Egyptian ankhs, Bolga baskets, masks and banners and framed pictures of silhouetted men and women on African National Congress black, green and yellow. Posters too: Malcolm X, Martin Luther King Jr., Tina, Tupac, Beyoncé, Chris Rock, Shaq . . . And dozens of pictures of Jam Master Jay, the brilliant and generous vinyl-spinning rapper with Run-D.M.C., gunned down by some asshole in his Queens recording studio a few years back.

Jax was hit left and right by memories. He glanced at another corner. Well, lookit that. Now a fast food place, it had been the site of Jax's first crime, committed when he was fifteen — the crime that had launched him on the path to becoming righteously notorious. Because what he racked wasn't liquor or cigarettes or guns or cash, but a case of phat Krylon from a hardware store. Which he went on to use up over the next twenty-four hours, compounding the larceny with trespass and criminal property damage by spray-painting the graffitied bubble letters *Jax 157* throughout Manhattan and the Bronx.

Over the next few years Jax bombed that tag of his on thousands of surfaces: overpasses, bridges,

174

viaducts, walls, billboards, stores, city buses, private buses, office buildings — he tagged Rockefeller Center, right beside that gold statue, before getting tackled by two massive security bulls, who laid into him hard with Mace and nightsticks.

If young Alonzo Jackson found himself with five minutes of privacy and a flat surface, *Jax 157* appeared.

Struggling to get through high school, the son of divorced parents, bored to death with normal jobs, steady in trouble, he found comfort as a writer (graffiti guerrillas were 'writers,' not 'artists' — what Keith Haring, the Soho galleries and claimer ad agencies told everybody). He ran with some local Blood posses for a time, but he changed his mind one day when he was hanging with his set on 140th, and the Trey-Sevens drove by, and pop, pop, pop, Jimmy Stone, standing right next to him, went down with two holes in the temple, dead 'fore he hit the ground. All on account of a small bag of rock, or on account of no reason at all.

Fuck that. Jax went out on his own. Less money. But a hell of a lot safer (despite spraying his tag on places like the Verrazano Bridge and a *moving* A train car — which was one phat story that even brothers in prison had heard of).

Alonzo Jackson, unofficially but permanently renamed Jax, dove into his craft. He started out simply bombing his tag throughout the city. But, he learned early that if that's all you do, even if you lay it in every borough of the city, you're nothing but a lame 'toy,' and graffiti kings

175

wouldn't give you the time of day.

So, skipping school, working in fast food restaurants during the day to pay for paint, or racking what he could steal, Jax moved on to throw-ups — tags written fast but a lot bigger than bombing. He became a master of the top-to-bottom: doing the entire vertical height of a subway car. The A train, supposedly the longest route through town, was his personal favorite. Thousands of visitors would travel from Kennedy Airport into the city on a train that didn't say *Welcome to the Big Apple*; it offered the mysterious message: *Jax 157*.

By the time Jax was twenty-one he'd done two total end-to-ends — covering the entire side of a subway car with his graffiti — and had come close to doing a whole train, every graffiti king's dream. He did his share of 'pieces too. Jax had tried to describe what a graffiti masterpiece was. But all he could come up with was that a 'piece was something *more*. Something breathtaking. A work that a cluckhead crack addict sitting in a gutter and a Wall Street trader on New Jersey Transit could both look at and think, Man, that is so fucking cool.

Those were the days, Jax reflected. He was a graffiti king, in the middle of the most powerful black cultural movement since the Harlem Renaissance: hip-hop.

Sure, the Renaissance must've been def. But to Jax it was a smart person's thing. It came from the head. Hip-hop burst from the soul and from the heart. It wasn't born in colleges and writer's lofts, it came right from the fucking streets, from the angry and striving and despairing kids who had impossibly hard lives and broken homes, who walked on sidewalks littered with cookie vials discarded by the crackheads and dotted with brown, dried blood. It was the raw shout from people who *had* to shout to be heard . . . Hip-hop's four legs delivered everything: music in DJ'ing, poetry in MC rapping, dance in the b-boy's breakdancing and art in Jax's own contribution, graffiti.

In fact, here on 116th Street, he paused and looked at the place where the Woolworth's five-and-dime had stood. The store hadn't survived the chaos after the famous blackout of 1977 but what had sprouted in its place was a righteous miracle, the number-one hip-hop club in the nation, Harlem World. Three floors of every kind of music you could imagine, radical, addictive, electrifying. B-boys spinning like tops, writhing like stormy waves. DJs spinning vinyl for the packed dance floors, and MCs making love to their microphones and filling the room with their raw, don't-fuck-with-me poems, pounding in time to the rhythm of a real heart. Harlem World was where the throw-downs started, the battles of the rappers. Jax had been lucky enough to see what was considered the most famous of all time: the Cold Crush Brothers and the Fantastic Five . . .

Harlem World was long gone, of course. Also gone — scrubbed or worn away or painted over — were the thousands of Jax's tags and 'pieces, along with those by the other graffiti legends of the early hip-hop era, Julio and Kool and Taki.

The kings of graffiti.

Oh, there were those lamenting the demise of hip-hop, which had become BET, multimillion-aire rappers in chrome Humvees, *Bad Boys II*, big business, suburban white kids, iPods and MP3 downloads and satellite radio. It was . . . well, case in point: Jax was watching a double-decker tour bus ease to the curb nearby. On the side was the sign *Rap/Hip-Hop Tours. See the Real Harlem.* The passengers were a mix of black and white and Asian tourists. He heard snatches of the driver's rehearsed spiel and the promise that they'd soon be stopping for lunch at an 'authentic soul food' restaurant.

But Jax didn't agree with the claimers bitching that the old days were gone. The heart of Uptown remained pure. Nothing could ever touch it. Take the Cotton Club, he reflected, that 1920s institution of jazz and swing and stride piano. Everybody thought it was the real Harlem, right? How many people knew that it was for white-only audiences (even the famed Harlem resident W. C. Handy, one of the greatest American composers of all time, was turned away at the door, while his own music was playing inside).

Well, guess what? The Cotton Club was fucking gone. Harlem wasn't. And it never would be. The Renaissance was done and hip-hop had changed. But percolating right now in the streets around him was some brand-new movement. Jax wondered what exactly *this* one would be. And if he'd even be around to see it — if he didn't handle this thing with Geneva Settle right he'd be dead or back in prison within twenty-four hours.

Enjoy your soul food, he thought to the tourists as the bus pulled away from the curb.

Continuing up the street for a few blocks, Jax finally found Ralph, who was — sure enough — leaning against a boarded-up building.

'Dog,' Jax said.

'S' up?'

Jax kept on walking.

'Where we goin'?' Ralph asked, speeding up to keep pace beside the large man.

'Nice day for a walk.'

'It cold out.'

'Walking'll warm you up.'

They kept going for a time, Jax ignoring whatever the fuck Ralph was whining about. He stopped at Papaya King and bought four dogs and two fruit drinks, without asking Ralph if he was hungry. Or a vegetarian or puked when he drank mango juice. He paid and walked out onto the street again, handing the skinny man his lunch. 'Don't eat it here. Come on.' Jax looked up and down the street. Nobody was following. He started off again, moving fast. Ralph followed. 'We walkin' 'cause you don' trust me?'

'Yeah.'

'So why you ain't trust me all of a sudden?'

''Cause you had time to dime me out since I saw you last. What *exactly* is the mystery here?'

'Nice day fo' a walk,' was Ralph's answer. He snuck a bite of hot dog.

They continued for a half block to a street that seemed deserted and the pair turned south. Jax

179

stopped. Ralph did too and leaned against a wrought-iron fence in front of a brownstone. Jax ate his hot dogs and sipped the mango juice. Ralph wolfed down his own lunch.

Eating, drinking, just two workers on their meal break from a construction job or window washing. Nothing suspicious about this.

'That place, shit, they make good dogs,' Ralph said.

Jax finished the food, wiped his hands on his jacket and patted down Ralph's T-shirt and jeans. No wires. 'Let's get to it. What'd you find?'

'The Settle girl, okay? She goin' to Langston Hughes. You know it? The high school.'

'Sure, I know it. She there now?'

'I don't know. You ask where, not when. Only I hear something else from my boys in the hood.'

The hood . . .

'They be saying somebody got her back. Stayin' on her steady.'

'Who?' Jax asked. 'Cops?' Wondering why he even bothered. Of course it'd be them.

'Seem to be.'

Jax finished his fruit juice. 'And the other thing?'

Ralph frowned.

'That I asked for.'

'Oh.' The pharaoh looked around. Then pulled a paper bag from his pocket and slipped it into Jax's hand. He could feel the gun was an automatic and that it was small. Good. Like he asked. Loose bullets clicked in the bottom of the sack.

'So,' Ralph said cautiously.

180

'So.' Jax pulled some benjamins from his pocket and handed them to Ralph and then leaned close to the man. He smelled malt and onion and mango. 'Now, listen up. Our business's done with. If I hear you told anybody 'bout this, or even mention my name, I will find you and cap your fucked-up ass. You can ask DeLisle and he will tell you I am one coal-bad person to cross. You know what I'm saying?'

'Yes, sir,' Ralph whispered to his mango juice.

'Now get the fuck outa here. No, go that way. And don't look back.'

Then Jax was moving in the opposite direction, back to 116th Street, losing himself in the crowds of shoppers. Head down, moving fast, despite the limp, but not so fast as to attract attention.

Up the street another tour bus squealed to a stop in front of the site of the long-dead Harlem World, and some anemic rap dribbled from a speaker inside the gaudy vehicle. But at the moment the blood-painting King of Graffiti wasn't reflecting on Harlem, hip-hop or his criminal past. He had his gun. He knew where the girl was. The only thing he was thinking about now was how long it would take him to get to Langston Hughes High.

12

The petite Asian woman eyed Sachs cautiously.

The uneasiness was no wonder, the detective supposed, considering that she was surrounded by a half dozen officers who were twice her size — and that another dozen waited on the sidewalk outside her store.

'Good morning,' Sachs said. 'This man we're looking for? It's very important we find him. He may've committed some serious crimes.' She was speaking a bit more slowly than she supposed was politically correct.

Which was, it turned out, a tidy faux pas.

'I understand that,' the woman said in perfect English, with a French accent, no less. 'I told those other officers everything I could think of. I was pretty scared. With him trying the stocking cap on, you understand. Pulling it down like it was a mask. Scary.'

'I'm sure it was,' Sachs said, picking up her verbal pace a bit. 'Say, you mind if we take your fingerprints?'

This was to verify that they were her prints on the receipt and merchandise found at the museum library scene. The woman agreed, and a portable analyzer verified that they were hers.

Sachs then asked, 'You're sure you don't have any idea who he is or where he lives?'

'None. He's only been in here once or twice. Maybe more, but he's the sort of person you

182

never seem to notice. Average. Didn't smile, didn't frown, didn't say anything. Totally average.'

Not a bad look for a killer, Sachs reflected. 'What about your other employees?'

'I asked them all. None of them remember him.'

Sachs opened the suitcase, replaced the fingerprint analyzer and pulled out a Toshiba computer. In a minute she'd booted it up and loaded the Electronic Facial Identification Technique software. This was a computerized version of the old Identikit, used to re-create images of suspects' faces. The manual system used preprinted cards of human features and hair, which officers combined and showed to witnesses to create a likeness of a suspect. EFIT used software to do the same, producing a nearly photographic image.

Within five minutes, Sachs had a composite picture of a jowly, cleanshaven white man with trim, light brown hair, in his forties. He looked like any one of a million middle-aged business-men or contractors or store clerks you'd find in the metro area.

Average . . .

'Do you remember what he wore?'

There's a companion program to EFIT, which will dress the suspect's image in various outfits — like mounting clothes on paper dolls. But the woman couldn't recall anything other than a dark raincoat.

She added, 'Oh, one thing. I think he had a Southern accent.'

183

Sachs nodded and jotted this into her notebook. She then hooked up a small laser printer and soon had two dozen five-by-seven-inch copies of Unsub 109's image, with a short description of his height, weight and the fact he might be wearing a raincoat and had an accent. She added the warning that he targeted innocents. These she handed to Bo Haumann, the grizzled, crew-cut former drill instructor who was now head of the Emergency Services Unit, which was New York's tactical group. He in turn distributed the pictures to his officers and the uniformed patrolmen who were here with the team. Haumann divided the law enforcers up — mixing Patrol with ESU, which had heavier firepower — and ordered them to start canvassing the neighborhood.

The dozen officers dispersed.

NYPD, the constabulary of the city of cool, put their tactical teams not in army-style armored personnel carriers but in off-the-shelf squad cars and vans and carted their equipment around in an ESU bus — a nondescript blue-and-white truck. One of these was now parked near the store as a staging vehicle.

Sachs and Sellitto pulled on body armor with shock plates over the heart and headed into Little Italy. The neighborhood had changed dramatically in the past fifteen years. Once a huge enclave of working-class Italian immigrants, it had shrunk to nearly nothing, owing to the spread of Chinatown from the south, and young professionals from the north and west. On Mulberry Street the two detectives now passed

184

an emblem of this change: the building that was the former Ravenite Social Club, home of the Gambino crime family, which long-gone John Gotti had headed. The club had been seized by the government — resulting in the inevitable nickname 'Club Fed' — and was now just another commercial building looking for a tenant.

The two detectives picked a block and began their canvass, flashing their shields and the picture of the unsub to street vendors and clerks in stores, teenagers cutting classes and sipping Starbucks coffee, retirees on benches or front stairs. They'd occasionally hear reports from the other officers. '*Nothing . . . Negative on Grand, K . . . Copy that . . . Negative on Hester, K . . . We're trying east . . .*'

Sellitto and Sachs continued along their own route, having no more luck than anyone else.

A loud bang behind them.

Sachs gasped — not at the noise, which she recognized immediately as a truck backfire — but at Sellitto's reaction. He'd jumped aside, actually taking cover behind a phone kiosk, his hand on the grip of his revolver.

He blinked and swallowed. Gave a shallow laugh. 'Fucking trucks,' he muttered.

'Yeah,' Sachs said.

He wiped his face and they continued on.

★ ★ ★

Sitting in his safe house, smelling garlic from one of the nearby restaurants in Little Italy,

185

Thompson Boyd was huddled over a book, reading the instructions it offered and then examining what he'd bought at the hardware store an hour ago.

He marked certain pages with yellow Post-it tabs and jotted notes in the margins. The procedures he was studying were a bit tricky but he knew he'd work through them. There wasn't anything you couldn't do if you took your time. His father taught him that. Hard tasks or easy.

It's only a question of where you put the decimal point . . .

He pushed back from the desk, which, along with one chair, one lamp and one cot, was the only piece of furniture in the place. A small TV set, a cooler, a garbage can. He also kept a few supplies here, things he used in his work. Thompson pulled the latex glove away from his right wrist and blew into it, cooling his skin. Then he did the same with his left. (You always assumed a safe house would get tossed at some point so you took precautions there'd be no evidence to convict you, whether it was wearing gloves or using a booby trap.) His eyes were acting up today. He squinted, put drops in, and the stinging receded. He closed his lids.

Whistling softly that haunting song from the movie *Cold Mountain*.

Soldiers shooting soldiers, that big explosion, bayonets. Images from the film cascaded through his mind.

Wssst . . .

That song disappeared, along with the images, and up popped a classical tune. 'Bolero.'

Where the tunes came from, he generally couldn't tell. It was like in his head there was a CD changer that somebody else had programmed. But with 'Bolero' he knew the source. His father had the piece on an album. The big, crew-cut man had played it over and over on the green-plastic Sears turntable in his workshop.

'Listen to this part, son. It changes key. Wait . . . wait . . . *There!* You hear that?'

The boy believed he had.

Thompson now opened his eyes and returned to the book.

Five minutes later: *Wsssst* . . . 'Bolero' went away and another melody started easing out through his pursed lips: 'Time After Time.' That song Cyndi Lauper made famous in the eighties.

Thompson Boyd had always liked music and from an early age wanted to play an instrument. His mother took him to guitar and flute lessons for several years. After her accident his father drove the boy himself, even if that made him late to work. But there were problems with Thompson's advancement: His fingers were too big and stubby for fret boards and flute keys and piano, and he had no voice at all. Whether it was church choir or Willie or Waylon or Asleep at the Wheel, nope, he couldn't get more than a croak out of the old voice box. So, after a year or two, he turned away from the music and filled his time with what boys normally did in places like Amarillo, Texas: spending time with his family, nailing and planing and sanding in his father's work shed, playing touch then tackle football, hunting, dating shy girls, going for walks in the desert.

And he tucked his love of music wherever failed hopes go.

Which usually isn't very far beneath the surface. Sooner or later they crawl out again.

In his case this happened to be in prison a few years ago. A guard on the maximum security block came up and asked Thompson, 'What the fuck was *that*?'

'How do you mean?' asked the ever-placid Average Joe.

'That song. You were whistling.'

'I was whistling?'

'Fuck yes. You didn't know?'

He said to the guard, 'Just something I was doing. Wasn't thinking.'

'Damn, sounded good.' The guard wandered off, leaving Thompson to laugh to himself. How 'bout that? He had an instrument all along, one he'd been born with, one he carried around with him. Thompson went to the prison library and looked into this. He learned that people would call him an 'orawhistler,' which was different from a tin-whistle player, say — like in Irish bands. Orawhistlers are rare — most people have very limited whistling range — and could make good livings as professional musicians in concerts, advertising, TV and movies (*everybody* knew the *Bridge on the River Kwai* theme, of course; you couldn't even think about it without whistling the first few notes, at least in your head). There were even orawhistling competitions, the most famous being the International Grand Championship, which featured dozens of performers — many of them appeared regularly with orchestras around the world and had their own cabaret acts.

Wssst . . .

Another tune came into his head. Thompson Boyd exhaled the notes softly, getting a soft trill. He noticed he'd moved his .22 out of reach. That *wasn't* doing things by the book . . . He pulled the pistol closer then returned to the instruction booklet again, sticking more Post-it notes onto pages, glancing into the shopping bag to make sure he had everything he needed. He thought that he had the technique down. But, as always when he approached something new, he was going to learn everything cold before executing the job.

★   ★   ★

'Nothing, Rhyme,' Sachs said into the microphone dangling near her ample lips.

That his prior good mood had vanished like steam was evident when he snapped, '*Nothing?*'

'Nobody's seen him.'

'Where are you?'

'We've covered basically all of Little Italy. Lon and I're at the south end. Canal Street.'

'Hell,' Rhyme muttered.

'We could . . . ' Sachs stopped speaking. 'What's that?'

'What?' Rhyme asked.

'Hold on a minute.' To Sellitto she said, 'Come on.'

Displaying her badge she forced her way

189

through four lanes of thick, attitudinal traffic. She looked around then started south on Elizabeth Street, a dark canyon of tenements, retail shops and warehouses. She stopped again. 'Smell that?'

Rhyme asked caustically, 'Smell?'

'I'm asking Lon.'

'Yeah,' the big detective said. 'What *is* that? Something, you know, sweet.'

Sachs pointed to a wholesale herbal products, soap and incense company, two doors south of Canal on Elizabeth Street. A strong flowery scent wafted from the open doors. It was jasmine — the aroma that they'd detected on the rape pack and that Geneva herself had smelled at the museum.

'We might have a lead, Rhyme. I'll call you back.'

★   ★   ★

'Yeah, yeah,' the slim Chinese man in the herbal wholesaler said, gazing at the EFIT composite picture of Unsub 109. 'I see him some. Upstair. He not there a lot. What he do?'

'Is he up there now?'

'Don't know. Don't know. Think I saw him today. What he do?'

'Which apartment?'

The man shrugged.

The herbal import company took up the first floor, but at the end of the dim entryway, past a security door, were steep stairs leading up into darkness. Sellitto pulled out his radio and called

190

in on the operations frequency. 'We've got him.'

'Who's this?' Haumann snapped.

'Oh, sorry. It's Sellitto. We're two buildings south of Canal on Elizabeth. We've got a positive ID on the tenant. Might be in the building now.'

'ESU Command, all units. You copy, K?'

Affirmative responses filled the airwaves.

Sachs identified herself and transmitted, 'Make it a silent roll-up and stay off Elizabeth. He can see the street from the window in the front.'

'Roger, five-eight-eight-five. What's the address? I'm calling in for a no-knock warrant, K.'

Sachs gave him the street number. 'Out.'

Less than fifteen minutes later the teams were on site and S and S officers were checking out the front and rear of the building with binoculars and infrared and sonic sensors. The lead Search and Surveillance officer said, 'There're four floors in the building. Import warehouse is on the ground. We can see into the second and the fourth floors. They're occupied — Asian families. Elderly couple on the second and the top's got a woman and four or five kids.'

Haumann said, 'And the third floor?'

'Windows are curtained, but the infrared scans positive for heat. Could be a TV or heater. But could be human. And we're getting some sounds. Music. And the creaking of floors, sounds like.'

Sachs looked at the building directory. The plate above the intercom button for the third floor was empty.

An officer arrived and gave Haumann a piece

of paper. It was the search warrant signed by a state court judge and had just been faxed to the ESU command post truck. Haumann looked it over, made sure the address was correct — a wrong no-knock could subject them to liability and jeopardize the case against the unsub. But the paper was in order. Haumann said, 'Two entry teams, four people each, front stairwell and back fire escape. A battering ram at the front.' He pulled eight officers from the group and divided them into two groups. One of them — A team — was to go through the front. B was on the fire escape. He told the second group, 'You take out the window on the three count and hit him with a flash-bang, two-second delay.'

'Roger.'

'On zero, take out the front door,' he said to the head of the A team. Then he assigned other officers to guard the innocents' doors and to be backup. 'Now deploy. Move, move, move!'

The troopers — mostly men, two women — moved out, as Haumann ordered. The B team went around to the back of the building, while Sachs and Haumann joined the A team, along with an officer manning the battering ram.

Under normal circumstances a crime scene officer wouldn't be allowed on an entry team. But Haumann had seen Sachs under fire and knew she could pull her own. And, more important, the ESU officers themselves welcomed her. They'd never admit it, at least not to her, but they considered Sachs one of them and were glad to have her. It didn't hurt, of course,

192

that she was one of the top pistol shots on the force.

As for Sachs herself, well, she just plain liked doing kick-ins.

Sellitto volunteered to remain downstairs and keep an eye on the street.

Her knees aching from arthritis, Sachs climbed with the other officers to the third floor. She stepped close to the door and listened. She nodded to Haumann. 'I can hear something,' she whispered.

Haumann said into his radio, 'Team B, report.'

'We're in position,' Sachs heard in her earpiece. 'Can't see inside. But we're ready to go.'

The commander looked at the team around them. The huge officer with the battering ram — a weighted tube about three feet long — nodded. Another cop crouched beside him and closed his fingers around the doorknob to see if it was locked.

Into his mike Haumann whispered, 'Five . . . four . . . three . . . '

Silence. This was the moment when they should've heard the sound of breaking glass and then the explosion of the stun grenade.

Nothing.

And something was wrong here too. The officer gripping the knob was shivering fiercely, moaning.

Jesus, Sachs thought, staring at him. The guy was having a fit or something. A tactical entry officer with epilepsy? Why the hell hadn't that shown up in his medical?

193

'What's wrong?' Haumann whispered to him.

The man didn't reply. The quaking grew worse. His eyes were wide and only the whites showed.

'B team, report,' the commander called into his radio. 'What's going on, K?'

'Command, the window's boarded up,' the B team leader transmitted. 'Plywood. We can't get a grenade in. Status of Alpha, K?'

The officer at the door had slumped now, his hand frozen on the knob, still shivering. Haumann whispered in a harsh voice, 'We're wasting time! Get him out of the way and take the door out. Now!' Another officer grabbed the seizing one.

The second one began to shake too.

The other officers stepped back. One muttered, 'What's going — '

It was then that the first officer's hair caught fire.

'He wired the door!' Haumann was pointing to a metal plate on the floor. You saw these often in old buildings — they were used as cheap patches on hardwood floors. This one, though, had been used by Unsub 109 to make an electric booby trap; high voltage was coursing through both men.

Fire was sprouting from the first officer's head, his eyebrows, the backs of his hands, then his collar. The other cop was unconscious now, but still quivering horribly.

'Jesus,' an officer whispered in Spanish.

Haumann tossed his H&K machine gun to a nearby officer, took the battering ram and swung

194

it hard at the wrist of the officer gripping the knob. Bones probably shattered, but the ram knocked his fingers loose. The circuit broken, the two men collapsed. Sachs beat out the flames, which were filling the hallway with the revolting smell of burnt hair and flesh.

Two of the backup officers began CPR on their unconscious colleagues, while an A-team cop grabbed the handles of the battering ram and swung it into the door, which burst open. The team raced inside, guns up. Sachs followed.

It took only five seconds to learn that the apartment was empty.

13

Bo Haumann called into his radio, 'B Team, B team, we're inside. No sign of the suspect. Get downstairs, sweep the alley. But remember — he waited around at the last scene. He goes for innocents. And he goes for cops.'

A desk lamp burned and when Sachs touched the seat of the chair she found it was warm. A small closed-circuit TV sat on the desk, the fuzzy screen showing the hallway in front of the door. He'd had a security camera hidden somewhere outside and seen them coming. The killer had gotten away only moments ago. But where? The officers looked around for an escape route. The window by the fire escape was covered with plywood. The other was uncovered but it was thirty feet above the alley. 'He *was* here. How the hell'd he get away?'

The answer came a moment later.

'Found this,' an officer called. He'd been looking under the bed. He pulled the cot away from the wall, revealing a hole just big enough for a person to crawl through. It looked like the unsub had cut through the plaster and removed the brick wall between this building and the one next door. When he saw them on the TV monitor he'd simply kicked out the plaster on the other side of the wall and slipped into the adjoining building.

Haumann sent more officers to check the roof

and nearby streets, others to find and cover the entrances into the building next door.

'Somebody into the hole,' the ESU commander ordered.

'I'll go, sir,' a short officer said.

But with his bulky armor, even he couldn't fit through the gap.

'I'll do it,' Sachs said, by far the slimmest of the officers present. 'But I need this room cleared. To save the evidence.'

'Roger that. We'll get you inside then pull back.' Haumann ordered the bed moved aside. Sachs knelt down and shone her flashlight through the hole, on the other side of which was a catwalk in a warehouse or factory. To reach it she had a four-foot crawl through the tight space.

'Shit,' muttered Amelia Sachs, the woman who'd drive 160 miles per hour and trade shots face to face with cornered perps but came close to paralysis at the hint of claustrophobia.

Headfirst or feet?

She sighed.

Headfirst would be spookier but safer; at least she'd have a few seconds to find the unsub's firing position before he could draw a target. She looked into the tight, dark space. A deep breath. Pistol in hand, she started forward.

★   ★   ★

What the hell's the matter with me? Lon Sellitto thought, standing in front of the warehouse beside the herbal goods importer, the building

197

whose front door he was supposed to be guarding. He stared at this doorway and at the windows, looking for the escaped unsub, praying the perp would show up so he could nail him.

Praying that he wouldn't.

What the hell's the matter?

In his years on the force Sellitto had been in a dozen firefights, taken weapons off cranked-up psychos, even wrestled a suicide off the roof of the Flatiron Building, with nothing but six inches of ornate trim separating him from heaven. He'd gotten shook sometimes, sure. But he'd always bounced right back. Nothing'd ever affected him like Barry's death this morning. Being in the line of fire had spooked him, no denying that. But this was something else. Something to do with being so close to a person at that one moment . . . the moment of death. He couldn't get the librarian's voice out of his head, his last words as a living person.

I didn't really see —

Couldn't forget the sound of the three bullets striking his chest either.

Tap . . . tap . . . tap . . .

They were soft, barely audible, faint slaps. He'd never heard a noise like that. Lon Sellitto now shivered and felt nauseous.

And the man's brown eyes . . . They were looking right into Sellitto's when the slugs hit. In a fraction of an instant there was surprise, then pain, then . . . nothing. It was the oddest thing Sellitto had ever seen. Not like drifting off to sleep, not distracted. The only way to describe it: one moment there was something complicated

198

and real behind the eyes and then, an instant later, even before he crumpled to the sidewalk, there was nothing.

The detective had remained frozen, staring at the limp doll lying in front of him — despite the fact that he knew he should be trying to run down the shooter. The medics had actually jostled him aside to get to Barry; Sellitto had been unable to move.

Tap . . . tap . . . tap . . .

Then, when it came time to call Barry's next of kin, Sellitto had balked again. He'd made plenty of those difficult calls over the years. None of them easy, of course. But today he simply couldn't face it. He'd made up some bullshit excuse about his phone and let someone else do the duty. He was afraid his voice would crack. He was afraid he'd cry, which he'd never done in his decades of service.

Now, he heard the radio report on the futile pursuit of the perp.

Hearing, *tap, tap, tap . . .*

Fuck, I just want to go home.

He wanted to be with Rachel, have a beer with her on their porch in Brooklyn. Well, too early for beer. A coffee. Or maybe it wasn't too early for a beer. Or a scotch. He wanted to be sitting there, watching the grass and trees. Talking. Or not saying anything. Just to be with her. Suddenly the detective's thoughts shifted to his teenage son, who lived with Sellitto's ex. He hadn't called the boy for three or four days. Had to do that.

He —

Shit. Sellitto realized that he was standing in the middle of Elizabeth Street with his back to the building he was supposed to be guarding, lost in thought. Jesus Christ! What're you doing? The shooter's loose around here somewhere, and you're fucking *daydreaming*? He could be waiting in that alley there, or the other one, just like he was that morning.

Crouching, Sellitto turned back, examining the dark windows, smudged or shaded. The perp could be behind any one of them, sighting down on him right now with that fucking little gun of his. *Tap, tap* . . . The needles from the bullets tearing flesh to shreds as they fanned out. Sellitto shivered and stepped back, taking refuge between two parked delivery trucks, out of sight of the windows. Peering around the side of one van, he watched the black windows, he watched the door.

But those weren't what he saw. No, he was seeing the brown eyes of the librarian in front of him, a few feet away.

I didn't . . .

Tap, tap . . .

Life becoming no life.

Those eyes . . .

He wiped his shooting hand on his suit trousers, telling himself that he was sweating only because of the body armor. What was with the fucking weather? It was too hot for October. Who the hell *wouldn't* sweat?

★ ★ ★

200

'I can't see him, K,' Sachs whispered into her microphone.

'Say again?' was Haumann's staticky reply.

'No sign of him, K.'

The warehouse into which Unsub 109 had fled was essentially one big open space divided by mesh catwalks. On the floor were pallets of olive oil bottles and tomato sauce cans, sealed in shrink-wrap. The catwalk she stood on was about thirty feet up, around the perimeter — level with the unsub's apartment in the building next door. It was a working warehouse, though probably used only sporadically; there were no signs that employees had been here recently. The lights were out but enough illumination filtered through greasy skylights to give her a view of the place.

The floors were swept clean and she could find no footprints to reveal which way Unsub 109 had gone. In addition to the front door and back loading-dock door, there were two others on the ground-floor level, to the side. One labeled *Restroom*, the other unmarked.

Moving slowly, swinging her Glock ahead of her, her flashlight beam seeking a target, Amelia Sachs soon cleared the catwalks and the open area of the warehouse. She reported this to Haumann. ESU officers then kicked in the loading-dock door of the warehouse and entered, spreading out. Relieved for the reinforcements, she used hand signals to point to the two side doors. The cops converged on them.

Haumann radioed, 'We've been canvassing but nobody's seen him outside. He might still be inside, K.'

Sachs quietly acknowledged the transmission. She walked down the stairs to the main floor, joining up with the other officers.

She pointed to the bathroom. 'On three,' she whispered.

They nodded. One pointed to himself but she shook her head, meaning she was going in on point. Sachs was furious — that the perp had gotten away, that he had a rape pack in a smiley-face bag, that he'd shot an innocent simply for diversion. She wanted this guy nailed and she wanted to make sure she had a piece of him.

She was in the armored vest, of course, but she couldn't help thinking about what would happen if one of those needle bullets hit her face or arm.

Or throat.

She held up a single finger. *One* . . .

Go in fast, go in low, with two pounds of pressure on the two-and-a-half-pound trigger.

You sure about this, girl?

An image of Lincoln Rhyme came to mind.

Two . . .

Then a memory of her patrolman father imparting his philosophy of life from his deathbed, 'Remember, Amie, when you move they can't getcha.'

So, *move!*

Three.

She nodded. An officer kicked the door open — nobody was going near any metal doorknobs — and Sachs lunged forward, dropping into a painful crouch and spraying the flashlight beam around the small, windowless bathroom.

Empty.

She backed out and turned to the other door. The same routine here.

On three, another powerful kick. The door cracked inward.

Guns and flashlights up. Sachs thought, Brother, never easy, is it? She was looking down a long stairway that descended into pitch-black darkness. She noted that there were no backs on the stairs, which meant that the unsub could stand behind them and shoot into their ankles, calves or backs as they descended.

'Dark,' she whispered.

The men shut out their flashlights, mounted to the barrels of their machine guns. Sachs went first, knees aching. Twice she nearly tumbled down the uneven, loose steps. Four ESU officers followed her.

'Corner formation,' she whispered, knowing she wasn't technically in charge, but unable to stop herself at this point. The troops didn't question her. Touching one another's shoulders to orient themselves, they formed a rough square, each facing outward and guarding a quadrant of the basement.

'Lights!'

The beams of the powerful halogens suddenly filled the small space as the guns sought targets.

She saw no threat, heard no sounds. Except one fucking loud heartbeat, she thought.

But that's mine.

The basement contained a furnace, pipes, oil tanks, about a thousand empty beer bottles. Piles of trash. A half dozen edgy rats.

Two officers probed the stinking garbage bags, but the perp was clearly not here.

She radioed Haumann what they'd found. No one else had seen a sign of the unsub. All the officers were going to rendezvous at the command post truck to continue the canvass of the neighborhood, while Sachs searched the scenes for evidence — with everybody keeping in mind that, as at the museum earlier, the killer might still be nearby.

. . . *watch your back.*

Sighing, she replaced her weapon and turned toward the stairs. Then paused. If she took the same flight of steps back up to the main floor — a nightmare on her arthritic knees — she'd still have to walk down another flight to street level. An easier alternative was to take the much shorter stairway directly to the sidewalk.

Sometimes, she reflected, turning toward it, you just have to pamper yourself.

★   ★   ★

Lon Sellitto had become obsessed with one particular window.

He'd heard the transmission that the warehouse was clear, but he wondered if ESU had actually gotten into all the nooks and crannies. After all, everybody'd missed the unsub that morning at the museum. He'd easily gotten within pistol range.

Tap, tap, tap.

That one window, far right, second floor . . . It

204

seemed to Sellitto that it had quivered once or twice.

Maybe just the wind. But maybe the motion was from somebody trying to open it.

Or aiming through it.

Tap.

He shivered and stepped back.

'Hey,' he called to an ESU officer, who'd just come out of the herbal importer's. 'Take a look — you see anything in that window?'

'Where?'

'That one.' Sellitto leaned out of cover just a bit and pointed to the black glass square.

'Naw. But the place's cleared. Didn't you hear?'

Sellitto leaned out from cover a bit farther, hearing *tap, tap, tap,* seeing brown eyes going lifeless. He squinted and, shivering, looked the window over carefully. Then in his periphery he suddenly saw motion to his left and heard the squeal of a door opening. A flash of light as the cold sun reflected off something metallic.

It's him!

'God,' Sellitto whispered. He went for his gun, crouching and spinning toward the glint. But instead of following procedures when speed-drawing a weapon and keeping his index finger outside the trigger guard, he yanked the Colt from his holster in a panic.

Which is why the gun discharged an instant later, sending the slug directly toward the spot where Amelia Sachs was emerging from the basement door to the warehouse.

14

Standing at the corner of Canal and Sixth, a dozen blocks from his safe house, Thompson Boyd waited for the light to change. He caught his breath and wiped his damp face.

He wasn't shaken, he wasn't freaked out — the breathlessness and sweat were from the sprint to safety — but he *was* curious how they'd found him. He was always so careful with his contacts and the phones he used, and always checking to see if he was being followed, that he guessed it had to be through physical evidence. Made sense — because he was pretty sure that the woman in white, walking through the museum library scene like a sidewinder snake, had been in the hallway outside the apartment on Elizabeth Street. What had he left behind at the museum? Something in the rape bag? Some bits of trace from his shoes or clothes?

They were the best investigators he'd ever encountered. He'd have to keep that in mind.

Gazing at the traffic, he reflected on the escape. When he'd seen the officers coming up the stairs, he'd quickly placed the book and the purchases from the hardware store into the shopping bag, grabbed his attaché case and gun, then clicked on the switch that turned the doorknob live. He'd kicked through the wall and escaped into the warehouse next door, climbed to its roof and then hurried south to the end of the block. Climbing down a fire escape, he'd turned west and started sprinting, taking the course he'd charted out and practiced dozens of times.

Now, at Canal and Sixth, he was lost in a crowd waiting for the light to change, hearing the sirens of the police cars joining in the search for him. His face was emotionless, his hands didn't shake, he wasn't angry, he wasn't panicked. This was the way he had to be. He'd seen it over and over again — dozens of professional killers he'd known had been caught because they panicked, lost their cool in front of the police and broke down under routine questioning. That, or they got rattled during the job, leaving evidence or living witnesses. Emotion — love, anger, fear — makes you sloppy. You had to be cool, distant.

Numb . . .

Thompson gripped his pistol, hidden in his raincoat pocket, as he watched several squad cars speed up Sixth Avenue. The vehicles skidded around the corner and turned east on Canal. They were pulling out all the stops looking for him. Not surprising, Thompson knew. New York's finest would frown on a perp electrocuting one of their own (though in Thompson's opinion it was the cop's own fault for being careless).

Then a faint tone of concern sounded in his brain as he watched another squad car skid to a stop three blocks away. Officers got out and began interviewing people on the street. Then another rolled to a stop only two hundred feet from where he now stood. And they were moving this way. His car was parked near Hudson, about five minutes away. He had to get to it now. But still the stoplight remained red.

More sirens filled the air.

This was becoming a problem.

Thompson looked at the crowd around him, most of them peering east, intent on the police cars and the officers. He needed some distraction, some cover to get across the street. Just something . . . didn't have to be flamboyant. Just enough to deflect people's attention for a time. A fire in a trash bin, a car alarm, the sound of breaking glass . . . Any other ideas? Glancing south, to his left, Thompson noticed a large commuter bus headed up Sixth Avenue. It was approaching the intersection where the cluster of pedestrians stood. Set fire to the trash bin, or this? Thompson Boyd decided. He eased closer to the curb, behind an Asian girl, slim, in her twenties. All it took was an easy push in her lower back to send her into the bus's path. Twisting in panic, gasping, she slid off the curb.

'She fell!' Thompson cried in a drawl-free shout. 'Get her!'

Her wail was cut off as the right sideview mirror of the bus struck her shoulder and head and flung her body, tumbling, along the sidewalk. Blood spattered the window and those standing nearby. The brakes screamed. So did several of the women in the crowd.

The bus skidded to a stop in the middle of Canal, blocking traffic, where it would have to remain until the accident investigation. A fire in a trash basket, a breaking bottle, a car alarm — they might've worked. But he'd decided that killing the girl was more efficient.

Traffic was instantly frozen, including two approaching police cars on Sixth Avenue.

He crossed the street slowly, leaving the gathering crowd of horrified passersby, who were crying, or shouting, or just staring in shock at the limp, bloody body, crumpled against a chain-link fence. Her unseeing eyes stared blankly skyward. Apparently nobody thought the tragedy was anything more than a terrible accident.

People running toward her, people calling 911 on mobile phones . . . chaos. Thompson now calmly crossed the street, weaving through the stopped traffic. He'd already forgotten the Asian girl and was considering more important matters: He'd lost one safe house. But at least he'd escaped with his weapons, the things he'd bought at the hardware store and his instruction book. There were no clues at the apartment to lead to him or the man who'd hired him; not even the woman in white could find any connection. No, this wasn't a serious problem.

He paused at a pay phone, called voice mail and received some good news. Geneva Settle, he learned, was attending Langston Hughes High School in Harlem. She was also, he found out, being guarded by police, which was no surprise, of course. Thompson would find out more details soon — presumably where she lived or even, with some luck, the fact that an opportunity had presented itself, and the girl had already been shot to death, the job finished.

Thompson Boyd then continued on to his car — a three-year-old Buick, in a boring shade of blue, a medium car, an *average* car, for Average Joe. He pulled into traffic and circled far around the bus accident congestion. He made his way toward the Fifty-ninth Street bridge, his thoughts occupied about what he'd learned in the book he'd been studying for the past hour, the one bristling with Post-it tabs, thinking about how he'd put his new skills to use.

★ ★ ★

'I don't . . . I don't know what to say.'

Miserable, Lon Sellitto was looking up at the captain who'd come directly here from Police Plaza as soon as the brass learned of the shooting incident. Sellitto sat on the curb, hair askew, belly over his belt, pink flesh showing between the buttons. His scuffed shoes pointed outward. Everything about him was rumpled at the moment.

'What happened?' The large, balding African-American captain had taken possession of Sellitto's revolver and was holding it at his side, unloaded, the cylinder open, following NYPD procedures after an officer has discharged a weapon.

Sellitto looked into the tall man's eyes and said, 'I fumbled my piece.'

The captain nodded slowly and turned to Amelia Sachs. 'You're okay?'

She shrugged. 'It was nothing. Slug hit nowhere near me.'

Sellitto could see that the captain knew she was being cool about the incident, making light of it. Her protecting him made the big detective even more miserable.

'You were in the line of fire, though,' the captain said.

'It wasn't any — '

'You *were* in the line of fire?'

'Yes, sir,' Sachs said.

The 38-caliber slug had missed her by three feet. Sellitto knew it. She knew it.

Nowhere near me . . .

The captain looked over the warehouse. 'This hadn't happened, the perp would still've gotten away?'

'Yep,' Bo Haumann said.

'You sure it had nothing to do with his escape? It's going to come up.'

The ESU commander nodded. 'It's looking now like the unsub got onto the roof of the warehouse and headed north or south — probably south. The shot' — He nodded toward Sellitto's revolver — 'was after we'd secured the adjacent buildings.'

Sellitto again thought, What's happening to me?

Tap, tap, tap . . .

The captain asked, 'Why'd you draw your weapon?'

'I wasn't expecting anybody to come through the basement door.'

'Didn't you hear any transmissions about the building being cleared?'

A hesitation. 'I missed that.' The last time Lon

211

Sellitto had lied to brass had been to protect a rookie who'd failed to follow procedure when trying to save a kidnap victim, which he'd managed to do. That had been a good lie. This was a cover-your-own-ass lie, and it hurt like a broken bone to utter it.

The captain looked around the scene. Several ESU cops milled about. None of them was looking at Sellitto. They seemed embarrassed for him. The brass finally said, 'No injury, no serious property damage. I'll do a report, but a shooting review board's optional. I won't recommend it.'

The relief flooded through Sellitto. An SRB for an accidental discharge was a short step away from an Internal Affairs investigation as far as what it did to your reputation. Even if you were cleared, grime stuck to you for a long, long time. Sometimes forever.

'Want some time off?' the captain asked.

'No, sir,' Sellitto said firmly.

The worst thing in the world for him — for any cop — was downtime after a thing like this. He'd brood, he'd eat himself drunk on junk food, he'd be in a shitty mood to everybody around him. And he'd get even more spooked than he was now. (He still recalled with shame how he'd jumped like a schoolgirl at the truck backfire earlier.)

'I don't know.' The captain had the power to order a mandatory leave of absence. He wanted to ask Sachs's opinion but that would be out of line. She was a new, junior detective. Still, the captain's hesitation in deciding was meant to give her the chance to pipe up. To say, maybe,

Hey, Lon, yeah, it'd be a good idea. Or: It's okay. We'll manage without you.

Instead she said nothing. Which they all knew was a vote in his favor. The captain asked, 'I understand some wit got killed right in front of you today, right? That have anything to do with this?'

Fuck yes, fuck no . . .

'Couldn't say.'

Another long debate. But say what you will about brass, they don't rise through the ranks in the NYPD without knowing all about life on the street and what it does to cops. 'All right, I'll keep you active. But go see a counselor.'

His face burned. A shrink. But he said, 'Sure. I'll make an appointment right away.'

'Good. And keep me in the loop on how it goes.'

'Yes, sir. Thanks.'

The captain returned his weapon and walked back to the CP with Bo Haumann. Sellitto and Sachs headed for the Crime Scene Unit rapid response vehicle, which had just arrived.

'Amelia . . . '

'Forget it, Lon. It happened. It's over with. Friendly fire happens all the time.' Statistically cops had a much higher chance of being shot by their own or fellow cops' bullets than by a perp's.

The heavyset detective shook his head. 'I just . . . ' He didn't know where to go from there.

Silence for a long moment as they walked to the bus. Finally Sachs said, 'One thing, Lon.

213

Word'll go around. You know how that is. But nobody civilian'll hear. Not from me.' Not being hooked into the wire — the network of police scuttlebutt — Lincoln Rhyme would only learn about the incident from one of them.

'I wasn't going to ask that.'

'I know,' she said. 'Just telling you how I'm going to handle it.' She started unloading crime scene equipment.

'Thanks,' he said in a thick voice. And realized that the fingers of his left hand had returned to the stigmata of blood on his cheek.

Tap, tap, tap . . .

★　★　★

'It's a lean one, Rhyme.'

'Go ahead,' he said through the headset.

In her white Tyvek suit, she was walking the grid in the small apartment — a safe house, they knew, because of its sparseness. Most pro killers had a place like this. They kept weapons and supplies there and used it as a staging spot for nearby hits and a hidey-hole if a gig went bad.

'What's inside?' he asked.

'A cot, bare desk and chair. Lamp. A TV hooked up to a security camera mounted in the hall outside. It's a Video-Tect system but he's removed the serial number stickers so we don't know when and where it was bought. I found wires and some relays for the electric charge he rigged on the door. The electrostatics match the Bass walking shoes. I've dusted everywhere and can't find a single print. Wearing gloves inside his hidey-hole — what's up with that?'

Rhyme speculated, 'Aside from the fact he's goddamn smart? Probably he wasn't guarding the place very carefully and knew it'd get tossed at some point. I'd just *love* to get a print. He's definitely on file someplace. Maybe a lot of places.'

'I found the rest of the tarot card deck, but there're no store labels on it. And the only card missing is number twelve, the one he left at the scene. Okay, I'm going to keep searching.'

She continued walking the grid carefully — even though the apartment was small and you could see most of it simply by standing in the center and turning three-sixty. Sachs found one piece of hidden evidence: As she passed the cot she noticed a small sliver of white protruding from under the pillow. She lifted it out, opened the folded sheet carefully.

'Got something here, Rhyme. A map of the street the African-American museum's on. There're a lot details of the alleys and entrances and exits for all the buildings around it, loading zones, parking spaces, hydrants, manholes, pay phones. Man's a perfectionist.'

Not many killers would go to this much trouble for a hired clip. 'Stains on it too. And some crumbs. Brownish.' Sachs sniffed. 'Garlic. Crumbs look like food.' She slipped the map into a plastic envelope and continued the search.

'I've got some more fibers, like the other ones — cotton rope, I'd guess. A bit of dust and dirt. That's it, though.'

'Wish I could see the place.' His voice trailed to silence.

'Rhyme?'

'I'm picturing it,' he whispered. Another pause. Then: 'What's on the surface of the desk?'

'There's nothing. I told — '

'I don't mean what's *sitting* on it. I mean, is it stained with ink? Doodles? Knife marks? Coffee cup rings?' He added acerbically, 'When perps are rude enough not to leave their electric bill lying around, we take what we can get.'

Yep, the good mood was officially deceased.

She examined the wooden top. 'It's stained, yes. Scratched and scarred.'

'It's wood?'

'Yes.'

'Take some samples. Use a knife and scrape the surface.'

Sachs found a scalpel in the examination kit. Just like the ones used in surgery it was sterilized and sealed in paper and plastic. She carefully scraped the surface and placed the results in small plastic bags.

As she glanced down she noticed a flash of light from the edge of the table. She looked.

'Rhyme, found some drops. Clear liquid.'

'Before you sample them, hit one with some Mirage. Go with Exspray Two. This guy likes deadly toys way too much.'

Mirage Technologies makes a convenient, explosives detection system. Exspray No. 2 would detect Group B explosives, which include the highly unstable, clear liquid nitroglycerine, even a drop of which could blow off a hand.

216

Sachs tested the sample. Had the substance been explosive, its color would have turned pink. There was no change. She hit the same sample with Spray No. 3, just to be sure — this would show the presence of *any* nitrates, the key element in most explosives, not just nitro-glycerine.

'Negative, Rhyme.' She collected a second dot of the liquid and transferred the sample to a glass tube, then sealed it.

'Think that's about it, Rhyme.'

'Bring it all back, Sachs. We need to get a jump on this guy. If he can get away from an ESU team that easily, it means he can get close to Geneva just as fast.'

15

She'd aced it.

Cold.

Twenty-four multiple choices — all correct, Geneva Settle knew. And she'd written a seven-page answer to an essay question that called for only four.

Phat . . .

She was chatting with Detective Bell about how she'd done and he was nodding — which told her he wasn't listening, just checking out the halls — but at least he kept a smile on his face and so she pretended he was. And it was wack, she felt good rambling like this. Just telling him about the curveball the teacher'd thrown them in the essay, the way Lynette Tompkins had whispered, 'Jesus, save me,' when she realized she'd studied for the wrong subject. Nobody else except Keesh'd be interested in listening to her go on and on like this.

Now, she had the math test to tackle. She didn't enjoy calc much but she knew the material, she'd studied, she had the equations nailed cold.

'Girlfriend!' Lakeesha fell into step beside her. 'Damn, you still here?' Her eyes were wide. 'You nearly got your own ass killed this morning and you don't stress it none. That some mad shit, girl.'

'Gum. You sound like you're cracking a whip.'

Keesh kept right on snapping, which Geneva knew she would.

'You got a A already. Why you need to take them tests?'

'If I don't take *those* tests, it won't be *an* A.'

The big girl glanced at Detective Bell with a frown. 'You ask me, you oughta be out looking for that prick done attack my girlfriend here.'

'We've got plenty of people doing that.'

'How many? And where they be?'

'Keesh!' Geneva whispered.

But Mr. Bell gave a faint smile. 'Plenty of 'em.'

Snap, snap.

Geneva asked her friend, 'So, how'd the WC test go?'

'The world *ain't* civilized. The world fucked up.'

'But you didn't skip?'

'Told you I'd go. Was def, girl. I was all on it. Pretty sure I got myself *an* C. Least that. Maybe even *an* B.'

'Funny.'

They came to an intersection of hallways and Lakeesha turned to the left. 'Later, girl. Call me in the p.m.'

'You got it.'

Geneva laughed to herself as she watched her friend steam through the halls. Keesh seemed like any other fine, hooked-up, off-the-rack homegirl, with her flashy skintight outfits, scary nails, taut braids, cheap bling. Dancing like a freak to L.L. Cool J, Twista and Beyoncé. Ready to jump into fights — even going right in the face of gangsta girls (she sometimes carried a

219

box cutter or a flick knife). She was an occasional DJ who called herself Def Mistress K when she spun vinyl at school dances — and at clubs too, where the bouncers chose to let her pass for twenty-one.

But the girl wasn't quite as ghetto as she fronted. She'd wear the image the way she'd put on her crazy nails and three-dollar extensions. The clues were obvious to Gen: If you listened closely you could tell that standard English was her first language. She was like those black stand-up comics who sound like homies in their act but they get the patter wrong. The girl might say, 'I be at Sammy's last night.' But somebody really talking ebonics — the new politically correct phrase was 'African-American vernacular English' — wouldn't say that; they'd say 'I was at Sammy's.' 'Be' was only used for ongoing or future activity, like 'I be working at Blockbuster every weekend.' Or: 'I be going to Houston with my aunt next month.'

Or Keesh would say, 'I the first one to sign up.' But that wasn't AAVE, where you never dropped the verb 'to be' in the first person, only the second or third: 'He the first one to sign up' was right. But to the casual listener, the girl sounded bred in the hood.

Other things too: A lot of project girls bragged about perping merch from stores. But Keesh'd never lifted so much as a bottle of fingernail polish or pack of braids. She didn't even buy street jewelry from anybody who might've fiended it from a tourist, and the big girl was fast to whip out her cell phone and 911 suspicious kids hanging around apartment lobbies during 'hunting season' — the times of the month when the welfare, ADC or social security checks started hitting the mailboxes.

Keesh paid her way. She had two jobs — doing extensions and braids on her own and working the counter in a restaurant four days a week (the place was in Manhattan, but miles south of Harlem, to make sure she wouldn't run into people from the neighborhood, which would blow her cover as the DJing bling-diva of 124th Street). She spent carefully and socked away her earnings to help her family.

There was yet one other aspect of Keesh that set her apart from many girls in Harlem. She and Geneva were both in what was sometimes called the 'Sistahood of None.' Meaning, no sex. (Well, fooling around was okay, but, as one of Geneva's friends said, 'Ain't no boy putting his ugly in me, and that's word.') The girls had kept the virgin pact she and Geneva had made in middle school. This made them a rarity. A huge percentage of the girls at Langston Hughes had been sleeping with boys for a couple of years.

Teenage girls in Harlem fell into two categories and the difference was defined by one image: a baby carriage. There were those who pushed buggies through the streets and those who didn't. And it didn't matter if you read Ntozake Shange or Sylvia Plath or were illiterate, didn't matter if you wore orange tank tops and store-bought braids or white blouses and pleated skirts . . . if you ended up on the baby carriage side, then your life was headed in a way different direction from that of girls in the other category. A baby wasn't automatically the end of school and a profession but it often was. And even if not, a carriage girl could look forward to a heart-breakingly tough time of it.

Geneva Settle's inflexible goal was to flee Harlem at the very first opportunity, with stops in Boston or New Haven for a degree or two and then on to England, France or Italy. Even the slightest risk that something like a baby might derail her plan was unacceptable. Lakeesha was lukewarm about higher education but she too had her ambitions. She was going to *some* four-year college and, as a coal-savvy business-woman, take Harlem by storm. The girl was going to be the Frederick Douglass or Malcolm X of Uptown business.

It was these common views that made sistas of these otherwise opposite girls. And like most deep friendships the connection ultimately defied definition. Keesh put it best once by waving her bracelet-encrusted hand, tipped in polka-dotted nails, and offering, in a proper use of AAVE's third-person-singular nonagreement rule, 'Wha-ever, girlfriend. It work, don't it?'

And, yeah, it did.

Geneva and Detective Bell now arrived at math class. He stationed himself outside the door. 'I'll be here. After the test, wait inside. I'll have the car brought 'round front.'

The girl nodded then turned to go inside. She hesitated, glanced back. 'I wanted to say something, Detective.'

'What's that?'

'I know I'm not too agreeable sometimes. Pigheaded, people say. Well, mostly they say I'm a pain in the ass. But, thanks for what you're doing.'

'Just my job, miss. 'Sides, half the witnesses and folk I protect aren't worth the concrete they walk on. I'm happy to be looking after somebody decent. Now, go for another twenty-four multiple choice in a row.'

She blinked. 'You were listening? I thought you weren't paying attention.'

'I was listening, yes'm. *And* looking out for you. Though I'll fess up, doing *two* things at once's pretty much my limit. Don't go expecting more than that. Okay, now — I'll be here when you get out.'

'And I *am* going to pay you back for lunch.'

'I told you that's on the mayor.'

'Only, you paid for it yourself — you didn't get a receipt.'

'Well, now, lookit that. You notice stuff too.'

Inside the classroom she saw Kevin Cheaney standing in the back, talking to a few of his crew. He lifted his head, acknowledging her with a big smile, and strode over to her. Nearly every girl in class — whether pretty or plain — followed his stroll. Surprise — then shock — flashed in their eyes when they saw where he was headed.

Hey, she thought to them triumphantly, wrap your minds round *that*.

I'm in heaven. Geneva Settle looked down, face hot with pumping blood.

'Yo, girl,' he said, walking up close. She smelled his aftershave. Wondered what it was.

Maybe she'd find out his birthday and buy him some.

'Hi,' she said, voice trembling. She cleared her throat. 'Hi.'

Okay, she'd had her moment of glory in front of the class — which would last forever. But now, once again, all she could think of was keeping him at a distance, making sure he didn't get hurt because of her. She'd tell him how dangerous it was to be around her. Forget snapping, forget yo' momma jokes. Get serious. Tell him what you really feel: that you're worried about him.

But before she could say anything he gestured her to the back of the classroom. 'Come on over here. Got something for you.'

For me? she thought. A deep breath and she walked after him to the corner of the room.

'Here. Got you a present.' He slipped something into her hand. Black plastic. What was it? A cell phone? Pager? You weren't allowed to have them in school. Still, Geneva's heart pounded hard, wondering about the purpose of the gift. Was it to call him if she was in danger? Or could it be so that he could get in touch with her whenever he wanted to?

'This's phat,' she said, looking it over. She realized that it wasn't a phone or beeper, but one of those organizer things. Like a Palm Pilot.

'Got games, Internet, email. All wireless. Wack how those things work.'

'Thanks. Only . . . well, it looks expensive, Kevin. I don't know about this . . . '

'Oh, it's cool, girl. You'll earn it.'

She looked up at him. 'Earn it?'

224

'Listen up. Nothing to it. My boys and me tried it out. It's already hooked up to mine.' He tapped his shirt pocket. 'What you do is, first thing to remember, keep it 'tween yo' legs. Better if you wear a skirt. Teachers don't go lookin' there, or they get their ass sued, you know? Now, the first question on the test, you push the one button there. See it? Then push that space button and then type in the answer. You down with that?'

'The answer?'

'Then, listen up, this's important. You gotta push this button to send it to me. That little button with the antenna on it. You don't push it, it don't send. Second question, push two. Then the answer.'

'I don't understand.'

He laughed, wondering why she wasn't getting it. 'Whatchu think? We got a deal, girl. I'll cover your back on the street. You cover mine in class.'

The realization hit her like a slap. Her eyes looked up, bored into his. 'You mean cheat.'

He frowned. 'Don't go talking that shit out loud.' Looking around.

'You're kidding. This's a joke.'

'Joke? No, girl. You gonna help me.'

Not a question. An order.

She felt she was about to choke or be sick. Her breathing came fast. 'I'm not going to do it.' She held the organizer out. He didn't take it.

'What's yo' problem? Lotta girls help me.'

'Alicia,' Geneva whispered angrily, nodding and recalling a girl who'd been in math class with them until recently, Alicia Goodwin, a smart girl, a whiz in math. She'd left school when her family had moved to Jersey. She and Kevin had been tight. So that's what this was all about: When he'd lost his partner, Kevin'd gone looking for a new one and picked Geneva, a better student than her predecessor but not nearly as good-looking. Geneva wondered how far down on the list she'd fallen. Anger and pain raged in her like fire in a boiler. This was even worse than what had happened at the museum this morning. At least the man in the mask hadn't pretended to be her friend.

Judas . . .

Geneva raged, 'You got a stable of girls feeding you the answers . . . What'd your GPA be if it weren't for them?'

'I'm not stupid, girl,' he whispered angrily. 'Just, I don't need to learn this shit. I'll be playing ball and getting tall paper for endorsements the rest of my life. Better for everybody for me to practice, 'sted of study.'

' 'For everybody.' ' She gave a sour laugh. 'So that's where your grades come from: You steal them. Like you'd fiend somebody in Times Square for a gold chain.'

'Yo, girl, I telling you, watch yo' mouth,' he whispered ominously.

'I'm not helping you,' she muttered.

Then he smiled, giving her a lowered-lid gaze. 'I'll make it worth yo' while. You come over to my place anytime you want. I'll fuck you good. I'll even go down on you. I know what I'm about in *that* department.'

'Go to hell,' she shouted. Heads turned.

'Listen up,' he growled, gripping her arm hard. Pain surged. 'You got the booty of a ten-year-old and you go round like some blondie from Long Island, thinking you're better'n everybody. A peasy-haired bitch like you can't be too choosy when it comes to a man, you know what I'm saying? Where you gonna find somebody good as me?'

Geneva gasped at the insult. 'You're disgusting.'

'Okay, girl, fine. You frigid, that's cool. I pay you to help me. How much you want? A C-note. Two? I got tall paper. Come on, name yo' price. I gotta pass this test.'

'Then study,' she snapped and flung the organizer at him.

He caught it in one hand and yanked her close to him with the other.

'Kevin,' a man's voice called sternly.

'Fuck,' the boy whispered in disgust, closing his eyes momentarily, letting go of her arm.

Mr. Abrams, the math teacher, walked up and took the organizer away. He looked at it. 'What's this?'

'He wanted me to help him cheat,' Geneva said.

'The bitch's wack. It's hers and she — '

'Come on, we're going to the office,' he said to Kevin.

The boy stared at her with cold eyes. She glared right back.

The teacher asked, 'You all right, Geneva?'

She was rubbing her arm where he'd gripped her. She lowered her hand and nodded. 'Just want to go to the bathroom for a few minutes.'

'Go ahead.' He said to the class, all staring, all quiet, 'We'll have a study period for ten minutes before the test.' The teacher escorted Kevin out the back door of the classroom. Which filled suddenly with rapid-fire gossip, as if somebody had clicked off the mute button on a TV. Geneva waited a few seconds then followed.

Looking up the corridor, she saw Detective Bell, standing with his arms crossed, near the front door. He didn't see her. She stepped into the hallway and plunged into the crowd of students heading for their classes.

Geneva Settle didn't make for the girls' room, however. She came to the end of the hallway and pushed through the door into the deserted school yard, thinking: Nobody on earth's going to see me cry.

★　★　★

There! Not a hundred feet from him.

Jax's heart gave a fast thud when he saw Geneva Settle standing by herself in the school yard.

The Graffiti King was in the mouth of an alley across the street, where he'd been for the past hour, waiting for a glimpse of her. But this was even better than he hoped. She was alone. Jax looked over the block. There was an unmarked police car, with a cop inside, in front of the school, but it was some ways from the girl and the cop wasn't looking at the school yard; he wouldn't be able to see her from where he was

228

even if he turned around. This might be easier than he'd thought.

So quit standing around, he told himself. Get your ass moving.

He pulled a black do-rag out of his pocket, slicked down his 'fro with it. Easing forward, pausing beside a battered panel truck, the ex-con scanned the playground (which reminded him a lot of the yard at prison, minus, of course, the razor wire and gun towers). He decided he could cross the street here and use the cover of a Food Emporium tractor-trailer that was parked along the sidewalk, its engine idling. He could get to within maybe twenty-five feet of her without being seen by Geneva or the cop. That'd be plenty close enough.

As long as the girl continued to look down, he could slip through the chain link unnoticed. She'd be spooked after everything that'd happened to her, and if she got a glimpse of him approaching, she'd probably turn and run, shouting for help.

Go slow, be careful.

But move now. You may not get a chance like this again.

Jax started for the girl, picking his steps carefully to keep his limping leg from shuffling leaves and giving him away.

16

Was that the way it always worked?

Did boys *always* want something from you?

In Kevin's case, he wanted her mind. Well, wouldn't she have been just as upset if she'd been built like Lakeesha and he'd hit on her for booty or boobs?

No, she thought angrily. That was different. That was normal. The counselors at school talked a lot about rape, about saying no, about what to do if a boy got too pushy. What to do after, if it happened.

But they never said a word about what to do if somebody wanted to rape your mind.

Shit, shit, shit!

Her teeth ground together and she wiped the tears, flung them away on her fingertips. Forget him! He's a lame asshole. The calc test — that's all that's important.

d over dx times x to the nth equals . . .

Motion to her left. Geneva looked in that direction and, squinting against the sun, saw a figure across the street, in the shadows of a tenement, a man with a black do-rag on his head and wearing a dark green jacket. He'd been walking toward the school yard but then disappeared behind a big truck nearby. Her first panicked thought: The man from the library had come for her. But, no, this guy was black. Relaxing, she glanced at her Swatch. Get back inside.

Only . . .

Despairing, she thought about the looks she'd get. Kevin's boys, who'd give her the bad eye. The bling girls, who'd stare and laugh.

Get her down, get the bitch down . . .

Forget about them. Who gives a shit what they think? The test is all that matters.

d over dx times x to the nth equals nx to the nth minus one . . .

As she started back for the side door she wondered if Kevin would be suspended. Or maybe expelled. She hoped so.

d over dx times . . .

It was then that she heard the scrape of footsteps from the street. Geneva stopped and turned. She couldn't see anyone clearly, because of the glare of the bright sun. Was it the black man in the green jacket coming toward her?

The sound of footsteps paused. She turned away, started toward the school, pushing aside every thought but the power rule of calculus.

. . . equals nx to the nth minus one . . .

Which is when she heard footsteps again, moving fast now. Somebody was charging forward, headed straight for her. She couldn't see. Who is it? She held her hand up to block the fierce sunlight.

And heard Detective Bell's voice call, 'Geneva! Don't move!'

The man was sprinting forward, with someone else — Officer Pulaski — at his side. 'Miss, what happened? Why'd you come outside?'

'I was — '

Three police cars squealed up nearby. Detective Bell looked up, toward the large truck, squinting into the sun. 'Pulaski! That's *him*. Go, go, go!'

They were looking at the receding form of the man she'd seen a minute ago, the one in the green jacket. He was jogging away quickly, with a slight limp, down an alley.

'I'm on it.' The officer sprinted after him. He squeezed through the gate and disappeared into the alley, in pursuit of the man. Then a half dozen police officers appeared in the school yard. They fanned out and surrounded Geneva and the detectives.

'What's going on?' she asked.

Hurrying her toward the cars, Detective Bell explained that they'd just heard from an FBI agent, somebody named Dellray, who worked with Mr. Rhyme. One of his informants had learned that a man in Harlem had been asking about Geneva that morning, trying to find which school she went to and where she lived. He was African-American and wearing a dark green army jacket. He'd been arrested on a murder charge a few years ago and was now armed. Because the attacker in the museum that morning was white and might not know Harlem very well, Mr. Rhyme concluded, he'd decided to use an accomplice who knew the neighborhood.

After Mr. Bell learned this, the detective had gone into the classroom to get her and found out that she'd slipped out the back door. But Jonette Monroe, the undercover cop, had been keeping an eye on her and followed her. She'd then alerted the police to where Geneva was.

Now, the detective said, they had to get her back to Mr. Rhyme's immediately.

'But the test. I — '

'No tests, no school until we catch this guy,' Bell said firmly. 'Now, come on, miss.'

Furious at Kevin's betrayal, furious that she'd been dragged into the middle of this mess, she crossed her arms. 'I have to take that test.'

'Geneva, you don't know what kind of muley I can be. I aim to keep you alive and if that means picking you up and carrying you to my car rest assured I will do just that.' His dark eyes, which had seemed so easygoing, were now hard as rocks.

'All right,' she muttered.

They continued toward the cars, the detective looking around them, checking the shadows. She noticed his hand was near his side. Close to his gun. The blond-haired officer trotted up to them a moment later. 'Lost him,' he gasped, catching his breath. 'Sorry.'

Bell sighed. 'Any description?'

'Black, six feet, solid build. Limp. Black do-rag. No beard or mustache. Late thirties, early forties.'

'Did you see anything else, Geneva?'

She shook her head sullenly.

Bell said, 'Okay. Let's get out of here.'

She climbed into the back of the detective's Ford, with the blond officer beside her. Mr. Bell started for the driver's side. The counselor they'd met earlier, Mrs. Barton, hurried up, a frown on her face. 'Detective, what's wrong?'

'We have to get Geneva out of here. Might be that one of the people wants to hurt her was close by. Still could be, for all we know.'

The heavy woman looked around, frowning. 'Here?'

'We aren't sure. A possibility, all I'm saying. Just better to play it safe.' The detective added, 'We're thinking he was here about five minutes ago. African-American, good-sized fella. Wearing a green army jacket and do-rag. Clean-shaven. Limping. He was on the far side of the school yard, by that big truck there. Could you ask students and teachers if they know him or saw anything else?'

'Of course.'

He asked her too to see if any school security tapes might have picked him up. They exchanged phone numbers, then the detective dropped into the driver's seat, started the engine. 'Buckle up, everybody. We aren't exactly going to be moseyin' on out of here.'

Just as Geneva clicked her seat belt on, the policeman hit the gas and the car skidded away from the curb and started a roller-coaster ride through the ragged streets of Harlem, as Langston Hughes High School — her last fortress of sanity and comfort — disappeared from view.

★   ★   ★

As Amelia Sachs and Lon Sellitto organized the evidence she'd collected at the safe house on Elizabeth Street, Rhyme was thinking about Unsub 109's accomplice — the man who'd just gotten real damn close to Geneva at her school.

There was a possibility that the unsub had been using this man solely for surveillance, except that with the ex-con's violent background and the fact he was armed, he too was probably prepared to kill her himself. Rhyme had hoped that the man had shed some evidence near the school yard, but no — a crime scene team had looked over the area carefully and found nothing. And a canvass team had located no witnesses on the street who'd seen him or how he got away. Maybe —

'Hi, Lincoln,' a male voice said.

Startled, Rhyme looked up and saw a man standing nearby. In his midforties, with broad shoulders, a close-cropped cap of silver hair, bangs in the front. He wore an expensive, dark gray suit.

'Doctor. Didn't hear the bell.'

'Thom was outside. He let me in.'

Robert Sherman, the doctor supervising Rhyme's physical therapy, ran a clinic that specialized in working with spinal cord injury patients. It was he who'd developed Rhyme's regimen of therapy, the bicycle and the locomotor treadmill, as well as aquatherapy and the traditional range-of-motion exercises that Thom performed on Rhyme.

The doctor and Sachs exchanged greetings,

then he glanced at the lab, noting the bustle of activity. From a therapeutic point of view, he was pleased that Rhyme had a job. Being engaged in an activity, he'd often said, vastly improved one's will and drive to improve (though he caustically urged Rhyme to avoid situations where he could be, say, burned to death, which had nearly happened in a recent case).

The doctor was talented and amiable and damn smart. But Rhyme had no time for him at the moment, now that he knew *two* armed perps were after Geneva. He greeted the medico in a distracted mood.

'My receptionist said you canceled the appointment today. I wondered if you were okay.'

A concern that could easily have been addressed via telephone, the criminalist reflected.

But that way the doctor couldn't have put the same pressure on Rhyme to take the tests as he could in person.

And Sherman had indeed been pressuring him. He wanted to know that the exercise plan was paying off. Not only for the patient's sake but also so that the doctor himself could incorporate the information into his ongoing studies.

'No, everything's fine,' Rhyme said. 'A case just fell into our laps.' He gestured toward the evidence board. Sherman eyed it.

Thom stuck his head in the doorway. 'Doctor, you want some coffee? Soda?'

'Oh, we don't want to take up the doctor's precious time,' Rhyme said quickly. 'Now that he

236

knows that there's nothing wrong, I'm sure he'll want to — '

'A case?' Sherman asked, still looking over the board.

After a moment Rhyme said in a brittle voice, 'A tough one. Very bad man out there. One we were in the process of trying to catch when you stopped by.' Rhyme wasn't inclined to give an inch and didn't apologize for his rude behavior. But doctors or therapists who deal with SCI patients know that they come with some bonuses: anger, bad attitudes and searing tongues. Sherman was completely unaffected by Rhyme's behavior. The doctor continued to study Rhyme as he responded: 'No, nothing for me, Thom, thank you. I can't stay long.'

'You sure?' A nod toward Rhyme. 'Don't mind him.'

'I'm fine, yes.'

But even though he didn't want a refreshing beverage, even though he couldn't stay long, nonetheless here he was, not making any immediate move to depart. In fact, he was pulling up a fucking chair and sitting down.

Sachs glanced toward Rhyme. He gave her a blank look and turned back to the doctor, who scooted his chair closer. Then he leaned forward and whispered, 'Lincoln, you've been resisting the tests for months now.'

'It's been a whirlwind. Four cases we've been working on. And now five. Time-consuming, as you can imagine . . . And fascinating, by the way. Unique issues.' Hoping the doctor would ask him for some details, which would at least

237

deflect the course of the conversation.

But the man didn't, of course. SCI doctors never went for the bait. They'd seen it all. Sherman said, 'Let me say one thing.'

And how the hell can I stop you? thought the criminalist.

'You've worked harder on our exercises than any other patient of mine. I know you're resisting the test because you're afraid it won't've had any effect. Am I right?'

'Not really, Doctor. I'm just busy.'

As if he hadn't heard, Sherman said, 'I know you're going to find considerable improvement in your overall condition and functional status.'

Doctor-talk could be as prickly as cop-talk, Rhyme reflected. He replied, 'I hope so. But if not, believe me, it doesn't matter. I've got the muscle mass improvement, the bone density improvement . . . Lungs and heart are better. That's all I'm after. Not motor movement.'

Sherman eyed him up and down. 'You really feel that way?'

'Absolutely.' Looking around, he lowered his voice as he said, 'These exercises won't let me walk.'

'No, that won't happen.'

'So why would I want some tiny improvement in my left little toe? That's pointless. I'll do the exercises, keep myself in the best shape I can and in five or ten years, when you folks come up with a miracle graft or clone or something, I'll be ready to start walking again.'

The doctor smiled and clapped his hand on Rhyme's leg, a gesture he did not feel. Sherman nodded. 'I'm so glad to hear you say that, Lincoln. The biggest problem I have is patients' giving up because they find that all the exercise and hard work doesn't really change their lives very much. They want big wins and cures. They don't realize that this kind of war is won with small victories.'

'I think I've already won.'

The doctor rose. 'I'd still like those scans done. We need the data.'

'As soon as — hey, Lon, are you listening? Incoming clichè! As soon as the deck is cleared.'

Sellitto, who had no clue what Rhyme was talking about, or didn't care, gave him a hollow look.

'All right,' Sherman said and walked to the door. 'And good luck with the case.'

'We'll hope for the best,' Rhyme said cheerily.

The man of small victories left the town house and Rhyme immediately turned back to the evidence boards.

Sachs took a call and listened for a moment, hung up. 'That was Bo Haumann. Those guys on the entry team? The ones who took the electricity? The first one's got some bad burns, but he'll live. The other one's been released.'

'Thank God,' Sellitto said, seeming hugely relieved. 'Man, what that must've been like. All that juice going through you.' He closed his eyes momentarily. 'The burns. And the smell. Jesus. His hair was fucking burnt off . . . I'll send him something. No, I'll take him a present myself. Maybe flowers. Think he'd like some flowers?'

This reaction, like his earlier behavior, wasn't

typical of Sellitto. Cops got hurt and cops got killed, and everybody on the force accepted that reality in his or her own way. There were plenty of officers who'd say, 'Thank God he's alive,' and bless themselves and trot to the closest church to pray their thanks. But Sellitto's way was to nod and get on with the job. Not to act like this.

'No clue,' Rhyme said.

Flowers?

Mel Cooper called out, 'Lincoln, I've got Captain Ned Seely on the line.' The tech had been talking to the Texas Rangers about the killing in Amarillo that VICAP had reported was similar to the incident at the museum.

'Speaker it.'

He did and Rhyme asked, 'Hello, Captain?'

'Yes, sir,' came the response, a drawl. 'Mr. Rhyme?'

'That's right.'

'Got your associate's request for information on the Charlie Tucker case. I pulled what he had but it wasn't much. You think it's the same fellow causing a stir up your way?'

'The M.O.'s similar to an incident we had here this morning. His shoes were the same brand — so was the tread wear. And he left some fake evidence to lead us off, the same way he left those candles and occult markings at Tucker's killing. Oh, and our perp's got a Southern accent. There was also a similar killing in Ohio a few years later. That one was a contract hit.'

'So y'all're thinkin' somebody hired this fella to kill Tucker?'

'Maybe. Who was he?'

'Tucker? Ordinary fellow. Just retired from the Department of Justice — that's our corrections outfit down here. Was happily married, a grandfather. Never in any trouble. Went to church regular.'

Rhyme frowned. 'What'd he do for prisons?'

'Guard. In our maximum security facility in Amarillo ... Hmmm, you thinkin' maybe a prisoner hired somebody to get even for something that happened inside? Prisoner abuse, or some such?'

'Could be,' Rhyme said. 'Did Tucker ever get written up?'

'Nothing in the file here about it. You might wanta check with the prison.'

Rhyme got the name of the warden of the facility where Tucker had worked and then said, 'Thanks, Captain.'

'Nothing to it. Y'all have a good day.'

A few minutes later Rhyme was on the line with Warden J. T. Beauchamp of the Northern Texas Maximum Security Correction Facility in Amarillo. Rhyme identified himself and said he was working with the NYPD. 'Now, Warden — '

'J. T., if you please, sir.'

'All right, J. T.' Rhyme explained the situation to him.

'Charlie Tucker? Sure, the guard who was killed. Lynching, or whatever. I wasn't here then. Tucker retired just before I moved from Houston. I'll pull his file. Put you on hold.' A moment later the warden returned. 'I've got it right here. Nope, no formal complaints against him, 'cepting from one prisoner. He said Charlie was ridin' him pretty hard. When Charlie didn't stop they got into a little scuffle 'bout it.'

'That could be our man,' Rhyme pointed out.

''Cepting the prisoner was executed a week later. And Charlie didn't get hisself killed for another year.'

'But maybe Tucker hassled another prisoner, who hired somebody to even the score.'

'Possible. Only hiring a pro for that? Little sophisticated for our lot down here.'

Rhyme tended to agree. 'Well, maybe the perp was a prisoner himself. He went after Tucker as soon as he got out, then set up the murder to look like some ritual killing. Could you ask some of your guards or other employees? We'd be looking for a white male, forties, medium build, light brown hair. Probably doing time for a violent felony. And probably released or escaped — '

'No escapes, not from here,' the warden added.

'Okay then, *released* not long before Tucker was killed. That's about all we know. Oh, and he has a knowledge of guns and's a good shot.'

'That won't help. This's Texas.' A chuckle.

Rhyme continued, 'We have a computer composite of his face. We'll email a copy to you. Could you have somebody compare it to the pictures of releasees around that time?'

'Yes, sir, I'll have my gal do it. She's got a pretty good eye. But may take a while. We've had ourselves a lotta inmates go through here.' He gave them his email address and they hung up.

Just as the call was disconnected, Geneva, Bell

242

and Pulaski arrived.

Bell explained about the accomplice's escape at the school. He added a few details about him, though, and told them that somebody was going to canvass the students and teachers and dig up a security tape if there was one.

'I didn't get to take my last test,' Geneva said angrily, as if this were Rhyme's fault. This girl could definitely get on your nerves. Still, he said patiently, 'I have some news you might be interested in. Your ancestor survived his swim in the Hudson.'

'He did?' Her face brightened and she eagerly read the printout of the 1868 magazine article. Then she frowned. 'They make him sound pretty bad. Like he'd planned it all along. He wasn't that way. I know it.' She looked up. 'And we still don't know what happened to him if he was ever released.'

'We're still searching for information. I hope we can find out more.'

The tech's computer chimed and he looked it over. 'Maybe something here. Email from a professor at Amherst who runs an African-American history website. She's one of the people I emailed about Charles Singleton.'

'Read it.'

'It's from Frederick Douglass's diary.'

'Who was he again?' Pulaski asked. 'Sorry, I probably should know. Got a street named after him and all.'

Geneva said, 'Former slave. *The* abolitionist and civil rights leader of the nineteenth century. Writer, lecturer.'

The rookie was blushing. 'Like I say, should've known.'

Cooper leaned forward and read from the screen, "May third, 1866. Another evening at Gallows Heights — "

'Ah,' Rhyme interrupted, 'our mysterious neighborhood.' The word 'gallows' again reminded him of The Hanged Man tarot card, the placid figure swinging by his leg from a scaffold. He glanced at the card, then turned his attention back to Cooper.

" . . . discussing our vital endeavor, the Fourteenth Amendment. Several members of the Colored community in New York and myself met with, *inter alia*, the Honorable Governor Fenton and members of the Joint Committee on Reconstruction, including Senators Harris, Grimes and Fessenden, and Congressmen Stevens and Washburne and the Democrat, Andrew T. Rogers, who proved far less partisan than we had feared.

"Governor Fenton began with a moving invocation, whereupon we began to present to the members of the committee our opinions on the various draft versions of the Amendment, which we did at length. (Mr. Charles Singleton was particularly articulate in his view that the amendment should incorporate a requirement of universal suffrage for all citizens, Negroes and Caucasians, women as well as men, which the members of the committee took under advisement.) Lengthy debates lasted well into the night."

Geneva leaned over his shoulder and read.

''Particularly articulate,'' she whispered out loud. 'And he wanted voting for women.'

'Here's another entry,' Cooper said.

''June twenty-fifth, 1867. I am troubled by the slow progress. The Fourteenth Amendment was presented to the states for ratification one year ago, and with expediency twenty-two blessed the measure with their approval. Only six more are required, but we are meeting with stubborn resistance.

''Willard Fish, Charles Singleton and Elijah Walker are traveling throughout those states as yet uncommitted and doing what they can to implore legislators therein to vote in favor of the amendment. But at every turn they are faced with ignorance in perceiving the wisdom of this law — and personal disdain and threats and anger. To have sacrificed so much, and yet not achieve our goal . . . Is our prevailing in the War to be hollow, merely a Pyrrhic victory? I pray the cause of our people does not wither in this, our most important effort.'' Cooper looked up from the screen. 'That's it.'

Geneva said, 'So Charles was working with Douglass and the others on the Fourteenth Amendment. They were friends, sounds like.'

Or were they? Rhyme wondered. Was the newspaper article right? Had he worked his way into the circle to learn what he could about the Freedmen's Trust and rob it?

Although, for Lincoln Rhyme, truth was the only goal in any forensic investigation, he harbored a rare sentimental hope that Charles Singleton had not committed the crime.

245

He stared at the evidence board, seeing far more question marks than answers.

'Geneva, can you call your aunt? See if she's found any more letters or anything else about Charles?'

The girl called the woman with whom Aunt Lilly was living. There was no answer but she left a message for one of them to call back at Rhyme's. She then placed another call. Her eyes brightened. 'Mom! Are you home?'

Thank God, Rhyme thought. Her parents were back at last.

But a frown crossed the girl's face a moment later. 'No . . . What happened? . . . When?'

A delay of some sort, Rhyme deduced. Geneva gave her mother an update, reassured them she was safe and being looked out for by the police. She handed the phone to Bell, who spoke to her mother at some length about the situation. He then gave the phone back and Geneva said good-bye to her and to her father. She reluctantly hung up.

Bell said, 'They're stuck in London. The flight was canceled, and they couldn't get anything else today. They're on the earliest plane out tomorrow — it goes to Boston and they'll catch the next flight here.'

Geneva shrugged, but Rhyme could see the disappointment in her eyes. She said, 'I better get back home. I have some projects for school.'

Bell checked with his SWAT officers and Geneva's uncle. Everything seemed safe, he reported.

'You'll stay out of school tomorrow?'

246

A hesitation. She grimaced. Would there be another battle?

Then someone spoke. It was Pulaski, the rookie. 'The fact is, Geneva, it's not just you anymore. If that guy today, the one in the combat jacket, had gotten close, and started shooting, there might've been other students hurt or killed. He might try again when you're in a crowd outside of school or on the street.'

Rhyme could see in her face that his words affected her. Maybe she was reflecting about Dr. Barry's death.

So he's dead because of me . . .

'Sure,' she said in a soft voice. 'I'll stay home.'

Bell nodded at her. 'Thanks.' And cast a grateful glance toward the rookie.

The detective and Pulaski ushered the girl out the door and the others returned to the evidence from the unsub's safe house.

Rhyme was upset to see there wasn't much. The diagram of the street in front of the African-American museum, which Sachs had found hidden in the man's bed, yielded no prints. The paper was off-the-shelf generic, the sort sold at Staples and Office Depot. The ink was cheap and untraceable. The sketch contained far more details of the alleys and buildings across the street than of the museum itself — this map was for the man's escape route, Rhyme assumed. But Sachs had already searched those locations carefully and detectives had canvassed potential witnesses in the jewelry exchange and other buildings shown on the plan.

There were more fibers from the rope — his garrotte, they speculated.

Cooper ran a portion of the map through the GC/MS, and the only trace found in the paper was pure carbon. 'Charcoal from a street fair vendor?' he wondered.

'Maybe,' Rhyme said. 'Or maybe he burned evidence. Put it on the chart. Maybe we'll find a connection later.'

The other trace evidence on the map — stains and crumbs — were more food: yogurt and ground chickpeas, garlic and corn oil.

'Falafel,' Thom, a gourmet cook, offered. 'Middle Eastern. And often served with yogurt. Refreshing, by the way.'

'And extremely common,' Rhyme said sourly. 'We can narrow down the sources to about two thousand in Manhattan alone, wouldn't you think? What the hell else do we have?'

On the way back here Sachs and Sellitto had stopped at the real estate company managing the Elizabeth Street building and had gotten information on the lessee of the apartment. The woman running the office had said the tenant had paid three months' rent in cash, plus another two months' security deposit, which he'd told her to keep. (The cash, unfortunately, had been spent; there was none left to fingerprint.) He'd given his name as Billy Todd Hammil on the lease, former address, Florida. The composite picture that Sachs had done bore a resemblance to the man who'd signed the lease, though he'd worn a baseball cap and glasses. The woman confirmed that he had a Southern accent.

A search of identification databases revealed 173 hits for Billy Todd Hammils throughout the country in the past five years. Of the ones who were white and between thirty-five and fifty, none was in the New York area. The ones in Florida were all elderly or in their twenties. Four Billy Todds had criminal records, and of these, three were still in prison and one had died six years ago.

'He picked the name out of a hat,' Rhyme muttered. He looked over the computer-generated image.

Who are you, Unsub 109? he wondered.

And *where* are you?

'Mel, email the picture to J.T.'

'To?'

'Our good ole boy warden down in Amarillo.' A nod toward the picture. 'I'm still leaning toward the theory our boy's an inmate who had a run-in with that guard who was lynched.'

'Got it,' Cooper said. After he'd done so he took the sample of liquid that Sachs had found in the safe house, carefully opened it up and prepared it for the gas chromatograph/mass spectrometer.

A short time later the results popped up on the screen.

'This's a new one to me. Polyvinyl alcohol, povidone, benzalkonium chloride; dextrose; potassium chloride; water; sodium bicarbonate; sodium chloride — '

'More salt,' Rhyme chimed in. 'But it ain't popcorn this time.'

'And sodium citrate and sodium phosphate. Few other things.'

'Fucking Greek to me.' Sellitto shrugged and wandered into the hall, turning toward the bathroom.

Cooper nodded at the list of ingredients. 'Any clue what it is?'

Rhyme shook his head. 'Our database?'

'Nothing.'

'Send it down to Washington.'

'Will do.' The tech sent the information off to the FBI's lab and then turned to the final item of evidence that Sachs had found: wood scrapings of the stains on top of the desk. Cooper prepared a sample for the chromatograph.

As they waited for the results Rhyme scanned the evidence chart. He was looking over the entries when he saw some fast motion from the corner of his eye. Startled, he turned toward it. But no one was in that portion of the lab. What had he seen?

Then he saw movement again and realized what he was looking at: a reflection in the glass front of a cabinet. It was Lon Sellitto, alone in the hallway, apparently believing no one could see him. The fast motion had been the big detective's practicing a fast draw of his pistol. Rhyme couldn't see the man's face clearly but his expression appeared distressed.

What was *this* about?

The criminalist caught Sachs's eye and nodded toward the doorway. She edged closer to the door and looked out, watching the detective draw his weapon several more times then shake his head, grimacing. Sachs shrugged. After three or four minutes of the exercise, the detective put his gun away, stepped into the bathroom and without closing the door flushed the toilet and stepped out again a second later.

He returned to the lab. 'Jesus, Linc, when're you going to put in a classy john in this place? Didn't yellow and black go out in the seventies?'

'You know, I just don't hold a lot of meetings in the toilet.'

The big man laughed, but too loudly. The sound, like the banter that inspired it, rang false.

But whatever was troubling the man instantly ceased to occupy Rhyme's mind when the results of the GC/MS analysis flashed onto the computer screen — the scrapings from the unsub's desktop at the safe house. Rhyme frowned. The analysis had reported that the substance that had stained the wood was pure sulfuric acid, news that Rhyme found particularly discouraging. For one thing, from an evidentiary point of view, it was readily available and therefore virtually impossible to trace to a single source.

But more upsetting was the fact that it was perhaps the most powerful — and dangerous — acid you could buy; as a weapon, even a tiny quantity could, within seconds, kill or permanently disfigure.

ELIZABETH STREET SAFE HOUSE SCENE

- Used electrical booby trap.
- Fingerprints: None. Glove prints only.
- Security camera and monitor; no leads.
- Tarot deck, missing the twelfth card; no leads.
- Map with diagram of museum where G. Settle was attacked and buildings across the street.
- Trace:
  - Falafel and yogurt.
  - Wood scrapings from desk with traces of pure sulfuric acid.
  - Clear liquid, not explosive. Sent to FBI lab.
  - More fibers from rope. Garrotte?
  - Pure carbon found in map.
- Safe house was rented, for cash, to Billy Todd Hammil. Fits Unsub 109's description, but no leads to an actual Hammil.

AFRICAN-AMERICAN MUSEUM SCENE

- Rape pack:
  - Tarot card, twelfth card in deck, the Hanged Man, meaning spiritual searching.
  - Smiley-face bag.
    - Too generic to trace.
  - Box cutter.
  - Trojan condoms.
  - Duct tape.
  - Jasmine scent.
  - Unknown item bought for $5.95. Probably a stocking cap.
  - Receipt, indicating store was in New York City, discount variety store or drugstore.
  - Most likely purchased in a store on Mulberry Street, Little Italy. Unsub identified by clerk.
- Fingerprints:
  - Unsub wore latex or vinyl gloves.
  - Prints on items in rape pack belonged to person with small hands, no IAFIS hits. Positive ID for clerk's.
- Trace:
  - Cotton rope fibers, some with traces of human blood. Garrotte?
    - Sent to CODIS.
      - No DNA match in CODIS.
  - Popcorn and cotton candy with traces of canine urine.

- Weapons:
  - Billy club or martial arts weapon.
  - Pistol is a North American Arms .22 rimfire magnum, Black Widow or Mini-Master.
  - Makes own bullets, bored-out slugs filled with needles. No match in IBIS or DRUGFIRE.

- Motive:
  - Uncertain. Rape was probably staged.
  - True motive may have been to steal microfiche containing July 23, 1868, issue of *COLOREDS' WEEKLY ILLUSTRATED* magazine and kill G. Settle because of her interest in an article for reasons unknown. Article was about her ancestor Charles Singleton (see accompanying chart).
  - Librarian victim reported that someone else wished to see article.
    - Requesting librarian's phone records to verify this.
      - No leads.
    - Requesting information from employees as to other person wishing to see story.
      - No leads.
  - Searching for copy of article.
    - Several sources report man requested same article. No leads to identity. Most issues missing or destroyed. One located. (See accompanying chart.)
  - Conclusion: G. Settle still at risk.

- Profile of incident sent to VICAP and NCIC.
  - Murder in Amarillo, TX, five years ago. Similar M.O. — staged crime scene (apparently ritual killing, but real motive unknown).
    - Victim was a retired prison guard.
    - Composite picture sent to Texas prison.
  - Murder in Ohio, three years ago. Similar M.O. — staged crime scene (apparently sexual assault, but real motive probably hired killing). Files missing.

PROFILE OF UNSUB 109

- White male.
- 6 feet tall, 180 lbs.

- Middle-aged.
- Average voice.
- Used cell phone to get close to victim.
- Wears three-year-old, or older, size-11 Bass walkers, light brown. Right foot slightly outturned.
- Additional jasmine scent.
- Dark pants.
- Ski mask, dark.
- Will target innocents to help in killing victims and escaping.
- Most likely is a for-hire killer.
- Possibly a former prisoner in Amarillo, TX.
- Talks with a Southern accent.
- Has trim, light brown hair, clean-shaven.
- Nondescript.
- Seen wearing dark rain-coat.

PROFILE OF PERSON HIRING UNSUB 109

- No information at this time.

PROFILE OF UNSUB 109'S ACCOMPLICE

- Black male.
- Late 30's, early 40's.

- Six feet.
- Solidly built.
- Wearing green combat jacket.
- Ex-convict.
- Has a limp.
- Reportedly armed.
- Clean-shaven.
- Black do-rag.
- Awaiting additional witnesses and security tapes.

PROFILE OF CHARLES SINGLETON

- Former slave, ancestor of G. Settle. Married, one son. Given orchard in New York state by master. Worked as teacher, as well. Instrumental in early civil rights movement.
- Charles allegedly committed theft in 1868, the subject of the article in stolen microfiche.
- Reportedly had a secret that could bear on case. Worried that tragedy would result if his secret was revealed.
- Attended meetings in Gallows Heights neighborhood of New York.
  - Involved in some risky activities?
- Worked with Frederick

254

Douglass and others in getting the 14th Amendment to the Constitution ratified.

- The crime, as reported in *Coloreds' Weekly Illustrated*:
  - Charles arrested by Det. William Simms for stealing large sum from Freedmen's Trust in NY. Broke into the trust's safe, witnesses saw him leave shortly after. His tools were found nearby. Most money was recovered. He was sentenced to five years in prison. No information about him after sentencing. Believed to have used his connections with early civil rights leaders to gain access to the trust.
- Charles's correspondence:
- Letter 1, to wife: Re: Draft Riots in 1863, great anti-black sentiment throughout NY state, lynchings, arson. Risk to property owned by blacks.
- Letter 2, to wife: Charles at Battle of Appomattox at end of Civil War.
- Letter 3, to wife: Involved in civil rights movement. Threatened for this work. Troubled by his secret.

17

Walking down a street in Queens, carrying his shopping bag and briefcase, Thompson Boyd paused suddenly. He pretended to look at a newspaper in a vending machine and, cocking his head in concern at the state of world affairs, glanced behind him.

Nobody following, nobody paying any attention to Average Joe.

He didn't really think there was a chance of a tail. But Thompson always minimized risks. You could never be careless when your profession was death, and he was particularly vigilant after the close call on Elizabeth Street with the woman in white.

They'll kill you in a kiss . . .

He now doubled back to the corner. Saw no one ducking into buildings or turning away fast.

Satisfied, Thompson continued in the direction he'd been heading originally.

He glanced at his watch. It was the agreed-upon time. He walked to a phone kiosk and placed a call to a pay phone in downtown Manhattan. After one ring he heard, 'Hello?'

'It's me.' Thompson and the caller went through a little song and dance — security stuff, like spies — to make certain each knew for sure who was on the other end of the line. Thompson was minimizing his drawl, just like his client was altering his voice too. Wouldn't fool a voiceprint analyzer, of course. Still, you did what you could.

The man would already know the first attempt had failed since the local news had broken the story. His client asked, 'How bad is it? We have a problem?'

The killer tilted his head back and put Murine into his eyes. Blinking as the pain dissipated, Thompson replied in a voice as numb as his soul, 'Oh, well now, you gotta understand 'bout what we're doing here. It's like everything else in life. Nothing ever goes smooth one hundred percent. Nothing runs just the way we'd like. The girl outsmarted me.'

'A high school girl?'

'The girl's got street smarts, simple as that. Good reflexes. She lives in a jungle.' Thompson felt a brief pang that he'd made this comment, thinking the man might believe it referred to the fact she was black, a racist thing, though he only meant she lived in a tough part of town and had to be savvy. Thompson Boyd was the least prejudiced person on earth. His parents had taught him that. Thompson himself had known people of all races and backgrounds and he'd responded to them solely on the basis of their behavior and attitudes, not what color they were. He'd worked for whites, blacks, Arabs, Asians, Latinos, and he'd killed people of those same races. He could see no difference between them. The people who'd hired him all avoided his eyes and acted edgy and cautious. The people who'd died by his hand had gone to their rewards with varying degrees of dignity and fear, which had

257

nothing to do with color or nationality.

He continued, 'Wasn't what you wanted. It wasn't what *I* wanted, bet your bottom dollar. But what happened was a reasonable possibility. She's got good people watching her. Now we know. We'll just rerig and keep going. We can't get emotional about it. Next time we'll get her. I've brought in somebody knows Harlem pretty good. We've already found out where she goes to school, we're working on where she lives. Trust me, we've got everything covered.'

'I'll check for messages later,' the man said. And hung up abruptly. They'd spoken for no more than three minutes, Thompson Boyd's limit.

By the book . . .

Thompson hung up — there was no need to wipe prints; he was wearing leather gloves. He continued down the street. The block was a pleasant strip of bungalows on the east side of the street and apartments on the west, an old neighborhood. There were a few children nearby, just getting home from school. Inside the houses here Thompson could see the flicker of soap operas and afternoon talk shows, as the women ironed and cooked. Whatever life was like in the rest of the city, a lot of this neighborhood had never dug out of the 1950s. It reminded him of the trailer park and the bungalow of his childhood. A nice life, a comforting life.

His life before prison, before he grew numb as a missing arm or a snakebit leg.

A block ahead of him Thompson saw a young blonde girl dressed in a school uniform approach

258

a beige bungalow. His heart sped up a bit — just a beat or two — watching her climb the few concrete stairs, take a key from her book bag, open the door and walk inside.

He continued on to this same house, which was as neat as the others, perhaps slightly more so, and featured a hitching-post jockey, with black features painted politically correct tan, and a series of small ceramic deer grazing on the tiny, yellowing lawn. He walked past the bungalow slowly, looking into the windows, and then continued up the block. A gust of wind blew the shopping bag in an arc and the cans clanked dully against each other. Hey, careful there, he told himself. And steadied the bag.

At the end of the block he turned and looked back. A man jogging, a woman trying to parallel park, a boy dribbling a basketball on a leaf-covered driveway. No one paid him any attention.

Thompson Boyd started back toward the house.

★   ★   ★

Inside her Queens bungalow Jeanne Starke told her daughter, 'No book bags in the hall, Brit. Put 'em in the den.'

'Mom,' the ten-year-old girl sighed, managing to get at least two syllables out of the word. She tossed her yellow hair, hung her uniform jacket on the hook and picked up the heavy knapsack, groaning in exasperation.

'Homework?' her pretty, mid-thirties mother

asked. She had a mass of curly brunette hair, today tied back with a rosy red scrunchy.

'Don't have any,' Britney said.

'None?'

'Nope.'

'Last time you said no homework, you had homework,' her mother said pointedly.

'It wasn't really homework. It was a report. Just cutting something out of a magazine.'

'You had work for school to do at home. Homework.'

'Well, I don't have *any* today.'

Jeanne could tell there was more. She lifted an eyebrow.

'It's just we have to bring in something Italian. For show-and-tell. You know, for Columbus Day. Did you know he was Italian? I thought he was Spanish or something.'

The mother of two did happen to know this fact. She was a high school graduate and the holder of an associate degree in nursing. She could have worked, if she'd wanted to, but her boyfriend made good money as a salesman and was happy to let her to take care of the house, go shopping with her girlfriends and raise the children.

Part of which was making sure they did their homework, whatever form it took, including show-and-tell.

'That's all? Loving, loving, tell the truth?'

'Mommmmm.'

'The truth?'

'Yeah.'

' 'Yes.' Not 'yeah.' What're you going to take?'

'I don't know. Something from Barrini's deli maybe. Did you know that Columbus, like, was wrong? He thought he'd found Asia, not America. And he came here three times and still never got it right.'

'Really?'

'Yeah . . . *yes*.' Britney vanished.

Jeanne returned to the kitchen, thinking *this* fact she hadn't known. Columbus really thought he'd found Japan or China? She dredged the chicken in flour, then egg, then bread crumbs, and started to lose herself in a fantasy about the family traveling in Asia — the images courtesy of cable TV. The girls would love that. Maybe . . . It was then that she happened to glance outside and, through the opaque curtain, saw the form of a man slow as he approached the house.

This made her uneasy. Her boyfriend, whose company made computer components for government contractors, had stirred up some paranoia inside her. Always be on the lookout for strangers, he'd say. You notice anybody slowing down as they drive past the house, anybody who seems unusually interested in the children . . . tell me about it right away. Once, not long ago, they'd been in the park up the street with the girls, who were playing on the swings, when a car slowed up and the driver, wearing sunglasses, glanced at the children. Her boyfriend had gotten all freaked and made them go back to the house.

He'd explained: 'Spies.'

'What?'

'No, not like CIA spies. *Industrial* spies

— from our competitors. My company made over six billion dollars last year and I'm responsible for a good chunk of that. People would love to find out what I know about the market.'

'Companies really do that?' Jeanne had asked.

'You never really know about people,' had been his response.

And Jeanne Starke, who had a rod imbedded in her arm where it'd been shattered by a whisky bottle a few years ago, had thought: You never did, true. She now wiped her hands on her apron, walked to the curtain and looked out.

The man was gone.

Okay, stop spooking yourself. It's —

But wait . . . She saw motion on the front steps. And believed she saw a corner of a bag — a shopping bag — sitting on the porch. The man was here!

What was going on?

Should she call her boyfriend?

Should she call the police?

But they were at least ten minutes away.

'There's somebody outside, Mommy,' Britney called.

Jeanne stepped forward fast. 'Brit, you stay in your room. I'll see.'

But the girl was opening the front door.

'No!' Jeanne called.

And heard: 'Thanks, honey,' Thompson Boyd said in a friendly drawl as he stepped inside the house, toting the shopping bag she'd seen.

'You gave me a fright,' Jeanne said. She hugged him and he kissed her.

'Couldn't find my keys.'

'You're home early.'

He grimaced. 'Problems with the negotiations this morning. They were postponed till tomorrow. Thought I'd come home and do some work here.'

Jeanne's other daughter, Lucy, eight, ran into the hallway. 'Tommy! Can we watch *Judge Judy*?'

'Not today.'

'Aw, please. What's in the bag?'

'That's the work I have to do. And I need your help.' He set the bag down on the floor in the hallway, looked at the girls solemnly and said, 'You ready?'

'I'm ready!' Lucy said.

Brit, the older girl, said nothing but that was because it wouldn't be cool to agree with her sister; she was definitely ready to help too.

'After we postponed my meeting I went out and bought these. I've been reading up on it all morning.' Thompson reached into the shopping bag and pulled out cans of paint, sponges, rollers and brushes. Then he held up a book bristling with yellow Post-it tabs, *Home Decor Made Easy. Volume 3: Decorating Your Child's Room.*

'Tommy!' Britney said. 'For our rooms?'

'Yep,' he drawled. 'Your mom and I sure don't want Dumbo on our walls.'

'You're going to paint *Dumbo*?' Lucy frowned. 'I don't want Dumbo.'

Neither did Britney.

'I'll paint whoever y'all want.'

'Let me look first!' Lucy took the book from him.

'No, me!'

'We'll all look together,' Thompson said. 'Let me hang up my coat and put my briefcase away.' He headed into his office, in the front of the house.

And returning to the kitchen, Jeanne Starke thought that despite his incessant travel, the paranoia about his job, the fact that his heart didn't join into either his joy or his sadness, the fact that he wasn't much of a lover, well, she knew she could do a lot worse in the boyfriend department.

★   ★   ★

Escaping down the alley from the police at the Langston Hughes school yard, Jax had piled into a cab and told the driver to head south, fast, ten bucks extra you roll through that light. Then five minutes later he'd told the man to circle back, dropping him off not far from the school.

He'd been lucky, getting away. The police were obviously going to do whatever was necessary to keep people from getting close to the girl. He was uneasy; it was almost like they'd known about him. Had that asshole claimer Ralph dimed him, after all?

Well, Jax'd have to be smarter. Which is what he was trying to do right now. Just like in prison — never make your move until you'd checked everything out.

And he knew where to look for help.

City men always gravitated together, whether they were young or old, black or Hispanic or white, lived in East New York or Bay Ridge or Astoria. In Harlem they'd gather in churches, bars, rap and jazz clubs and coffee shops, living rooms, on park benches and doorsteps. They'd be on front stairs and fire escapes in the summer, around burning trash drums in the winter. Barbershops too — just like the movie from a few years ago (Jax's real first name, Alonzo, in fact, had come from Alonzo Henderson, the former Georgia slave who became a millionaire by creating a popular chain of barbershops — a man whose drive and talent Jax's father had hoped would rub off on the boy, vainly, as it turned out).

But the most popular place for men to congregate in Harlem was on basketball courts.

They'd go there to play ball, sure. But they'd also go just to bullshit, to solve the world's problems, to speak of women fine and women mean, to argue sports, to dis, and to boast — in a modern, freewheeling version of signifying and toasting: the traditional art of telling the tales of mythical characters in black culture, like the criminal Stackolee or the stoker on the *Titanic* who survived the ice disaster by swimming to safety.

Jax now found the closest park to Langston Hughes with basketball courts. Despite the chill autumn air and low sun, they were plenty crowded. He eased up to the nearest one and took off his combat jacket, which the cops had probably tipped to, turned it inside out and slung it over his arm. He leaned against the chain link, smoking and looking like a big version of Pharaoh Ralph. He pulled off the do-rag and brushed his 'fro up with his fingers.

Just as well he changed his look. He saw a squad car drive past, slow, along the street across from the playground. Jax stayed right where he was. Nothing draws cops faster than walking away (he'd been stopped dozens of times for the criminal offense of WWB — walking while black). At the court in front of him a handful of high school boys moved magically over the scuffed gray asphalt of a half court, while another dozen watched. Jax saw the dusty brown ball smack into the ground, then heard the delayed crack. He watched hands grapple, watched bodies collide, watched the ball sailing toward the board.

The squad car vanished and Jax pushed away from the fence and approached the boys standing on the edge of the court. The ex-con looked them over. Not a posse, no Glock-toting gangstas. Just a bunch of boys — some with tats, some without, some draped with chain, some with a single cross, some with bad intentions, some with good. Preening for the girls, lording over the little kids. Talking, smoking. Being young.

Watching them, Jax slipped into melancholy. He'd always wanted a big family but, like so many other things, that dream hadn't worked out. He'd lost one child to the foster system and another to his girlfriend's fateful visit to the clinic on 125th Street. One January years ago, to

Jax's delight, she'd announced she was pregnant. In March she'd had some pains and they'd gone to a free clinic, which was their only health care option. They'd spent hours in the filthy, overcrowded waiting room. By the time she'd finally gotten to see a doctor she'd miscarried.

Jax had grabbed the man and come close to beating him bloody. 'Not my fault,' said the tiny Indian, cowering beside a gurney. 'They cut our budget. The city did, I'm saying.' Jax was plunged into rage and depression. He *had* to get even with somebody, to make sure this didn't happen again — to her or to anyone else. It was no consolation when the doctor explained that at least they'd saved his girlfriend's life — which probably wouldn't've happened if other planned budget cutbacks for healthcare to the poor had gone through.

How could a fucking government do that to people? Wasn't the whole point of city hall and the state capital to be there for the welfare of citizens? How could they let a little baby die?

Neither the doctor, nor the police who led him out of the hospital that night in handcuffs, had been inclined to answer those questions.

The sorrow and blistering anger at that memory made him all the more determined to get over with what he was about now.

Grim-faced, Jax looked over the boys on the courts and nodded to the one that he'd pegged as a leader of some kind. Wearing baggy shorts, hightop sneakers and a sports jersey. His hair was a gumby — thin on one side, rounded high on the other. The boy looked him over. 'S'up, grandpa?'

Some guffaws from the others.

Grandpa.

In the old Harlem — well, maybe the old everywhere — being an adult carried respect. Now it got you dissed. A playa would've taken the piece out of his sock and make this little claimer hop to. But Jax had been seasoned by his years on the street and years inside prison and knew that wasn't the way to go, not here. He laughed it off. Then whispered, 'Tall paper?'

'You want some?'

'I wanta give *you* some. If you're interested, asshole.' Jax tapped his pocket, where his wad of benjamins resided, curled up fat.

'I ain't selling nothing.'

'And I ain't buying what you think. Come on. Let's stroll.'

The kid nodded and they walked away from the court. As they did, Jax felt the boy looking him over, noticing the man's limp. Yeah, it was an I-got-shot limp but it *could've* been a playa-gangsta limp just as easy. And then he looked at Jax's eyes, cold as dirt, and then the muscles and the prison tat. Maybe thinking: Jax's age would've made him head-high O.G. — who you fucked with at your peril. Original Gangstas had AKs and Uzis and Hummers and a dozen badasses in their posses. O.G.s were the ones used twelve-year-olds to cap witnesses and rival dealers 'cause courts couldn't send them into the system forever, like they did when you were seventeen or eighteen.

An O.G. would bust you up bad for calling him 'grandpa.'

The kid started to look uneasy. 'Yo, yo, whatchu want exactly, man? Where we goin'?'

'Just over there. Don't want to talk in front of the whole world.' Jax stopped behind some bushes. The boy's eyes darted around. Jax laughed. 'I'm not going to fuck you up, boy. Chill.'

The kid laughed too. But nervous. 'I'm down, man.'

'I need to find somebody's crib. Somebody going to Langston Hughes. You go there?'

'Yeah, most of us.' He nodded toward the courts.

'I'm looking for the girl was on the news this morning.'

'Her? Geneva? Saw some dude get capped or something? The straight-A bitch?'

'I don't know. She get straight A's?'

'Yeah. She smart.'

'Where's she live?'

He fell silent, cautious. Debating. Was he going to get fucked up for asking what he wanted to? He decided he wasn't. 'You were talking 'bout paper?'

Jax slipped him some bills.

'I myself don' know the bitch, man. But I can hook you up with a brother who does. Nigger of mine name of Kevin. Want me to give him a call?'

'Yeah.'

A tiny cell phone emerged from the boy's shorts. 'Yo, dog. It's Willy . . . The half courts

. . . Yeah. Listen, dude here with some benjamins, looking fo' yo' bitch . . . Geneva. The Settle bitch . . . Hey, chill, man. S'a joke, you know what I'm saying? . . . Right. Now, this dude, he — '

Jax snatched the phone from Willy's hand and said, 'Two hundred, you give up her address.'

A hesitation.

'Cash?' Kevin asked.

'No,' Jax snapped, 'American Fuckin' Express. Yeah, cash.'

'I'ma come by the courts. You got those C-notes on you?'

'Yeah, they're sitting right next to my Colt, you're interested. And when I say Colt I don't mean malt in a forty.'

'I'm down, man. Just askin'. I don't go round fielding folk.'

'I'll be hanging with my *crew*,' Jax said, grinning at the uneasy Willy. He disconnected the phone and tossed it to the kid. Then he walked back to the fence and leaned against it and watched the game.

Ten minutes later Kevin arrived — unlike Willy, he was a *real* playa, tall, handsome, poised. Looked like some actor Jax couldn't place. To show off for the old dude, show he wasn't too eager to earn any C-notes — and to impress a few of the bling girls, of course — Kevin took his time. Paused, tapped fists, hugged a boy or two. Tossed out, 'Yo, yo, my man,' a few times and then stepped onto the court, commandeered the ball and did a couple of impressive dunks.

Man could play hoops, no question.

Finally Kevin loped up to Jax and looked him over, because that was what you did when an outsider walked into a pack — whether it was on half courts or in a bar or even in Alonzo Henderson's Victorian-era barbershops, Jax guessed. Kevin tried to figure out where Jax was carrying the piece, how much paper he really had on him, what he was about. Jax asked, 'Just lemme know how long you're going keep giving me the bad-eye, okay? 'Cause it's gettin' boring.'

Kevin didn't smile. 'Where's the benjamins?'

Jax slipped Kevin the money.

'Where's the girl?'

'Come on. I'll show you.'

'Just the address.'

'You afraid of me?'

'Just the address.' Eyes not wavering.

Kevin grinned. 'Don't know the number, man. I know the building. I walked her home last spring. I gotta point it out.'

Jax nodded.

They started west and south, surprising Jax; he thought the girl would live in one of the tougher neighborhoods — farther north toward the Harlem River, or east. The streets here weren't elegant but they were clean, and many of the buildings had been renovated, it seemed. There was also a lot of new construction underway.

Jax frowned, looking around at the nice streets. 'You sure we're talking Geneva Settle.'

'That's the bitch you ask about. That's the crib I'm showing you . . . Yo, man, you wanta buy some weed, some rock?'

'No.'

'Sure? I got some good shit.'

'A damn shame, you going deaf and all at your young age.'

Kevin shrugged.

They came to a block near Morningside Park. On top of the rocky incline was the Columbia University campus, a place he had frequently bombed with *Jax 157* years ago.

They started to turn the corner but both of them stopped fast.

'Yo, check it out,' Kevin whispered. There was a Crown Vic — clearly an unmarked police car — double-parked in front of an old building.

'That's her crib? The car's in front of?'

'Naw. Hers's two buildings closer. That one there.' He pointed.

It was old but in perfect shape. Flowers in the window boxes, everything clean. Nice curtains. Paint looked new.

Kevin asked, 'You going to fuck up the bitch?' He looked Jax up and down.

'What I'm about is my business.'

'Your business, your business . . . Sure it is,' Kevin said in a soft voice. 'Only . . . the reason I'm asking is, 'cause if she *was* to get fucked up — which I have no problem with, I'm saying — but if something *was* to happen to her, yo, check it out: I'd know it was you. And somebody might come round and wanna talk to me 'bout it. So, I'm thinking, with all that tall paper you carrying around in your pocket there, maybe I had a little more of it, I might forget I even seen you. On th' other hand, it's possible I could remember a *lot* 'bout you and that you was

272

interested in the little bitch.'

Jax had seen quite a bit of life. Been a graffiti king, been a soldier in Desert Storm, known gangstas in prison and outside, been shot at . . . If there was a rule in this crazy world it was that however stupid you thought people were, they were always happy to be stupider.

In a fraction of a second, Jax grabbed the boy's collar with his left hand and swung his fist up hard into the boy's gut, three times, four, five . . .

'Fuck — ' was all the boy got out.

The way you fought in prison. Never give 'em a single second to recover.

Again, again, again . . .

Jax let go and the kid rolled into the alley, groaning in pain. With the deliberate, slow movement of a baseball player picking out a bat, Jax bent down and pulled the gun from his sock. As terrified Kevin watched helplessly, the ex-con worked the slide of the automatic to chamber a round then wrapped his do-rag around the barrel a number of times. This was, Jax had learned from DeLisle Marshall on S block, one of the best, and cheapest, ways to muffle the sound of a gunshot.

18

That evening, 7:30 P.M., Thompson Boyd had just finished painting a cartoon bear on the wall of Lucy's room. He stepped back and glanced at his work. He'd done what the book had told him to do and, sure enough, it looked pretty much like a bear. It was the first picture in his life he'd ever painted, outside of school — which is why he'd worked so hard studying the book in his safe house earlier today.

The girls seemed to love it. He thought he himself should be pleased with the picture. But he wasn't sure. He stared at it for a long time, waiting to feel proud. He didn't. Oh, well. He stepped into the hallway, glanced at his cell phone. 'Got a message,' he said absently. He dialed. 'Hey, it's Thompson. How you doing? Saw you called.'

Jeanne glanced at him then returned to drying the dishes.

'No, kidding?' Thompson chuckled. For a man who didn't laugh, he thought he sounded real. Of course, he'd done the same thing that morning, in the library, laughing to put the Settle girl at ease, and *that* hadn't worked so well. He reminded himself not to overact. 'Man, that's a bummer,' he said into the dead phone. 'Sure. Won't take too long, will it? Got that negotiation again tomorrow, yeah, the one we postponed . . . Gimme ten and I'll see you there.'

He folded the phone closed and said to Jeanne, 'Vern's over at Joey's. He's got a flat.'

Vernon Harber had once existed but no longer did. Thompson had killed him some years ago. But because he'd known Vern before he died, Thompson had turned him into a fictional neighborhood buddy he saw occasionally, a sidekick. Like the dead real Vern, the live fictional one drove a Supra and had a girlfriend named Renee and told plenty of funny stories about life on the docks and at the pork store and in his neighborhood. Thompson knew a lot more about Vern and he kept the details in mind. (When you lie, he knew, lie big, ballsy and specific.)

'He drove his Supra over a beer bottle.'

'Is he all right?' Jeanne asked.

'He was just parking. The putz can't get the lug nuts off by himself.'

Alive and dead, Vern Harber was a couch potato.

Thompson took the paintbrush and cardboard bucket to the laundry room and set them in the basin, ran water to soak the brush. He slipped on his jacket.

Jeanne asked, 'Oh, could you get some two-percent on the way home?'

'Quart?'

'That's fine.'

'And some roll-ups!' Lucy called.

'What flavor?'

'Grape.'

'All right. Brit?'

'Cherry!' the girl said. Her memory nudged

her. 'Please,' she added.

'Grape and cherry and milk.' Pointing at each of the females, according to her order.

Thompson stepped outside and started walking in a convoluted path up and down the streets of Queens, glancing back occasionally to make sure he wasn't being followed. Breathing cold air into his lungs, exhaling it hotter and in the form of soft musical notes: the Celine Dion song from *Titanic*.

The killer had kept an eye on Jeanne when he'd told her he was going out. He'd noted that her concern for Vern seemed real and that she wasn't the least suspicious, despite the fact he was going to see a man she'd never met. But this was typical. Tonight, he was helping a friend. Sometimes he said he wanted to place an OTB bet. Or he was going to see the boys at Joey's for a fast one. He rotated his lies.

The lean, curly-haired brunette never asked much about where he went, or about the phoney computer salesman job he claimed he had, which required him to be away from home frequently. Never asked details about why his business was so secret he had to keep his home office door locked. She was smart and clever, two very different things, and most any other smart and clever woman would have insisted on being included more in his life. But not Jeanne Starke.

He'd met her at a lunch counter here in Astoria a few years ago after he'd gone to ground following the murder of a Newark drug dealer he'd been hired to kill. Sitting next to Jeanne at the Greek diner, he'd asked her for the ketchup and then apologized, noting that she had a broken arm and couldn't reach it. He asked if she was all right, what had happened? She'd deflected the question, though tears filled her eyes. They'd continued to talk.

Soon they were dating. The truth about the arm finally came out and one weekend Thompson paid a visit to her ex-husband. Later, Jeanne told him that a miracle had happened: Her ex had left town and wasn't even calling the girls anymore, which he'd done once a week, drunk, to rage at them about their mother.

A month later Thompson moved in with her and the children.

It was a good arrangement for Jeanne and her daughters, it seemed. Here was a man who didn't scream or take a belt to anyone, paid the rent and showed up when he said he would — why, they felt he was the greatest catch on earth. (Prison had taught Thompson a great deal about setting low bars.)

A good arrangement for them, and good for a professional killer too: Someone in his line of work who has a wife or girlfriend and children is far less suspicious than a single person.

But there was another reason he was with her, more important than simple logistics and convenience. Thompson Boyd was waiting. Something had been missing from his life for a long time and he was awaiting its return. He believed that someone like Jeanne Starke, a woman without excessive demands and with low expectations, could help him find it.

And what was this missing thing? Simple:

Thompson Boyd was waiting for the numbness to go away and for the feeling in his soul to return, the way your foot comes back to life after it's fallen asleep.

Thompson had many recollections of his childhood in Texas, images of his parents and his aunt Sandra, cousins, friends from school. Watching Texas A&M games on the tube, sitting around the Sears electric organ, Thompson pushing the button for the chords while his aunt or father played the melody as best they could with their pudgy fingers (they ran in the family line). Singing 'Onward Christian Soldiers' and 'Tie a Yellow Ribbon' and the theme from *The Green Berets*. Playing hearts. Learning how to use tools with his father in the perfectly neat work shed. Walking beside the big man in the desert, marveling at the sunsets, the lava beds, coyotes, the sidewinders, which moved like music but could still sting you to death in a flash.

He recalled his mother's life of church, packing sandwiches, sun-bathing, sweeping Texas dust out the trailer door and sitting in aluminum chairs with her girlfriends. He recalled his father's life of church, collecting LP records, spending Saturdays with his boy and weekdays wildcatting on the derricks. He recalled those wonderful Friday evenings, going to the Goldenlight Café on Route 66 for Harleyburgers and fries, Texas swing music pumping through the speakers.

Thompson Boyd wasn't numb then.

Even during that hard time after a June twister took their double-wide and his mother's right

278

arm, and nearly her life, even when his father lost his job in the layoffs that swept the Panhandle like an Okie dust storm, Thompson wasn't numb.

And he sure wasn't numb when he watched his mother gasp and stifle tears on the streets of Amarillo after some kid called her 'one-arm' and Thompson had followed and made sure the boy never made fun of anybody again.

But then came the prison years. And somewhere in those Lysol-stinking halls numbness crawled over feeling and put it to sleep. So deep asleep that he didn't even feel a blip when he got the word that a driver snoozing at the cab of a Peterbilt killed his parents and aunt simultaneously, the only thing that survived being the shoe-shine kit the boy had made his father for the man's fortieth birthday. So deep asleep that when, after he left prison and tracked down the guard Charlie Tucker, Thompson Boyd felt nothing as he watched the man die slowly, face purple from the noose, struggling desperately to grip the rope and hoist himself up to stop the strangulation. Which you just can't do, no matter how strong you are.

Numb, as he'd watched the pendulum of the guard's corpse, twisting slowly to stillness. Numb, as he'd set the candles on the ground at Tucker's feet to make the murder look like some psycho, satanic thing and glanced up into the man's glazed eyes.

Numb . . .

But Thompson believed he could repair himself, just like he fixed the bathroom door and the loose stair railing at the bungalow. (They were both tasks, the only difference being where you put the decimal point.) Jeanne and the girls would bring the feelings back. All he had to do was go through the motions. Do what other people did, normal people, people who weren't numb: Paint the children's rooms, watch *Judge Judy* with them, go on picnics in the park. Bring them what they'd asked for. Grape, cherry, milk. Grape, cherry, milk. Try an occasional cuss word, fuck, fuck, shit . . . Because that's what people said when they were angry. And angry people *felt* things.

This was also why he whistled — he believed music could transport him back to those earlier days, before prison. People who liked music weren't numb. People who whistled felt things, they had families, they'd turn the heads of strangers with a good trill. They were people you could stop on the street corner and talk to, people you could offer a french fry to, right off your Harleyburger plate, with giddy music pounding in the next room, ain't them musicians something, son? How 'bout that?

Do it by the book and the numbness would go away. The feeling would return.

Was it working, he wondered, the regimen he'd set up for himself to get the feeling back in his soul? The whistling, reciting the things he felt he should recite, grape and cherry, cussing, laughing? Maybe a little, he believed. He remembered watching the woman in white that morning, back and forth, back and forth. He could honestly say that he'd enjoyed watching her at work. A small pleasure, but it was a feeling nonetheless. Pretty good.

Wait: 'Pretty *fucking* good,' he whispered.

There, a cuss word.

Maybe he should try the sex thing again (usually once a month, in the morning, he could manage, but truth was he just didn't want to — if the *mood*'s not there, even Viagra won't do you much good). He now debated. Yes, that's what he'd do — give it a couple of days and try with Jeanne. The thought made him uneasy. But maybe he'd give it a shot. That'd be a good test. Yeah, he'd try it and see if he was getting better.

Grape, cherry, milk . . .

Thompson now stopped at a pay phone in front of a Greek deli. He dialed the voice-mail box number again and punched in the code. He listened to a new message, which told him that there'd nearly been a chance to kill Geneva Settle at the school but too many police had been guarding her. The message continued, giving her address, on 118th Street, and reporting that at least one unmarked police car and a squad car were parked nearby, changing positions occasionally. The number of officers guarding her seemed to vary from one to three.

Thompson memorized the address and erased the message then continued on his complicated walk to a six-story apartment building that was considerably more dilapidated than Jeanne's bungalow. He went around to the back and opened the door. He climbed the stairs to the apartment that was his main safe house. He stepped inside, locked the door then disarmed

281

the system he'd set up to stop intruders.

This place was a little nicer than the one on Elizabeth Street. It was covered in blond paneling carefully tacked up and featured brown shag carpet that smelled just like what brown shag would smell. There were a half dozen pieces of furniture. The place reminded Thompson of the rec room he and his father had built weekends in the Amarillo bungalow, which had replaced the tornado-shredded trailer.

From a large utility cabinet he carefully removed several jars and carried them to the desk, whistling the theme from *Pocahontas*. The girls had just loved that movie. He opened the toolbox, put on thick rubber gloves and a face mask and goggles and assembled the device that tomorrow would kill Geneva Settle — and anyone near her.

Wssst . . .

The tune became something else: no longer Disney. Bob Dylan's 'Forever Young.'

When he finished the device he examined it carefully and was satisfied. He put everything away and then walked into the bathroom, stripped off the gloves and washed his hands three times. The whistling faded as he began mentally reciting the mantra for today.

Grape, cherry and milk . . . Grape, cherry and milk.

He never stopped getting ready for the day when the numbness would go away.

★   ★   ★

'How you doing there, miss?'

'Okay, Detective.'

Mr. Bell stood in the doorway of her room and looked over her bed, which was covered with schoolbooks and papers.

'My, I must say you do work hard.'

Geneva shrugged.

'I'm going home to my boys now.'

'You have sons?'

'That I do. Two of 'em. Maybe you'll meet them someday. If you'd like.'

'Sure,' she said. Thinking: That'll never happen. 'Are they at home with your wife?'

'They're at their grandfolks right now. I was married but she passed on.'

These words flicked Geneva's heart. She could see pure pain behind them — in the way, oddly enough, that his expression didn't change as he spoke them. It was like he practiced saying this to people and not crying. 'I'm sorry.'

'Oh, that was some years ago.'

She nodded. 'Where's Officer Pulaski?'

'He's gone home. He's got a daughter. And his wife's expecting.'

'Boy or girl?' Geneva asked.

'I honestly couldn't tell you. He'll be back tomorrow early. We can ask him then. Your uncle's in the next room and Miss Lynch'll be staying here tonight.'

'Barbe?'

'Yes'm.'

'She's nice. She was telling me about some of the dogs she owns. And about some of the new TV shows.' Geneva nodded down at her books. 'I

283

don't have much time for TV.'

Detective Bell laughed. 'My boys could use a bit of your influence, miss. I will sure as rain get y'all together. Now, you shout out for Barbe, any reason you want.' He hesitated. 'Even you have a bad dream. I know it's tough sometimes, your parents not home.'

'I do fine being alone,' she said.

'I don't doubt it. Still, holler if you need to. That's what we're here for.' He walked to the window, peeked out through the curtains, made sure the window was locked and let the drapes fall back. ' 'Night, miss. Don't you worry. We'll catch ourselves this fellow. Only a matter of time. There's nobody better than Mr. Rhyme and the people he's got working with him.'

' 'Night.' Glad he was leaving. Maybe he meant well but Geneva hated to be treated like a child as much as she hated to be reminded of this terrible situation. She cleared her books off the bed and stacked them neatly by the door so that if she had to leave fast she could find them in the dark and take them with her. She did this every night.

She now reached into her purse and found the dried violet that that illusionist woman, Kara, had given her. She looked at it for a long moment then put it carefully into the book that was on the top of the stack and closed the cover.

A fast trip to the bathroom, where she cleaned the pearl-colored basin after washing up and brushing her teeth. She laughed to herself, thinking of the unholy mess that was Keesh's john. In the hallway Barbe Lynch said good night to her. Back in the bedroom, Geneva locked the door, then hesitated and, feeling foolish, propped the desk chair under the knob. She undressed and pulled on shorts and a faded T-shirt and got back into bed. She shut the light out and lay on her back, anxious and frenzied, for twenty minutes, thinking of her mother, then her father, then Keesh.

Kevin Cheaney's image made an entrance; she shoved it angrily away.

Then her thoughts ended up on her ancestor, Charles Singleton.

Running, running, running . . .

The leap into the Hudson.

Thinking of his secret. What was so important that he'd risk everything to keep it hidden?

Thinking of the love he had for his wife, his son.

But the terrible man from the library that morning kept barging into her mind. Oh, she talked big in front of the police. But of *course* she was scared. The ski mask, the *thonk* as the club hit the mannequin, the slap of his feet after her. And now the other one too, the black man at the school yard with the gun.

Those memories killed sleep quickly.

She opened her eyes and lay awake, restless, thinking of another sleepless night, years ago: Seven-year-old Geneva had crawled out of bed and wandered into the living room of their apartment. There she'd turned on the TV and watched some stupid sitcom for ten minutes before her father stepped into the living room.

'What're you doing there, watching that?'

He'd blinked at the light.

'I can't sleep.'

'Read a book. Better for you.'

'I don't feel like reading.'

'All right. I will.' He'd walked to the shelves. 'You'll like this one. One of the best books ever.'

As he sat in his armchair, which creaked and hissed under his weight, she glanced at the limp paperback but couldn't see the cover.

'You comfy?' he asked.

'Yeah.' She was lying on the couch.

'Close your eyes.'

'I'm not sleepy.'

'Close your eyes so you'll picture what I'm reading.'

'Okay. What's — ?'

'Hush.'

'Okay.'

He'd started the book, *To Kill a Mockingbird*. For the next week, his reading it out loud to her at bedtime became a ritual.

Geneva Settle decided it was one of the best books ever — and even at that age, she'd read, or heard, a lot of books. She loved the main characters — the calm, strong, widower father; the brother and sister (Geneva'd always wanted a sibling). And the story itself, about courage in the face of hatred and stupidity, was spellbinding.

The memory of the Harper Lee book stayed with her. And funny, when she went back and reread it at age eleven, she got a lot more of it. Then at fourteen she understood even more. She'd read it again last year and wrote a paper on it for English. She got an A-plus.

To Kill a Mockingbird was one of the books on the stack that sat beside the bedroom door at the moment, the in-case-of-fire-grab-this pile. It was a book that she tended to cart around in her book bag, even if she wasn't reading it. This was the book that she'd slipped Kara's good-luck-charm violet into.

Tonight, though, she picked another one from the stack. Charles Dickens. Oliver Twist. She lay back, rested the book on her chest and opened it to her flattened straw bookmark (she'd never turn down the pages in any book, even a paperback). She began to read. At first the creaks of the town house spooked her, and the image of the man in the mask came back, but soon she lost herself in the story. And not long after that, an hour or so, Geneva Settle's eyes grew heavy and she was finally lulled to sleep — not by a mother's good-night kiss, or a father's deep voice reciting a prayer, but by the litany of a stranger's beautiful words.

19

'Time for bed.'

'What?' Rhyme asked, looking up from his computer screen.

'Bed,' Thom repeated. He was a bit wary. Sometimes it was a battle to get Rhyme to stop working.

But the criminalist said, 'Yep. Bed.'

He was, in fact, exhausted — discouraged too. He was reading an email from Warden J. T. Beauchamp in Amarillo reporting that nobody in the prison recognized the computer composite of Unsub 109.

The criminalist dictated a brief thank-you and logged off. Then he said to Thom, 'Just one call, then I'll go willingly.'

'I'll straighten up some,' the aide said. 'Meet you upstairs.'

Amelia Sachs had gone back to her place to spend the night, and to see her mother, who lived near her and had been sick lately — some cardiac problems. Sachs spent the night with Rhyme more often than not, but she'd kept her apartment in Brooklyn, where she had other family members and friends. (Jennifer Robinson — the patrolwoman who'd delivered the teenagers to Rhyme's that morning — lived right up the street.) Besides, Sachs, like Rhyme, needed solitude from time to time, and this arrangement suited them both.

Rhyme called and talked briefly to her mother, wished her well. Sachs came on the line and he told her about the latest developments — few though they were.

'You okay?' Sachs asked him. 'You sound preoccupied.'

'Tired.'

'Ah.' She didn't believe him. 'Get some sleep.'

'You too. Sleep well.'

'Love you, Rhyme.'

'Love you.'

After he disconnected, he rolled toward the evidence chart.

He wasn't, however, gazing at Thom's precise entries about the case. He was looking at the printout of the tarot card, taped to a board, the twelfth card, The Hanged Man. He reread the block about the meaning of the card. He studied the man's placid, inverted face. Then he turned and wheeled to the small elevator that connected the laboratory on the first floor to the bedroom on the second, instructed the elevator to ascend and then wheeled out.

He reflected on the tarot card. Just like Kara, their illusionist friend, Rhyme didn't believe in spiritualism or the psychic. (They were both, in their own ways, scientists.) But he couldn't help but be struck by the fact that a card showing a scaffold just happened to be a piece of evidence in a case in which the word 'Gallows' figured prominently. The word 'Hanged' too was a curious coincidence. Criminalists must know about all methods of death, of course, and Rhyme understood exactly how hanging worked.

It snapped the neck high, just below the base of the skull. (The actual cause of death in execution-style hangings was suffocation, though not from squeezing the throat shut, but from cutting off the neuron messages to the lungs.) This is what had nearly happened to Rhyme at the subway crime scene accident some years ago.

Gallows Heights . . . The Hanged Man . . .

The meaning of the tarot card, though, was the most significant aspect of the happenstance: *Its appearance in a reading indicates spiritual searching leading to a decision, a transition, a change of direction. The card often foretells a surrendering to experience, ending a struggle, accepting what is. When this card appears in your reading you must listen to your inner self, even if that message seems to be contrary to logic.*

He was amused because he'd been doing plenty of seeking lately — before the Unsub 109 case and the appearance of the fortune-telling card. Lincoln Rhyme needed to make a decision.

A change of direction . . .

Now he didn't remain in the bedroom but instead drove to the room that was the epicenter of this churning debate: his therapy room, where he'd spent hundreds of hours hard at work on Dr. Sherman's exercise regimen.

Parking the wheelchair in the doorway, he studied the rehab equipment in the dim room — the ergometer bike, the treadmill. Then he glanced down at his right hand, strapped at the wrist to the padded arm of his red Storm Arrow wheelchair.

Decision . . .

Go on, he told himself.

Try it. Now. Move your hand.

Breathing hard. Eyes riveted to his right hand.

No . . .

His shoulders slumped, to the extent they could, and he looked into the room. Thinking of all the grueling exercise. Sure, the effort had improved his bone density and muscle mass and circulation, reducing infections and the chance of a neurovascular episode.

But the real question surrounding the exercise could be summed up in a two-word euphemism from the medical specialists: functional benefit. Rhyme's translation was less foggy: feeling and moving.

The very aspects of his recovery he'd dismissed when speaking to Sherman earlier today.

To put it frankly, he'd lied to the doctor. In his heart, not confessed to anyone, was the burning need to know one thing: Had those tortured hours of exercise let him regain sensation and given him the ability to move muscles that had not moved in years? Could he now turn the knob on a Bausch & Lomb microscope to bring a fiber or hair into focus? Could he feel Amelia Sachs's palm against his?

As for the sensation, perhaps there had been some slight improvement. But a quadriplegic with a C4 level of injury floats in a sea of phantom pain and phony sensation, all ginned up by the brain to taunt and confuse. You feel flies crawling on skin where no flies have landed.

You feel no sensation whatsoever as you look down and realize that a spill of scalding coffee is burning off layers of your flesh. Rhyme believed, though, that he had a bit of improved sensation.

Ah, but about the big payoff — movement? This was the jewel in the crown of spinal-cord-injury recovery.

He looked down at his hand once again, his right hand, which he hadn't been able to move since the accident.

This question could be answered simply and definitively. No phantom-pain issues, no I-think-maybe-I-feel-something responses. It could be answered right now. Yes or no. He didn't need MRI scans or a dynamic resistance gauge or whatever contraption the doctors had in their little black bags. Right now he could simply send tiny impulses shooting to the muscle along the highway of neurons and then see what happened.

Would the messengers arrive and make the finger curl — which would be the equivalent of a world-record long jump? Or would they crash to a stop on a dead strand of nerve?

Rhyme believed he was a brave man, both physically and morally. In the days before the accident, there was nothing he wouldn't do for the job. Protecting a crime scene once, he and another officer had held off a crazed mob of forty people trying to loot the store where a shooting had taken place, when the cops could easily have dodged to safety. Another time, he'd run a scene fifty feet from a barricaded perp taking potshots at him, in order to find evidence

292

that might lead them to the location of a kidnapped girl. Then there was the time he'd put his entire career on the line by arresting a senior police officer who was contaminating a scene simply to grandstand for the press.

But now his courage failed him.

His eyes boring into the right hand, staring.

Yes, no . . .

If he tried to move his finger and wasn't able to, if he couldn't even claim one of Dr. Sherman's small victories in this exhausting battle he'd been fighting, he believed that it would be the end for him.

The dark thoughts would return, like a tide rolling higher and higher on the shore, and finally he'd call up a doctor once more — oh, but not Sherman. A very different doctor. The man from the Lethe Society, a euthanasia group. A few years ago when he'd tried to end his life he hadn't been as independent as he was now. There'd been fewer computers, no voice-activated ECU systems and phones. Ironically, now that his lifestyle was better, he was also more self-sufficient at killing himself. The doctor could help him rig some contraption to the ECU, and leave pills or a weapon nearby.

Of course, he had people in his life now, not like a few years ago. His suicide would be devastating to Sachs, yes, but death had always been an aspect of their love. With cop blood in her veins, she was often first through the door in a suspect takedown, even though she didn't need to be. She'd been decorated for her courage in firefights, and she drove like hot lightning

— some would even say she herself had a suicidal streak within her.

In Rhyme's case, when they'd met — on a hard, hard case, a crucible of violence and death some years ago — he'd been very close to killing himself. Sachs understood this about him.

Thom too accepted it. (Rhyme had told the aide at the first interview, 'I might not be around too much longer. Be sure to cash your paycheck as soon as you get it.')

Still, he hated the thought of what his death would do to them, and the other people he knew. Not to mention the fact that crimes would go unsolved, victims would die, if he wasn't on earth to practice the craft that was the essential part of his soul.

This was why he'd been putting off the test. If he'd had no improvement it could be enough to push him over the edge.

Yes . . .

The card often foretells a surrendering to experience, ending a struggle, accepting what is.

. . . or no?

When this card appears in your reading you must listen to your inner self.

And it was at this moment that Lincoln Rhyme made his decision: He would give up. He'd stop the exercises, would stop considering the spinal cord operation.

After all, if you don't have hope, then hope can't be destroyed. He'd made a good life for himself. His existence wasn't perfect but it was tolerable. Lincoln Rhyme would accept his course, and he'd be content to be what Charles

Singleton had rejected: a partial man, a three-fifths man.

Content, more or less.

Using his left ring finger, Rhyme turned his wheelchair around and drove back toward the bedroom just in time to meet Thom at the doorway,

'You ready for bed?' the aide asked.

'As a matter of fact,' Rhyme said cheerfully, 'I am.'

III

GALLOWS HEIGHTS

Wednesday, October 10

20

At 8 A.M. Thompson Boyd retrieved his car from the alley garage near the bungalow in Astoria where he'd parked it yesterday after escaping from the Elizabeth Street safe house. He pulled the blue Buick into congested traffic, headed for the Queensborough Bridge and, once in Manhattan, made his way Uptown.

Recalling the address from the message on the voice mail, he drove into western Harlem and parked two blocks away from the Settles' town house. He was armed with his .22 North American Arms pistol and his club and carting the shopping bag, which contained no decorating books today; inside was the device he'd made last night and he treated it very gingerly as he moved slowly down the sidewalk. He looked up and down the street casually several times, seeing people presumably headed for work, an equal mix of blacks and whites, many in business suits, on their way to work, and students heading to Columbia — bikes, backpacks, beards . . . But he saw nothing threatening.

Thompson Boyd paused by the curb and studied the building the girl lived in.

There was a Crown Vic, parked several doors away from the apartment — smart of them not to flag it. Around the corner was a second unmarked car near a hydrant. Thompson thought he saw some motion on the apartment roof. Sniper? he wondered. Maybe not, but somebody was definitely there, undoubtedly a cop. They were taking this case real serious.

Average Joe turned around and walked back to his average car, climbed in and started the engine. He'd have to be patient. It was too risky for an attempt here; he'd have to wait for the right opportunity. Harry Chapin's 'Cat's in the Cradle' started to play on the radio. He shut it off but continued to whistle the tune to himself, never missing a single note, never a fraction of a tone off pitch.

★ ★ ★

Her great-aunt had found something.

In Geneva's apartment Roland Bell got a call from Lincoln Rhyme, who reported that Geneva's father's aunt, Lilly Hall, had found some boxes of old letters and souvenirs and artifacts in the storage space of the building where she was staying. She didn't know if there was anything helpful — her eyes were hopeless — but the cartons were chockablock with papers. Did Geneva and the police want to look through them?

Rhyme had wanted to have everything picked up but the aunt said, no, she'd only give it to her great-niece in person. She didn't trust anyone else.

'Police included?' Bell had asked Rhyme, who'd answered, 'Police especially.'

Amelia Sachs had then broken into the conversation to offer what Bell realized was the

300

real explanation: 'I think she wants to see her niece.'

'Ah, yes'm. Got it.'

Not surprisingly Geneva was more than eager to go. Roland Bell truly preferred guarding nervous people, people who didn't want to set foot on the concrete of New York City sidewalks, who liked to curl up with computer games and long books. Put them in an interior room, no windows, no visitors, no roof access and order out Chinese or pizza every day.

But Geneva Settle was unlike anybody he'd ever guarded.

Mr. Goades, please . . . I was a witness to a crime, and I'm being held by the police. It's against my will and —

The detective arranged for two cars for security. There'd be Bell, Geneva and Pulaski in his Crown Vic. Luis Martinez and Barbe Lynch would be in their Chevy. A uniformed officer in another blue-and-white would remain parked near the Settles' apartment while they were gone.

As he waited for the second squad car to show up, Bell asked if there'd been any more word from her parents. She said that they were at Heathrow now, awaiting the next flight.

Bell, a father of two boys, had some opinions about parents who left their daughter in the care of an uncle while they traipsed off to Europe. (This uncle in particular. No lunch money for the girl? That was a tough row.) Even though Bell was a single father with a demanding job, he still made his boys breakfast in the morning, packed them lunch and made supper most nights, however lame and starchy the meals might be ('Atkins' was not a word to be found in the Roland Bell encyclopedia of cuisine).

But his job was to keep Geneva Settle alive, not comment on parents who weren't much skilled at child-rearing. He now put aside thoughts of personal matters and stepped outside, hand near his Beretta, scanning the façades and windows and rooftops of nearby buildings and cars, looking for anything out of the ordinary.

The relief squad car pulled up outside and parked, while Martinez and Lynch climbed into the Chevrolet, around the corner from Geneva's apartment.

Into his Handi-Talkie, Bell said, 'Clear. Bring her out.'

Pulaski appeared, hustling Geneva into the Crown Victoria. He jumped in beside her, and Bell took the driver's seat. In tandem, the two cars sped across town and eventually arrived at an old tenement east of Fifth Avenue, in *el barrio*.

The majority of this area was Puerto Rican and Dominican, but other Latin nationalities lived here too, those from Haiti, Bolivia, Ecuador, Jamaica, Central America — both black and nonblack. There were also pockets of new immigrants, legal and otherwise, from Senegal, Liberia and the Central African nations. Most of the hate crimes here weren't white versus Hispanic or black; they were American-born versus immigrant, of whatever race or nationality. The way of the world, Bell reflected sadly.

The detective now parked where Geneva indicated and he waited until the other officers climbed out of the squad car behind them and checked out the street. A thumbs-up from Luis Martinez and together they hustled Geneva inside.

The building was shabby, the lobby smelling of beer and sour meat. Geneva seemed embarrassed about the condition of the place. As at the school she again suggested the detective wait outside, but it was half-hearted, as if she expected his response, 'Prob'ly better I go with you.'

On the second floor she knocked and an elderly voice asked, 'Who there?'

'Geneva. I'm here to see Auntie Lilly.'

Two chains rattled and two deadbolts were undone. The door opened. A slight woman in a faded dress looked at Bell cautiously.

'Morning, Mrs. Watkins,' the girl said.

'Hi, honey. She's in the living room.' Another uncertain glance at the detective.

'This's a friend of mine.'

'He yo' friend?'

'That's right,' Geneva told her.

The woman's face suggested that she didn't approve of the girl spending time in the company of a man three times her age, even if he was a policeman.

'Roland Bell, ma'am.' He showed his ID.

'Lilly said there was something about the police,' she said uneasily. Bell continued to smile and said nothing more. The woman repeated, 'Well, she's in the living room.'

Geneva's great-aunt, a frail, elderly woman in a pink dress, was staring at the television through large, thick glasses. She looked over at the girl and her face broke into a smile. 'Geneva, darling. How are you? And who's this?'

'Roland Bell, ma'am. Pleased to meet you.'

'I'm Lilly Hall. You're the one interested in Charles?'

'That's right.'

'I wish I knew more. I told Geneva everything I know 'bout him. Got hisself that farm, then got arrested. That was all I heard. Didn't even know if he went to jail or not.'

'Looks like he did, Auntie. We don't know what happened after that. That's what we want to find out.'

On the stained floral wallpaper behind her were three photographs: Martin Luther King, Jr., John F. Kennedy and the famous picture of Jackie Kennedy in mourning with young John John and Caroline beside her.

'There's the boxes right there.' The woman nodded toward three large cartons of papers and dusty books and wooden and plastic objects. They sat in front of a coffee table whose leg had been broken and duct-taped together. Geneva stooped and looked through the largest box.

Lilly watched her. After a moment the woman said, 'I feel him sometime.'

'You . . . ?' Bell asked.

'Ou' kin, Charles. I feel him. Like the other haints.'

304

Haint . . . Bell knew the word from North Carolina. An old black term for ghost.

'He restless, I'm feeling,' the great-aunt said.

'I don't know about that,' her grandniece said with a smile.

No, Bell thought, Geneva hardly seemed like the sort who'd believe in ghosts or anything supernatural. The detective, though, wasn't so sure. He said, 'Well, maybe what we're doing here'll bring him some rest.'

'You know,' the woman said, pushing her thick glasses higher on her nose, 'you *that* interested in Charles, there some other relations of ou's round the country. You 'member yo' father's cousin in Madison? And his wife, Ruby? I could call him an' ask. Or Genna-Louise in Memphis. Or I *would*, only I don't have no phone of my own.' A glance at the old Princess model sitting on a TV table near the kitchen, her grim expression evidence of past disputes with the woman she was staying with. The great-aunt added, 'And phone cards, they be so expensive.'

'*We* could call, Auntie.'

'Oh, I wouldn't mind talking to some of 'em. Been a while. Miss having family around.'

Bell dug into his jeans pocket. 'Ma'am, since this is something Geneva and I're working on together, let me get you a phone card.'

'No.' This was from Geneva. 'I'll do it.'

'You don't — '

'I've got it,' she said firmly, and Bell put the money away. She gave the woman a twenty.

The great-aunt looked reverently at the bill, said, 'I'ma get me that card and call today.'

305

Geneva said, 'If you find out anything, call us again at that number you called before.'

'Why's the police all interested in Charles? Man musta died a hundred years ago, at least.'

Geneva caught Bell's eye and shook her head; the woman hadn't heard that Geneva was in danger, and the niece wanted to keep it that way. Through her Coke-bottle lenses the woman didn't catch the look. Geneva said, 'They're helping me prove he didn't commit that crime he was accused of.'

'Are they now? After all them years?'

Bell wasn't sure the woman exactly believed her niece. The detective's own aunt, about this woman's age, was sharp as a needle. Nothing got by her.

But Lilly said, 'Be right nice of y'all. Bella, let's make these folk some coffee. And cocoa for Geneva. I remember that's what she likes.'

As Roland Bell looked out carefully through a space between the drawn curtains, Geneva started through the box once again.

★   ★   ★

On this Harlem street:

Two boys tried to outdo each other at skateboarding down the tall banister of a brownstone, flaunting the laws both of gravity and of truancy.

A black woman stood on a porch, watering some spectacular red geraniums that the recent frost hadn't killed.

A squirrel buried, or dug up, something in the

306

largest plot of dirt nearby: a five-by-four-foot rectangle dusted with yellow grass, in the middle of which rested the carcass of a washing machine.

And on East 123rd Street, near the Iglesia Adventista Church, with the soaring approach to the Triborough Bridge in the background, three police officers looked diligently out over a shabby brownstone and the surrounding streets. Two — a man and a woman — were in plain clothes; the cop in the alley was in uniform. He marched up and down the alley like a recruit on guard duty.

These observations were made by Thompson Boyd, who'd followed Geneva Settle and her guards here and was now standing in a boarded-up building across the street and several doors west. He peered through the cracks in a defaced billboard advertising home equity loans.

Curious that they'd brought the girl out into the open. Not by the book. But that was their problem.

Thompson considered the logistics: He assumed this was a short trip — a hit-and-run, so to speak, with the Crown Victoria and the other car double-parked and no attempt made to hide them. He decided to move fast to take advantage of the situation. Hurrying out of the ruined building, via the back door, Thompson now circled the block, pausing only long enough to buy a pack of cigarettes in a bodega. Easing into the alley behind the tenement where Geneva now was, Thompson peered out. He carefully set the shopping bag on the asphalt and moved forward a few more feet. Hiding behind a pile of garbage bags, he watched the blond officer on his patrol in the alley. The killer began counting the young man's footsteps. *One, two* . . .

At *thirteen* the officer reached the back of the building and turned around. He was covering a lot of ground in his guard detail; he must've been told to watch the entire alleyway, both front and back, and to keep an eye on the windows in the opposite building too.

At *twelve* he reached the front sidewalk and turned, started back. *One, two, three* . . .

It took twelve steps again to get to the rear of the building. He glanced around then paced his way to the front, stepping thirteen times.

The next trip was eleven steps, then twelve.

Not clockwork, but close enough. Thompson Boyd would have at least eleven steps to slip unseen to the rear of the building, while the boy's back was turned. He'd then have another eleven until he appeared at the rear again. He pulled the ski mask over his head.

The officer now turned and headed toward the street once more.

In an instant Thompson was out of cover and sprinting to the back of the apartment building, counting . . . *three, four, five, six* . . .

Quiet on his Bass walking shoes, Thompson kept his eyes on the boy's back. The cop didn't look around. The killer reached the wall on *eight*, pressed against it, catching his breath; he turned toward the alleyway where the uniformed cop would soon be appearing.

Eleven. The cop would have just reached the street and be turning and starting back. *One, two, three . . .*

Thompson Boyd, slowing his breathing.

Six, seven . . .

Thompson Boyd, gripping the club in both hands.

Nine, ten, eleven . . .

Feet scraped on the gritty cobblestones.

Thompson stepped quickly out of the alley, swinging the club like a baseball bat, fast as a sidewinder striking. He noted the pure shock on the boy's face. He heard the whistling of the stick and the cop's gasp, which stopped at the same moment the club struck his forehead. The boy dropped to his knees, a gurgling sound coming from his throat. The killer then clocked the man on the crown of the head.

The officer fell face forward to the filthy ground. Thompson dragged the quivering young man, still partly conscious, around the back of the building, where they couldn't be seen from the street.

★   ★   ★

At the sound of the gunshot, Roland Bell leapt to the window of the apartment, looked out carefully. He unbuttoned his jacket and grabbed his radio.

He ignored Aunt Lilly's wide-eyed friend, who said, 'Lord, what's going on?'

The great-aunt herself stared silently at the huge gun on the detective's hip.

309

'Bell,' the detective said into the microphone. 'What've we got?'

Luis Martinez replied breathlessly, 'Gunshot. Came from the back of the building, boss. Pulaski was there. Barbe's gone to check.'

'Pulaski,' Bell called into his radio. 'Respond.'

Nothing.

'Pulaski!'

'What's this about?' Lilly demanded, terrified. 'Lord.'

Bell held up a finger. Into his radio: 'Positions. Report.'

'I'm still on the front porch,' Martinez responded. 'Nothing from Barbe.'

'Move to the middle of the ground-floor corridor, keep your eye on the back door. That's the way I'd come in, I was him. But cover both entrances.'

'Roger.'

Bell turned to Geneva and the two elderly women. 'We're leaving. Now.'

'But — '

'Now, miss. I'll carry you if I have to but that'll put us more at risk.'

Barbe Lynch finally transmitted. 'Pulaski's down.' She called in a 10-13, officer needs assistance, and requested medics.

'Back entrance intact?' he asked.

Lynch answered, 'Door's closed and locked. That's all I can tell you.'

'Stay in position, cover the back alley. I'm taking her out.

'Let's go,' he said to the girl.

The defiance faded but she said, 'I'm not

310

leaving them.' Nodding toward the women.

'You tell me right now what's this about,' her great-aunt said, eyeing Bell angrily.

'It's a police matter. Somebody might be trying to hurt Geneva. I want you to leave. Is there a friend's apartment here you can stay in for a spell?'

'But — '

'Gonna have to insist here, ladies. Is there? Tell me quick.'

They glanced at each other with frightened eyes and nodded. 'Ann-Marie's, I guess,' the aunt said. 'Up the hall.'

Bell walked to the doorway and looked out. The empty corridor yawned at him.

'Okay, now. Go.'

The older women moved quickly down the hall. Bell saw them knock on a door. It opened and there were some hushed voices, then the face of an elderly black woman looked out. The women vanished inside, the door closed and the sound of chains and locks followed. The detective and the girl hurried down the stairs, with Bell pausing at every landing to make sure the lower level was cleared, his large, black automatic in hand.

Geneva said nothing. Her jaw was set; fury had blossomed inside her once again.

They paused in the lobby. The detective directed Geneva into the shadows behind him. He shouted, 'Luis?'

'This level's clear, boss, for now at least,' the cop called in a harsh whisper from halfway up the dim corridor that led to the back door.

Barbe's calm voice said, 'Pulaski's still alive. I found him holding his gun — he got off one round. That was the shot we heard. No sign he hit anything.'

'What's he say?'

'He's unconscious.'

So maybe the guy's rabbited, Bell thought.

Or maybe he planned something else. Was it safer to wait here for backup? That was the logical answer. The real issue, though: Was it the right answer to the question of what Unsub 109 had in mind?

Bell made a decision.

'Luis, I'm taking her out of here. Now. Need your help.'

'With you, boss.'

★   ★   ★

Thompson Boyd was once again in the burnt-out building across the street from the tenement Geneva Settle and the cops had gone into.

So far, his plan was working.

After beaning the cop, he'd ejected a shell from the man's Glock. This he'd rubber-banded to a lit cigarette — a fuse, in effect — and set the homemade firecracker in the alley. He'd placed the gun in the unconscious cop's hand.

He'd stripped off the mask, slipped through another alley, east of the building, into the street. When the cigarette burned down and detonated the bullet, and the two plainclothes cops disappeared, he'd run to the Crown Victoria. He had a slim jim to pop the door but hadn't needed it; the car had been unlocked. From the shopping bag he took several of the items he'd prepared last night, then assembled and hid them under the driver's seat and carefully closed the car door.

The improvised device was quite simple: a low, wide jar of sulfuric acid, in which rested a short glass candleholder. And sitting on top of that was a foil ball containing several tablespoons of finely ground cyanide powder. Any motion of the car would roll the ball into the acid, which would melt the foil and dissolve the poison. The lethal gas would spread upward and overcome the occupants before they had time to open a door or window. They'd be dead — or brain dead — soon after.

He peeked out through the crack between the billboard and what was left of the building's front wall. On the porch was the brown-haired detective who seemed to be in charge of the guard detail. Beside him was the male plainclothes cop and between them the girl.

The trio paused on the porch as the detective scanned the street, the rooftops, cars, alleys.

A gun was in his right hand. Keys in his other. They were going to make a run for the deadly car.

Perfect.

Thompson Boyd turned and left the building quickly. He had to put some distance between himself and this place. Other cops were already on their way; sirens were growing louder. As he slipped out of the back of the building he heard the detective's car start. The squeal of tires followed.

Breathe deep, he thought to the occupants of the car. He thought this for two reasons: First, of course, he wanted this hard job over with. But he also sent the message to them for another reason: Dying by cyanide can be extremely unpleasant. Wishing them a speedy, painless death was what a person with feeling would think, a person who was no longer numb.

Grape, cherry, milk . . .

Breathe deep.

* * *

Sensing the wild rattle of the engine — it shook her hands and legs and back — Amelia Sachs sped toward Spanish Harlem. She was doing sixty before she shifted into third gear.

She'd been at Rhyme's when they got the report: Pulaski was down, and the killer had managed to get some sort of device into Roland Bell's car. She'd run downstairs, fired up her red 1969 Camaro and hurried toward the scene of the attack in East Harlem.

Roaring through green lights, slowing to thirty or so at the reds — check left, check right, downshift, punch it!

Ten minutes later she skidded onto East 123rd Street, going against traffic, missing a delivery truck by inches. Ahead of her she could see the flashing lights of the ambulances and three squad cars from the local house. Also: a dozen uniforms and a handful of ESU troops, working

314

their way along the sidewalks. They moved cautiously, as if they were soldiers under fire.

Watch your backs . . .

She brought the Chevy to a tire-smoking stop and jumped out, glancing at the nearby alleyways and vacant windows for any sign of the killer and his needle gun. Jogging into the alley, flashing her shield, she could see medics working on Pulaski. He was on his back and they'd cleared an airway — at least he was alive. But there was a lot of blood and his face was hugely swollen. She'd hoped he'd be able to tell them something but he was unconscious.

It looked like the kid had been surprised by his attacker, who'd lain in wait as he'd walked down the alley. The rookie had been too close to the side of the building. There would've been no warning when the man attacked. You always walked down the center of sidewalks and alleys so nobody could jump out and surprise you.

You didn't know . . .

She wondered if he'd live to learn this lesson.

'How's he doing?'

The medic didn't look up. 'No guess. We're lucky he's still with us.' Then to his partner: 'Okay, let's move him out. Now.'

As they got Pulaski onto a backboard and hustled him toward the ambulance, Sachs cleared everybody away from the scene to preserve whatever evidence might be there. Then she returned to the mouth of the alley and dressed in the white Tyvek suit.

Just as she zipped it up a sergeant from the

local house walked up to her. 'You're Sachs, right?'

She nodded. 'Any sign of the perp?'

'Nothing. You going to run the scenes?'

'Yep.'

'You want to see Detective Bell's car?'

'Sure.'

She started forward.

'Wait,' the man said. He handed her a face mask.

'That bad?'

He pulled his own on. Through the thick rubber she heard his troubled voice say, 'Follow me.'

21

With ESU backing them up, two Bomb Squad Unit cops from the Sixth Precinct were crouched in the backseat of Roland Bell's Crown Victoria. They weren't wearing bomb suits but were in full biohazard outfits.

Wearing the thinner, white suit, Amelia Sachs stood back ten yards.

'What've you got, Sachs?' Rhyme called into the microphone. She jumped. Then turned the volume down. The line from her radio was plugged into the gas mask.

'I haven't gotten close yet; they're still removing the device. It's cyanide and acid.'

'Probably the sulfuric we found traces of on the desk,' he said.

Slowly, the team removed the glass-and-foil device. They sealed up the pieces in special hazardous materials containers.

Another transmission — from one of the Bomb Squad officers: 'Detective Sachs, we've rendered it safe. You can run the car, you want. But keep the mask on inside. There's no gas but the acid fumes could be dangerous.'

'Right. Thanks.' She started forward.

Rhyme's voice crackled again. 'Hold on a minute . . . ' He came back on. 'They're safe, Sachs. They're at the precinct.'

'Good.'

The 'they' were the intended victims of the

poison left in the Crown Victoria, Roland Bell and Geneva Settle. They'd come very close to dying. But, as they'd prepared to rush out of the great-aunt's apartment to the car, Bell had realized that something about the crime scene of Pulaski's assault seemed odd. Barbe Lynch had found the rookie holding his weapon. But this unsub was too smart to leave a gun in the hand of a downed cop, even if he was unconscious. No, he'd at least pitch it away, if he didn't want to take it with him. Bell had concluded that somehow the unsub himself had fired the shot and left the gun behind to make them think that the rookie had fired. The purpose? To draw the officers away from the front of the apartment.

And why? The answer was obvious: so that they'd leave the cars unguarded.

The Crown Vic had been unlocked, which meant the unsub might have slipped an explosive device inside. So he'd taken the keys to the locked Chevy that Martinez and Lynch had driven here and used that vehicle to speed Geneva out of danger, warning everyone to stay clear of the unmarked Ford until the Bomb Squad had a chance to go over it. Using fiberoptic cameras they searched under and inside the Crown Vic and found the device under the driver's seat.

Sachs now ran the scenes: the car, the approach to it and the alley where Pulaski had been attacked. She didn't find much other than prints of Bass walking shoes, which confirmed the attacker had been Unsub 109, and another device, a homemade one: a bullet from Pulaski's service automatic had been rubber-banded to a lit cigarette. The unsub had left it burning in the alley and snuck around toward the front of the building. When it went off, the 'gunshot' had drawn the officers to the back, giving him a chance to plant the device in Bell's car.

Damn, that's slick, she thought with dark admiration.

There was no sign that his partner, the black man in the combat jacket, had been — or still was — nearby.

Donning the mask again, she carefully examined the glass parts of the poison device itself, but they yielded no prints or other clues, which surprised nobody. Maybe the cyanide or acid would tell them something. Discouraged, she reported her results to Rhyme.

He asked, 'And what did you search?'

'Well, the car and the alleyway around Pulaski. And then the entrance and exit routes into and out of the alley, the street where he approached the Crown Vic — both directions.'

Silence for a moment, as Rhyme considered this.

She felt uneasy. Was she missing something? 'What're you thinking, Rhyme?'

'You searched by the book, Sachs. Those were the right places. But did you take in the totality of the scene?'

'Chapter Two of your book.'

'Good. At least *somebody*'s read it. But did you *do* what I say?'

Although time was always of the essence when searching a crime scene, one of the practices

Rhyme insisted on was taking a few moments to get a sense of the entire scene in light of the particular crime. The example he cited in his forensic science textbook was an actual murder in Greenwich Village. The primary crime scene was where the strangled victim was found, his apartment. The secondary was the fire escape by which the killer had gotten away. It was the *third* scene, though, an unlikely one, at which Rhyme had found the matches bearing the killer's fingerprints: a gay bar three blocks away. No one would've thought to search the bar, except that Rhyme found some gay porno tapes in the victim's apartment; a canvass of the nearest gay bar turned up a bartender who identified the victim and recalled him sharing a drink with a man earlier that night. The lab raised latents from the book of matches resting on the bar near where the two men had sat; the prints led them to the murderer.

'Let's keep thinking, Sachs. He sets up this plan — improvised but elaborate — to distract our people and get the device into a car. That meant he had to know where all the players were, what they were doing and how he could make enough time to set the device. Which tells us what?'

Sachs was already scanning the street. 'He was watching.'

'Yes, indeed, Sachs. Good. And where might he have been doing that from?'

'Across the street'd have the best visibility. But there're dozens of buildings he could've been in. I have no idea which one.'

320

'True. But Harlem's a neighborhood, right?'

'I . . .'

'Understand what I'm saying?'

'Not exactly.'

'Families, Sachs. Families live there, extended families living together, not yuppie singles. A home invasion wouldn't go unnoticed. Neither would somebody skulking about in lobbies or alleys. Good word, isn't that? Skulking. Says it all.'

'Your point, Rhyme?' His good mood had returned but she was irritated that he was more interested in the puzzle of the case than he was about, say, Pulaski's chances for recovery or that Roland Bell and Geneva Settle had nearly been killed.

'Not an apartment. Not a rooftop — Roland's people always look there. There'll be someplace *else* he was watching from, Sachs. Where do *you* think it might be?'

Scanning the street again . . . 'There's a billboard on an abandoned building. It's full of graffiti and handbills — real busy, you know, hard to spot anybody looking out from behind it. I'm going to see.'

Checking carefully for signs that the unsub was nearby, and finding none, she crossed the street and walked to the back of the old building — a burnt-out store, it seemed. Climbing through the back window, she saw that the floor was dusty — the perfect surface for footprints and, sure enough, she spotted Unsub 109's Bass walker shoes right away. Still, she slipped rubber bands around the booties of the Tyvek overalls

— a trick Rhyme invented to make certain that an officer exploring the crime scene didn't confuse his or her own prints with those of the suspect. The detective started into the room, her Glock in hand.

Following the unsub's prints to the front, she paused from time to time, listening for noises. Sachs heard a skitter or two but, no stranger to the sound track of seamier New York, she knew immediately that the intruder was a rat.

In the front she looked out through a gap in the plywood panels of the billboard where he'd stood and noticed that, yes, it provided a perfect view of the street. She collected some basic forensic equipment then returned and hit the walls with ultraviolet spray. Sachs turned the alternative light source wand on them.

But the only marks she found were latex glove prints.

She told Rhyme what she'd found and then said, 'I'll collect trace from where he stood but I don't see very much. He's just not leaving anything.'

'Too professional,' Rhyme said, sighing. 'Every time we outsmart him, he's already outsmarted us. Well, bring in what you've got, Sachs. We'll look it over.'

★　★　★

As they waited for Sachs to return, Rhyme and Sellitto made a decision: While they believed that Unsub 109 had fled the area around the apartment they still arranged to have Geneva's great-aunt, Lilly Hall, and her friend moved to a hotel room for the time being.

As for Pulaski, he was in intensive care, still unconscious from the beating The doctors couldn't say whether he'd live or not. In Rhyme's lab, Sellitto slammed his phone shut angrily after getting this news. 'He was a fucking rookie. I had no business recruiting him for Bell's team. I should've gone myself.'

A curious thing to say. 'Lon,' Rhyme said, 'you've got rank. You graduated from guard detail, when? Twenty years ago?'

But the big cop wouldn't be consoled. 'Put him in over his head. Stupid of me. Goddamn.'

Once again the hand rubbed at the hotspot on his cheek. The detective was edgy and looked particularly rumpled today. He usually wore pretty much what he wore now: light shirt and dark suit. Rhyme wondered, though, if these were the same clothes he'd had on yesterday. It seemed so. Yes, there was a dot of blood from the library shooting on the jacket sleeve — as if he were wearing the clothing as penance.

The doorbell rang.

Thom returned a moment later with a tall, lanky man. Pale skin, bad posture, unruly beard and brown, curly hair. He was dressed in a tan corduroy jacket and brown slacks. Birkenstocks.

His eyes scanned the laboratory then glanced at Rhyme and looked him over. Unsmiling, he asked, 'Is Geneva Settle here?'

'Who're you?' Sellitto asked.

'I'm Wesley Goades.'

Ah, the legal Terminator — who was not

323

fictional, Rhyme was somewhat surprised to find. Sellitto checked his ID and nodded.

The man's long fingers continually adjusted thick wire-rimmed glasses or tugged absently at his long beard and he never looked anyone in the eye for more than a half second. The constant ocular jitters reminded Rhyme of Geneva's friend, the gum-snapping Lakeesha Scott.

He offered a card to Thom, who showed it to Rhyme. Goades was director of the Central Harlem Legal Services Corporation and was affiliated with the American Civil Liberties Union. The fine print at the bottom said that he was licensed to practice law in New York state, the federal district courts in New York and Washington, D.C., and before the U.S. Supreme Court.

Maybe his days representing capitalist insurance companies had turned him to the other side.

In response to the querying glances from Rhyme and Sellitto, he said, 'I've been out of town. I got the message that Geneva called my office yesterday. Something about her being a witness. I just wanted to check on her.'

'She's fine,' Rhyme said. 'There've been some attempts on her life but we have a full-time guard on her.'

'She's being held here? Against her will?'

'Not *held*, no,' the criminalist said firmly. 'She's staying in her home.'

'With her parents?'

'An uncle.'

'What's this all about?' the unsmiling lawyer

324

asked, his eyes flitting from face to face, taking in the evidence boards, the equipment, the wires.

Rhyme was, as always, reluctant to discuss an active case with a stranger, but the lawyer might have some helpful information. 'We think somebody's worried about what Geneva's been researching for a project for school. About an ancestor of hers. Did she ever mention anything to you?'

'Oh, something about a former slave?'

'That's it.'

'That's how I met her. She walked into my office last week and asked if I knew where she could get records of old crimes in the city — back in the eighteen hundreds. I let her look through a few of the old books I have but it's almost impossible to find trial court records going back that far. I couldn't help her.' The skinny man raised an eyebrow. 'She wanted to pay me for my time. Most of my *clients* don't even do that.'

With another look around the town house, Goades seemed satisfied that the situation was what it seemed to be. 'Are you close to catching this guy?'

'We have some leads,' Rhyme said noncommittally.

'Well, tell her I came by, would you? And if there's anything she needs, anytime, have her call me.' He nodded at his card and then left.

Mel Cooper chuckled. 'A hundred bucks he's represented a spotted owl at one point or another in his career.'

'No takers on that one,' Rhyme muttered.

'And what'd we do to deserve all these distractions? Back to work. Let's *move*!'

Twenty minutes later Bell and Geneva arrived with a box of documents and other material from her great-aunt's apartment, which a patrolman had delivered to them at the precinct house.

Rhyme told her that Wesley Goades had come by.

'To check on me, right? I told you he was good. If I ever sue anybody I'm going to hire him.'

Lawyer of Mass Destruction . . .

Amelia Sachs walked inside with the evidence from the scene, nodding a greeting to Geneva and the others.

'Let's see what we've got,' Rhyme said eagerly.

The cigarette that Unsub 109 had used as a fuse for the distracting 'gunshot' was a Merit brand, common and untraceable. The cigarette had been lit but not smoked — or at least they could detect no teeth marks or saliva on the filter. This meant he was not a habitual smoker, most likely. No fingerprints on the cigarette, of course. Nor was there anything distinctive about the rubber band he'd affixed the cigarette to the bullet with. They found no manufacturer's markers in the cyanide. The acid could be purchased in many locations. The contraption that would mix the acid and poison in Bell's car was made of household objects: a glass jar, foil and a glass candleholder. Nothing had any markings or indications that could be traced to a particular location.

In the abandoned building where the killer had done his surveillance Sachs had found additional traces of the mysterious liquid she'd recovered from the Elizabeth Street safe house (and whose FBI analysis Rhyme was still impatiently awaiting). In addition she'd recovered a few tiny flakes of orange paint the shade of roadside signs or construction or demolition site warnings. Sachs was sure these were from the unsub because she'd located flakes in two different locations, right next to his footprints, and nowhere else in the abandoned store. Rhyme speculated that the unsub might have masqueraded as a highway, construction or utility worker. Or maybe this was his real job.

Meanwhile Sachs and Geneva had been searching through the box of family memorabilia from her aunt's house. It contained dozens of old books and magazines, papers, scraps, notes, recipes, souvenirs and postcards.

And, it turned out, a yellowed letter filled with Charles Singleton's distinctive handwriting. The lettering on this page was, however, far less elegant than in his other correspondence.

Understandable, given the circumstances.

Sachs read it out loud:

' 'July fifteenth, 1868.' '

'The day after the theft at the Freedmen's Trust,' Rhyme noted. 'Go on.'

' 'Violet — What madness this is! As near as I have been able to discern, these events are a plan to discredit me, to shame me in the eyes of my colleagues and of the honorable soldiers in the war for freedom.

327

''Today I learned where I might find justice, and this evening, I went to Potters' Field, armed with my Navy Colt. But my efforts ended in disaster, and the one hope for salvation now lies forever hidden beneath clay and soil.

''I will spend the night in hiding from the constables — who now search everywhere for me, — and in the morning, I will steal to New Jersey. You and our son must flee too; I fear they will try to visit their vengeance upon you, as well. Tomorrow at noon-time meet me at the John Stevens Pier in New Jersey. Together, we will repair to Pennsylvania, if your sister and her husband will agree to harbor us.

''There is a man who lives in the building above the stable where I am now hiding, who seems not unsympathetic to my plight. He has assured me he will get you this message.''

Sachs looked up. 'Something's crossed out here. I can't make it out. Then he goes on: 'It is dark now. I am hungry and tired, as tested as Job. And yet the source of my tears — the stains you see on this paper, my darling, — are not from pain but from regret for the misery I have visited upon us. All because of my d — ed secret! Had I shouted the truth from the top of City Hall, perhaps these sorrowful events would not have transpired. Now it is too late for the truth. Please forgive my selfishness, and the destruction wrought by my deceit.''

Sachs looked up. 'He signs it only 'Charles.''

The next morning, Rhyme recalled, came the pursuit and arrest described in the magazine Geneva had been reading when she was attacked.

'His one hope? 'Hidden beneath clay and soil.'' Rhyme looked over the letter again, Sachs holding it up for him. 'Nothing specific about the secret — And what happened in Potters' Field? That's the pauper's graveyard, isn't it?'

Cooper went online and browsed for a few moments. He reported that the city cemetery for indigents was located on Hart's Island, near the Bronx. The island had been a military base, and the graveyard had just opened on it shortly before Charles went there on his mysterious mission, armed with his Colt pistol.

'Military?' Rhyme asked, frowning. Something had clicked in his memory. 'Show me the other letters.'

Cooper produced them.

'Look, Charles's division was mustered there. Wonder if that's the connection. Anything else about the graveyard?'

Cooper read. 'No. There were only two or three hits.'

Rhyme scanned the white board. 'What the hell was Charles up to? Gallows Heights, Potters' Field, Frederick Douglass, civil rights leaders, congressmen, politicians, the Fourteenth Amendment . . . What ties them all together?' After a lengthy silence the criminalist said, 'Let's call in an expert.'

'Who's more expert that you, Lincoln?'

'I don't mean forensic science, Mel,' Rhyme said. 'I'm speaking of history. There are a few subjects I'm not proficient in.'

22

Professor Richard Taub Mathers was lean and tall, with skin dark as mahogany, sharp eyes and an intellect that suggested several post-graduate degrees were tucked into his résumé. He sported a throwback short Afro hairstyle and a self-effacing manner. He was dressed, well, professorially: tweed jacket and bow tie (missing only the de rigueur suede elbow patches).

He nodded to Rhyme, with a brief double-take at the wheelchair, and shook hands with the rest of those present.

Rhyme occasionally lectured at local colleges on forensic science, mostly at John Jay and Fordham; he rarely appeared at such lofty venues as Columbia, but a professor he knew at George Washington down in D.C. had put him in touch with Mathers, who was, it seemed, an institution unto himself in Morningside Heights. He was a professor in the law school — teaching criminal, constitutional and civil rights law as well as various esoteric graduate courses — and lectured in African-American studies in the undergrad program.

Mathers listened attentively as Rhyme related what they knew about Charles Singleton and the civil rights movement, his secret, how it was possible that he'd been framed for robbery. Then he told the professor what had happened to Geneva over the past two days.

The professor blinked in shock at this news. 'Tried to kill you?' he whispered.

Geneva said nothing. Holding his eye, she gave a faint nod.

Rhyme said to Sachs, 'Show him what we have so far. The letters.'

Mathers unbuttoned his jacket and pulled on thin, stylish glasses. He read Charles Singleton's correspondence carefully, unhurried. He nodded once or twice, gave one faint smile. When he was finished he looked over them again. 'Fascinating man. A freedman, farmer, served in the Thirty-first U.S. Colored Troops — and was at Appomattox.'

He read the letters yet again as Rhyme stifled the urge to tell him to hurry. Finally the man removed his glasses, polished the lenses carefully with a tissue and mused, 'So he was involved in the enactment of the Fourteenth Amendment?' The professor gave another smile. He was clearly intrigued. 'Well, this could be interesting. This could be something.'

Struggling to remain patient, Rhyme asked, 'Yes, and what would that be exactly? The 'interesting something'?'

'I'm speaking of the controversy, of course.'

Had he been able to, Rhyme might've grabbed the man's lapels and shouted for him to speed up. But he offered a casual frown. 'And what's the controversy?'

'A bit of history?' he asked.

Rhyme sighed. Sachs gave him a dark look and the criminalist said, 'Go right ahead.'

'The United States Constitution's the document that set up the American government

— the presidency, Congress and the Supreme Court. It still controls how we operate and supersedes every other law and regulation in the land.

'Now, in this country we've always wanted a balance: a government strong enough to protect us from foreign powers and to regulate our lives, but not so strong it becomes oppressive. When the nation's founders read over the Constitution after it was signed they were worried that it was too powerful — that it could lead to a repressive central government. So they revised it — they passed ten amendments, the Bill of Rights. The first eight are really the crucial ones. They list basic rights that protect citizens against abuse from the federal government. For instance: the FBI can't arrest you without probable cause. Congress can't take your house away from you to build an interstate highway without compensation. You get a fair trial with an impartial jury. You can't be subject to cruel and unusual punishments, and so on. But, did you note the key word?'

Rhyme thought he was actually testing them. But Mathers continued before anyone could speak. 'Federal. We're ruled by two different governments in America: the federal government in Washington and the government of the state we live in. The Bill of Rights only limits what the federal government can do to us: Congress and federal agencies, like the FBI or the DEA. The Bill of Rights gives us virtually no protection against human and civil rights violations by state governments. And state laws are the ones that

332

affect our lives much more directly than the federal government — most criminal police matters, public works, real estate, cars, domestic relations, wills, civil lawsuits are all state issues.

'Got that so far? The Constitution and Bill of Rights protect us from Washington only, not from abuse by New York or Oklahoma.'

Rhyme nodded.

The man eased his lanky frame onto a lab stool, glancing uncertainly at a petri dish containing green mold, and continued, 'Let's go back to the eighteen sixties. The pro-slavery South lost the Civil War so we enact the Thirteenth Amendment, which prohibits slavery. The country was reunified, involuntary servitude was outlawed . . . freedom and harmony would reign. Right?'

A cynical laugh. 'Wrong. Banning slavery wasn't enough. There was even more bad feeling toward blacks than before the war — even in the North — because so many young men had died on behalf of freeing them. State legislatures enacted hundreds of laws discriminating against blacks. They were barred from voting, from holding office, owning property, using public facilities, testifying in court . . . Life for most of them was nearly as bad as under slavery.

'But these were *state* laws, remember; the Bill of Rights couldn't stop them. So Congress decided the citizens needed protection from the state governments. They proposed the Fourteenth Amendment to remedy that.' Mathers glanced at a computer. 'You mind if I go on-line?'

'No, not at all,' Rhyme told him.

The professor typed in an Alta Vista search and a moment later had downloaded some text. He cut and pasted a passage into a separate window, which everyone in the room could see on the flat-screen monitors around the room.

No State shall make or enforce any law which shall abridge the privileges or immunities of citizens of the United States; nor shall any State deprive any person of life, liberty, or property, without due process of law; nor deny to any person within its jurisdiction the equal protection of the laws.

'This is part of section one of the Fourteenth,' he explained. 'It drastically limits what states can do to their citizens. Another part, which I didn't print out, gave states incentives to give blacks — well, black men — the right to vote. So, we're clear so far?' asked the educator.

'We're with you,' Sachs said.

'Now, the way an amendment to the Constitution works is that it has to be approved by Congress in Washington and then by three-fourths of the states themselves. Congress approved the Fourteenth in the spring of 1866, and it went to the states for ratification. Two years later it was finally ratified by the required number of states.' He shook his head. 'But ever since then there've been rumors that it was never properly enacted and ratified. That's the controversy I was referring to. A lot of people think it's invalid.'

Rhyme frowned. 'Really? What do they say is wrong with the enactment?'

'There were a number of arguments. Several states withdrew approval after they'd voted to ratify but Congress ignored the withdrawals. Some people say it wasn't properly presented or approved in Washington. There were also claims of vote fraud in the state legislatures, bribery and even threats.'

'Threats?' Sachs nodded at the letters. 'Like Charles said.'

Mathers explained: 'Political life was different then. That was an era when J. P. Morgan got together a private army to shoot it out with troops hired by his competitors Jay Gould and Jim Fisk in a railroad takeover. And the police and the government just sat back and watched it happen.

'And you must understand too that people were utterly passionate about the Fourteenth Amendment: Our country had nearly been destroyed, a half million people died — about as many as we've lost in all other wars combined. Without the Fourteenth Amendment, Congress could've ended up controlled by the South, and we might see the country split up again. Maybe even a second civil war.'

He waved his hand at the material in front of him. 'Your Mr. Singleton was apparently one of the men who went out to the states to lobby in favor of the amendment. What if he found proof that the amendment was invalid? That certainly could be the sort of secret that would torment him.'

'So maybe,' Rhyme speculated, 'a pro-amendment group set up the fake theft to discredit him. So if he *did* tell what he knew nobody'd believe him.'

'Not the great leaders back then, of course, not Frederick Douglass or Stevens or Sumner. But, yes, there were certainly plenty of politicians who'd want the amendment passed, and they'd do anything to make sure that happened.' The professor turned toward Geneva. 'And that would explain why this young lady's in danger.'

'Why?' Rhyme asked. He'd followed the history just fine but the broader implications were a bit elusive.

It was Thom who said, 'All you have to do is open a newspaper.'

'And what does *that* mean?' Rhyme snapped.

Mathers replied, 'He means that every day there're stories about how the Fourteenth Amendment affects our lives. You may not hear it mentioned specifically but it's still one of the most powerful weapons in our human rights arsenal. The language is very vague — what does 'due process' mean? Or 'equal protection'? 'Privileges and immunities'? The vagueness was intentional, of course, so Congress and the Supreme Court could create new protections to meet the circumstances of every generation.

'Out of those few words have come hundreds of laws about everything imaginable, much more than just racial discrimination. It's been used to invalidate discriminatory tax laws, to protect homeless people and underage laborers, to guarantee basic medical services for the poor. It's the basis for gay rights and for thousands of prisoners' rights cases every year. Maybe the most controversial was using the amendment to protect the right to abortions.

'Without it, states could decide that abortion doctors are capital murderers. And now, after September eleventh, in our Homeland Security frame of mind, it's the Fourteenth Amendment that stops the states from rounding up innocent Muslims and keeping them detained for as long as the police want.' His face was a mask of ill ease. 'If it's invalid, because of something your Charles Singleton learned, it could be the end of liberty as we know it.'

'But,' Sachs said, 'let's say he *did* find that out, and it *was* invalid. The amendment could simply be reratified, couldn't it?'

This time the professor's laugh was clearly cynical. 'Wouldn't happen. The one thing that all scholars agree on is that the Fourteenth was approved at the only window of time in our history when it could have been passed. No, if the Supreme Court invalidated the amendment, oh, we might reenact a few of the laws, but the main weapon for civil rights and civil liberties would be gone forever.'

'If that's the motive,' Rhyme asked, 'who'd be behind the attack on Geneva? Who should we be looking for?'

Mathers shook his head. 'Oh, the list's endless. Tens of thousands of people want to make sure the amendment stays in force. They'd be politically liberal or radical, a member of a minority group — racially or in sexual orientation — or in favor of social programs, medical services to the poor, abortion rights, gay rights, prisoners' rights, workers' rights . . . We think of extremists being the religious right — mothers who have their children lie down in abortion clinic driveways — or people who bomb federal buildings. But they don't have a monopoly on killing for their principles. Most European terrorism has been carried out by left-wing radicals.' He shook his head. 'I couldn't even begin to guess who was behind it.'

'We need to narrow it down somehow,' Sachs said.

Rhyme nodded slowly, thinking: The main focus of their case had to be catching Unsub 109 and hoping he'd tell them who'd hired him, or finding evidence that would lead to that person. But he instinctively sensed this was an important lead too. If there were no answers in the present as to who was behind the attempts on Geneva Settle's life, they'd have to look to the past. 'Whoever it is obviously knows something more about what happened in 1868 than we do. If we can find that out — about what Charles learned, what he was up to, his secret, about the robbery — it might point us somewhere. I want more information on that time period in New York, Gallows Heights, Potters' Field, everything we can find.' He frowned as a memory returned. He said to Cooper, 'When you looked up Gallows Heights the first time you found an article about that place near here, the Sanford Foundation.'

'Right.'

'You still have it?'

Mel Cooper saved everything. He called up the *Times* article on his computer. The text popped up on his screen. 'Got it here.'

Rhyme read the article and learned that the Sanford Foundation had an extensive archive on Upper West Side history. 'Call up the director of the place — William Ashberry. Tell him we need to go through his library.'

'Will do.' Cooper lifted a phone. He had a brief conversation, then hung up and reported, 'They're happy to help. Ashberry'll hook us up with a curator in the archives.'

'Somebody's got to go check it out,' Rhyme said, looking at Sachs with a raised eyebrow.

''Somebody'? I drew the short straw without drawing?'

Who else did she have in mind? Pulaski was in the hospital. Bell and his team were guarding Geneva. Cooper was a lab man. Sellitto was too senior to do grunt work like that. Rhyme chided, 'There are no small crime scenes, there are only small crime scene investigators.'

'Funny,' she said sourly. She pulled on her jacket, grabbed her purse.

'One thing,' Rhyme said, serious now.

She lifted an eyebrow.

'We know he'll target us.'

Police, he meant.

'Keep that orange paint in mind. Watch out for construction or highway workers . . . Well, with him, watch out for anybody.'

'Got it,' she said. Then took the address of the

foundation and left.

After she'd gone, Professor Mathers looked though the letters and other documents once more then handed them back to Cooper. He glanced at Geneva. 'When I was your age they didn't even have African-American studies in high school. What's the program like nowadays? Do you take two semesters?'

Geneva frowned. 'AAS? I'm not taking it.'

'Then what's your term paper for?'

'Language arts.'

'Ah. So you're taking black studies next year?'

A hesitation. 'I'm not taking it at all.'

'Really?'

Geneva obviously sensed some criticism in his question. 'It's pass/fail. All you have to do is show up. I don't want that kind of grade on my record.'

'It can't hurt.'

'What's the point?' she asked bluntly. 'We've heard it all over and over . . . *Amistad*, slavers, John Brown, the Jim Crow laws, *Brown versus the Board of Education*, Martin Luther King, Jr., Malcolm X . . . ' She fell silent.

With the detachment of a professional teacher, Mather asked, 'Just whining about the past?'

Geneva finally nodded. 'I guess that's how I see it, yeah. I mean, this is the twenty-first century. Time to move on. All those battles are over with.'

The professor smiled, then he glanced at Rhyme. 'Well, good luck. Let me know if I can help some more.'

'We'll do that.'

The lean man walked to the door. He paused and turned.

'Oh, Geneva?'

'Yes?'

'Just think about one thing — from somebody who's lived a few years longer than you. I sometimes wonder if the battles really aren't over with at all.' He nodded toward the evidence chart and Charles's letters. 'Maybe it's just harder to recognize the enemy.'

23

Guess what, Rhyme, there *are* small crime scenes.

I know it because I'm looking at one.

Amelia Sachs stood on West Eighty-second Street, just off Broadway, in front of the impressive Hiram Sanford Mansion, a large, dark Victorian structure. This was the home of the Sanford Foundation. Appropriately, around her were trappings of historical New York: In addition to the mansion, which was more than a hundred years old, there was an art museum that dated 1910 and a row of beautiful, landmark town houses. And she didn't need unsubs wearing orange-paint-stained overalls to feel spooked; right next door to the foundation was the ornate and eerie Sanford Hotel (rumor was that *Rosemary's Baby* was originally going to have been filmed in the Sanford).

A dozen gargoyles looked down at Sachs from its cornices as if they were mocking her present assignment.

Inside, she was directed to the man Mel Cooper had just spoken with, William Ashberry, the director of the foundation and a senior executive at Sanford Bank and Trust, which owned the nonprofit organization. The trim, middle-aged man greeted her with a look of bemused excitement. 'We've never had a policeman here, excuse me, police*woman*, I meant to say, well, never had *either* here actually.' He seemed disappointed when she gave a vague explanation that she merely needed some general background on the history of the neighborhood and didn't need to use the foundation for a stakeout or undercover operation.

Ashberry was more than happy to let her prowl through the archives and library, though he couldn't help her personally; his expertise was finance, real estate, and tax law, not history. 'I'm really a banker,' he confessed, as if Sachs couldn't tell this from his outfit of dark suit, white shirt and striped tie and the incomprehensible business documents and spreadsheets sitting in precise stacks on his desk.

Fifteen minutes later she was in the care of a curator — a young, tweedy man who led her down dark corridors into the sub-basement archives. She showed him the composite of Unsub 109, thinking maybe the killer had come here too, looking for the article about Charles Singleton. But the curator didn't recognize his picture and didn't recall anybody asking about any issues of *Coloreds' Weekly Illustrated* recently. He pointed out the stacks and a short time later she was sitting, edgy and frazzled, on a hard chair in a cubicle small as a coffin, surrounded by dozens of books and magazines, printouts, maps and drawings.

She approached this search the same way Rhyme had taught her to run a crime scene: looking over the whole first, then organizing a logical plan, then executing the search. Sachs first separated the material into four stacks: general information, West Side history and Gallows Heights, civil rights in the mid-1800s and Potters' Field. She started on the graveyard first. She read every page, confirmed Charles Singleton's reference to his regiment's being mustered at Hart's Island. She learned how the graveyard came into being, and how busy it had been, especially during the cholera and influenza epidemics of the mid- and late-nineteenth century, when cheap pine coffins would litter the island, stacked high, awaiting burial.

Fascinating details, but not helpful. She turned to the civil rights material. She read a mind-numbing amount of information, including references to the Fourteenth Amendment controversy but nothing that touched on the issues Professor Mathers had suggested to them as a motive for setting up Charles Singleton. She read in an 1867 *New York Times* article that Frederick Douglass and other prominent civil rights leaders of the time had appeared at a church in Gallows Heights. Douglass had told the reporter afterward that he had come to the neighborhood to meet with several men in the fight for the amendment's passage. But this they already knew, from Charles's letters. She found no mention of Charles Singleton but did come across a reference to a lengthy article in the *New York Sun* about the former slaves and freedmen who were assisting Douglass. That particular issue, though, was not in the archives.

Page after page, on and on . . . Hesitating sometimes, worrying that she'd missed those vital few sentences that could shed light on the case. More than once she went back and reread a paragraph or two that she'd looked at without really reading. Stretching, fidgeting, digging at her fingernails, scratching her scalp.

Then plowing into the documents once more. The material she'd read piled up on the table but the pad of paper in front of her held not a single notation.

Turning to New York history, Sachs learned more about Gallows Heights. It was one of a half-dozen early settlements on the Upper West Side of New York, separate villages really, like Manhattanville and Vandewater Heights (now Morningside). Gallows Heights extended west from present-day Broadway to the Hudson River and from about Seventy-second Street north to Eighty-sixth. The name dated from colonial times, when the Dutch built a gallows atop a hill in the center of the settlement. When the British purchased the land, their hangmen executed dozens of witches, criminals and rebellious slaves and colonists on the spot until the various sites of justice and punishment in New York City were consolidated downtown.

In 1811 city planners divided all of Manhattan into the blocks that are used today, though for the next fifty years in Gallows Heights (and much of the rest of the city) those grids could be found only on paper. In the early 1800s the land there was a tangle of country lanes, empty fields, forests, squatters' sheds, factories and dry docks on the Hudson River, and a few elegant, sprawling estates. By the mid-nineteenth century

345

Gallows Heights had developed a multiple personality, reflected in the map that Mel Cooper had found earlier: The big estates existed side by side with working-class apartments and smaller homes. Shantytowns infested with gangs were moving in from the south, on the tide of city sprawl. And — just as crooked as street thieves, though on a larger and slicker scale — William 'Boss' Tweed ran much of the corrupt Tammany Hall Democratic political machine from the bars and dining rooms in Gallows Heights (Tweed was obsessed with profiting from the development of the neighborhood; in a typical scheme the man pocketed $6,000 in fees for the sale to the city of a tiny lot worth less than $35).

The area was now a prime Upper West Side neighborhood and among the nicest and most affluent in the city, of course. Apartments were going for thousands of dollars a month. (And, as an irritated Amelia Sachs now reflected from her 'small crime scene' dungeon, the present-day Gallows Heights was home to some of the best delis and bagel bakeries in the city; she hadn't eaten today.)

The dense history reeled past her but nothing bore on the case. Damnit, she ought to be analyzing crime scene material, or better yet, working the streets around the unsub's safe house, trying to find some connections to where he lived, what his name was.

What the hell was Rhyme thinking of?

Finally she came to the last book in the stack. Five hundred pages, she estimated (she was getting a good eye by this point); it turned out to be 504. The index didn't reveal anything important for the search. Sachs skimmed the pages but finally could take it no longer. Tossing the book aside, she stood, rubbed her eyes and stretched. Her claustrophobia was kicking in, thanks to the suffocating ambiance of the archives, located two flights underground. The foundation may have been renovated last month but this place was still the original basement of the Sanford Mansion, she supposed; it had low ceilings and dozens of stone columns and walls, making the space even more confining.

That was bad enough but the worst was the sitting. Amelia Sachs hated to sit still.

When you move they can't getcha . . .

No small crime scenes, Rhyme? Brother . . .

She started to leave.

But at the door, she paused, looking back over the material, thinking: A few sentences in one of these musty books or yellowing newspapers could make the difference between life and death for Geneva Settle — and the other innocents that Unsub 109 might one day kill.

Rhyme's voice came back to her. *When you're walking the grid at the scene, you search it once and then again and when you're finished, you search it once more. And when you're done with that, you search it again. And* . . .

She glanced at the last book — the one that had defeated her. Sachs sighed, sat back down, pulled the 504-pager toward her and read through it properly and then flipped through the photographs in the middle.

Which, it turned out, was a good idea.

She froze, staring at a photograph of West Eightieth Street, taken in 1867. She gave a laugh, read the caption and the text on the opposite page. Then pulled her cell phone off her belt and hit speed-dial button 1.

★ ★ ★

'I found Potters' Field, Rhyme.'

'We *know* where it is,' he snapped into the microphone near his mouth. 'An island in the — '

'There's *another* one.'

'A second cemetery?'

'Not a cemetery. It was a tavern. In Gallows Heights.'

'A tavern?' Well, this was interesting, he thought.

'I'm looking at the photo, or daguerreotype, whatever it is. A bar named Potters' Field. It was on West Eightieth Street.'

So, they'd been wrong, Rhyme reflected. Charles Singleton's fateful meeting may not have been on Hart's Island at all.

'And, it gets better — the place burned down. Suspected arson. Perpetrators and motive unknown.'

'Am I right in supposing that it was the same day Charles Singleton went there to — what did he say? To find justice?'

'Yep. July fifteenth.'

Forever hidden beneath clay and soil . . .

'Anything else about him? Or the tavern?'

'Not yet.'

'Keep digging.'

'You bet, Rhyme.'

They disconnected the call.

Sachs had been on the speakerphone; Geneva had heard. She asked angrily, 'You think Charles burned that place down?'

'Not necessarily. But one of the major reasons for arson is to destroy evidence. Maybe that's what Charles was up to, covering up something about the robbery.'

Geneva said, 'Look at his letter . . . he's saying that the theft was set up to discredit him. Don't you think he's innocent by now?' The girl's voice was low and firm, her eyes bored into Rhyme's.

The criminalist returned her gaze. 'I do, yes.'

She nodded. Gave a faint smile at this acknowledgement. Then she looked at her battered Swatch. 'I should get home.'

Bell was concerned that the unsub had learned where Geneva lived. He'd arranged a safe house for her, but it wouldn't be available until tonight. For the time being, he and the protection team would simply have to remain particularly vigilant.

Geneva gathered up Charles's letters.

'We'll have to keep those for the time being,' Rhyme said.

'Keep them? Like, for evidence?'

'Just until we get to the bottom of what's going on.'

Geneva was looking at them hesitantly. There seemed to be a longing in her eye.

'We'll keep them in a safe place.'

'Okay.' She handed them to Mel Cooper.

He looked at her troubled expression. 'Would you like copies of his letters?'

She seemed embarrassed. 'Yeah, I would. Just . . . they're, you know, from family. That makes 'em kind of important.'

'No problem at all.' He made copies on the Xerox machine and handed them to her. She folded them carefully and they disappeared into her purse.

Bell took a call, listened for a moment and said, 'Great, get it over here as soon as you can. Much appreciated.' He gave Rhyme's address, then hung up. 'The school. They found the security tape of the school yard when the unsub's partner was there yesterday. They're sending it over.'

'Oh, my God,' Rhyme said sourly, 'you mean there's a real lead in the case? And it's not a hundred years old?'

Bell switched to the scrambled frequency and radioed Luis Martinez about their plans. He then radioed Barbe Lynch, the officer guarding the street in front of Geneva's house. She reported the street was clear and she'd be awaiting them.

Finally the North Carolinian hit the speaker-phone button on Rhyme's phone and called the girl's uncle to make sure he was home.

''Lo?' the man answered.

Bell identified himself.

'She's okay?' the uncle asked.

'She's fine. We're headed back now. Everything all right there?'

'Yes, sir, sure is.'

'Have you heard from her parents?'

'Her folk? Yeah, my brother call me from th' airport. Had some delay or 'nother. But they'll be leaving soon.'

Rhyme used to fly to London frequently to consult with Scotland Yard and other European police departments. Travel overseas had been no more complicated than flying to Chicago or California. Not so anymore. Welcome to the post-9/11 world of international travel, he thought. He was angry that it was taking so long for her mom and dad to get home. Geneva was probably the most mature child he'd ever met but she was a child nonetheless and should be with her parents.

Then Bell's radio crackled and Luis Martinez's staticky voice reported, 'I'm outside, boss. The car's in front, door open.'

Bell hung up the phone and turned to Geneva. 'Ready when you are, miss.'

★　★　★

'Here you be,' said Jon Earle Wilson to Thompson Boyd, who was sitting in a restaurant in downtown Manhattan, on Broad Street.

The skinny white guy with a mullet haircut and wearing beige jeans, none too clean, handed the shopping bag to Boyd, who glanced inside.

Wilson sat down in the booth across from him. Boyd continued to study the bag. Inside was a large UPS box. A smaller bag sat beside it. From Dunkin' Donuts, though the contents

351

most definitely were not pastries. Wilson used the chain shop's bags because they were slightly waxed and protected against moisture.

'Are we eating?' Wilson asked. He saw a salad go past. He was hungry. But although he often met Boyd in coffee shops or restaurants they'd never actually broken bread together. Wilson's favorite meal was pizza and soda, which he'd have by himself in his one-room apartment, chockablock with tools and wires and computer chips. Though he sort of felt, for all the work he did for Boyd, the man could stand him to a fucking sandwich or something.

But the killer said, 'I've got to leave in a minute or two.'

A plate of lamb shish kebab sat half eaten in front of the killer. Wilson wondered if he was going to offer it to him. Boyd didn't. He just smiled at the waitress when she came to collect it. Boyd smiling — that was new. Wilson'd never seen it before (though he had to admit it was a pretty fucking weird smile).

Wilson asked, 'Heavy, huh?' Glancing toward the bag. He had a proud look in his eyes.

'Is.'

'Think you'll like it.' He was proud of what he'd made and a little pissed that Boyd didn't respond.

Wilson then asked, 'So how's it going?'

'It's going.'

'Everything's cool?'

'Little set-back. That's why . . . ' He nodded toward the bag and said nothing else. Boyd gave a faint whistle, trying to match the notes of

352

ethnic music coming out of the speaker above them. The music was bizarro. Sitars or something from India or Pakistan or who knew where. But Boyd hit the notes pretty good. Killing people and whistling — the two things this man knew how to do.

The counter girl dropped a plate of dishes into the busboy pan with a huge crash. As the diners turned to look, Wilson felt something tap his leg under the booth. He touched the envelope, slipped it into his bell-bottoms pocket. It seemed surprisingly thin to be holding $5,000. But Wilson knew it was all there. One thing about Boyd: He paid what he owed, and he paid on time.

A moment passed. So, they weren't eating together. They were sitting and Boyd was drinking tea and Wilson was being hungry. Even though Boyd had to leave in a 'minute or two.'

What was this about?

Then he got the answer. Boyd glanced out the window and saw a battered, unmarked white van slow and turn into the alley that led to the back of the restaurant. Wilson got a glimpse of the driver, a small man with light brown skin and a beard.

Boyd's eyes watched it closely. When it disappeared into the alley he rose, hefting the shopping bag. He left money on the table for his bill and nodded to Wilson. Then he started toward the door. He stopped, turned back. 'Did I thank you?'

Wilson blinked. 'Did you — '

'Did I thank you?' A nod down to the bag.

353

'Well, no.' Thompson Boyd smiling *and* thanking people. Must be a fucking full moon.

'I appreciate it,' the killer said. 'Your hard work, I mean. Really.' The words came out as if he were a bad actor. Then, this was odd too, he winked a good-bye to the counter girl and walked out the door onto the bustling streets of the financial district, circling through the alley to the back of the restaurant, with the heavy bag at his side.

24

On 118th Street, Roland Bell eased his new Crown Victoria up in front of Geneva's building.

Barbe Lynch nodded from her guard station: the Chevy Malibu, which Bell had returned to them. He hustled Geneva inside and hurried up the stairs to the apartment, where her uncle gave her a big hug and shook Bell's hand again, thanking him for looking out for the girl. He said he was going to pick up a few things at the grocery store and stepped outside.

Geneva went on to her room. Bell glanced in and saw her sitting on the bed. She opened her book bag and rummaged through it.

'Anything I can do for you, miss? You hungry?'

'I'm pretty tired,' she said. 'I think I'll just do my homework now. Maybe take a nap.'

'Now that's a fine idea, after all you've been through.'

'How's Officer Pulaski?' she asked.

'I talked to his commander earlier. He's still unconscious. They don't know how he'll be. Wish I could tell you different, but there it is. I'm going to go stop by and check in on him later.'

She found a book and handed it to Bell. 'Could you give him this?'

The detective took it. 'I will, you bet . . . Don't know that, even if he wakes up, he'll be in any shape to read it, I oughta say.'

'We'll hope for the best. If he does wake up, maybe somebody could read it to him. Might help. Sometimes it does. Just hearing a story. Oh, and tell him or his family there's a good luck charm inside.'

'That's right kind of you.' Bell closed her door and walked to the living room to call his boys and tell them that he'd be home in a little while. He then checked with the other guards on his SWAT team, who reported that all was secure.

He settled down in the living room, hoping that Geneva's uncle was doing some serious grocery shopping. That poor niece of his surely needed some meat on her bones.

★   ★   ★

On his route to Geneva Settle's apartment, Alonzo 'Jax' Jackson slowly made his way down one of the narrow passages separating the brownstones in western Harlem.

He wasn't, however, at this particular moment Jax the limpin' ex-con, the blood-spraying Graffiti King of Harlem past. He was some unnamed, wack homeless dude in dusty jeans and a gray sweatshirt, pushing a perped grocery cart, which held five dollars' worth of newspapers, all wadded up. And a bunch of empties he'd racked from a recycling bin. He doubted that up close anybody would buy the role — he was a little too clean for your typical homeless guy — but there were only a few people he needed to fool: like the cops staying steady on Geneva Settle.

Out of one alleyway, across the street, into another. He was about three blocks from the back door of the apartment building that poor-ass Kevin Cheaney had pointed out.

Nice place, damn.

Feeling shitty again, thinking of his own plans for family gone bad.

Sir, I must talk to you. I am sorry. The baby . . . We could not save him.

Was a him?

I'm sorry, sir. We did what we could, I promise you but . . .

It was a him . . .

He pushed those thoughts away. Fighting a bum wheel on the cart, which kept veering to the left, talking to himself a bit, Jax moved slowly but with determination, thinking: Man, funny if I got nailed for jacking a shopping cart. But then he decided, no, it wouldn't be so funny at all. It'd be just like a cop to decide to roust him for something little like that and find the gun. Then run the ID and he'd get his ass violated back to Buffalo. Or someplace even worse.

Clatter, clatter — the littered passageway was hell on the broken wheel of the cart. He struggled to keep it straight. But he had to stick to this dark canyon. To approach a nice town house from the sidewalk, in this fancy part of Harlem, would flag him as suspicious. In the alley, though, pushing a cart wasn't that wack. Rich people throw their empties out more'n the poor. And as for the garbage, it was a better quality round here. Naturally a homeless dude'd rather scrounge in West Harlem than in Central.

How much farther?

Jax the homeless dude looked up and squinted. Two blocks to the girl's apartment.

Almost there. Almost done.

★　★　★

He felt an itch.

In Lincoln Rhyme's case this could be literal — he had sensation on his neck, shoulders and head, and, in fact, this was a nondisabled, sensate condition he could do without; for a quadriplegic, not being able to scratch an itch was the most fucking frustrating thing in the world.

But this was a figurative itch he was feeling.

Something wasn't right. What was it?

Thom asked him a question. He didn't pay attention.

'Lincoln?'

'I'm thinking. Can't you see?'

'No, that happens on the inside,' the aide retorted.

'Well, be quiet.'

What was the problem?

More scans of the evidence charts, the profile, the old letters and clippings, the curious expression on the inverted face of The Hanged Man . . . But somehow the itch didn't seem to have anything to do with the evidence.

In which case he supposed he should just ignore it.

Get back to —

Rhyme cocked his head. Almost grabbed the

thought. It jiggled away.

It was some anomaly, words someone had said recently that didn't quite mesh.

Then:

'Oh, goddamn it,' he snapped. 'The uncle!'

'What?' Mel Cooper asked.

'Jesus, Geneva's uncle.'

'What about him?'

'Geneva said he was her mother's brother.'

'And?'

'When we just talked to him, he said that he'd talked to *his* brother.'

'Well, he probably meant brother-in-law.'

'If you mean brother-in-law, that's what you say . . . Command, dial Bell.'

* * *

The phone rang and the detective answered on the first note of the cell phone tone that meant the call was from Lincoln Rhyme's town house.

'Bell here.'

'Roland, you're at Geneva's?'

'Right.'

'Your cell doesn't have a speaker, does it?'

'No. Go ahead.' The detective instinctively pulled his jacket aside and unsnapped the thong holding the larger of his two pistols. His voice was as steady as his hand, though his heart ratcheted up a few beats per second.

'Where's Geneva?'

'Her room.'

'Uncle?'

'Don't know. He just went to the store.'

'Listen. He flubbed the story about how he's related to her. He said he's her father's brother. She said he's her mother's.'

'Hell, he's a ringer.'

'Get to Geneva and stay with her until we figure it out. I'm sending another couple of RMPs over there.'

Bell walked fast to the girl's room. He knocked but got no response.

Heart pumping fast now, he drew his Beretta. 'Geneva!'

Nothing.

'Roland,' Rhyme called, 'what's going on?'

'Just a second,' the detective whispered.

In a combat shooting crouch, he pushed the door open and, lifting his weapon, stepped inside.

The room was empty. Geneva Settle was gone.

25

'Central, I have a ten twenty-nine, possible abduction.'

In his calm drawl Bell repeated the ominous message and gave his location. Then: 'Vic is a black female, age sixteen, five-two, one hundred pounds. Suspect is a black male, stocky, early to mid forties, short hair.'

'Roger. Units en route, K.'

Bell clipped his radio to his belt and sent Martinez and Lynch to search the apartment building itself while he hurried downstairs. The street in front of the building had been under surveillance by Lynch, while Martinez had been on the roof. But they'd been expecting Unsub 109 or his accomplice to be heading *toward* the building, not going away from it. Martinez thought he'd seen a girl and a man, who could have been the uncle, walking away from the apartment about three minutes ago. He hadn't paid attention.

Scanning the street, Bell saw no one but a few businesspeople. He jogged down the service alley beside the building. He noticed a homeless man pushing a grocery cart but he was two blocks away. Bell'd talk to him in a minute and find out if he'd seen the girl. Now, he opted for the other possible witnesses, some young girls playing double-Dutch jump rope.

'Hi.' The rope went slack as they looked up at the detective.

'Hey there. I'm a police officer. I'm looking for this teenage girl. She's black, thin, got short hair. She'd be with an older man.'

The sirens from the responding officers' cars filled the air, growing closer.

'You got a badge?' one girl asked.

Bell tamped down his anxiety, kept smiling and flashed his shield.

'Wow.'

'Yeah, we saw 'em,' one tiny, pretty girl offered. 'They went up that street there. Turned right.'

'No, left.'

'You weren't looking.'

'Was too. You gotta gun, mister?'

Bell jogged to the street they'd pointed to. A block away, to his right, he saw a car pulling away from the curb. He grabbed his radio. 'Units responding to that ten two nine. Anybody close to One One Seven Street . . . there's a maroon sedan moving west. Stop it and check occupants. Repeat: We're looking for a black female, sixteen. Suspect is black male, forties, K. Assume he's armed.'

'RPM Seven Seven Two. We're almost there, K . . . Yeah, we've got a visual. We'll light him up.'

'Roger, Seven Seven Two.'

Bell saw the squad car, its lights flashing, speed toward the maroon sedan, which skidded to a stop. His heart beating fast, Bell started toward them, as a patrolman climbed from the squad car, stepped to the sedan's window and

362

bent down, his hand on the butt of his pistol.

Please, let it be her.

The officer waved the car on.

Damn, Bell said to himself angrily as he jogged up to the officer.

'Detective.'

'Wasn't them?'

'No, sir. A black female. In her thirties. She's alone.'

Bell ordered the RMP to cruise up and down the nearby streets to the south, and radioed the others to cover the opposite directions. He turned and picked another street at random, plunged down it. His cell phone rang.

'Bell here.'

Lincoln Rhyme asked what was happening.

'Nobody's spotted her. But I don't get it, Lincoln. Wouldn't Geneva know her own uncle?'

'Oh, I can think of a few scenarios where the unsub could get a substitute in. Or maybe he's working *with* the unsub. I don't know. But something's definitely wrong. Think about how he speaks. Hardly sounds like the brother of a professor. He's got some street in him.'

'That's true . . . I want to check with my team. I'll call you back.' Bell hung up then radioed his partners. 'Luis, Barbe, report in. What'd y'all find?'

The woman said that the people she'd canvassed on 118th hadn't seen either the girl or the uncle. Martinez reported that they weren't in any of the common areas of the building and there'd been no sign of intruders or forced entry. He asked Bell, 'Where're you?'

'Block east of the building, heading east. I got RMPs sweeping the streets. One of y'all get over here with me. The other keep the apartment covered.'

'K.'

'Out.'

Bell jogged across a street and looked to his left. He saw the homeless man again, pausing, glancing toward him then bending down and scratching his ankle. Bell started in his direction to ask if he'd seen anything.

But then he heard the sound of a car door slamming shut. Where had it come from? The sound reverberated off the walls and he couldn't tell.

An engine began grinding.

In front of him . . . He started forward.

No, to the right.

He sprinted up the street. Just then he saw a battered gray Dodge pull away from the curb. It started forward but skidded to a stop as a patrol car cruised slowly into the intersection. The driver of the Dodge put the car into reverse and rolled backward over the curb, into a vacant lot, out of sight of the RMP. Bell believed he saw two people inside . . . He squinted. Yes! It was Geneva and the man who'd claimed to be her uncle. The car bucked slightly as he put it in gear.

Bell grabbed his radio and called the RMPs, ordering them to blockade both intersections.

But the patrolman at the wheel of the closest squad car turned into the street, rather than just barricading it; Geneva's uncle saw him. He slipped his car into reverse, flooring the accelerator and skidding in a circle around the vacant lot and into the alley behind a row of buildings. Bell lost sight of the Dodge. He didn't know which way it had turned. Sprinting toward where he'd last seen the car, the detective ordered the squad cars to circle the block.

He ran into the alley and looked to his right, just in time to see the rear fender of the car disappearing. He raced for it, pulling his Beretta from his holster. He sprinted at full speed and turned the corner.

Bell froze.

Tires squealing, the old Dodge was racing in reverse right toward him, escaping from the squad car that was blocking the man's escape route.

Bell stood his ground. He lifted the Beretta. He saw the uncle's panicked eyes, Geneva's horrified expression, her mouth open in a scream. But he couldn't fire. The squad car was directly behind the Dodge. Even if he hit the kidnapper, the jacketed rounds could go right through their target and the car and hit the officers.

Bell jumped aside, but the cobblestones were slick with garbage and he went down hard on his side, grunting. He lay directly in the path of the Dodge. The detective tried to pull himself to safety. But with the car going so fast he wasn't going to make it.

But . . . but what was happening?

The uncle was hitting the brakes. The car skidded to a stop five feet from Bell. The doors flew open and both Geneva and her uncle were out, running to him, the man shouting, 'You all right? You all right?'

'Detective Bell,' Geneva said, frowning, bending down and helping him up.

Wincing in pain, Bell trained the big gun on the uncle and said, 'Don't move a damn muscle.'

The man blinked and frowned.

'Lie down. And your arms — stretch 'em out.'

'Detective Bell — ' Geneva began.

'Just a minute, miss.'

The uncle did as he was told. Bell cuffed him, as the uniforms from the RMP trotted through the alley.

'Frisk him.'

'Yes, sir.'

The uncle said, 'Look, you don't know what you doin', sir.'

'Quiet,' Bell said to him and took Geneva aside, put her in a recessed doorway so she'd be out of the line of fire from anyone on rooftops nearby.

'Roland!' Barbe Lynch hurried down the alley.

Bell leaned against the brick wall, catching his breath. He glanced to the left, seeing the homeless guy he'd noticed earlier squint uneasily at the police and turn around, then head in the opposite direction. Bell ignored him.

'You didn't need to do that,' Geneva said to the detective, nodding at the cuffed man.

'But he's not your uncle,' the detective said, calming slowly, 'is he?'

'No.'

'What was he doing with you just now?'

She looked down, a sorrowful expression on her face.

'Geneva,' Bell said sternly, 'this's serious. Tell me what's going on.'

'I asked him to take me someplace.'

'Where?'

She lowered her head. 'To work,' she said. 'I couldn't afford to miss my shift.' She opened her jacket, revealing a McDonald's uniform. The cheery name tag read, *Hi, my name's Gen*.

26

'What's the story?' Lincoln Rhyme asked. He was concerned but, despite the fright at her disappearance, there was no accusation in his voice.

Geneva was sitting in a chair near his wheelchair, on the ground floor of the town house. Sachs stood beside her, arms crossed. She'd just arrived with a large stack of material she'd brought from the Sanford Foundation archives where she'd made the Potters' Field discovery. It sat on the table near Rhyme, ignored now that this new drama had intruded.

The girl looked defiantly into his eyes. 'I hired him to play my uncle.'

'And your parents?'

'I don't have any.'

'You don't — '

' — *have* any,' she repeated through clenched teeth.

'Go on,' Sachs said kindly.

She didn't speak for a moment. Finally: 'When I was ten, my father left us, my moms and me. He moved to Chicago with this woman and got married. Had himself a whole new family. I was torn up — oh, it hurt. But deep down I didn't really blame him much. Our life was a mess. My moms, she was hooked on crack, just couldn't get off it. They'd have these bad fights — well, *she* fought. Mostly he tried to straighten her out and she'd get mad at him. To pay for what she needed she'd perp stuff from stores.' Geneva held Rhyme's eyes as she added, 'And she'd go to girlfriends' places and they'd have some men over — you know what for. Dad knew all about it. I guess he put up with it for as long as he could then moved on.'

She took a deep breath and continued, 'Then moms got sick. She was HIV positive but didn't take any medicine. She died of an infection. I lived with her sister in the Bronx for a while but then she moved back to Alabama and left me at Auntie Lilly's apartment. But *she* didn't have any money either and kept getting evicted, moving in with friends, just like now. She couldn't afford to have me with her anyway. So I talked to the superintendent of the building where my moms had worked some, cleaning. He said I could stay in the basement — if I paid him. I have a cot down there, an old dresser, a microwave, a bookshelf. I put his apartment down as my address for mail.'

Bell said, 'You didn't seem real at home in that place. Whose was it?'

'This retired couple. They live here half the year and go to South Carolina for the fall and winter. Willy has an extra key.' She added, 'I'll pay them back for the electric bill and replace the beer and things that Willy took.'

'You don't have to worry about that.'

'Yes, I do,' she said firmly.

'Who'd I talk to before, if it wasn't your mother?' Bell asked.

'Sorry,' Geneva said, sighing. 'That was

369

Lakeesha. I asked her to front she was my moms. She's kind of an actress.'

'She had me fooled.' The detective grinned at being taken in so completely.

'And your own language?' Rhyme asked. 'You sure sound like a professor's daughter.'

She slipped into street talk. 'Don't be talkin' like no homegirl, you sayin'?' A grim laugh. 'I've worked on my Standard English ever since I was seven or eight.' Her face grew sad. 'The only good thing about my father — he always had me into books. He used to read to me some too.'

'We can find him and — '

'No!' Geneva said in a harsh voice. 'I don't want anything to do with him. Anyway, he's got his own kids now. He doesn't want anything to do with me.'

'And nobody found out you were homeless?' Sachs asked.

'Why would they? I never applied for welfare or food stamps so no social workers came to see me. I never even signed up for free meals at school 'cause it'd blow my cover. I forged my parents' names on the school papers when I needed their signatures. And I have a voice-mail box at a service. That was Keesh again. She recorded the outgoing message, pretending to be my mother.'

'And the school never suspected?'

'Sometimes they asked why I never had anybody at parent-teacher conferences, but nobody thought anything about it because I have straight A's. No welfare, good grades, no problems with the police . . . Nobody notices you if there's nothing wrong.' She laughed. 'You know the Ralph Ellison book, *Invisible Man*? No, not that science fiction movie. It's about being black in America, being invisible. Well, I'm the invisible girl.'

It made sense now: the shabby clothes and cheap watch, not at all what jet-setting parents would buy for their girl. The public school, not a private one. Her friend, the homegirl Keesh — not the sort who'd be close to the daughter of a college professor.

Rhyme nodded. 'We never *saw* you actually call your parents in England. But you *did* call the super yesterday, after what happened at the museum, right? Had him pretend to be your uncle?'

'He said he'd agree if I paid him extra, yeah. He wanted me to stay in his place — but *that* wouldn't be a good idea. You know what I'm saying? So I told him to use Two-B, with the Reynolds being away. I had him take their name off the mailbox.'

'Never thought that man seemed much like kin,' Bell said and Geneva responded with a scoffing laugh.

'When your parents never showed up, what were you going to say?'

'I didn't know.' Her voice broke and for an instant she looked hopelessly young and lost. Then she recovered. 'I've had to improvise the whole thing. When I went to get Charles's letters yesterday?' She glanced at Bell, who nodded. 'I snuck out the back door and went down to the basement. That's where they were.'

'You have *any* family here?' Sachs asked. 'Other than your aunt?'

'I don't have no — 'The flash of true horror in the girl's eyes was the first that Rhyme had seen. And its source was not a hired killer but the near slip into hated nonstandard grammar. She shook her head. 'I don't have anybody.'

'Why *don't* you go to Social Services?' Sellitto asked. 'That's what they're there for.'

Bell added, 'You more'n anybody're entitled to it.'

The girl frowned and her dark eyes turned darker. 'I don't take anything for free.' A shake of the head. 'Besides, a social worker'd come to check things out and see my situation. I'd get sent down to my aunt's in 'Bama. She lives in a town outside of Selma, three hundred people in it. You know what kind of education I'd get there? Or, I stay here, and end up in foster in Brooklyn, living in one room with four gangbanger girls, boxes playing hip-hop and BET on, twenty-four hours a day, dragged to church . . . ' She shivered and shook her head.

'That's why the job.' Rhyme glanced at the uniform.

'That's why the job. Somebody hooked me up with this guy makes fake driver's licenses. According to it, I'm eighteen.' A laugh. 'I don't look it, I know. But I applied to a place where the manager's an old white guy. He didn't have a clue how old I was from looking at me. Been at the same place ever since. Never missed a single shift. Until today.' A sigh. 'My boss'll find out. He'll have to fire me. Shit. And I just lost my other job last week.'

'You had *two* jobs?'

The girl nodded. 'Scrubbing graffiti. There's all this renovation going on in Harlem. You see it everywhere now. Some big insurance or real estate companies fix up old buildings and rent 'em for a lot of money. The crews hired some kids to clean the walls. It was great money. But I got fired.'

'Because you were underage?' Sachs asked.

'No, because I saw these workers, three big white guys who worked for some real estate company. They were hassling this old couple who'd lived in the building forever. I told 'em to stop or I'd call the police . . . ' She shrugged. 'They fired me. I did call the police but they weren't interested . . . So much for doing good deeds.'

'And that's why you didn't want that Mrs. Barton, the counselor, to help,' Bell said.

'She finds out I'm homeless, and, bang, my ass's in foster.' She shuddered. 'I was so close! I could've done it. A year and a half and I'd be gone. I'd be in Harvard or Vassar. Then that guy shows up at the museum yesterday and ruins everything!'

Geneva rose and walked to the chart that had the details about Charles Singleton on it. She gazed at it. 'That's why I was writing about him. I *had* to find out he was innocent. I wanted him to be nice and be a good husband and father. The letters were so wonderful. He could write so pretty, all his words. Even his handwriting was beautiful.' She added breathlessly, 'And he was a

373

hero in the Civil War and taught children and saved the orphans from the draft rioters. Suddenly I had a relative who was good, after all. Who was smart, who knew famous people. I wanted him to be somebody I could admire, not like my father or mother.'

Luis Martinez stuck his head in the doorway. 'He checks out. Right name and address, no priors, no warrants.' He'd run the name of the phony uncle. Rhyme and Bell weren't trusting *anybody* at this point.

'You must be lonely,' Sachs said.

A pause. 'My daddy took me to church some, 'fore he ran off. I remember this gospel song. It used to be our favorite. It's called 'Ain't Got Time to Die.' That's what my life's like. I ain't got time to be lonely.'

But Rhyme knew Geneva well by now. She was fronting. He said, 'So you've got a secret just like your ancestor. Who knows yours?'

'Keesh, the super, his wife. That's all.' She fixed Rhyme with a defiant look. 'You're going to turn me in, aren't you?'

'You can't live alone,' Sachs said.

'I have for two years,' she snapped. 'I have my books, school. I don't *need* anything else.'

'But — '

'No. If you tell, it'll ruin everything.' She added, 'Please.' The word was muted, as if saying it came very hard to her.

Silence for a moment. Sachs and Sellitto looked at Rhyme, the one person in the room who didn't have to answer to city brass and regulations. He said, 'No need to make any

374

decisions right away. We've got our hands full catching the unsub. But I'm thinking you ought to stay here, not a safe house.' He glanced at Thom. 'I think we can find room for you upstairs, can't we?'

'You bet we can.'

'I'd rather — ' the girl started.

Rhyme said with a smile, 'I think we'll insist this time.'

'But my job. I can't afford to lose it.'

'I'll take care of it.' Rhyme got the number from her and called the girl's boss at McDonald's and explained in general terms about the attack and said that Geneva wouldn't be coming in for a few days. The manager sounded truly concerned and told him that Geneva was their most conscientious employee. She could take as much time off as she needed and could be sure that her job would be waiting for her when she returned.

'She's the best employee we've got,' the man said over the speakerphone. 'A teenager who's more responsible than somebody twice that age. You don't see that very often.'

Rhyme and Geneva shared a smile and he disconnected the call.

It was then that the doorbell rang. Bell and Sachs immediately grew vigilant, their hands slipping toward their weapons. Sellitto, Rhyme noted, still looked spooked, and though he glanced down at his weapon, he didn't reach for it. His fingers remained on his cheek, rubbing gently, as if the gesture could conjure up a genie to calm his troubled heart.

Thom appeared in the doorway. He said to Bell, 'There's a Mrs. Barton here, from the school. She's brought a copy of some security video.'

The girl shook her head in dismay. 'No,' she whispered.

'Send her in,' Rhyme said.

A large African-American woman walked in, wearing a purple dress. Bell introduced her. She nodded to everyone and, like most of the counselors Rhyme himself had met, had no reaction to his disabled condition. She said, 'Hello, Geneva.'

The girl nodded. Her face was a still mask. Rhyme could tell she was thinking about the threat this woman represented to her: rural Alabama or a foster home.

Barton continued, 'How're you doing?'

'Okay, fine, thank you,' the girl said with a deference that wasn't typical of her.

'This's got to be tough on you,' the woman said.

'I've been better.' Geneva now tried a laugh. It sounded flat. She glanced at the woman once and then looked away.

Barton said, 'I spoke to maybe a dozen or so people about that man near the school yard yesterday. Only two or three remember seeing anybody. They couldn't describe him, except he was of color, wore a green combat jacket and old work shoes.'

'That's new,' Rhyme said. 'The shoes.' Thom wrote this on the board.

'And here's the tape from our security

department.' She handed a VHS cassette to Cooper, who played it.

Rhyme wheeled close to the screen and felt his neck straining with the tension as he studied the images.

It wasn't much help. The camera was aimed mostly at the school yard, not the surrounding sidewalks and streets. In the periphery it was possible to see some vague images of passersby, but nothing distinctive. Without much hope that they'd pick up anything, Rhyme ordered Cooper to send the cassette off to the lab in Queens to see if it could be digitally enhanced. The tech filled out the chain-of-custody card and packed it up, called for a pickup.

Bell thanked the woman for her help.

'Anything we can do.' She paused and looked the girl over. 'But I really do need to talk to your parents, Geneva.'

'My parents?'

She nodded slowly. 'I have to say — I've been talking to some of the students and teachers, and to be honest, most of them say your folks haven't been very involved in your classes. In fact, I haven't found anybody who's actually met them.'

'My grades're fine.'

'Oh, I know that. We're real happy with your academic work, Geneva. But school's about children and parents working together. I'd really like to talk to them. What's their cell number?'

The girl froze.

A dense silence.

Which Lincoln Rhyme finally broke. 'I'll tell you the truth.'

Geneva looked down. Her fists were clenched.

Rhyme said to Barton, 'I just got off the phone with her father.'

Everyone else in the room turned and stared at him.

'Are they back home?'

'No, and they won't be for a while.'

'No?'

'I asked them not to come.'

'You did? Why?' The woman frowned.

'It's my decision. I did it to keep Geneva safe. As Roland Bell here will tell you' — a glance at the Carolina detective, who nodded, a fairly credible gesture, considering he had no clue what was going on — 'when we set up protection details, sometimes we have to separate the people we're guarding from their families.'

'I didn't know that.'

'Otherwise,' Rhyme continued, vamping, 'the attacker could use their relatives to draw them into public.'

Barton nodded. 'Makes sense.'

'What's it called, Roland?' Rhyme glanced at the detective again. And filled in the answer himself, 'Isolation of Dependents, right?'

'IOD,' Bell said, nodding. 'What we call it. Very important technique.'

'Well, I'm glad to know that,' the counselor said. 'But your uncle'll be looking out for you, right?'

Sellitto said, 'No, we think it's probably best if Geneva stays here.'

'We're running an IOD with her uncle too,' Bell said. The fabrication sounded particularly slick coming from a law enforcer with a Southern drawl. 'Want to keep him out of sight.'

Barton bought it all, Rhyme could see. The counselor said to Geneva, 'Well, when this is over, please have them call me. Seems like you're handling it pretty well. But psychologically it has to be taking a toll. We'll all sit down together and work through some of the issues.' She added with a smile, 'There's nothing broke that can't be fixed.'

A sentence that was probably emblazoned on a desk plaque or coffee mug in her office.

'Okay,' Geneva said cautiously. 'We'll see.'

After the woman was gone, Geneva turned to Rhyme. 'I don't know what to say. It means so much to me, what you did.'

'Mostly,' he muttered, uneasy with the gratitude, 'it was for *our* convenience. I can't very well go calling up Child Welfare and tracking you down in foster homes every time we have a question about the case.'

Geneva laughed. 'Front all you want,' she said. 'Thanks anyway.' Then she huddled with Bell and told him what books, clothes and other items she needed from the basement on 118th Street. The detective said he'd also get back from the phony uncle whatever she'd paid him for the scam.

'He won't give it back,' she said. 'You don't know him.'

Bell smiled and said amiably, 'Oh, he'll give it back.' This, from the man with two guns.

Geneva called Lakeesha and told her girlfriend that she'd be staying at Rhyme's, then, hanging up, she followed Thom upstairs to the guest room.

Sellitto asked, 'What if the counselor finds out, Linc?'

'Finds out what?'

'Well, how 'bout that you lied about Geneva's parents and made up some department procedures? What the hell was it? The DUI?'

'IOD,' Bell reminded.

'And what's she going to do?' Rhyme growled. 'Make me stay after school?' He gave an abrupt nod at the evidence board. 'Now can we get back to work? There *is* a killer out there. And he's got a partner. *And* somebody hired them. Recall that? I'd like to figure out who the hell they are *sometime* this decade.'

Sachs walked to the table and began organizing the folders and copies of materials that William Ashberry had let her borrow from the foundation library — the 'small crime scene.' She said, 'This's mostly about Gallows Heights — maps, drawings, articles. Some things on Potters' Field.'

She handed the documents to Cooper one by one. He taped up several drawings and maps of Gallows Heights, which Rhyme stared at intently as Sachs told them what she'd learned about the neighborhood. She then walked to the drawing and touched a two-story commercial building. 'Potters' Field was right about here. West Eightieth Street.' She skimmed some of the documents. 'Seems like it was pretty disreputable, a lot of crooks hung out there, people like Jim Fisk and Boss Tweed and politicians

380

connected to the Tammany Hall machine.'

'See how valuable small crime scenes can be, Sachs? You're a *wealth* of helpful information.'

She gave him a minor scowl, then picked up a photocopy. 'This's an article about the fire. It says that the night Potters' Field burned down, witnesses heard an explosion in the basement and then, almost immediately, the place was engulfed. Arson was suspected but nobody was ever arrested. No fatalities.'

'What did Charles go there for?' Rhyme mused aloud. 'What did he mean by 'justice'? And what's 'forever hidden beneath clay and soil'?'

Was it a clue, a bit of evidence, a scrap of document that could answer the question of who wanted to murder Geneva Settle?

Sellitto shook his head. 'Too bad it was a hundred and forty years ago. Whatever, it's gone now. We'll never know.'

Rhyme looked at Sachs. She caught his eye. She smiled.

27

'Oh, you're lucky in one way,' explained David Yu, a spiky-haired young engineer who worked for the city.

'We could use some,' Amelia Sachs said. 'Luck, I mean.'

They were standing on West Eightieth Street, about a half block east of Riverside Park, looking up at a three-story brownstone. A crime scene bus waited nearby, as did another friend of Sachs's, a policewoman named Gail Davis, from the K9 unit, and her dog Vegas. Most police dogs were German shepherds, Malinois and — for bomb detail — Labrador retrievers. Vegas, though, was a briard, a French breed with a long history of military service; these dogs are known for having keen noses and an uncanny ability to sense threats to livestock and humans. Rhyme and Sachs had thought that running a 140-year-old crime scene might benefit from some old-fashioned search methods, in addition to the high-tech systems that would be employed.

The engineer, Yu, nodded at the building that had been constructed on the site where Potters' Field tavern had burned. The date on the cornerstone read 1879. 'To build a tenement like this back then they wouldn't have excavated and laid a slab. They'd dig a perimeter foundation, pour concrete and set the walls. That was the load-bearing part. The basement floor would have been dirt. But building codes changed. They would've put a concrete floor in sometime early in this century. Again, though, it wouldn't be structural. It'd be for health and safety. So the contractors wouldn't've excavated for that either.'

'So the lucky part is that whatever was under there in the eighteen sixties might still be there,' Sachs said.

Forever hidden . . .

'Right.'

'And the unlucky part is that it's under concrete.'

'Pretty much.'

'A foot deep?'

'Maybe less.'

Sachs walked around the building, which was grimy and plain, though she knew the apartments in it would rent for $4,000 or so a month. There was a service entrance in the back that led below ground to the basement.

She was returning to the front of the structure when the phone rang. 'Detective Sachs.'

Lon Sellitto was on the other end. He'd found the name of the building's owner, a businessman who lived several blocks way. The man was on his way to the place to let them inside. Rhyme came on the phone a moment later and she told him what Yu had said.

'Good luck, bad luck,' he said, the scowl clear. 'Well, I've ordered an S and S team there with SPR and ultrasound.'

Just then the owner of the building arrived, a

short, balding man in a suit and white shirt open at the collar. Sachs disconnected the cell call with Rhyme and explained briefly to the man that they needed to examine the basement. He looked her up and down suspiciously then opened the basement door and stood back, crossing his arms, near Vegas. The police dog didn't seem to like him very much.

A Chevy Blazer pulled up and three members of the NYPD Search and Surveillance Unit climbed out. S and S officers were a mixed breed of cop, engineer and scientist, whose job was to back up the tactical forces by locating perps and victims at scenes with telescopes, night vision imagers, infrared, microphones and other equipment. They nodded to the crime scene techs and then unloaded battered black suitcases, very much like the ones that held Sachs's own crime scene equipment. The owner watched them with a frown.

The S and S officers walked down into the dank, chill basement, smelling of mold and fuel oil, followed by Sachs and the owner. They hooked up probes that resembled vacuum cleaner heads to their computerized equipment,

'The whole area?' one asked Sachs.

'Yup.'

'That's not going to hurt anything, is it?' the owner asked.

'No, sir,' a tech replied.

They got to work. The men decided to use SPR first. Surface Penetrating Radar sent out radio waves and returned information on objects it struck, just like traditional radar on board a ship or airplane. The only difference was that SPR could go through objects like dirt and rubble. It was as fast as the speed of light and, unlike ultrasound, didn't have to be in contact with the surface to get a reading.

For an hour they scanned the floor, clicking computer buttons, making notations, while Sachs stood to the side, trying not to tap her foot or fidget impatiently, figuring that it wouldn't be good for the instrument's readings.

After they'd swept the floor with the radar, the team consulted the unit's computer screen and then, based on what they learned, walked around the floor again, touching the ultrasound sensor to the concrete in a half dozen areas they'd targeted as important.

When they were finished they called Sachs and Yu over to the computer, flipped through some images. The dark gray screen was unreadable to her: It was filled with blotches and streaks, many of which had small boxes of indecipherable numbers and letters beside them.

One of the techs said, 'Most of these are what you'd expect under a building this age. Boulders, a bed of gravel, pockets of decayed wood. That's a portion of a sewer here.' Pointing to part of the screen.

'There's an easement for a storm drain that feeds into the main drain going to the Hudson,' Yu said. 'That must be it.'

The owner leaned over his shoulder.

'You mind, sir?' Sachs grumbled. The man grudgingly stepped back.

The tech nodded. 'But here . . . ' He tapped a

spot next to the back wall. 'We got a ping but no hit.'

'A — ?'

'When something comes back that the computer's seen before, it suggests what it might be. But this was negative.'

Sachs saw only a less dark area on the dark screen.

'So we ran the ultrasound and got this.'

His partner typed in a command and a different screen appeared, one much lighter and with a clearer image on it: a rough ring, inside of which was a round, opaque object that seemed to have a strand of something coming off it. Filling the ring, in the space below the smaller object, was what appeared to be a pile of sticks or boards — maybe, Sachs speculated, a strongbox that had broken apart over the years.

One officer said, 'The outer ring's about twenty-four inches across. The inner one's three-dimensional — a sphere. It's eight, nine inches in diameter.'

'Is it close to the surface?'

'The slab's about seven inches deep, and this thing's about six to eight feet below that.'

'Where exactly?'

The man looked from the computer screen to the floor and back again. He walked over to a spot right beside the wall in the back of the basement, near the door that led outside. He drew a chalk mark. The object was right against the wall. Whoever had built the wall had missed it by only inches.

'I'm guessing it was a well or a cistern. Maybe a chimney.'

'What would it take to get through the concrete?' Sachs asked Yu.

'My permission,' said the owner. 'Which you ain't getting. You're not breaking up my floor.'

'Sir,' Sachs said patiently, 'this is police business.'

'Whatever that thing is, it's mine.'

'Ownership isn't the issue. It may be relevant to a police investigation.'

'Well, you'll have to get a court order. I'm a lawyer. You're not breaking up my floor.'

'It's really important we find out what that is.'

'Important?' the man asked. 'Why?'

'It has to do with a criminal case from a few years ago.'

'Few years?' the man said, picking up on the weakness of her case immediately. 'How 'few'?' He was probably a really good lawyer.

You lie to people like this and it comes back to get you. She said, 'A hundred and forty. Give or take.'

He laughed. 'This isn't an investigation. This is the Discovery Channel. No jackhammer. Uh-uh.'

'A little cooperation here, sir?'

'Get a court order. I don't have to cooperate until I'm forced to.'

'Then it's not really cooperation, is it?' Sachs snapped back. She called Rhyme.

'What's going on?' he asked.

She briefed him about what they'd found.

'An old strongbox in a well or cistern inside a burned-down building. Hiding places don't get

387

much better than that.' Rhyme asked for S and S to send him the images via wireless email. They did so.

'I've got the picture here, Sachs,' he said after a moment. 'No clue what it is.'

She told him about the unconcerned citizen.

'And I'll fight it,' the lawyer said, hearing the conversation. 'I'll appear before the magistrate myself. I know 'em all. We're on a first-name basis.'

She heard Rhyme discussing the matter with Sellitto. When he came back on the line he wasn't happy. 'Lon's going to try to get a warrant, but it'll take time. And he's not even sure the judge'd issue paper in a case like this.'

'Can't I just clock this guy?' she muttered and hung up. She turned to the owner. 'We'll repair your floor. Perfectly.'

'I have tenants. They'll complain. And *I'll* have to deal with it. You won't. You'll be long gone.'

Sachs waved her hand in disgust, actually thinking about placing him under arrest for — well, for something — and then digging through the damn floor anyway. How long would a warrant take? Probably forever, she imagined, considering that judges needed a 'compelling' interest in order to allow police to invade someone's home.

Her phone rang again and she answered.

'Sachs,' Rhyme asked, 'is that engineer fellow there?'

'David? Yeah. He's right next to me.'

'I have a question.'

'What?'
'Ask him who owns the alleys?'

★　★　★

The answer, in this particular instance, though not all, was: the city. The lawyer owned only the footprint of the building itself and what was inside.

Rhyme said, 'Have the engineers get some equipment next to the exterior wall and dig down then tunnel under his wall. Would that work?'

Out of hearing of the owner, she posed the question to Yu, who said, 'Yeah, we could do that. No risk of structural damage if you keep the hole narrow.'

Narrow, thought the claustrophobic police-woman. Just what I need . . . She hung up and then said to the engineer, 'Okay, I want a . . . ' Sachs frowned. 'What are those things called with the big scoop on them?' Her knowledge of vehicles whose top speed was ten miles an hour was severely limited.

'Backhoe?'

'Sounds right. How soon can you get one here?'

'A half hour.'

She gave him a pained look. 'Ten minutes?'

'I'll see what I can do.'

Twenty minutes later, with a loud reverse warning beep, a city backhoe rolled up to the side of the building. There was no way to hide their strategy anymore. The owner stepped forward, waving his hands. 'You're going underneath from outside! You can't do that either. I own this property from the heavens to the center of the earth. That's what the law says.'

'Well, sir,' said slim, young civil servant Yu. 'There's a public utility easement under the building. Which we have a right to access. As I'm sure you know.'

'But the fucking easement's on the other side of the property.'

'I don't think so.'

'It's on that screen right there.' He pointed to a computer — just as the screen went dark.

'Ooops,' said one of the S and S officers, who'd just shut it off. 'Damn thing's always breaking down.'

The owner scowled at him, then said to Yu, 'There is no easement where you're going to dig.'

Yu shrugged. 'Well, you know, when somebody disputes the location of an easement, the burden's on *him* to get a court order stopping us. You might want to give some of your magistrate friends a call. And you know what, sir? You better do it pretty fast, 'cause we're going in now.'

'But — '

'Go ahead!' he shouted.

'Is that true?' Sachs whispered to him. 'About the easements?'

'Don't know. But he seemed to buy it.'

'Thanks.'

The backhoe went to work. It didn't take long. Ten minutes later, guided by the S and S team, the backhoe had dug out a four-foot-wide, ten-foot-deep foxhole. The foundation of the building ended about six feet below the surface and beneath that was a wall of dark soil and gray clay. Sachs would have to climb to the bottom of the excavation and dig horizontally only about eighteen inches until she found the cistern or well. She donned the Tyvek suit and a hard hat with a light on the top. She called Rhyme back on her radio — not sure how cell phone reception would be in the pit. 'I'm ready,' she told him.

K9 officer Gail Davis walked over with Vegas, straining on the leash, pawing at the edge of the hole. 'Something's down there,' the police-woman said.

As if I'm not spooked enough, Sachs thought, looking at the dog's alert face.

'What's that noise, Sachs?'

'Gail's here. Her dog's got a problem with the site.'

'Anything specific?' Sachs asked Davis.

'Nope. Could be sensing anything.'

Vegas then growled and pawed Sachs's leg. Davis had told Sachs that another skill of briards was battlefield triage — they'd been used by corpsmen to determine which of the wounded could be saved and which could not. She wondered if Vegas was marking her for the latter ahead of time.

'Keep close,' Sachs said to Davis, with an uneasy laugh. 'In case I need digging out.'

Yu volunteered to go down into the pit (he said he liked tunnels and caves, a fact that astonished Amelia Sachs). But she said no. This was, after all, a crime scene, even if it was 140 years old, and the sphere and strongbox, whatever they might be, were evidence to be collected and preserved, according to CS procedure.

The city workers lowered a ladder into the shaft, which Sachs looked down into, sighing.

'You okay?' Yu asked.

'Fine,' she said cheerfully and started into the hole. Thinking: The claustrophobia in the Sanford Foundation's archives was nothing compared to this. At the bottom she took the shovel and pickax Yu had given her and began the excavation.

Sweating from the effort, shivering from the waves of panic, she dug and dug, picturing with every scoop the foxhole collapsing and trapping her.

Pulling out rocks, dislodging the dense earth.

Forever hidden beneath clay and soil . . .

'What's in view, Sachs?' Rhyme asked through the radio.

'Dirt, sand, worms, a few tin cans, rocks.'

She progressed about one foot under the building, then two.

Her spade gave a *tink* and stopped cold. She scraped away soil and found herself facing a rounded brick wall, very old, the mortar clumsily smeared between the bricks.

'Got something here. The side of the cistern.'

Dirt from the edges of the foxhole skittered to the floor. It scared her more than if a rat had traipsed across her thigh. A fast image came to mind: being held immobile while dirt flooded around her, crushing her chest, then filling her nose and mouth. Drowning on dirt . . .

Okay, girl, relax. Sachs took several deep breaths. Scraped away more soil. Another gallon or so of it spilled out on her knees. 'Should we shore this up, you think?' she called to Yu.

'What?' Rhyme asked.

'I'm taking to the engineer.'

Yu called, 'I think it'll probably hold. The soil's damp enough to be cohesive.'

Probably.

The engineer continued, 'If you want we can, but it'll take a few hours to build the frame.'

'Never mind,' she called to him. Into the speaker she asked, 'Lincoln?'

There was a pause.

She felt a jolt, realizing she'd used his first name. Neither of them was superstitious but there was one rule they stuck to: It was bad luck to use their first names on the job.

The hesitation told her that he too was aware she'd broken the rule. Finally he said, 'Go ahead.'

Gravel and dry dirt again trickled down the side of the foxhole and sprayed her neck and shoulders. It hit the Tyvek suit, which amplified the sound. She jumped back, thinking the walls were coming down. A gasp.

'Sachs? You all right?'

She looked around. No, the walls were holding. 'Fine.' She continued to scrape away dirt from the rounded brick cistern. With the pickax she chipped away mortar. She asked Rhyme, 'Any more thoughts about what's

393

inside?' The question was meant mostly for the comfort of hearing his voice.

A sphere with a tail.

'No idea.'

A fierce bash with the ax. One brick came out. Then two. Earth poured out from inside the well and covered her knees.

Damn, I hate this.

More bricks, more sand and pebbles and dirt. She stopped, cleared the heavy pile off her kneeling legs and turned back to her task.

'How you doing?' Rhyme asked.

'Hanging in there,' she said softly and removed several more bricks. A dozen of them lay around her. She turned her head, shining the light on what was behind the bricks: a wall of black dirt, ash, bits of charcoal and scraps of wood.

She started to dig into the dense dry earth that was inside the cistern. Nothing cohesive about *this* goddamn dirt, she thought, watching the loose brown rivulets stream downward, glistening in the beam from her hard-hat light.

'Sachs!' Rhyme shouted. 'Stop!'

She gasped. 'What's — '

'I just looked over the story of the arson again. It said there was an explosion in the basement of the tavern. Grenades back then were spheres with fuses. Charles must've taken *two* with him. That's the sphere in the well! You're right next to the one that didn't go off. The bomb could be as unstable as nitroglycerine. That's what the dog was sensing, the explosives! Get out of there fast.'

She gripped the side of the well to pull herself to her feet.

But the brick she was holding suddenly gave way, and she fell onto her back as an avalanche of dry earth from inside the well poured out into the foxhole. Stones and gravel and dirt flowed around her, pinning her bent, cramping legs and spreading fast toward her chest and face.

She screamed, trying desperately to climb to her feet. But she couldn't; the flood had reached her arms.

'Sa — ' She heard Rhyme's voice as the headset cord was ripped from the radio.

More dirt cascaded over her body, helplessly frozen under the crushing weight that rose like flooding water.

Then Sachs screamed once more — as the sphere, carried by the current of dirt, dropped from the gaping hole in the brick wall and rolled against her immobilized body.

★ ★ ★

Jax was out of his area.

He'd left Harlem behind, both the place and the state of mind. Left behind the empty lots filled with malt liquor bottles, left behind the storefront tabernacles, the faded, weather-battered posters for Red Devil lye, which black men had used to conk their hair straight in the Malcolm X era, left behind the teenage rapper wannabees and bucket percussion ensembles in Marcus Garvey Park, the stands selling toys and sandals and bling and kente-cloth wall hangings.

395

Left behind all the new redevelopment construction, left behind the tour buses.

He was now in one of the few places where he'd never bombed a *Jax 157*, never painted a throw-up. The elegant part of Central Park West.

Staring at the building where Geneva Settle now was.

After the incident in the alley, near her house on 118th Street, with Geneva and the guy in the gray car, Jax had jumped in another cab and followed the police cars here. He didn't know what to make of this place: the two police cars out front, and from the stairs to the sidewalk a ramp, like they make for people in wheelchairs.

Limping slowly through the park, scoping the building out. What was the girl doing inside? He tried to get a look. But the blinds were drawn.

Another car — a Crown Vic, the kind the police drive a lot — pulled up and two cops got out, carrying a cheap suitcase, taped together, and boxes of books. Probably Geneva's, he guessed. She was moving in.

Protecting her even steadier, he thought, discouraged.

He stepped into the bushes to get a better view when the door opened, but just then another squad car drove past, slow. It seemed that a cop inside was scanning the park as well as the sidewalk. Jax memorized the number of the building, then turned away and disappeared into the park. He headed north, walking back toward Harlem.

Feeling the gun in his sock, feeling the tug of his parole officer two hundred miles to the

396

north, who might be thinking about a surprise visit to his Buffalo apartment at this very moment, Jax remembered a question that Ralph the leaning Egyptian prince had asked him: Was what he was doing worth all the risk?

He considered this now, as he returned home.

And he thought: Had it been worth the risk twenty years ago, perching on the six-inch iron ledge of the overpass on the Grand Central Parkway, to tag *Jax 157* thirty feet above traffic streaming by at sixty miles an hour?

Had it been worth the risk six years ago, chambering a 12-gauge shell in the breakdown and shoving the muzzle into the face of the armored-truck driver, just to get that $50,000 or $60,000? Enough to help him get over, get his life back on track?

And he knew that, fuck, Ralph's wasn't a question that made any sense, because it suggested there was a choice. Then and now, right or wrong, didn't matter. Alonzo 'Jax' Jackson was going right ahead. If this worked out he'd get back his righteous life in Harlem, his home, the place that for good and bad had made him what he was — and the place that he himself had helped form, with his thousands of cans of spray paint. He was simply doing what he had to do.

★　★　★

Careful.

In his safe house in Queens, Thompson Boyd was wearing a gas mask/respirator and thick gloves. He was slowly mixing acid and water, then checking the concentration.

Careful . . .

This was the tricky part. Certainly the potassium cyanide powder sitting nearby was dangerous — enough to kill thirty or forty people — but in its dried form it was relatively stable. Just like the bomb he'd planted in the police car, the white powder needed to be mixed with sulfuric acid to produce the deadly gas (the infamous Zyklon-B used by the Nazis in their extermination showers).

But the big 'if' is the sulfuric acid. Too weak a concentration will produce the gas slowly, which could give the victims a chance to detect the odor and escape. But too strong an acid — over 20 percent concentration — will cause the cyanide to explode before it's dissolved, dissipating much of the desired deadly effect.

Thompson needed the concentration to be as close to 20 percent as possible — for a simple reason: The place he was going to plant the device — that old Central Park West town house where Geneva Settle was staying — would hardly be airtight. After learning that this was where the girl was hiding, Thompson had conducted his own surveillance of the town house and had noted the unsealed windows and an antiquated heating and air-conditioning system. It would be a challenge to turn the large structure into a death chamber.

. . . *you gotta understand 'bout what we're doing here. It's like everything else in life. Nothing ever goes one hundred percent.*

Nothing runs just the way it ought . . .

Yesterday he'd told his employer that the next attempt on Geneva's life would be successful. But now he wasn't too sure about that. The police were far too good.

We'll just re-rig and keep going. We can't get emotional about it.

Well, he wasn't emotional or concerned. But he needed to take drastic measures — on several fronts. If the poison gas in the town house now killed Geneva, fine. But that wasn't his main goal. He had to take out at least some of the people inside — the investigators searching for him and his employer. Kill them, put them in a coma, cause brain damage — it didn't matter. The important thing was to debilitate them.

Thompson checked the concentration once again, and altered it slightly, making up for how the air would alter the pH balance. His hands were a bit unsteady, so he stepped away for a moment to calm himself.

Wssst . . .

The song he'd been whistling became 'Stairway to Heaven.'

Thompson leaned back and thought about how to get the gas bomb into the town house. A few ideas occurred to him — including one or two he was pretty sure would work quite well. He again tested the concentration of the acid, whistling absently through the mouthpiece of the respirator. The analyzer reported that the strength was 19.99394 percent.

Perfect.

Wssst . . .

The new tune that popped into his head was the 'Ode to Joy' from Beethoven's Ninth Symphony.

★ ★ ★

Amelia Sachs had been neither crushed to death by clay and soil nor blown up by unstable nineteenth-century ordnance.

She was now standing, showered and in clean clothes, in Rhyme's lab, looking over what had tumbled from the dry cistern into her lap an hour earlier.

It wasn't an old bomb. But there was little doubt now that it'd been left in the well by Charles Singleton on the night of July 15, 1868.

Rhyme's chair was parked in front of the examination table beside Sachs, as they peered into the cardboard evidence collection box. Cooper was with them, pulling on latex gloves.

'We'll have to tell Geneva,' Rhyme said.

'Do we?' Sachs said reluctantly. 'I don't want to.'

'Tell me what?'

Sachs turned quickly. Rhyme backed away from the table and reluctantly rolled the Storm Arrow in a circle. Thinking: Damnit. Should've been more careful.

Geneva Settle stood in the doorway.

'You found out something about Charles in the basement of that tavern, didn't you? You found out that he really *did* steal the money. Was that his secret, after all?'

A glance at Sachs, then Rhyme said, 'No,

400

Geneva. No. We found something else.' A nod toward the box. 'Here. Take a look.'

The girl walked closer. She stopped, blinking, staring down at the brown human skull. It was this that they'd seen on the ultrasound image and that had rolled out into Sachs's lap. With the help of Vegas, Gail Davis's briard, the detective had recovered the remaining bones. These bones — what Sachs had thought were the slats from a strongbox — were those of a man, Rhyme had determined. The body had apparently been stuffed vertically into the cistern in the basement of Potters' Field tavern just before Charles had ignited the fire. The ultrasound imaging had picked up the top of the skull and a rib beneath it, which gave the appearance of a fuse for a bomb.

The bones were in a second box on the worktable.

'We're pretty sure it's a man that Charles killed.'

'No!'

'And then he burned down the tavern to cover up the crime.'

'You couldn't *know* that,' Geneva snapped.

'We don't, no. But it's a reasonable deduction.' Rhyme explained: 'His letter said he was going to Potters' Field, armed with his Navy Colt revolver. That was a pistol from the Civil War. It didn't work like guns nowadays, where you load a bullet into the back of the cylinder. You had to load each chamber from the front with a ball and gunpowder.'

She nodded. Her eyes were on the brown and

black bones, the eyeless skull.

'We found some information on guns like his in our database. It's a .36-caliber but most Civil War soldiers learned to use .39-caliber balls in them. They're a little bigger and fit more tightly. That makes the gun more accurate.'

Sachs picked up a small plastic bag. 'This was in the skull cavity.' Inside was a little sphere of lead. 'It's a .39-caliber ball that was fired out of a .36-caliber gun.'

'But that doesn't prove anything.' She was staring at the hole in the forehead of the skull.

'No,' Rhyme said kindly. 'It suggests. But it suggests very *strongly* that Charles killed him.'

'Who was he?' Geneva asked.

'We don't have any idea. If he had any ID on him it burned up or disintegrated, along with his clothes. We found the bullet, a small gun that he probably had with him, some gold coins and a ring with the word . . . what was the word, Mel?'

' 'Winskinskie.' ' He held up a plastic bag with the gold signet ring inside. Above the inscription was an etched profile of an American Indian.

Cooper had quickly found that the word meant 'doorman' or 'gatekeeper' in the language of the Delaware Indians. This might be the dead man's name, though his cranial bone structure suggested he wasn't Native-American. More likely, Rhyme felt, it was a fraternal, school or lodge slogan of some sort and Cooper had queried some anthropologists and history professors via email to see if they'd heard of the word.

'Charles wouldn't do it,' his descendant said softly. 'He wouldn't murder anyone.'

'The bullet was fired into the forehead,' Rhyme said. 'Not from behind. And the Derringer — the gun — that Sachs found in the cistern probably belonged to the victim. That suggests the shooting could've been in self-defense.'

Though the fact remained that Charles had voluntarily gone to the tavern armed with a gun. He would have anticipated some sort of violence.

'I should never have started this in the first place,' Geneva muttered. 'Stupid. I don't even like the past. It's pointless. I hate it!' She turned and ran into the hallway, then up the stairs.

Sachs followed. She returned a few minutes later. 'She's reading. She said she wants to be alone. I think she'll be all right.' Her voice didn't sound very certain, though.

Rhyme looked over the information on the oldest scene he'd ever run — 140 years. The whole point of the search was to learn something that might lead them to whoever had hired Unsub 109. But all it had done was nearly get Sachs killed and disappoint Geneva with the news that her ancestor had killed a man.

He looked at the copy of The Hanged Man tarot card, staring at him placidly from the evidence board, mocking Rhyme's frustration.

Cooper said, 'Hey, have something here.' He was looking at his computer screen.

'Winskinskie?' Rhyme asked.

'No. Listen. An answer to our mystery substance — the one that Amelia found in the unsub's Elizabeth Street safe house and near Geneva's aunt's. The liquid.'

'Damn well about time. What the hell is it? Toxin?' Rhyme asked.

'Our bad boy's got dry eyes,' Cooper said.

'What?'

'It's Murine.'

'Eyedrops?'

'That's right. The composition's exactly the same.'

'Okay. Add that to the chart,' Rhyme ordered Thom. 'Might just be temporary — because he'd been working with acid. In which case, won't help us. But it might be chronic. That'd be good.'

Criminalists loved perps with physical maladies. Rhyme had a whole section in his book on tracing people through prescription or over-the-counter drugs, disposed hypodermic needles, prescription eyeglasses, unique shoe-tread wear from orthopedic problems, and so on.

It was then that Sachs's phone rang. She listened for a moment. 'Okay. I'll be there in fifteen minutes.' The policewoman disconnected, glanced at Rhyme. 'Well, this's interesting.'

28

When Amelia Sachs walked into the Critical Care Unit at Columbia-Presbyterian Hospital she saw two Pulaskis.

One was in bed, swathed in bandages and hooked up to creepy clear plastic tubes. His eyes were dull, his mouth slack.

The other sat at his bedside, awkward in the uncomfortable plastic chair. Just as blond, just as fresh-faced, in the same crisp blue NYPD uniform Ron Pulaski had been wearing when Sachs had recruited him in front of the African-American museum yesterday and told him to act concerned about a pile of garbage.

How many sugars? . . .

She blinked at the mirror image.

'I'm Tony. Ron's brother. Which you probably guessed.'

'Hi, Detective,' Ron managed breathlessly. His voice wasn't working right. It was slurred, sloppy.

'How you feeling?'

'How ish Geneva?'

'She's all right. I'm sure you heard — we stopped him at her aunt's place but he got away . . . You hurting? Must be.'

He nodded toward the IV drip. 'Happy soup . . . Don't feel a thing.'

'He'll be okay.'

'I'll be okay,' Ron echoed his brother's words.

He took a few deep breaths, blinked.

'A month or so,' Tony explained. 'Some therapy. He'll be back on duty. Some fractures. Not much internal damage. Thick skull. Which Dad always said.'

'Shkull.' Ron grinned.

'You were at the academy together?' She pulled up a chair and sat.

'Right.'

'What's *your* house?'

'The Six,' Tony answered.

The Sixth Precinct was in the heart of west Greenwich Village. Not many muggings or carjackings or drugs. Mostly breakins, gay domestics and incidents by emotionally disturbed artists and writers off their meds. The Six was also home to the Bomb Squad.

Tony was shaken, sure, but angry too. 'The guy kept at him, even when he was down. He didn't need to.'

'But maybe,' came Ron's stumbling words, 'it took for time . . . took *more* time on me. So he didn't get . . . didn't get a good chance to go after Geneva.'

Sachs smiled. 'You're kind of a glass-is-half-full sorta guy.' She didn't tell him that he'd been beaten nearly to death simply so Unsub 109 could use a bullet from his weapon for a distraction.

'Sorta am. Thank Sheneva. *Gen*-eva for me. For the book.' He couldn't really move his head but his eyes slipped to the side of the bedside table, where a copy of *To Kill a Mockingbird* lay. 'Tony'sh reading to me. He

406

even can read the big wordsh.'

His brother laughed. 'You putz.'

'So what can you tell us, Ron? This guy's smart and he's still out there. We need something we can use.'

'I don't know, ma — I don't know, Detective. I wasssh goin' up and down th'alley. He hid when I want to . . . *went* to the street. Came back to the back, the alley . . . I washn't expecting hih. *Him*. He was around the corner of the, you know, the bidling . . . the *building*. I got to the corner. I shaw this guy, in a mask like a ski mashk. And then this thing. Club, bat. Came too fasht. Couldn't shee it really. Got me good.' He blinked again, closed his eyes. 'Careless. Washhh, was too close to the wall. Won't do that again.'

You didn't know. Now you do.

'A woosh.' He winced.

'You okay?' his brother asked.

'I'm okay.'

'A woosh,' Sachs encouraged, nudged her chair closer.

'What?'

'You heard a woosh.'

'Yes, I heard it, ma'am. Not 'ma'am.' Detective.'

'It's okay, Ray. Call me whatever. You see *anything*? Anything at all?'

'This thing. Like a bat. No, not Batman and Robin. Ha. A baseball bat. Right at my face. Oh, I told you that. And I went down. I mean, Detective. Not 'ma'am.''

'That's okay, Ron. What do you remember then?'

407

'I don't know. I remember lying on the ground. Thinking . . . I was thinking he was going for my weapon. I tried to control my weapon. Wash . . . was in the book, not to let it go. 'Always control your weapon.' But I didn't. He got it anyway. I wash dead. I knew I *was* dead.'

She encouraged softly, 'What do you remember seeing?'

'A tangle.'

'A what?'

He laughed. 'I didn't mean tangle. A *triangle*. Cardboard. On the ground. I couldn't move. It was all I could see.'

'And this cardboard. It was the unsub's?'

'The trangle? No. I mean, triangle. No, it was jusht trash. I mean, it's all I could see. I tried to crawl. I don't think I did.'

Sachs sighed. 'You were found on your back, Ron.'

'I washhh? . . . I was on my back?'

'Think back. Did you see the sky maybe?'

He squinted.

Her heart beat faster. Did he get a look at something?

'Bluh.'

'What?'

'Bluh in my eyes by then.'

'Blood?' his brother offered.

'Yeah. Blood. Couldn't shee anything then. No trangles, no building. He got my piece. He stayed neareye for a few minutes. Then I don't remember anything elshe.'

'He was nearby? How close?'

'I don't know. Not close. Couldn't see. Too much bluh.'

Sachs nodded. The poor man looked exhausted. His breathing was labored, his eyes much more unfocused than when she'd arrived. She rose. 'I'll let him get some rest.' She asked, 'You heard of Terry Dobyns?'

'No. Ishh he . . . Who ishh?' A grimace crossed the injured officer's face. 'Who *is* he?

'Department psychologist.' She glanced at Ron with a smile. 'This'll take the starch out of you for a while. You should talk to him about it. He's the man. He rules.'

Ron said, 'Don't need to — '

'Patrolman?' she said sternly.

He lifted an eyebrow, winced.

'It's an order.'

'Yes, ma'am. I mean . . . ma'am.'

Anthony said, 'I'll make sure he does.'

'You'll thank . . . Geneva for me? I like that book.'

'I will.' Sachs slung her bag over her shoulder and started for the door. She just stepped through it when she stopped abruptly, turned back. 'Ron?'

'Wusthat?'

She returned to his bedside, sat down again.

'Ron, you said the unsub was near you for a few minutes.'

'Yuh.'

'Well, if you couldn't see him, with the blood in your eyes, how did you know he was there?'

The young officer frowned. 'Oh . . . yeah. There's shomething I forgot to tell you.'

'Our boy's got a habit, Rhyme.'

Amelia Sachs was back in the laboratory.

'What's that?'

'He whistles.'

'For taxis?'

'Music. Pulaski heard him. After he'd been hit the first time and was lying on the ground the unsub took his weapon and, I'm guessing, spent a few minutes to hook the bullet to the cigarette. While he was doing that, he was whistling. Real softly, Ron said, but he's sure it was whistling.'

'No pro's going to whistle on the job,' Rhyme said.

'You wouldn't think. But *I* heard it too. At the safe house on Elizabeth Street. I thought it was the radio or something — he was good.'

'How's the rookie doing?' Sellitto asked. He hadn't rubbed his invisible bloodstain recently but he was still edgy.

'They say he'll be okay. A month of therapy or so. I told him to see Terry Dobyns. Ron was pretty out of it but his brother was there. He'll look after him. He's a uniform too. Identical twin.'

Rhyme wasn't surprised. Being on the force often ran in the family. 'Cop' could be the name of a human gene.

But Sellitto shook his head at the news of a sibling. He seemed all the more upset, as if it was his fault that an entire family had been affected by the attack.

There was no time, though, to deal with the

410

detective's demons. Rhyme said, 'All right. We've got some new information. Let's put it to use.'

'How?' Cooper asked.

'The murder of Charlie Tucker's still the closest lead we have to Mr. One-oh-nine. So, obviously,' the criminalist added, 'we call Texas.'

'Remember the Alamo,' Sachs offered and hit the speaker button on the phone.

POTTERS' FIELD SCENE (1868)

- Tavern in Gallows Heights — located in the Eighties on the Upper West Side, mixed neighborhood in the 1860s.
- Potters' Field was possible hangout for Boss Tweed and other corrupt New York politicians.
- Charles came here July 15, 1868.
- Burned down following explosion, presumably just after Charles's visit. To hide his secret?
- Body in basement, man, presumably killed by Charles Singleton.
  - Shot in forehead by .36 Navy Colt loaded with .39-caliber ball (type of weapon Charles Singleton owned).
  - Gold coins.
- Man was armed with Derringer.
- No identification.
- Had ring with name 'Winskinskie' on it.
  - Means 'doorman' or 'gatekeeper' in Delaware Indian language.
  - Currently searching other meanings.

EAST HARLEM SCENE (GENEVA'S GREAT-AUNT'S APARTMENT)

- Used cigarette and 9mm round as explosive device to distract officers. Merit brand, not traceable.
- Friction ridge prints: None. Glove-prints only.
- Poisonous gas device:
- Glass jar, foil, candle-holder. Untraceable.
- Cyanide and sulfuric acid.

Neither containing markers. Untraceable.

- Clear liquid similar to that found on Elizabeth Street.
- Determined to be Murine.
- Small flakes of orange paint. Posing as construction or highway worker?

ELIZABETH STREET SAFE HOUSE SCENE

- Used electrical booby trap.
- Fingerprints: None. Glove prints only.
- Security camera and monitor; no leads.
- Tarot deck, missing the twelfth card; no leads.
- Map with diagram of museum where G. Settle was attacked and buildings across the street.
- Trace:
  - Falafel and yogurt.
  - Wood scrapings from desk with traces of pure sulfuric acid.
  - Clear liquid, not explosive. Sent to FBI lab.
    - Determined to be Murine.
  - More fibers from rope. Garrotte?
  - Pure carbon found in map.
- Safe house was rented, for cash, to Billy Todd

Hammil. Fits Unsub 109's description, but no leads to an actual Hammil.

AFRICAN-AMERICAN MUSEUM SCENE

- Rape pack:
  - Tarot card, twelfth card in deck, The Hanged Man, meaning spiritual searching.
  - Smiley-face bag.
    - Too generic to trace.
  - Box cutter.
  - Trojan condoms.
  - Duct tape.
  - Jasmine scent.
  - Unknown item bought for $5.95. Probably a stocking cap.
  - Receipt, indicating store was in New York City, discount variety store or drugstore.
  - Most likely purchased in a store on Mulberry Street, Little Italy. Unsub identified by clerk.

- Fingerprints:
  - Unsub wore latex or vinyl gloves.
  - Prints on items in rape pack belonged to person with small hands, no IAFIS hits. Positive ID for clerk's.

- Trace:
  - Cotton-rope fibers, some with traces of human blood. Garrotte?
    - Sent to CODIS.
      - No DNA match in CODIS.
    - Popcorn and cotton candy with traces of canine urine.
- Weapons:
  - Billy club or martial arts weapon.
  - Pistol is a North American Arms .22 rimfire magnum, Black Widow or Mini-Master.
  - Makes own bullets, bored-out slugs filled with needles. No match in IBIS or DRUGFIRE.
- Motive
  - Uncertain. Rape was probably staged.
  - True motive may have been to steal microfiche containing July 23, 1868, issue of *Coloreds' Weekly Illustrated* magazine and kill G. Settle because of her interest in an article for reasons unknown. Article was about her ancestor Charles Singleton (see accompanying chart).
- Librarian victim reported that someone else wished to see article.
  - Requesting librarian's phone records to verify this.
  - No leads.
- Requesting information from employees as to other person wishing to see story.
  - No leads.
- Searching for copy of article.
  - Several sources report man requested same article. No leads to identity. Most issues missing or destroyed. One located. (See accompanying chart.)
- Conclusion: G. Settle still at risk.
- Motive may be to keep secret the fact that her ancestor found the Fourteenth Amendment to the Constitution is invalid, threatening most of the U.S. civil rights and civil liberties laws.
- Profile of incident sent to VICAP and NCIC.
  - Murder in Amarillo, TX, five years ago. Similar

413

M.O. — staged crime scene (apparently ritual killing, but real motive unknown).
- Victim was a retired prison guard.
- Composite picture sent to Texas prison.
  - Not recognized.
- Murder in Ohio, three years ago. Similar M.O. — staged crime scene (apparently sexual assault, but real motive probably hired killing). Files missing.

PROFILE OF UNSUB 109

- White male.
- 6 feet tall, 180 lbs.
- Middle-aged.
- Average voice.
- Used cell phone to get close to victim.
- Wears three-year-old, or older, size-11 Bass walkers, light brown. Right foot slightly outturned.
- Additional jasmine scent.
- Dark pants.
- Ski mask, dark.
- Will target innocents to help in killing victims and escaping.
- Most likely is a for-hire killer.

- Possibly a former prisoner in Amarillo, TX.
- Talks with a Southern accent.
- Has trim, light-brown hair, clean-shaven.
- Nondescript.
- Seen wearing dark rain-coat.
- Probably not a regular smoker.
- Construction, utility, highway worker?
- Uses Murine.
- Whistles.

PROFILE OF PERSON HIRING UNSUB 109

- No information at this time.

PROFILE OF UNSUB 109'S ACCOMPLICE

- Black male.
- Late 30's, early 40's.
- Six feet.
- Solidly built.
- Wearing green combat jacket.
- Ex-convict.
- Has a limp.
- Reportedly armed.
- Clean-shaven.
- Black do-rag.
- Awaiting additional witnesses and security tapes.

414

- Tape inconclusive, sent to lab for analysis.
- Old work shoes.

PROFILE OF CHARLES SINGLETON

- Former slave, ancestor of G. Settle. Married, one son. Given orchard in New York state by master. Worked as teacher, as well. Instrumental in early civil rights movement.
- Charles allegedly committed theft in 1868, the subject of the article in stolen microfiche.
- Reportedly had a secret that could bear on case. Worried that tragedy would result if his secret was revealed.
- Attended meetings in Gallows Heights neighborhood of New York.
  - Involved in some risky activities?
- Worked with Frederick Douglass and others in getting the 14th Amendment to the Constitution ratified.
- The crime, as reported in *Coloreds' Weekly Illustrated*:

- Charles arrested by Det. William Simms for stealing large sum from Freedman's Trust in NY. Broke into the Trust's safe, witnesses saw him leave shortly after. His tools were found nearby. Most money was recovered. He was sentenced to five years in prison. No information about him after sentencing. Believed to have used his connections with early civil rights leaders to gain access to the trust.
- Charles's correspondence:
  - Letter 1, to wife: Re: Draft Riots in 1863, great anti-black sentiment throughout NY state, lynchings, arson. Risk to property owned by blacks.
  - Letter 2, to wife: Charles at Battle of Appomattox at end of Civil War.
  - Letter 3, to wife: Involved in civil rights movement. Threatened for this work. Troubled by his secret.

- Letter 4, to wife: Went to Potters' Field with his gun for 'justice.' Results were disastrous. The truth is now hidden in Potters' Field. His secret was what caused all this heartache.

''Lo?'

'Hey there, J. T. This's Lincoln Rhyme in New York.' Speaking to someone who went by initials and lived in the Lone Star State — not to mention his drawl — made you tend to drop words like 'hey,' and 'listen here' into your speech.

'Oh, yes, sir, how you doing? Say, I read up on you after we talked last time. Didn't know you were famous.'

'Ah, just a former civil servant,' Rhyme said with a modesty that rang like dull tin. 'Nothing more or less than that. Any better luck with the picture we sent you?'

'Sorry, Detective Rhyme. Fact is, he looks like half the white guys who graduated from here. 'Sides, we're like most correctional outfits — got ourselves a big turnover. Aren't hardly any employees still here from the time when Charlie Tucker was killed.'

'We've got a little more information about him. This might help narrow down the list. You got a minute?'

'Shoot.'

'He may have an eye problem. He uses Murine regularly. That could be recent but maybe he did it when he was a prisoner there. And then we think he may've had the habit of whistling.'

416

'Whistling? Like at a woman or some such?'

'No, whistling a tune. Songs.'

'Oh. Okay. Hold on.' Five impossibly long minutes later he came back on the line. 'Sorry. Nobody could remember anything about anybody whistling, or having bad eyes, not particular. But we'll keep looking.'

Rhyme thanked him and disconnected. He stared at the evidence chart in frustration. In the early 1900s, one of the greatest criminalists who ever lived, Edmond Locard of France, came up with what he called the exchange principle, which holds that at every crime scene there is some exchange of evidence, however minute, between the criminal and the scene or the victim. Finding that evidence was the goal of the forensic detective. Locard's principle, however, didn't go on to guarantee that simply *establishing* that connection would lead you to the perp's door.

He sighed. Well, he'd known it would be a long shot. What'd they have? A vague computer drawing, a possible eye condition, a possible habit, a grudge against a prison guard.

What else should the — ?

Rhyme frowned. He was staring at the twelfth card in the tarot deck.

The Hanged Man does not refer to someone being punished . . .

Maybe not, but it still depicted a man dangling from a scaffold.

Something clicked in his mind. He glanced at the evidence chart again. Noting: the baton, the electricity hookup on Elizabeth Street, the poison gas, the cluster of bullets in the heart, the lynching of Charlie Tucker, the rope fibers with traces of blood . . .

'Oh, hell!' he spat out.

'Lincoln? What's the matter?' Cooper glanced over at his boss, concerned.

Rhyme shouted, 'Command, redial!'

The computer responded on the screen: *I did not understand what you said. What would you like me to do?*

'Redial the number.'

I did not understand what you said.

'Fuck it! Mel, Sachs . . . *somebody* hit redial!'

Cooper did and a few minutes later the criminalist was speaking once again to the warden in Amarillo.

'J. T., it's Lincoln again.'

'Yes, sir?'

'Forget inmates. I want to know about *guards*.'

'Guards?'

'Somebody who used to be on your staff. With eye problems. Who whistled. And he might've worked on Death Row before or around the time Tucker was killed.'

'We all weren't thinkin' 'bout *employees*. And, again, most of our staff wasn't here five, six years ago. But hold on here. Lemme ask around.'

The image of The Hanged Man had put the thought into Rhyme's head. He then considered the weapons and the techniques that Unsub 109 had employed. They were methods of execution: cyanide gas, electricity, hanging, shooting a group of bullets into the heart, like a firing squad. And his weapon to subdue his victims was a baton, like a prison guard would carry.

A moment later he heard, 'Hey there, Detective Rhyme?'

'Go ahead, J. T.'

'Sure 'nough, somebody said that rings a bell. I called one of our retired guards at home, worked execution detail. Name of Pepper. He's agreed to come into the office and talk to you. Lives nearby. Should be here in just a few minutes. We'll call you right back.'

Another glance at the tarot card.

A change of direction . . .

Ten insufferably long minutes later the phone rang.

Fast introductions were made. Retired Texas Department of Justice officer Halbert Pepper spoke in a drawl that made J. T. Beauchamp's accent sound like the Queen's English. 'Thinkin' I might be able to help y'all out some.'

'Tell me,' Rhyme said.

'Till 'bout five years ago we had us a executions control officer fit the bill of who y'all were describin' to J. T. Had hisself eye trouble and he whistled up a storm. I was just 'bout to retire round then but I worked with him some.'

'Who was he?'

'Fella name of Thompson Boyd.'

IV

DEAD MAN WALKING

29

Through the speakerphone, Pepper was explaining, 'Boyd grew up round these parts. Father was a wildcatter — '

'Oil?'

'Field hand, yes, sir. Mother stayed at home. No other kids. Normal childhood, sounded like. Pretty nice, to hear tell. Always talkin' 'bout his family, loved 'em. Did a lot for his mother, who lost a arm or leg or whatnot in a twister. Always looking out for her. Like one time, I heard, this kid on the street made fun of her, and Boyd followed him and threatened to slip a sidewinder into the boy's bed some night if he didn't apologize.

'Anyway after high school and a year'r two of college he went to work at his daddy's company for a spell, till they had a string of layoffs. He got fired. His daddy too. Times was bad and he just couldn't get work round here, and so he moved outa the state. Don't know where. Got hisself a job at some prison. Started as a block guard. Then there was some problem — their executions officer went sick, I think — and there was nobody to do the job so Boyd done it. The burn went so good — '

'The what?'

'Sorry. The *electrocution* went so good they give him the job. He stayed for a while, but kept on movin' from state to state, 'cause he was in demand. Became an expert at executions. He knew chairs — '

'Electric chairs?'

'Like our Ol' Sparky down here, yes, sir. The famous one. And he knew gas too, was a expert at riggin' the chamber. Could also tie a hangman's noose and not many people in the U.S.'re licensed for *that* line of work, lemme tell you. The ECO job opened up here and he jumped at it. We'd switched to lethal injections, like most other places, and he became a whiz at them too. Even read up on 'em so he could answer the protesters. There's some people claim the chemicals're painful. I myself think that's the whale people and Democrats, who don't bother to know the facts. It's hogwash. I mean, we had these — '

'About Boyd?' asked impatient Lincoln Rhyme.

'Yes, sir, sorry. So he's back here and things go fine for a spell. Nobody really paid him much mind. He was just kinda invisible. 'Average Joe' was his nickname. But somethin' happened over time. Somethin' changed. After a time he started to go strange.'

'How so?'

'The more executions he ran, the crazier he got. Kind of blanker and blanker. That make sense? Like he wasn't quite all there. Give you a for-instance: Told you he and his folks was real tight, got along great. What happens but they get themselves killed in this car accident, his aunt too, and Boyd, he didn't blink. Hell, he didn't even go to the funeral. You would've thought he was in shock, but it wasn't that way.

He just didn't seem to care. He went to his normal shift and, when ever'body heard, they asked what he was doin' there. It was two days till the next execution. He coulda took time off. But he didn't want to. He said he'd go out to their graves later. Don't know if he ever did.

'See, it was like he kept gettin' closer and closer to the *prisoners* — too close, a lot of folk thought. You don't do that. Ain't healthy. He stopped hangin' out with other guards and spent his time with the condemned. He called 'em 'my people.' Word is that he one time even sat down in our old electric chair itself, which is in this sort of museum. Just to see what it was like. Fell asleep. Imagine that.

'Somebody asked Boyd about it, how'd it feel, bein' in a electric chair. He said it didn't feel like nothin'. It just felt 'kinda numb.' He said that a lot toward the end. He felt numb.'

'You said his parents were killed? Did he move into their house?'

'Think he did.'

'Is it still there?'

The Texans were on a speakerphone too and J. T. Beauchamp called out, 'I'll find that out, sir.' He posed a question to somebody. 'Should see in a minute or two, Mr. Rhyme.'

'And could you find out about relatives in the area?'

'Yes, sir.'

Sachs asked, 'You recall he whistled a lot, Officer Pepper?'

'Yes'm. And he was right good at it.

Sometimes he'd give the condemned a song or two to send 'em off.'

'What about his eyes?'

'That too,' Pepper said. 'Thompson had hisself bad eyes. The story is he was runnin' a electrocution — wasn't here — and somethin' went bad. Happened sometimes, when you'd use the chair. A fire started — '

'The man being executed?' Sachs asked, wincing.

'That's right, ma'am. Caught hisself on fire. He mighta been dead already, or unconscious. Nobody knows. He was still movin' round but they always do that. So Thompson runs in with a riot gun, gonna shoot the poor fella, put him out of his misery. Now, that's not part of protocol, I'll tell you. It's murder to kill the condemned before they die under the writ of execution. But Boyd was gonna do it anyway. Couldn't let one of 'his people' die like that. But the fire spread. Insulation on the wire or some plastic or somethin' caught and the fumes knocked Boyd out. He was blinded for a day or two.'

'The inmate?' Sachs asked.

'Thompson didn't hafta shoot him. The juice did the trick.'

'And he left five years ago?' Rhyme asked.

''Bout that,' Pepper drawled. 'Quit. Think he went up to some place, some prison, in the Midwest. Never heard nothin' 'bout him after that.'

Midwest — maybe Ohio. Where the other murder that fit the profile took place. 'Call

426

somebody at Ohio Corrections,' Rhyme whispered to Cooper, who nodded and grabbed another phone.

'What about Charlie Tucker, the guard who was killed? Boyd left around the time of the murder?'

'Yes, sir, that's right.'

'There bad blood between them?'

Pepper said, 'Charlie worked under Thompson for a year 'fore he retired. Only Charlie was what we'd call a Bible thumper, a hard-shell Baptist. He'd lay chapter and verse on pretty thick to the condemned sometimes, tell 'em they was goin' to hell, and so on. Thompson didn't hold with that.'

'So maybe Boyd killed him to pay him back for making prisoners' lives miserable.'

My people . . .

'Could've been.'

'What about the picture we sent? Was that Boyd?'

'J. T. just showed it to me,' Pepper said. 'And, yeah, it could be him. Though he was bigger, fatter, I mean, back then. And he had a shaved head and goatee — lotta us did that, tryin' to look as mean as the prisoners.'

''Sides,' the warden said, 'we were looking for inmates, not guards.'

Which was *my* mistake, Rhyme thought angrily.

'Well, damn.' The voice of the warden again.

'What's that, J. T.?'

'My gal went to pull Boyd's personnel file. And — '

427

'It's missing.'

'Sure is.'

'So he stole his record to cover up any connection to Charlie Tucker's murder,' Sellitto said.

'I'd reckon,' J. T. Beauchamp said.

Rhyme shook his head. 'And he was worried about fingerprints because he'd been printed as a state *employee*, not a criminal.'

'Hold on,' the warden drawled. A woman was speaking to him. He came back on the speakerphone. 'We just heard from a fella at county records. Boyd sold the family house five years ago. Didn't buy anything else in the state. At least not under his name. Must've just took the cash and disappeared . . . And nobody knows about any other relations of his.'

'What's his full name?' Rhyme asked.

Pepper said, 'Think his middle initial was *G*, but I don't know what it stood for.' Then he added, 'One thing I'll say for him, Thompson Boyd knew what he was doin'. He knew the EP backward and forward.'

'EP?'

'The Execution Protocol. It's a big book we have, givin' all the details of how to execute somebody. He made ever'body who worked the detail memorize it, and made 'em walk around recitin' to themselves, 'I have to do it by the book, I have to do it by the book.' Thompson always said you can't never cut corners when it comes to death.'

★ ★ ★

428

Mel Cooper hung up the phone.

'Ohio?' Rhyme asked.

The tech nodded. 'Keegan Falls Maximum Security. Boyd only worked there for about a year. The warden remembers him because of the eye problem, and he did whistle. He said Boyd was a problem from the beginning. Got into fights with guards about the treatment of prisoners, and spent a lot of time socializing with inmates, which was against the rules. The warden thinks he was making contacts to use later to get jobs as a hitman.'

'Like hooking up with the man who hired him to kill that witness there.'

'Could be.'

'And *that* employment file? Stolen?'

'Missing, yep. Nobody knows where he lived or anything else about him. Fell off the radar.'

Average Joe . . .

'Well, he's not Texas's or Ohio's problem anymore. He's *ours*. Do the full search.'

'Right.'

Cooper ran the standard search — deeds, Department of Motor Vehicles, hotels, traffic tickets, taxes . . . everything. In fifteen minutes all the results were in. There were several listings of Thompson G. Boyd and one of T. G. Boyd. But their ages and descriptions weren't close to the suspect's. The tech also tried variant spellings of those names and had the same results.

'AKAs?' Rhyme asked. Most professional perps, particularly contract killers, used also-known-as names. The ones they picked were usually like passwords for computers and ATMs — they were some variation on a name that meant something to the perp. When you found out what they were, you could kick yourself for the simplicity of the choice. But guessing them was usually impossible. Still, they tried: They transposed the given- and surnames ('Thompson' was, of course, more common as a last name). Cooper even tried an anagram generator to rearrange the letters in 'Thompson Boyd,' but came up with no hits in the databases.

Nothing, Rhyme thought, inflamed with frustration. We know his name, we know what he looks like, we know he's in town . . .

But we can't goddamn *find* him.

Sachs squinted at the chart, cocked her head. She said, 'Billy Todd Hammil.'

'Who?' Rhyme demanded.

'The name he used to rent the safe house on Elizabeth Street.'

'What about it?'

She flipped through a number of sheets of paper. She looked up. 'Died six years ago.'

'Does it say where?'

'Nope. But I'm betting Texas.'

Sachs called the prison once more and asked about Hammil. A moment later she hung up the phone and nodded. 'That's it. Killed a clerk in a convenience store twelve years ago. Boyd supervised his execution. Seems like he's got this weird connection with the people he killed. His M.O. comes from the days when he was an executioner. Why not his identities too?'

Rhyme didn't know, or care, about 'weird

430

connections,' but whatever Boyd's motive, there was some logic to Sachs's suggestion. He barked, 'Get the list of everybody he's executed and match it to DMV here. Try Texas first then we'll move on to other states.'

J. T. Beauchamp sent them a list of seventy-nine prisoners Thompson Boyd had put to death as an execution officer in Texas.

'That many?' Sachs asked, frowning. Though Sachs would never hesitate to shoot to kill when it came to saving lives, Rhyme knew she had some doubts about the death penalty, because it was often meted out after trials involving circumstantial or faulty, and sometimes even intentionally altered, evidence.

Rhyme thought of the other implication of the number of executions: that somewhere along the line of nearly eighty executions, Thompson Boyd had lost any distinction between life and death.

What happens but they get themselves killed in this car accident . . . and Boyd, he didn't blink. Hell, he didn't even go to the funeral.

Cooper matched the names of the male prisoners executed to government records.

Nothing.

'Shit,' Rhyme snapped. 'We'll have to find out the other states he worked and who he executed there. It'll take forever.' Then a thought came to him. 'Hold on. Women.'

'What?' Sachs asked.

'Try the *women* he's executed. Variations on their names.'

Cooper took this, the smaller, list and ran the

431

names, and all possible spellings, through the DMV computer.

'Okay, may have something here,' the tech said excitedly. 'Eight years ago a woman named Randi Rae Silling — a prostitute — was executed in Amarillo for robbing and killing two of her johns. New York DMV's got one too, same last name, but it's a male, Randy with a *Y* and middle name *R-A-Y*. Right age and right description. Address in Queens — Astoria. Got a blue Buick Century, three years old.'

Rhyme ordered, 'Have somebody in plain clothes take the composite picture around to some neighbors.'

Cooper called the deputy inspector — the head of the local precinct, the 114. This house covered Astoria, a largely Greek neighborhood. He explained about the case and then emailed him the picture of Boyd. The dep inspector said he'd send some street-clothes officers out to subtly canvass tenants in Randy Silling's apartment.

For a tense half hour — with no word from the canvass team in Queens — Cooper, Sachs and Sellitto contacted public records offices in Texas, Ohio and New York, looking for any information they could find about Boyd or Hammil or Silling.

Nothing.

Finally they received a call back from the inspector at the 114. 'Captain?' the man asked. Many senior officers still referred to Rhyme by his old title.

'Go ahead.'

432

'We've had two people confirm that your man lives at the DMV address,' the man said. 'What are you thinking of in terms of prioritizing our approaches, sir?'

Brass, Rhyme sighed. He dispensed with any caustic responses to the bureaucrat-talk and settled for a slightly bemused, 'Let's go nail his ass.'

30

A dozen Emergency Services Unit tactical officers were moving into position behind Thompson Boyd's six-story apartment building on Fourteenth Street in Astoria, Queens.

Sachs, Sellitto and Bo Haumann were standing at the hastily set up command post behind an unmarked ESU van.

'We're here, Rhyme,' Sachs whispered into the stalk mike.

'But is *he* there?' the criminalist asked impatiently.

'We've got S and S in position . . . Hold on. Somebody's reporting.'

A Search and Surveillance Unit officer came up to them.

'Get a look inside?' asked Haumann.

'Negative, sir. He's masked the front windows.'

The S and S man in Team One explained he'd gotten as close to the apartment's front windows as he dared; the second team was around back. The officer now added, 'I could hear sounds, voices, water running. Children, it sounded like.'

'Kids, hell,' Haumann muttered.

'Might've been TV or radio. I just can't tell.'

Haumann nodded. 'CP to S and S Two. Report.'

'S and S Two. Little crack beside the shade — not much, though. Nobody in the back

434

bedroom I can see. But it's a narrow angle. Lights on in the front. Hear voices, I think. Music, K.'

'See kids' toys, anything?'

'Negative. But I've only got a ten-degree view of the bedroom. That's all I can see, K.'

'Movement?'

'Negative, K.'

'Roger. Infrared?' Infrared detectors can locate the position of animals, humans or other sources of heat inside a building.

A third S and S technician was playing a monitor over the apartment. 'I'm getting heat indications, but they're too weak to pinpoint the source, K.'

'Sounds, K?'

'Creaks and moans. Could be the structure settling, utilities, HVAC. Or could be him walking around or shifting in a chair. Assume he's there but I can't tell you where. He's really got the place blacked out, K.'

'Okay, S and S, keep monitoring. Out.'

Sachs said into her mike, 'Rhyme, you get any of that?'

'And how could I get it?' came his irritated voice.

'They think there's activity in his apartment.'

'Last thing we need is a firefight,' he muttered. A tactical confrontation was one of the most effective ways to destroy trace and other clues at a crime scene. 'We've got to secure as much evidence as we can — it could be our only chance to find out who hired him and who his partner is.'

Haumann looked over the apartment once again. He didn't seem pleased. And Sachs — who was half tactical officer at heart — could understand why. It would be a difficult take-down, requiring many officers. The unsub had two front, three back and six side windows. Boyd could easily leap through any one of them and try to escape. There was also a building next door, only four feet away — an easy jump from the roof if he made his way to the top. He could also have cover from behind the façade on the crown of the building and could target anyone below. Across the street, facing the killer's apartment, were other houses. If it came to a fight, a stray bullet could easily injure or kill a bystander. Boyd could also intentionally pepper those buildings with gunfire, hoping to inflict random injuries. Sachs was recalling his practice of targeting innocents solely for diversion. There was no reason to think he'd handle this situation any differently. They'd have to clear all these residences before the assault.

Haumann radioed, 'We just got somebody into the hallway. There're no cameras like Boyd had on Elizabeth Street. He won't know we're coming.' The tactical cop added darkly, though, 'Unless he's got some other way of telling. Which he very well may, knowing this prick.'

Sachs heard a hiss of breath next to her and turned. Decked out in body armor and absently touching the grip of his service pistol, snug in its holster, Lon Sellitto was examining the apartment. He too looked troubled. But Sachs knew immediately that it wasn't the difficulty of a

436

residential takedown that was bothering him. She could see how torn he was. As a senior investigating detective, there was no reason for him to be on an entry team — in fact, given his paunchy physique and rudimentary weapons skills, there was every reason for him *not* to do a kick-in.

But logic had nothing to do with the real reason for his being here. Seeing his hand rise once more compulsively to his cheek and worry the phantom bloodstain, and knowing that he was reliving the accidental discharge of his weapon yesterday, and Dr. Barry's being shot to death right in front of him, Sachs understood: This was Lon Sellitto's knuckle time.

The expression had come from her father, who'd done plenty of courageous things on the force but had probably been the bravest during his last fight, against the cancer that ended his life, though hardly defeated him. His girl was a cop by then and he'd taken to giving her advice about the job. Once, he'd told her that sometimes she'd find herself in situations where there was nothing to do but stand up to a risk or challenge all by yourself. 'I call it 'knuckle time,' Amie. Something you've got to muscle your way through. The fight might be against a perp, it might be against a partner. It might even be against the whole NYPD.'

Sometimes, he'd said, the hardest battle was within your own soul.

Sellitto knew what to do. He *had* to be the first man through the door.

But after the incident at the museum yesterday

he was paralyzed with fear at the thought.

Knuckle time . . . Would he stand up or not?

Haumann now divided his entry officers into three teams and sent several others to the street corners to halt traffic and another one into the shadows beside the building's front door to intercept anybody who happened to be entering the building — and to be prepared to take down Boyd himself if he happened to wander outside on an errand, unsuspecting. One officer climbed up to the roof. Several more ESU cops secured the apartments next door to Boyd's — in case he tried to escape the way he'd done on Elizabeth Street.

Haumann then glanced at Sachs. 'You're going in with us?'

'Yup,' she replied. 'Somebody from Crime Scene's got to secure the place. We still don't know who hired this SOB and we've got to find out.'

'Which team you want to be on?'

'With whoever's going through the front door,' she said.

'That'd be Jenkins's.'

'Yes, sir.' She then explained about the residences across the street and reminded them that Boyd might target the civilians living there in an attempt to escape. Haumann nodded. 'I need somebody to clear those places, at least get people away from the front windows and keep 'em off the streets.'

Nobody wanted this job, of course. If ESU cops had been cowboys, Haumann was asking for somebody to volunteer to be cook.

The silence was broken by a voice. 'Hell, I'll take it.' It was Lon Sellitto. 'Perfect for an old guy like me.'

Sachs glanced at him. The detective had just flunked his knuckle time. His nerve had broken. He gave a carefree grin, maybe the saddest smile Sachs had ever seen in her life.

Into his mike the ESU head said, 'All teams, deploy to holding perimeter. And S and S, let me know the minute there's a change in the premises, K.'

'Roger. Out.'

Sachs said into her microphone, 'We're going in, Rhyme. I'll let you know what happens.'

'Got it,' he said tersely.

Nothing more was said between them. Rhyme didn't like her going into combat. But he knew how driven she was, how any threat to an innocent infuriated her, how it was important for her to make sure people like Thompson Boyd didn't get away. This was part of her nature and he'd never suggested she stand down at times like this.

Didn't mean he was going to be cheerful about it, though.

But then thoughts of Lincoln Rhyme faded as they started into position.

Sachs and Sellitto were walking up the alley, she to join the entry team, he to continue on to the residences across the street and get the people there under cover. The lieutenant's phony grin was gone. The man's face looked puffy and was dotted with sweat, despite the cool temperature. He wiped it, scratched the invisible bloodstain and noticed her looking at him. 'Fucking body armor. Hot.'

'Hate it,' Sachs said. They continued steadily down the alley, until they got close to the back of Boyd's apartment, where the troops were deploying. Suddenly she grabbed Sellitto's arm and pulled him back. 'Somebody's watching . . . ' But as they stepped close to the building, Sachs tripped over a trash bag and went down hard on her leg. She gasped, wincing and cradling her knee.

'You okay?'

'Fine,' she said, climbing to her feet with a grimace. She called into her radio, in a breathless voice, 'Five Eight Eight Five, I saw movement in a second-floor window, rear of the building. S and S, can you confirm?'

'No hostiles. That's one of our people you're seeing, K.'

'Roger. Out.'

Sachs started forward, limping.

'Amelia, you're hurt.'

'Nothing.'

'Tell Bo.'

'It's not a problem.'

The fact that she suffered from arthritis was well known to the inner circle — Rhyme, Mel Cooper and Sellitto — but that was about it. She went to great lengths to hide her malady, worried that the brass would sideline her on a medical if they found out. She reached into her slacks pocket and pulled out a packet of painkillers, ripped it open with her teeth and swallowed the pills dry.

Over the radio they heard Bo Haumann's voice: 'All teams form up, K.'

Sachs moved forward to the main entry team. The limp was worse.

Sellitto pulled her aside. 'You can't go in.'

'It's not like I'm going to run him to ground, Lon. I'm just going to secure the scene.'

The detective turned toward the CP truck, hoping he'd find someone to ask about the situation, but Haumann and the others had already deployed.

'It's better. It's fine.' She limped forward.

One of the officers on Team A called in a whisper to Sachs, 'Detective, you ready?'

'Yeah.'

'No, she's not.' Sellitto turned to the officer. 'She's getting the civvies out of the way. I'm going in with you guys.'

'You?'

'Yeah, me. There a fucking problem?'

'No, sir.'

'Lon,' she whispered, 'I'm fine.'

The big detective responded, 'I know enough about crime scenes to secure the place. Rhyme's been busting my chops for years to get it right.'

'I'm not going to be sprinting.'

'Yeah, maybe not, but could you drop into a combat pose if he lights you up with that fucking gun of his?'

'Yes, I could,' she answered firmly.

'Well, I don't think so. So quit arguing and get the civvies safe.' He cinched his body armor tighter and drew his revolver.

She hesitated.

'That's an order, Detective.'

She looked at him darkly. But as independent as Sachs was — some would use the word 'renegade' — the portable's daughter knew her place in the ranks of the New York City Police Department. She said, 'All right . . . but here, take this.' She drew her fifteen-round Glock and handed it to him, along with an extra clip. She took his six-shot revolver.

He looked down at the large black automatic. It was a gun with a trigger pull as delicate as a moth's wing. If he handled this weapon wrong, like he'd done on Elizabeth Street yesterday, he could easily kill himself or somebody on the entry team. Rubbing his cheek once more, Sellitto glanced at the apartment. And hurried to join the others.

Crossing the street to clear the apartments and houses, Sachs glanced back and watched them go. She turned and continued on to the apartments and houses across the street.

The limp was gone.

In fact, she was fine. The only pain she felt was disappointment that she wasn't on point with the entry team. But she'd had to fake the fall and injury. For Lon Sellitto's sake. She couldn't think of any way to save him except by forcing him to take on the job. She'd assessed the risk of his going in on a team and decided that there was minimal threat to him or to anybody else — there'd be plenty of backup, everybody was in armor and they were catching their perp by surprise. Sellitto also seemed to have some measure of control over his fear. She recalled the deliberation with which he'd held and examined the Glock, how his quick eyes had looked over the perp's building.

But in any event there really was no choice. Sellitto was a great cop. But if he stayed skittish he'd cease to be any kind of cop at all and his life would be over with. Those splinters of self-doubt had a way of infecting your entire soul. Sachs knew; she battled them constantly herself. If he didn't go back into combat now, he'd give up.

She picked up her pace; after all, she *did* have an important job here, clearing the residences across the street, and she had to move fast; the entry team was going inside at any minute. Sachs started ringing doorbells and getting people out of front rooms and making sure they stayed inside for the time being behind locked doors. She radioed Bo Haumann on the secure tactical frequency and told him that the immediate houses were clear; she'd keep going with those that were farther away, up and down the street.

'Okay, we're going in,' the man said tersely and disconnected.

Sachs continued along the street. She found her fingernail digging into her thumb. Reflecting on the irony: Sellitto fidgeted going into a fight; Amelia Sachs was edgy when she had to stay out of harm's way.

31

Lon Sellitto followed the four officers up the dim stairs, to the second-floor landing of the apartment.

Breathing hard from the climb, he paused, caught his breath. The tactical cops huddled, waiting for word from Haumann that the electricity to the apartment had been cut — they didn't want any more electrocutions.

While they waited the big detective had a talk with himself: Are you ready for this?

Think about it. Now's the time to decide. Leave or stay?

Tap, tap, tap . . .

It all swirled around in his mind: the blood spattering him obscenely, the needles from the bullet ripping apart flesh. The brown eyes that were filled with life one second and then glazed with death a moment later. The icy rush of absolute panic when that basement door on Elizabeth Street opened and his gun went off with a huge, kicking explosion, Amelia Sachs cringing, reaching for her weapon, as the bullet dug chunks of stone out of the wall just a few feet from her.

The bullet from my own goddamn gun!

What was happening? he wondered. Was his nerve gone? He laughed grimly to himself, comparing the kind of nerve he was thinking of to Lincoln Rhyme's, whose physical nerve, the one in his spine, was literally destroyed. Well, Rhyme fucking well dealt with what happened to him. Why can't I?

It was a question that had to be answered, because if he stepped up now and he caved or flubbed the takedown again, people might die. Probably would, given the stone-cold perp they were after.

If he stayed back, took himself off the detail, his career would be over, but at least he wouldn't've jeopardized anyone else.

Can you do it? he asked himself.

The leader of the team said, 'Detective, we're going in in about thirty seconds. We'll batter the door, spread out and clear the apartment. You can come in and secure the crime scene after. That all right with you?'

Leave or stay? the lieutenant asked himself. You can just walk downstairs. That'll be it. Give up your shield, hire on as a security consultant with some corporation. Double your salary.

Never get shot at again.

Tap, tap, tap . . .

Never see eyes wincing and going lifeless inches from yours.

Tap . . .

'Is that okay?' the leader repeated.

Sellitto glanced at the cop 'No,' he whispered. 'No.'

The ESU officer frowned.

The detective said, 'Take the door out with the ram, then I'll go in. First.'

'But — '

Sellitto muttered, 'You heard Detective Sachs.

This perp isn't working alone. We need anything we can find that'll lead us to the prick who hired him. I'll know what to look for and I can save the scene if he tries to fuck it up.'

'Let me call in,' the ESU man said doubtfully.

'Officer,' the detective said calmly, 'that's the way it is. I'm senior here.'

The team leader looked at his second in command. They shrugged.

'It's your . . . decision.'

Sellitto supposed the third word of that sentence was originally going to be 'funeral.'

'As soon as they pull the juice we go in,' the ESU officer said. He put on his gas mask. The team pulled on theirs, Sellitto too. He gripped Sachs's Glock — kept his finger *outside* the trigger guard — and stepped to the side of the door.

In his earpiece he heard: 'We're cutting the electricity in three . . . two . . . one.'

The leader tapped the shoulder of the officer with the battering ram. The big man swung it hard and the door crashed open.

Flying on adrenaline, forgetting everything but the perp and the evidence, Sellitto charged inside, the tactical officers behind, covering him, kicking doors open and searching the rooms. The second team came in from the kitchen.

No immediate sign of Boyd. On a small TV a sitcom played — the source of the voices and most likely the source of heat and noise that S and S had found.

Most likely.

But maybe not.

Glancing left and right as he entered the small living room, seeing no one, Sellitto headed straight for Boyd's desk, piled high with evidence: sheets of paper, ammunition, several envelopes, bits of plastic wire, a digital timer, jars of liquid and of white powder, a transistor radio, rope. Using a tissue, Sellitto carefully checked a metal cabinet near the desk for traps. He found none and opened it, noting more jars and boxes. Two more guns. Several stacks of new bills — nearly $100,000, the detective estimated.

'Room's clear,' one of the ESU officers called. Then another, from a different room.

Finally a voice: 'Team Leader A to CP, we've cleared the scene, K.'

Sellitto laughed out loud. He'd done it. Confronted whatever the fuck it was that'd been torturing him.

But don't get too cocky, he told himself, pocketing Sachs's Glock. You came along on this sleigh ride for a reason, remember? You got work to do. So secure the fucking evidence.

As he looked over the place, though, he realized something was nagging.

What?

Looking over the kitchen, the hallway, the desk. What was odd? Something was wrong.

Then it occurred to him:

Transistor radio?

Did they even make those anymore? Well, if they did, you hardly ever saw 'em, with all the fancier players available for cheap: boom boxes, CD players, MP3s.

Shit. It's a booby trap, an explosive device!

447

And it's sitting right next to a big jar of clear liquid, with a glass stopper in the top, which Sellitto knew from science class was what you used to store acid in.

'Christ!'

How long did he have before it detonated? A minute, two?

Sellitto lunged forward and grabbed the radio, stepped to the bathroom, setting it in the sink.

One of the tactical officers asked, 'What's — ?'

'We've got an IED! Clear the apartment!' the detective shouted, ripping off his gas mask.

'Get the fuck out!' the officer cried.

Sellitto ignored him. When people make improvised explosive devices they never worry about obscuring fingerprints or other clues because once the devices blow up, most evidence is destroyed. They knew Boyd's identity, of course, but there could be some trace or other prints on the device that might lead to the person hiring him or his accomplice.

'Call the Bomb Squad,' somebody transmitted.

'Shut up. I'm busy.'

There was an on/off switch on the radio but he didn't trust that to deactivate the explosive charge. Cringing, the detective worked the black plastic back off the radio.

How long, how long?

What's a reasonable time for Boyd to get into his apartment and disarm the trap?

As he popped the back off and bent down, Sellitto found himself staring at a half stick of dynamite — not a plastic explosive but plenty powerful enough to blow off his hand and blind him. There was no display. It's only in the movies that bombs have easy-to-read digital timers that count down to zero. Real bombs are detonated by tiny microprocessor timing chips without displays. Sellitto held the dynamite itself in place with a fingernail — to keep from obliterating any prints. He started to work the blasting cap out of the explosive.

Wondering how sophisticated the unsub had been (serious bomb makers use secondary detonators to take out people like Sellitto who were fucking around with their handiwork), he pulled the blasting cap out of the dynamite.

No secondary detonators, or any —

The explosion, a huge ringing bang, echoed through the bathroom, reverberating off the tile.

'What was that?' Bo Haumann called. 'Somebody shooting? We have gunshots? All units report.'

'Explosion in the bathroom of the subject's unit,' somebody called. 'Medics to the scene, EMS to the scene!'

'Negative, negative. Everybody take it easy.' Sellitto was running his burned fingers under cold water. 'I just need a Band-Aid.'

'That you, Lieutenant?'

'Yeah. It was the blasting cap went off. Boyd had a booby trap rigged to take out the evidence. I saved most of it . . . ' He pressed his hand into his armpit and squeezed. 'Fuck, that stings.'

'How big a device?' Haumann asked.

Sellitto glanced at the desk in the other room. 'Big enough to blow the shit out of what looks like a gallon jar of sulfuric acid, I'd guess. And I see some jars of powder, probably cyanide. It would've taken out most of the evidence — and anybody who was nearby.'

Several of the ESU officers glanced with gratitude toward Sellitto. One said, 'Man, this's one perp I wanna take down personally.'

Haumann, ever the voice of a detached cop, asked matter-of-factly, 'Status of unsub?'

'No sign. Heat on the infrared was a fridge, TV and sunlight on furniture, looks like,' one cop transmitted.

Sellitto looked over the room and then radioed, 'Got an idea, Bo.'

'Go ahead.'

'Let's fix the door fast. Leave me and a couple other guys inside, clear everybody else off the streets. He might be back soon. We'll get him then.'

'Roger, Lon. I like it. Let's get moving. Who knows carpentry?'

'I'll do it,' Sellitto said. 'One of my hobbies. Just get me some tools. And what kind of fucking entry team is this? Doesn't anybody have a goddamn Band-Aid?'

★   ★   ★

Down the street from Boyd's apartment, Amelia Sachs was listening to the transmitted exchanges about the kick-in. It seemed that her plan for Sellitto might've worked — even better than she'd hoped. She wasn't exactly sure what had happened but it was clear that he'd done

450

something ballsy and she heard some newfound confidence in his voice.

She acknowledged the message about the plan to pull everybody off the street and wait for Boyd to return, then she added that she was going to warn the last residents across the street from the safe house and, after that, she'd join the others on the stake-out. She knocked on the front door and told the woman who answered to stay away from the front of the house until she heard it was safe to come out. There was a police action going on across the street.

The woman's eyes were wide. 'Is it dangerous?'

Sachs gave her the standard line: We're just being cautious, nothing to be alarmed about and so on. Noncommittal, reassuring. Half of being a cop is public relations. Sometimes it's *most* of being a cop. Sachs added that she'd seen some children's toys in the woman's yard. Were they home now?

It was then that Sachs saw a man emerge from an alleyway up the street. He was walking slowly in the direction of the apartment, head down, wearing a hat and a long overcoat. She couldn't see his face.

The woman was saying in a concerned voice, 'It's just my boyfriend and me here now. The children are at school. They usually walk home but should we go pick them up?'

'Ma'am, that man there, across the street?'

She stepped forward and glanced. 'Him?'

'Do you know him?'

'Sure. He lives in that building right there.'

'What's his name?'

'Larry Tang.'

'Oh, he's Chinese?'

'I guess. Or Japanese or something.'

Sachs relaxed.

'*He*'s not involved in anything, is he?' the woman asked.

'No, he's not. About your children, it probably would be best to — '

Oh, Jesus . . .

Looking past the woman, Amelia Sachs stared into a bedroom of the bungalow, which was in the process of being renovated. On the wall were some painted cartoon characters. One was from Winnie-the-Pooh — the character Tigger.

The orange shade of the paint was identical to the samples she'd found near Geneva's aunt's place in Harlem. Bright orange.

Then she glanced at the floor in the entry hall. On a square of newspapers was an old pair of shoes. Light brown. She could just see the label inside. They were Bass. About size 11.

Amelia Sachs understood suddenly that the boyfriend that the woman had referred to was Thompson Boyd and the apartment across the street wasn't his residence but was another of his safe houses. The reason it was empty at the moment, of course, was that he was somewhere in this very house.

452

32

Amelia Sachs, thinking: Get the woman outside. Her eyes aren't guilty. She's not part of it.

Thinking: Of course Boyd's armed.

Thinking: And I just traded my Glock for a fucking six-shooter.

Get her out of here. Fast.

Sachs's hand was easing toward her waistband, where Sellitto's tiny pistol rested. 'Oh, one more thing, ma'am,' she said calmly. 'I saw a van up the street. I wonder if you could tell me whose it is.'

What was that noise? Sachs wondered. Something from within the house. Metallic. But not like a weapon, a faint clatter.

'A van?'

'Yeah, you can't see it from here. It's behind that tree.' Sachs stepped back, gesturing her forward. 'Could you step outside and take a look, please? It'd be a big help.'

The woman, though, stayed where she was, in the entryway, glancing to her right. Toward where the sound had come from. 'Honey?' She frowned. 'What's wrong?'

The clattering, Sachs understood suddenly, had been venetian blinds. Boyd had heard the exchange with his girlfriend and had looked out the window. He'd seen an ESU officer or squad car near his safe house.

453

'It's really important,' Sachs tried. 'If you could just . . . '

But the woman froze, her eyes wide.

'No! Tom! What're you — ?'

'Ma'am, come over here!' Sachs shouted, drawing the Smith & Wesson. 'Now! You're in danger!'

'What're you doing with that? Tom!' She backed away from Boyd but remained in the corridor, a rabbit in headlights. 'No!'

'Get down!' Sachs said in a ragged whisper, dropping into a crouch and moving forward into the house.

'Boyd, listen to me,' Sachs shouted. 'If you've got a weapon, drop it. Throw it out where I can see it. Then get on the floor. I mean now! There're dozens of officers outside!'

Silence, except for the woman's sobbing.

Sachs executed a fast feint, looking low around the corner to the left. She caught a glimpse of the man, his face calm, a large, black pistol in his hand. Not the North American .22 magnum, but an automatic, which would have stopping-power bullets and a clip capacity of fifteen rounds or so. She ducked back to cover. Boyd'd been expecting her to present higher and the two slugs he fired missed her, though only by inches, blowing plaster and wood splinters into the air. The brunette was screaming with every breath, scrabbling away, looking from Sachs back to where Boyd was. 'No, no, no!'

Sachs called, 'Throw your weapon down!'

'Tom, please! What's going on?'

Sachs called to her, 'Get down, miss!'

454

A long moment of complete silence. What was Boyd up to? It was as if he was debating what to do next.

Then he fired a single round.

The detective flinched. The bullet was wide, though. It completely missed the wall where Sachs stood.

But, it turned out, Boyd hadn't been aiming at her at all, and the slug did indeed hit its target.

The brunette was dropping to her knees, her hands on her thigh, which gushed blood. 'Tom,' she whispered. 'Why? . . . Oh, Tom.' She rolled onto her back and lay clutching her leg, gasping in pain.

Just like at the museum, Boyd had shot someone to distract the police, to give him a chance to get away. But this time it was his girlfriend.

Sachs heard the crack of glass as Boyd broke through a window to escape.

The woman kept whispering words Sachs couldn't hear. She radioed Haumann about the woman's condition and location, and he immediately sent medics and backup. Then she thought: But it'll take a few minutes for EMS to get here. I *have* to save her. A tourniquet would slow the bleeding. I can save her life.

But then: No. He's not getting away. She looked around the corner, low, fast, and saw Boyd drop out of the hall window into the side yard.

Sachs hesitated, looking back at the woman. She'd passed out, and her hand had fallen away from the terrible wound on her leg. Already, blood pooled under her torso.

Christ . . .

She started toward her. Then stopped. No. You know what you have to do. Amelia Sachs ran to the side window. She looked out, fast again, in case he was waiting for her. But, no, Boyd expected that she'd save the woman. Sachs saw him sprinting away from the apartment down the cobblestoned alley without a glance back.

She looked down. A six-foot drop to the ground. Her story about the pain from the fall she'd told to Sellitto twenty minutes ago was fake; the chronic pain wasn't.

Oh, brother.

She scooted up onto the sill, clear of the broken glass, and swung her legs out, then pushed off. Trying to ease the shock of the landing, Sachs kept her knees bent. But it was a long drop and as she landed her left leg collapsed and she tumbled onto gravel and grass, crying out at the pain.

Breathing hard, she struggled to her feet and started off after Boyd, now with an honest limp slowing her up. God gets you for lying, she thought.

Shoving her way through a row of anemic bushes, Sachs broke from the yard into an alley that ran behind the houses and apartments. She looked right and left. No sign of him.

Then, a hundred feet ahead of her, she saw a large wooden door swing open. This was typical of older parts of New York — unheated, stand-alone garages lining alleys behind row and town houses. It made sense that Boyd would keep his car garaged; the Search and Surveillance team hadn't found it anywhere on the surrounding blocks. Jogging forward as best she could, Sachs reported his location to the command post.

'Copy, Five Eight Eight Five. We're on our way, K.'

Moving unsteadily over the cobblestones, she flipped open the cylinder of Sellitto's Smittie and grimaced to see that he was among the more cautious gun owners; the cylinder beneath the hammer was empty.

Five shots.

Versus Boyd's automatic with three times that many and possibly a spare clip or two in his pocket.

Running to the mouth of the alley, she could hear an engine start and a second later the blue Buick backed out, the rear toward her. The alley was too narrow to make the turn in one motion, so Boyd had to stop, drive forward then back up again. This gave Sachs the chance to sprint to within sixty or seventy feet of the garage.

Boyd finished the maneuver and, with the garage door as a shield between him and Sachs, accelerated away fast.

Sachs dropped hard to the cobblestones and saw that the only target she had was under a narrow gap at the bottom of the garage door: the rear tires.

Prone, Sachs sighted on the right one.

It's a rule in urban-combat shooting never to fire unless you 'know your backdrop,' that is, where the bullet will end up if you miss your shot — or if it penetrates your target and continues on. As Boyd's car peeled away from her, Sachs considered this protocol for a fraction of a second, then — thinking of Geneva Settle — came up with a rule of her own: This fucker's not getting away.

The best she could do to control the shot was to aim low so that the bullet would ricochet upward and lodge in the car itself if she missed.

Cocking the gun to single action, so the trigger pull was more sensitive, she aimed and squeezed off two rounds, one slightly higher than the other.

The slugs zipped under the garage door and at least one punctured the right rear tire. As the car lurched to the right and collided hard with the brick wall of the alley, Sachs rose and sprinted toward the wreck, wincing from the pain. At the garage door she paused and looked around it. It turned out that *both* right tires were flattened; she'd hit the front one as well. Boyd tried to drive away from the wall, but the front wheel was bent and frozen against the chassis. He climbed out, swinging the gun back and forth, searching for the shooter.

'Boyd! Drop the weapon!'

His response was to fire five or six shots toward the door. Sachs responded with one shot, which struck the car body inches from him, then she rolled to her right and rose fast, noting that Boyd was fleeing from her into the street beyond.

She could see the backdrop this time — a

458

brick wall across the far street — and squeezed off another round.

But just as the gun fired, Boyd turned aside as if he'd been expecting this. The slug sailed past him, also inches away. He returned fire, a barrage of shots, and she dropped hard to the slimy cobblestones again, her radio shattering. He disappeared around the corner, to the left.

One shot left. Should've used only one on the tire, she thought angrily, as she rose and hurried after him as best she could on the painful leg. A pause at the corner where the alley met the sidewalk, a fast glance to the left. She saw his solid form sprinting away from her.

She grabbed the Motorola and pressed transmit. Nope, it was gone. Shit. Call 911 on the cell? Too much to explain, too little time to relay a message. Somebody in one of the buildings had to've called in about the shots. She continued after Boyd, breath rasping, feet slapping on the ground.

At the far intersection, the end of the block, a blue-and-white rolled to a stop. The officers didn't climb out; they hadn't heard the shots and didn't know the killer and Sachs were here. Boyd looked up and saw them. He stopped fast and leapt over a small fence then ducked underneath the stairway of an apartment building leading to the first floor. She heard kicking as he tried to break into the basement apartment.

Sachs waved toward the officers but they were looking up and down the cross street and didn't see her.

It was then that a young couple stepped out

the front door of the apartment directly across from Boyd. Closing the door behind them, the young man zipped up his vest against the chill day and the woman took his arm. They started down the stairs.

The kicking stopped.

Oh, no . . . Sachs realized what was about to happen. She couldn't see Boyd but she knew what he was going to do. He was sighting on the couple now. He was going to shoot one or both, steal their keys and escape into the apartment — hoping again that the police would divide their forces to look after the wounded.

'Get down!' Sachs shouted.

Nearly a hundred feet away, the couple didn't hear.

Boyd would be drawing a target on them now, waiting for them to get closer.

'Get down!'

Sachs rose and limped toward them.

The couple noticed her but couldn't make out what she was saying. They paused, frowning.

'Get down!' she repeated.

The man cupped his hand behind his ear, shaking his head.

Sachs stopped, took a deep breath and fired her last bullet into a metal garbage can about twenty feet from the couple.

The woman screamed and they turned, scrabbling up the stairs into their apartment. The door slammed.

At least she'd managed to —

Beside Sachs a block of limestone exploded, pelting her with hot lead and bits of stone. A half second later she heard the loud pop of Boyd's gun.

Another shot and another, driving Sachs back, bullets striking feet from her. She stumbled through the yard, tripping over a foot-high wire edging fence and some plaster lawn ornaments, Bambis and elves. One slug grazed her vest, knocking the breath from her lungs. She went down hard in a planting bed. More slugs slammed home nearby. Boyd then turned toward the officers leaping out of their cruiser. He peppered the squad car with several rounds, flattening the tires and driving the officers to cover behind the car. The uniforms were staying put but at least they'd have called the assault in and other troops would be on the way.

Which meant of course that there was only one way for Boyd to go — toward her. She hunkered down for cover behind some bushes. Boyd had stopped firing but she could hear his footsteps getting closer. He was twenty feet away, she guessed. Then ten. She was sure that at any minute she'd see his face, followed by the muzzle of his weapon. Then she'd die . . .

Thud.

Thud.

Rising on an elbow, she could see the killer, close, kicking at another basement-apartment door, which was slowly starting to give way. His face was eerily calm — like that of The Hanged Man in the tarot card he'd intended to leave beside Geneva Settle's body. He must've believed he'd hit Sachs because he ignored where she'd fallen and was concentrating on

461

breaking through the doorway — the only escape route left. He looked behind him once or twice, toward the far end of the block, where the uniformed officers were making their way toward him — though slowly since he'd turn and fire at them occasionally.

He too would have to be out of ammo pretty soon, she figured. He probably —

Boyd ejected the clip from his pistol and slipped a new one in. Reloaded.

Okay, well . . .

She could stay where she was, safe, and hope that other officers would get here before he escaped.

But Sachs thought of the brunette lying bloody in the bungalow — maybe dead by now. She thought of the electrocuted officer, the librarian killed yesterday. She thought of the young rookie Pulaski, his face battered and bloody. And mostly she thought of poor young Geneva Settle, who'd be at risk every minute Boyd was free and walking the streets. Clutching the empty gun, she came to a decision.

★　★　★

Thompson Boyd delivered another powerful kick into the basement door. It was starting to give way. He'd get inside, he'd —

'Don't move, Boyd. Drop the weapon.'

Blinking his stinging eyes in surprise, Thompson turned his head. He lowered his foot, which was poised for another kick.

Well, now, what's this?

462

Keeping his gun low, he turned his head slowly and looked toward her. Yes, like he'd thought, it was the woman from the crime scene at the museum library yesterday morning. Walking back and forth, back and forth, like the sidewinder. Red hair, white jumpsuit. The one he'd enjoyed watching, admiring her. There was a lot to admire, he reflected. And a good shot, too.

He was surprised that she was alive. He thought for sure he'd hit her in the last barrage.

'Boyd, I will shoot. Drop your gun, lie down on the sidewalk.'

He thought a few more kicks at this door should break it in. Then into the alley behind the place. Or maybe the people who lived here had a car. He could take the keys and shoot whoever was inside, wound them, draw off more of the police. Escape.

But, of course, there was one question that had to be answered first: Did she have any ammunition left?

'You hearing me, Boyd?'

'So it's you.' Squinted his stinging eyes. Hadn't used any Murine lately. 'Thought it might be.'

She frowned. She didn't know what he meant. Maybe she was wondering if he'd seen her before, wondering how he knew her.

Boyd was careful not to move. He had to figure this out. Shoot her or not? But if he made the slightest motion toward her and she *did* have rounds left she'd fire. He knew that without a doubt. Nothing squeamish about this woman.

They'll kill you in a kiss . . .

He debated. Her gun was a six-round Smith & Wesson .38 special. She'd fired five times. Thompson Boyd always counted shots (he knew he himself had eight left in his present clip, and one more fourteen-round clip in his pocket).

Had she reloaded? If not, did she have one more round left?

There are police officers who keep an empty chamber under the hammer on revolvers on the rare chance that accidentally dropping it will cause the gun to fire. But she didn't seem to be that sort of person. She knew weapons too well. She'd never drop one accidentally. Besides, if she was doing tactical work, she'd want every round possible. No, she wasn't an empty-cylinder kind of cop.

'Boyd, I'm not telling you again!'

On the other hand, he was thinking, this gun wasn't hers. Yesterday at the museum she'd worn an automatic on her hip, a Glock. She still had a Glock holster on her belt now. Was the Smittie a backup piece? In the old days, when all cops had six-shooters, they sometimes carried another gun in an ankle holster. But these days, with automatics holding at least a dozen rounds and two extra clips on the belt, they usually didn't bother with a second weapon.

No, he bet that she'd either lost her automatic or loaned it to somebody and had borrowed this one, which meant she probably *didn't* have rounds to reload. Next question: Did the person she *borrowed* the Smittie from keep an empty chamber under the hammer? That, he'd have no

464

way of knowing, of course.

So the question came down to what kind of person she was. Boyd thought back to the museum, seeing her searching like a rattlesnake. Thinking of her in the hallway outside the Elizabeth Street safe house, going through the door after him. Thinking of her coming after him now — leaving Jeanne to die from the bullet wound in her thigh.

He decided: She was bluffing. If she had a round left she'd have shot him.

'You're out of ammo,' he announced. He turned toward her and raised his pistol.

She grimaced and the gun slumped. He'd been right. Should he kill her? No, just shoot to wound. But where was the best place? Painful and life-threatening. Screaming and copious blood both attract a lot of attention. She was favoring one leg; he'd shoot the painful one, the knee. When she was down, he'd park another round in her shoulder. And get away.

'So you win,' she said. 'What is it now? I'm a hostage?'

He hadn't thought of this. He hesitated. Did it make sense? Would it be helpful? Usually hostages were more trouble than they were worth.

No, better to shoot her. He began to pull the trigger as she pitched her gun to the sidewalk in defeat. He glanced at it, thinking, Something's wrong here . . . What was it?

She'd been holding the revolver in her *left* hand. But the holster was on her right hip.

Thompson's eyes returned to her and gasped

465

as he saw the flashing knife cartwheeling toward his face. She'd flung it with her right hand, when he'd glanced at her gun for a second.

The switchblade didn't stick into him, or even cut — it was the handle that collided with his cheek — but she'd tossed it directly at his poor eyes. Thompson ducked away instinctively, lifting his arm to protect them. Before he could step back and draw a target, the woman was on him, swinging a stone she'd picked up from the garden. He felt a stunning blow on his temple, gasped at the pain.

He pulled the trigger once, and the gun fired. But the shot missed and before he could fire again the rock slammed into his right hand. The gun dropped to the ground. He howled and cradled his wounded fingers.

Thinking she'd go for the gun, he tried to body-block her. But she wasn't interested in the pistol. She had all the weapon she needed; the rock crashed into his face once more. 'No, no . . . ' He tried to hit her, but she was big and strong, and another blow from the rock sent him to his knees, then his side, twisting away from the blows. 'Stop, stop,' he cried. But in response he felt another blow of the rock against his cheek. He heard a howl of rage coming from her throat.

They'll kill you . . .

What was she doing? he wondered in shock. She'd won . . . Why was she doing this, breaking the rules? How could she? This wasn't by the book.

. . . in a kiss.

466

In fact, when the uniformed officers sprinted up a moment later, only one of them grabbed Thompson Boyd and cuffed him. The other got his arm around the policewoman and struggled to wrestle the bloody stone from her grip. Through the pain, the ringing in his ears, Thompson heard the cop saying over and over, 'It's okay, it's okay, you got him, Detective. It's cool, you can relax. He's not going anywhere, he's not going anywhere, he's not going anywhere . . . '

33

Please, please . . .

Amelia Sachs was hurrying back to Boyd's bungalow as fast as she was able, ignoring the congratulations from fellow officers and *trying* to ignore the pain in her leg.

Sweating, breathless, she trotted up to the first EMS medic she saw and asked, 'The woman in that house?'

'There?' He nodded to the house.

'Right. The brunette who lives there.'

'Oh, her. I've got bad news, I'm afraid.'

Sachs inhaled a deep breath, felt the horror like ice on her flesh. She'd captured Boyd but the woman she could have saved was dead. She dug a fingernail into her thumb's cuticle and felt pain, felt blood. Thinking: I did exactly what Boyd did. I sacrificed an innocent life for the sake of the job.

The medic continued, 'She was shot.'

'I know,' Sachs whispered. Staring down at the ground. Oh, man, this would be hard to live with . . .

'You don't have to worry.'

'Worry?'

'She'll be okay.'

Sachs frowned. 'You said you had bad news.'

'Well, like, getting shot's pretty bad news.'

'Christ, I *knew* she was shot. I was there when it happened.'

468

'Oh.'

'I thought you meant she died.'

'Naw. Was a bleeder but we got it in time. She'll be all right. She's at St. Luke's ER. Stable condition.'

'Okay, thanks.'

I've got bad news . . .

Sachs wandered off, limping, and found Sellitto and Haumann in front of the safe house.

'You collared him with an empty weapon?' Haumann asked, incredulous.

'Actually I collared him with a rock.'

The head of ESU nodded, lifting an eyebrow — his sweetest praise.

'Boyd saying anything?' she asked.

'Understood his rights. Then clammed up.'

She and Sellitto swapped weapons. He reloaded. She checked her Glock and reholstered it.

Sachs asked, 'What's the story on the premises?'

Haumann ran a hand over his bristly crew cut and said, 'Looks like the bungalow he was living in was rented in his girlfriend's name, Jeanne Starke. They're her kids, two daughters. Not Boyd's. We've got Child Welfare involved. That place' — he nodded toward the apartment — 'was a safe house. Full of tools of the trade, you know.'

Sachs said, 'I better run the scene.'

'We kept it secure,' Haumann said. 'Well, *he* did.' A nod toward Sellitto. The ESU head said, 'I gotta debrief the brass. You'll be around after the scene? They'll want a statement.'

Sachs nodded. And together she and the heavy detective walked toward the safe house. A silence thick as sand rested between them. Finally Sellitto glanced at her leg and said, 'Limp's back.'

'Back?'

'Yeah, when you were clearing the houses, across the street, I looked out the window. Seemed like you were walking fine.'

'Sometimes it just fixes itself.'

Sellitto shrugged. 'Funny how stuff like that happens.'

'Funny.'

He knew what she'd done for him. He was telling her so. Then he added: 'Okay, we got the shooter. But that's only half the job. We need the prick that hired him and his partner — who we gotta assume just took over Boyd's assignment. Get on the grid, Detective.' Sellitto said this in a voice as gruff as any that Rhyme could muster.

This was the best thanks he could've given her: just knowing that he was back.

★   ★   ★

Often the most important piece of evidence is the last one you find.

Any good CS searcher'll assess the scene and immediately target the fragile items that are subject to evaporation, contamination by rain, dissipation by wind, and so on, leaving the obvious — like the literal smoking gun — to be collected later.

If the scene's secure, Lincoln Rhyme often

470

said, the good stuff ain't going anywhere.

In both Boyd's residence and the safe house across the street, Sachs had collected latent prints, rolled up the trace, collected fluid samples from the toilet for DNA analysis, scraped floor and furniture surfaces, cut portions of the carpet for fiber samples and photographed and videoed the entire sites. Only then did she turn her attention to the larger and more obvious things. She arranged to have the acid and cyanide transported to the department's hazardous-evidence holding center in the Bronx, and processed the improvised explosive device contained in the transistor radio.

She examined and logged in weapons and ammunition, the cash, coils of rope, tools. Dozens of other items that might prove helpful.

Finally Sachs picked up a small, white envelope that was sitting on a shelf near the front door of the safe house.

Inside was a single sheet of paper.

She read it. Then she gave a fast laugh. She read the letter again. And called Rhyme, thinking to herself: Brother, were we wrong.

★   ★   ★

'So,' Rhyme said to Cooper as both men stared at the computer screen. 'I'm betting a hundred bucks you're going to find more pure carbon, just like what was on the map hidden under his pillow on Elizabeth Street. You want to put some money on it? Any takers?'

'Too late,' said the tech, as the analyzer beeped

and the trace-elements analysis from the paper popped up in front of them. 'Not that I would've bet anyway.' He shoved his glasses higher on his nose and said, 'And, yep, carbon. One hundred percent.'

Carbon. Which could be found in charcoal or ash or a number of other substances.

But which could also be diamond dust.

'What's the business world's latest abomination of the English language?' the criminalist asked, his mood lighthearted once again. 'We were one-eighty on this one.'

Oh, they hadn't been off base about Boyd's being the perp or the fact he'd been hired to kill Geneva. No, it was the motive they'd blown completely. Everything they'd speculated about the early civil rights movement, about the present-day implications of Charles Singleton's setup in the Freedmen's Trust robbery, about the Fourteenth Amendment conspiracy . . . they'd been totally wrong.

Geneva Settle had been targeted to die simply because she'd seen something she shouldn't have: a jewelry robbery being planned.

The letter Amelia had found in his safe house contained diagrams of various buildings in Midtown, including the African-American museum. The note read:

A black girl, fifth floor in this window, 2 October, about 0830. She saw my delivery van when he was parked in a alley behind the Jewelry exchange. Saw enough to guess the plans of mine. Kill her.

The library window near the microfiche reader where Geneva was attacked was circled on the diagram.

In addition to the misspelling, the language of the note was unusual, which, to a criminalist, was good; it's far easier to trace the unusual than the common. Rhyme had Cooper send a copy to Parker Kincaid, a former FBI document examiner outside of D.C., currently in private practice. Like Rhyme, Kincaid was sometimes recruited by his old employer and other law enforcement agencies to consult in cases involving documents and handwriting. Kincaid's reply email said he'd get back to them as soon as he could.

As she looked over the letter Amelia Sachs shook her head angrily. She recounted the incident of the armed man she and Pulaski had seen outside the museum yesterday — the one who turned out to be a security guard, who'd told them about the valuable contents of the exchange, the multimillion-dollar shipments from Amsterdam and Jerusalem every day.

'Should've mentioned that,' she said, shaking her head.

But who could have guessed that Thompson Boyd had been hired to kill Geneva because she'd looked out the window at the wrong time?

'But why steal the microfiche?' Sellitto asked.

'To lead us off, of course. Which it did pretty damn well.' Rhyme sighed. 'Here we were running around, thinking of constitutional law conspiracies. Boyd probably had no clue what Geneva was reading.' He turned to the girl, who

473

sat nearby cradling a cup of hot chocolate. 'Someone, whoever wrote that note, saw you from the street. He or Boyd contacted the librarian to find out who you were and when you'd be back, so Boyd could be there, waiting for you. Dr. Barry was killed because he could connect you to them . . . Now, think back to a week ago. You looked out the window at eight-thirty and saw a van and somebody in the alley. Do you remember what you saw?'

The girl squinted and looked down. 'I don't know. I looked out the window a bunch. When I get tired of reading I walk around some, you know. I can't remember anything specific.'

For ten minutes Sachs talked with Geneva, trying to coax her recollections into coming up with an image. But to recall a specific person and a delivery van on the busy streets of Midtown from a glance a week ago was too much for the girl's memory.

Rhyme called the director of the American Jewelry Exchange and told him what they'd learned. Asked if he had any idea who might be trying a heist, the man replied, 'Fuck, no clue. It happens more than you'd think, though.'

'We found traces of pure carbon in some of the evidence. Diamond dust, we're thinking.'

'Oh, that'd mean they'd checked the alley near the loading dock probably. Nobody from outside gets near the cutting rooms, but, hey, you polish product, you get dust. It ends up in the vacuum cleaner bags and on everything we throw out.'

The man chuckled, not much troubled by the news of the impending burglary. 'I tell you, though, whoever's going after us's got some balls. We got the best fucking security in the city. Everybody thinks it's like on TV. We have guys come in to buy their girlfriends rings and they look around and ask where's those invisible beams that you wear goggles to see, you know? Well, the answer is they don't *make* any fucking invisible-beam machines. 'Cause if you can walk around the beams when you're wearing special goggles, then the bad guys are going to buy special fucking goggles and walk *around* them, right? Real alarms aren't like that. If a fly farts in our vault, the alarm goes off. And, fact is, the system's so tight a fly can't even *get* inside.'

'I should have known,' Lincoln Rhyme snapped after they hung up. 'Look at the chart! Look at what we found in the first safe house.' He nodded toward the reference to the map that had been found on Elizabeth Street. It showed only a basic outline of the library where Geneva was attacked. The jewelry exchange across the street was drawn in much greater detail, as were the nearby alleys, doors and loading docks — entrance and exit routes to and from the exchange, not the museum.

Two detectives from downtown had interrogated Boyd to find out the identity of the person behind the heist, the one who'd hired him, but he was stonewalling.

Sellitto then checked NYPD Larceny for suspicious activity reports in the diamond district but there were no particular leads that seemed relevant. Fred Dellray took time off from investigating the rumors of the potential terrorist bombings to look through the FBI's files about any federal investigations involving jewelry thefts. Since larceny isn't a federal crime, there weren't many cases, but several of them — mostly involving money laundering in the New York area — were active and he promised he'd bring the reports over right away.

They now turned to the evidence from Boyd's safe house and residence, in hopes of finding the mastermind of the theft. They examined the guns, the chemicals, the tools and the rest of the items, but there was nothing that they hadn't found before: more bits of orange paint, acid stains and crumbs of falafel and smears of yogurt, Boyd's favorite meal, it seemed. They ran the serial numbers on the money and came up with nothing from Treasury, and none of the bills yielded any fingerprints. To withdraw this much money from an account was risky for the man who hired Boyd because any such large transactions have to be reported under money laundering rules. But a fast check of recent large cash withdrawals from area banks came up with no leads. This was curious, Rhyme reflected, though he concluded that the perp had probably withdrawn small amounts of the cash over time for Boyd's fee.

The unsub was one of the few people on earth, it seemed, who didn't own a cell phone, or, if he did, his was an anonymous prepaid unit — there were no billing records — and he'd managed to dispose of it before he was caught. A look at Jeanne Starke's home phone bill yielded nothing suspicious except a half-dozen calls to

476

payphones in Manhattan, Queens or Brooklyn, but there was no regular pattern to the locations.

Sellitto's heroics had, however, yielded some good evidence: fingerprints on the dynamite and the guts of the explosive transistor radio. The FBI's IAFIS and local print databases resulted in a name: Jon Earle Wilson. He'd done time in Ohio and New Jersey for an assortment of crimes, including arson, bombmaking and insurance fraud. But he'd fallen off the radar of the local authorities, Cooper reported. LKA was Brooklyn but that was a vacant lot.

'I don't want the *last* known address. I want the *presently* known. Get the feds on it too.'

'Will do.'

The doorbell rang. Everybody was on edge with the main perp and accomplice still unaccounted for and they looked at the doorway cautiously. Sellitto had answered the bell and he stepped into the lab with an African-American boy, midteens, tall, wearing calf-length shorts and a Knicks jersey. He was carrying a heavy shopping bag. He blinked in surprise at the sight of Lincoln Rhyme — and then at everything else in the room.

'Yo, yo, Geneva. What happenin'?'

She looked at him with a frown.

'Yo, I'm Rudy.' He laughed. 'You ain't remember me.'

Geneva nodded. 'Yeah. I think so. You're — '

'Ronelle's brother.'

The girl said to Rhyme, 'A girl in my class.'

'How'd you know I was here?'

'Word up. Ronee hear it from somebody.'

'Keesh probably. I told her,' Geneva said to Rhyme.

The boy looked around the lab again then back to Geneva. 'Yo, what it is, some of the girls got some shit together for you. You know, you ain't be in school and all so they thought you might want something to read. I say, damn, give the girl a GameBoy, but they said, no, she like books. So they got it up for you with these.'

'Really?'

'Word. Ain't no homework or nothing like that. Shit you can read for the fun of it.'

'Who?'

'Ronelle, some other girls, don't know. Here. Weigh a ton.'

'Well, thanks.'

She took the bag.

'Girls tell me, say ever'thing gonna be cool.'

Geneva gave a sour laugh and thanked him again, told him to say hello to the other kids in her class. The boy left. Geneva glanced down into the bag. She lifted out a book by Laura Ingalls Wilder. Geneva gave another laugh. 'Don't know what they're thinking of. I read this, must be seven years ago.' She dropped it back in the bag. 'Anyway, it was nice of them.'

'And useful,' Thom said pointedly. 'Not much here for you to read, I'm afraid.' A sour glance at Rhyme. 'I keep working on him. Music. He listens to music a lot now. Even threatens to write some tunes himself. But reading fiction? We haven't gotten that far yet.'

Geneva gave him an amused smile and she took the heavy bag and walked toward the hallway as Rhyme said, 'Thank you for airing laundry, Thom. In any case, now Geneva can read to her heart's content, which I'm sure she'd rather do than listening to your tedious editorializing. And as for my *leisure* time? I guess I don't *have* much of it, you know, trying to catch killers and all.' His eyes returned to the evidence charts.

THOMPSON BOYD'S RESIDENCE AND PRIMARY SAFE HOUSE

- More falafel and yogurt, orange paint trace, as before.
- Cash (fee for job?) $100,000 in new bills. Untraceable. Probably withdrawn in small amounts over time.
- Weapons (guns, billy club, rope) traced to prior crime scenes.
- Acid and cyanide traced to prior crime scenes, no links to manufacturers.
- No cell phone found. Other telephone records not helpful.
- Tools traced to prior crime scenes.
- Letter revealing that G. Settle was targeted because she was a witness to a jewelry heist in the planning. More pure carbon — identified as diamond dust trace.
  - Sent to Parker Kincaid in Washington, D.C., for document examination.
- Improvised explosive device, as part of booby trap. Fingerprints are those of convicted bomb maker Jon Earle Wilson. Presently searching for him.

POTTERS' FIELD SCENE (1868)

- Tavern in Gallows Heights — located in the Eighties on the Upper West Side, mixed neighborhood in the 1860s.
- Potters' Field was possible hangout for Boss Tweed and other corrupt New York politicians.

- Charles came here July 15, 1868.
- Burned down following explosion, presumably just after Charles's visit. To hide his secret?
- Body in basement, man, presumably killed by Charles Singleton.
  - Shot in forehead by .36 Navy Colt loaded with .39-caliber ball (type of weapon Charles Singleton owned).
  - Gold coins.
  - Man was armed with Derringer.
  - No identification.
  - Had ring with name 'Winskinskie' on it.
    - Means 'doorman' or 'gatekeeper' in Delaware Indian language.
    - Currently searching other meanings.

EAST HARLEM SCENE (GENEVA'S GREAT-AUNT'S APARTMENT)

- Used cigarette and 9mm round as explosive device to distract officers. Merit brand, not traceable.
- Friction ridge prints: None. Glove-prints only.

- Poisonous gas device:
  - Glass jar, foil, candleholder. Untraceable.
  - Cyanide and sulfuric acid. Neither containing markers. Untraceable.
- Clear liquid similar to that found on Elizabeth Street.
  - Determined to be Murine.
- Small flakes of orange paint. Posing as construction or highway worker?

ELIZABETH STREET SAFE HOUSE SCENE

- Used electrical booby trap.
- Fingerprints: None. Glove prints only.
- Security camera and monitor; no leads.
- Tarot deck, missing the twelfth card; no leads.
- Map with diagram of museum where G. Settle was attacked and buildings across the street.
- Trace:
  - Falafel and yogurt.
  - Wood scrapings from desk with traces of pure sulfuric acid.
  - Clear liquid, not explosive. Sent to FBI lab.
    - Determined to be Murine.

- More fibers from rope. Garrotte?
- Pure carbon found in map.
- Determined to be additional diamond dust.
- Safe house was rented, for cash, to Billy Todd Hammil. Fits Unsub 109's description, but no leads to an actual Hammil.

AFRICAN-AMERICAN MUSEUM SCENE

- Rape pack:
  - Tarot card, twelfth card in deck, The Hanged Man, meaning spiritual searching.
  - Smiley-face bag.
    - Too generic to trace.
  - Box cutter.
  - Trojan condoms.
  - Duct tape.
  - Jasmine scent.
  - Unknown item bought for $5.95. Probably a stocking cap.
  - Receipt, indicating store was in New York City, discount variety store or drugstore.
  - Most likely purchased in a store on Mulberry Street, Little Italy. Unsub identified by clerk.
- Fingerprints:
  - Unsub wore latex or vinyl gloves.
  - Prints on items in rape pack belonged to person with small hands, no IAFIS hits. Positive ID for clerk's.
- Trace:
  - Cotton-rope fibers, some with traces of human blood. Garrotte?
    - Sent to CODIS.
      - No DNA match in CODIS.
  - Popcorn and cotton candy with traces of canine urine.
- Weapons:
  - Billy club or martial arts weapon.
  - Pistol is a North American Arms .22 rimfire magnum, Black Widow or Mini-Master.
  - Makes own bullets, bored-out slugs filled with needles. No match in IBIS or DRUGFIRE.
- Motive:
  - G. Settle was a witness to a crime in the planning — at the American Jewelry Exchange across the

street from the African-American museum.

- Profile of incident sent to VICAP and NCIC.
  - Murder in Amarillo, TX, five years ago. Similar M.O. — staged crime scene (apparently ritual killing, but real motive unknown).
    - Victim was a retired prison guard.
    - Composite picture sent to Texas prison.
      - Identified as Thompson G. Boyd, executions control officer.
  - Murder in Ohio, three years ago. Similar M.O. — staged crime scene (apparently sexual assault, but real motive probably hired killing). Files missing.

PROFILE OF UNSUB 109

- Determined to be Thompson G. Boyd, former executions control officer, from Amarillo, TX.
- Presently in custody.

PROFILE OF PERSON HIRING UNSUB 109

- No information at this time.

PROFILE OF UNSUB 109'S ACCOMPLICE

- Black male.
- Late 30's, early 40's.
- Six feet.
- Solidly built.
- Wearing green combat jacket.
- Ex-convict.
- Has a limp.
- Reportedly armed.
- Clean-shaven.
- Black do-rag.
- Awaiting additional witnesses and security tapes.
  - Tape inconclusive, sent to lab for analysis.
- Old work shoes.

PROFILE OF CHARLES SINGLETON

- Former slave, ancestor of G. Settle. Married, one son. Given orchard in New York state by master. Worked as teacher, as well. Instrumental in early civil rights movement.

482

- Charles allegedly committed theft in 1868, the subject of the article in stolen microfiche.
- Reportedly had a secret that could bear on case. Worried that tragedy would result if his secret was revealed.
- Attended meetings in Gallows Heights neighborhood of New York.
  - Involved in some risky activities?
- Worked with Frederick Douglass and others in getting the 14th Amendment to the Constitution ratified.
- The crime, as reported in *Coloreds' Weekly Illustrated*:
  - Charles arrested by Det. William Simms for stealing large sum from Freedmen's Trust in NY. Broke into the trust's safe, witnesses saw him leave shortly after. His tools were found nearby. Most money was recovered. He was sentenced to five years in prison. No information about him after sentencing. Believed to have used his connections with early civil rights leaders to gain access to the trust.
- Charles's Correspondence:
  - Letter 1, to wife: Re: Draft Riots in 1863, great anti-black sentiment throughout NY State, lynchings, arson. Risk to property owned by blacks.
  - Letter 2, to wife: Charles at Battle of Appomattox at end of Civil War.
  - Letter 3, to wife: Involved in civil rights movement. Threatened for this work. Troubled by his secret.
  - Letter 4, to wife: Went to Potters' Field with his gun for 'justice.' Results were disastrous. The truth is now hidden in Potters' Field. His secret was what caused all this heartache.

34

Minus the shopping cart, Jax was playing homeless again.

He wasn't being schizo at the moment, like before. The Graffiti King was fronting he was your typical fired-ass former vet, feeling sorry for himself, begging for change, a shabby Mets cap upturned on the gum-stained sidewalk and filled with, God bless you, thirty-seven cents.

Cheap pricks.

No longer in his olive-drab army jacket or the gray sweatshirt, but wearing a dusty black T-shirt under a torn beige sports coat (picked out of the garbage the way a real homeless person would do), Jax was sitting on the bench across from the town house on Central Park West, nursing a can wrapped up in a stained, brown-paper bag. Ought to be malt liquor, he thought sourly. Wished it was. But it was only Arizona iced tea. He sat back, like he was thinking about what kind of job he'd like to try for, though also enjoying the cool fall day, and sipped more of the sweet peach drink. He lit a cigarette and blew smoke toward the stunningly clear sky.

He was watching the kid from Langston Hughes walk up, the one who'd just left that town house on Central Park West, where he'd delivered the bag to Geneva Settle. Still no sign of anyone checking out the street from inside, but that didn't mean there wasn't anybody there.

Besides, two police cars sat out front, one squad car and one unmarked, right by that wheelchair ramp. So Jax had waited here, a block away, for the boy to make the delivery.

The skinny kid came up and plopped down on the bench next to the not-really-homeless Graffiti King of Blood.

'Yo, yo, man.'

'Why do you kids say 'yo' all the time?' Jax asked, irritated. 'And why the fuck do you say it twice?'

'Ever'body say it. Wus yo' problem, man?'

'You gave her the bag?'

'What up with that dude ain't got legs?'

'Who?'

'Dude in there ain't got no legs. Or maybe he got legs but they ain't work.'

Jax didn't know what he was talking about. He would rather've had a smarter kid deliver the package to the town house, but this was the only one he'd found around the Langston Hughes school yard who had any connection at all with Geneva Settle — his sister sort of knew her. He repeated, 'You give her the bag?'

'I give it to her, yeah.'

'What'd she say?'

'I don't know. Some shit. Thanks. I don't know.'

'She believed you?'

'She look like she ain't know who I be at first, then she was cool, yeah. When I mention my sister.'

He gave the kid some bills.

'Phat . . . Yo, you got anything else fo' me to

485

do, I'm down, man. I — '

'Get outa here.'

The kid shrugged and started away.

Jax said, 'Wait.'

The loping boy stopped. He turned back.

'What was she like?'

'The bitch? What she *look* like?'

No, that wasn't what he was curious about. But Jax didn't quite know how to phrase the question. And then he decided he didn't want to ask it. He shook his head. 'Go on 'bout your business.'

'Later, man.'

The kid strolled off.

Part of Jax's mind told him to stay here, where he was. But that'd be stupid. Better to put some distance between himself and the place. He'd find out soon enough, one way or the other, what happened when the girl looked through the bag.

★   ★   ★

Geneva sat on her bed, lay back, closed her eyes, wondering what she felt so good about.

Well, they'd caught the killer. But that couldn't be all of the feeling, of course, since the man who'd hired him was still out there somewhere. And then there was also the man with the gun, the one at the school yard, the man in the army jacket.

She should be terrified, depressed.

But she wasn't. She felt free, elated.

Why?

And then she understood: It was because

she'd told her secret. Unburdened her heart about living alone, about her parents. And nobody'd been horrified and shocked and hated her because of the lie. Mr. Rhyme and Amelia had even backed her up, Detective Bell too. They hadn't freaked, and dimed her out to the counselor.

Damn, it felt fine. How hard it'd been, carrying around this secret — just like Charles had carted *his* with him (whatever it was). If the former slave had told somebody, would he have avoided all the heartache that followed? According to his letter, he seemed to think so.

Geneva glanced at the shopping bag of books the girls at Langston Hughes had gotten for her. Curiosity got the better of her and she decided to look through them. She lifted the bag onto the bed. As Ronelle's brother had said, it weighed a ton.

She reached inside and lifted out the Laura Ingalls Wilder book. Then the next one: Geneva laughed out loud. This was even stranger: It was a Nancy Drew mystery. Was this wack, or what? She looked at a few of the other titles, books by Judy Blume, Dr. Seuss, Pat McDonald. Children's and young adult books. Wonderful authors, she knew them all. But she'd read their stories years ago. What was up with this? Didn't Ronelle and the kids know her? The most recent books she'd read for pleasure had been novels for adults: *The Remains of the Day* by Kazuo Ishiguro and *The French Lieutenant's Woman* by John Fowles. The last time she'd read *Green Eggs and Ham* had been ten years ago.

Maybe there was something better in the bottom. She started to reach into it.

A knock on the door startled her.

'Come in.'

Thom entered, carrying a tray with a Pepsi and some snacks on it.

'Hi there,' he said.

'Hi.'

'Thought you'd need some sustenance.' He opened the soda for her. She shook her head at the glass he was about to pour it into. 'The can's fine,' she said. She wanted to keep all the empties so she knew exactly how much to repay Mr. Rhyme.

'And . . . health food.' He handed her a Kit Kat candy bar, and they laughed.

'Maybe later.' Everybody was trying to fatten her up. Fact was, she just wasn't used to eating. That was something you did with family around a table, not by yourself, hunched over an unsteady table in a basement as you read a book or jotted notes for a paper about Hemingway.

Geneva sipped the soda, as Thom took over unloading the books for her. He held them up one by one. There was a novel by C. S. Lewis. Another: *The Secret Garden*.

Still nothing for adults.

'There's a big one at the bottom,' he said, lifting it out. It was a Harry Potter book, the first one in the series. She'd read it when it had first come out.

'You want it?' Thom asked.

She hesitated. 'Sure.'

The aide handed her the heavy volume.

★ ★ ★

A jogger, a man in his forties, approached, glancing toward Jax, the homeless vet, wearing his trash-picked jacket, sporting a hidden pistol in his sock and thirty-seven cents of charity in his pocket.

The jogger's expression didn't change as he ran past. But the man altered course just a tiny bit, to put an extra foot or so between him and the big black guy, a shift so little you could hardly see it. Except to Jax it was as clear as if the man had stopped, turned around and fled, calling out, 'Keep your distance, nigger.'

He was sick of this racial-dodgeball shit. Always the same. Is it *ever* going to change?

Yes. No.

Who the hell knew?

Jax bent down casually and adjusted the pistol that was stuffed into his sock and pressing uncomfortably against bone, then continued up the street, moving slow with his scar-tissue limp.

'Yo, you got some change?' He heard the voice from behind him as a man approached.

He glanced back at a tall, hunched-over man with very dark skin, ten feet behind him. The guy repeated, 'Yo, change, man?'

He ignored the beggar, thinking, This's pretty funny: All day he'd been fronting he was some homeless dude or another and here comes a real one. Serves me right.

'Yo, change?'

He said brusquely, 'No, I don't have any.'

'Come on. Ever'body got change. An' they

489

fuckin' hate it. They *wanta* get rid of it. All them coins be heavy and you can't buy shit with it. I be doing you a favor, brother. Come on.'

'Get lost.'

'I ain't ate for two days.'

Jax glanced back, snapped, 'Course not. 'Cause you spent all your paper on those Calvin Kleins.' He glanced at the man's clothes — a dirty but otherwise nice-looking set of royal-blue Adidas workout clothes. 'Go get a job.' Jax turned away and started up the street.

'Hokay,' the bum said. 'You ain't gimme any change, then how's 'bout you gimme your motherfuckin' hands?'

'My — ?'

Jax found his legs pulled out from underneath him. He slammed facedown onto the sidewalk. Before he could twist around and grab his gun both wrists were pinned behind his back and what seemed to be a large pistol was shoved into the nook behind his ear.

'The fuck you doing, man?'

'Shut up.' Hands patted him down and found the hidden pistol. Handcuffs ratcheted on and Jax was jerked into a sitting position. He found himself looking over an FBI identification card. The first name on it was Frederick. The second was Dellray.

'Oh, man,' Jax said, his voice hollow. 'I don't need this shit.'

'Well, guess what, sonny, there a lot more manure comin' yo' way. So you better get used to it.' The agent stood up and a moment later Jax heard, 'This is Dellray. I'm outside. I think I got

490

Boyd's boyfriend down. I just saw him slip some bills to a kid coming out of Lincoln's town house. Black kid, maybe thirteen. What was he doing there? . . . A bag? Fuck, it's a device! Probably gas. Boyd must've given it to this piece of crap to sneak inside. Get everybody out and call in a ten thirty-three . . . And get somebody to Geneva now!'

★   ★   ★

In Rhyme's lab the big man sat cuffed and leg-shackled in a chair, surrounded by Dellray, Rhyme, Bell, Sachs and Sellitto. He'd been relieved of a pistol, wallet, knife, keys, a cell phone, cigarettes, money.

For a half hour, utter chaos had reigned in Lincoln Rhyme's town house. Bell and Sachs had literally grabbed Geneva and hustled her out the back door and into Bell's car, which sped off in case there was yet another assailant planning to move on Geneva outside. Everyone else evacuated into the alley. The Bomb Squad, again in bio suits, had gone upstairs and X-rayed and then chemically tested the books. No explosives, no poison gas. They were just books, the purpose being, Rhyme assumed, to make them *think* there was a device in the bag. After they'd evacuated the town house, the accomplice would sneak in through the back door or enter with fire-fighters or police and wait for a chance to kill Geneva.

So this was the man Dellray had heard rumors about yesterday, who'd almost gotten to Geneva

491

at the Langston Hughes school yard, who'd found out where she lived and who'd followed her to Rhyme's to carry out yet another attempt on her life.

He was also the man, Rhyme hoped, who could tell them who'd hired Boyd.

The criminalist now looked him over carefully, this large, unsmiling man. He'd traded in his combat jacket for a tattered tan sports coat, probably assuming that they'd spotted him at the school yesterday in the green jacket.

He blinked and looked down at the floor, diminished by his arrest but not intimidated by the crescent of officers around him. Finally he said, 'Look, you don't — '

'Shhhhh,' Dellray said ominously and continued to rifle through the man's wallet, as he explained to the team what had happened. The agent had been coming to deliver reports about the FBI's jewelry district money-laundering investigations when he'd seen the teenage boy come out of Rhyme's. 'Saw the beast pass the kid some bills then get his ass up off a bench and leave. Descrip and the limp matched what we heard before. Looked funny to me, 'specially when I saw he had a de-formed ankle.' The agent nodded toward the small .32 automatic he'd found in the man's sock. Dellray explained that he'd pulled off his own jacket, wrapped it around the files and slipped them behind some bushes, then smeared some dirt on his running suit to impersonate a homeless man, a role he'd made famous in New York when he was an undercover agent. He'd then proceeded to collar the man.

'Let me say something,' Boyd's partner began.

Dellray wagged a huge finger at the man. 'We'll give ya this real clear little nod, we want any words trickling outa yo' mouth. We altogether on that?'

'I — '

'Al-to-gether?'

He nodded grimly.

The FBI agent held up what he'd found in the wallet: money, a few family pictures, a faded, shabby photograph. 'What's this?' he asked.

'My tag.'

The agent held the snapshot closer to Rhyme. It was an old boxy New York City subway. The colorful graffiti on the side read, *Jax 157*.

'Graffiti artist,' Sachs said, lifting an eyebrow. 'Pretty good, too.'

'You still go by Jax?' Rhyme asked.

'Usually.'

Dellray was holding up a picture ID card. 'You may've been Jax to the fine folk at the Transit Authority, but it's lookin' like you're Alonzo Jackson to the rest of the world. Also known by the illuminating moniker Inmate Two-two-oh-nine-three-fo', hailin' from the Department of Co-rrections in the *bee*-yootiful city of Alden, New York.'

'That's Buffalo, right?' Rhyme asked.

Boyd's accomplice nodded.

'The prison connection again. That how you know him?'

'Who?'

'Thompson Boyd.'

'I don't know anybody named Boyd.'

493

Dellray barked, 'Then who hired ya for the job?'

'I don't know what you're asking. 'Bout a job. I swear I don't.' He seemed genuinely confused. 'And all this other stuff, gas or whatever you're saying. I — '

'You were lookin' for Geneva Settle. You bought a gun and you showed up at her school yesterday,' Sellitto pointed out.

'Yeah, that's right.' He looked mystified at the level of their information.

'An' you showed up *here*,' Dellray continued. '*That*'s the job we're waggin' our tongues about.'

'There's no job. I don't know what you mean. Honest.'

'What's the story with the books?' Sellitto asked.

'Those're just books my daughter read when she was little. They were for her.'

The agent muttered, 'Wonnerful. But 'xplain to us why you paid somebody to deliver 'em to . . . ' He hesitated and frowned. For once words seemed to fail Fred Dellray.

Rhyme asked, 'You're saying — ?'

'That's right.' Jax sighed. 'Geneva. She's my little girl.'

35

'From the beginning,' Rhyme said.

'Okay. What it is — I got busted six years ago. Went six to nine at Wende.'

The DOC's maximum security prison in Buffalo.

'For what?' Dellray snapped. 'The AR and murder we heard about?'

'One count armed robbery. One count firearm. One count assault.'

'The twenty-five, twenty-five? The murder?'

He said firmly, 'That was *not* a righteous count. Got knocked down to assault. And I didn't do it in the first place.'

'Never heard *that* before,' Dellray muttered.

'But you did the robbery?' Sellitto asked.

A grimace. 'Yeah.'

'Keep going.'

'Last year I got upped to Alden, minimum security. Work-release. I was working and going to school there. Got paroled seven weeks ago.'

'Tell me about the AR.'

'Okay. Few years back, I was a painter, working in Harlem.'

'Graffiti?' Rhyme asked, nodding at the picture of the subway car.

Laughing, Jax said, '*House* painting. You don't make money at graffiti, 'less you were Keith Haring and his crowd. And they were just claimers. Anyway I was getting killed by the debt. See, Venus — Geneva's mother — had righteous problems. First it was blow, then smack then cookies — you know, crack. And we needed money for bail and lawyers too.'

The sorrow in his face seemed real. 'There were signs she was a troubled soul when we hooked up. But, you know, nothing like love to make you a blind fool. Anyways, we were going to be kicked out of the apartment and I didn't have money for Geneva's clothes or schoolbooks or even food sometimes. That girl needed a normal life. I thought if I could get together some benjamins I'd get Venus into treatment or something, get her straight. And if she wouldn't do it, then I'd take Geneva away from her, give the girl a good home.

'What happened was this buddy, Joey Stokes, told me 'bout this deal he had going on up in Buffalo. Word was up there was some armored car making fat runs every Saturday, picking up receipts from malls outside of town. Couple of lazy guards. It'd be a milk run.

'Joey and me left on Saturday morning, thinking we'd be back with fifty, sixty thousand each that night.' A sad shake of the head. 'Oh, man, I don't know what I was doing, listening to that claiming dude. The minute the driver handed over the money, everything went bad. He had this secret alarm we didn't know about. He hit it and next thing there're sirens all over the place.

'We headed south but came to a railroad crossing we hadn't noticed. This freight train was stopped. We turned around and took some roads that weren't on the map and had to go through a field. We got two flats and ran off on foot. The cops caught up with us a half hour later. Joey said let's fight and I said no and called out we were giving up. But Joey got mad and shot me in the leg. The state troopers thought we were shooting at *them*. That was the attempted murder.'

'Crime don't pay,' Dellray said, with the intonation, if not the grammar, of the amateur philosopher that he was.

'We were in a holding cell for a week, ten days 'fore they let me make a phone call. I couldn't call Venus anyway; our phone'd been shut off. My lawyer was some Legal Aid kid who didn't do shit for me. I called some friends but nobody could find Venus or Geneva. They'd been kicked out of our apartment.

'I wrote letters from prison. They kept coming back. I called everybody I could think of. I wanted to find her so bad! Geneva's mother and me lost a baby a while ago. And then I lost Geneva when I went into the system. I wanted my family back.

'After I got released I came here to look for her. Even spent what paper I had on this old computer to see if I could find her on the Internet or something. But I didn't have any luck. All I heard was Venus was dead and Geneva was gone. It's easy to fall through the cracks in Harlem. I couldn't find my aunt either, who they stayed with some. Then yesterday morning this woman I know from the old days, works in Midtown, saw this hubbub at that black museum, some girl getting attacked and heard her name was Geneva and she was sixteen and lived in Harlem. She knew I was looking for my girl and called. I got myself hooked up with this claimer hangs out Uptown and he checked out the schools yesterday. Found out she went to Langston Hughes High. I went there to find her.'

'When they spotted you,' Sellitto said. 'By the school yard.'

'That's right. I was there. When y'all came after me I took off. But I went back and found out from this kid where she lived, over in West Harlem, by Morningside. I went there today, was going to leave the books but I saw you put her in a car and take off.' He nodded at Bell.

The detective frowned. 'You were pushing a cart.'

'I was fronting that, yeah. I got a cab and followed y'all here.'

'With a gun,' Bell pointed out.

He snapped, 'Somebody'd tried to hurt my little girl! Hells yeah, I got myself that piece. I wasn't going to let anything happen to her.'

'You use it?' Rhyme asked. 'The weapon?'

'No.'

'We're going to test it.'

'All I did was pull it out and scare that asshole kid told me where Geneva lived, boy name of Kevin, who was speaking bad about my girl. Worst that happened to him was he peed his pants when I pointed it at him . . . which he deserved. But that's all I did — 'side from busting him up some. You can track him down and ask him.'

'What's her name, the woman who called you yesterday?'

'Betty Carlson. She works next to the museum.' He nodded at his phone. 'Her number's on the incoming-call list. Seven-one-eight — that's the area code.'

Sellitto took the man's mobile and stepped into the hallway.

'What about your family in Chicago?'

'My what?' He frowned.

'Geneva's mother said you moved to Chicago with somebody, married her,' Sachs explained.

Jax closed his eyes in disgust. 'No, no . . . That was a lie. I never even been to Chicago. Venus must've told her that to poison the girl against me . . . That woman, why'd I ever fall in love with her?'

Then Rhyme glanced at Cooper. 'Call DOC.'

'No, no, please,' Jax said, his face desperate. 'They'll violate me back. I can't be outside twenty-five miles of Buffalo. I asked permission to leave the jurisdiction twice and both times they denied it. I came anyway.'

Cooper considered this. 'I can run him through the general DOC database. It'll look routine. The P.O.'s won't see it.'

Rhyme nodded. A moment later a picture of Alonzo Jackson and his record popped up on the screen. Cooper read it. 'Confirms what he said. Good-behavior timely discharge. Got himself some college credits. And there's reference to a daughter, Geneva Settle, as next of kin.'

'Thank you for that,' Jax said, relieved.

'What's with the books?'

'I couldn't come up to y'all and just say who I was — I'd get violated back — so I got copies of a bunch of books Geneva read when she was young. So she'd know the note was really from me.'

'What note?'

'Wrote her a note, put it in one of the books.'

Cooper rummaged through the bag. In a battered copy of *The Secret Garden* was a slip of paper. In careful handwriting were the words: *Gen baby, this is from your father. Please call me.* Beneath this message was his phone number.

Sellitto stepped back into the doorway. He nodded. 'Talked to the Carlson woman. Everything he said checks out.'

Rhyme asked, 'Geneva's mother was your girlfriend, not wife. That's why Geneva's not 'Jackson'?'

'That's right.'

'Where do you live?' Bell asked.

'Got a room in Harlem. A Hundred Thirty-sixth. Once I found Geneva I was going to bring her back to Buffalo till I got permission to come back home.' His face grew still and Rhyme saw what he believed was pure sorrow in his eyes. 'But I don't think there's much chance of that happening now.'

'Why?' Sachs asked.

Jax gave a wistful grin. 'I saw where she lives, that nice place near Morningside. I was happy for her, of course, real happy. She'll have herself two good foster parents taking care of her, maybe a brother or sister, which she always wanted but that didn't work out, after Venus had such a bad time at the clinic. Why'd Geneva wanta come back with me? She's got the life she deserves, everything I couldn't give her.'

Rhyme glanced at Sachs with a raised eyebrow. Jax didn't catch it.

His story was sounding legit to Rhyme. But he had a thick vein of policeman's skepticism in him. 'I want to ask you a few questions.'

'Anything.'

'Who's the aunt you mentioned?'

'My father's sister. Lilly Hall. She helped raise me. Widow twice over. She'd've turned ninety this year. August. If she's still with us.'

Rhyme had no clue about her age or birthday but that was the name Geneva had given them. 'She's still alive, yes.'

A smile. 'I'm glad about that. I've missed her. I couldn't find her either.'

Bell said, 'You told Geneva something about the word 'sir.' What would that've been?'

'I told her even when she was little to look people in the eye and always be respectful, but never to call anyone 'sir' or 'ma'am' unless they earned it.'

The Carolina detective nodded to Rhyme and Sachs.

The criminalist asked, 'Who's Charles Singleton?'

Jax blinked in surprise. 'How d'you know about him?'

'Answer the man, scurv,' Dellray snapped.

'He's my, I don't know, great-great-great-great-grandfather or something.'

'Keep going,' Rhyme encouraged.

'Well, he was a slave in Virginia. His master freed him and his wife and gave 'em a farm up north. Then he volunteered to be in the Civil War, you know, like in that movie *Glory*. He came back home after, worked his orchard and taught at his school — an African free school. Made money selling cider to workers building boats up the road from his farm. I know he got medals in the war. He even met Abraham Lincoln once in Richmond. Just after the Union troops took it over. Or that's what my daddy said.' Another sad laugh. 'Then there was this story he got himself arrested for stealing some gold or payroll or something and went to jail. Just like me.'

'Do you know what happened to him after prison?'

'No. Never heard anything about that. So, you believe that I'm Geneva's father?'

Dellray looked at Rhyme, cocked an eyebrow.

The criminalist sized the man up. 'Almost. One last thing. Open your mouth.'

★   ★   ★

'You're my *father*?'

Breathless, nearly dizzy from the news, Geneva Settle felt her heart pounding. She looked him over carefully, her eyes scanning his face, his shoulders, his hands. Her first reaction had been utter disbelief but she couldn't deny that she recognized him. He still wore the garnet ring that her mother, Venus, had given him for

502

Christmas — when they were still celebrating Christmas. The memory she compared this man with, though, was vague, like looking at someone with bright sun behind them.

Despite the driver's license, the picture of her as a baby with him and her mother, the photo of one of his old graffiti drawings, she still would've denied the connection between them to the last, except for a DNA test that Mr. Cooper had run. There was no doubt they were kin.

They were alone upstairs — alone, of course, except for Detective Bell, her protective shadow. The rest of the police officers were downstairs working on the case, still trying to figure out who was behind the jewelry exchange robbery.

But Mr. Rhyme and Amelia and all the others — as well as the killer and everything else about the frightening events of the past few days — were, for the moment, forgotten. The questions that now consumed Geneva were: How had her father gotten here? And why?

And, most important: What does this mean for me?

A nod at the shopping bag. She picked up the Dr. Seuss book. 'I don't read children's books anymore.' It was all she could think of to say. 'I turned sixteen two months ago.' Her point, she guessed, was to remind him of all the birthdays she'd spent alone.

'I brought you those just so you'd know it was me. I know you're too old for them.'

'What about your other family?' she asked coldly.

Jax shook his head. 'They told me what Venus

said to you, Genie.'

She was pissed he was using the nickname he'd given her years ago. Short for both 'Geneva' and 'genius.'

'She was making that up. To turn you against me. No, no, Genie, I'd never leave you. I got arrested.'

'Arrested?'

'It's true, miss,' Roland Bell said. 'We've seen his files. He got arrested the day he left you and your mother. He's been in prison ever since. Just got out.'

He then told her a story about a robbery, about being desperate to get some money to make their life better, to help her mother.

But the words were tired, exhausted. He was giving her one of the thousands of limp excuses you heard so often in the neighborhood. The crack dealer, the shoplifter, the welfare scammer, the chain snatcher.

I did it for you, baby . . .

She looked down at the book in her hand. It was used. Who'd it been for when it was new? Where was the parent who'd bought it originally for his or her child? In jail, washing dishes, driving a Lexus, performing neuro-surgery?

Had her father stolen it from a used bookstore?

'I came back for you, Genie. I've been desperate to find you. And I was even more desperate when Betty called and told me you'd been attacked . . . What happened yesterday? Who's after you? Nobody ever told me.'

'I saw something,' she said dismissingly, not

wanting to give him too much information. 'Maybe somebody committing a crime.' Geneva had no interest in the direction of this conversation. She looked him over and said more cruelly than she intended, 'You know that Mom's dead.'

He nodded. 'I *didn't* know it till I came back. Then I heard. But I wasn't surprised. She was a troubled woman. Maybe she's happier now.'

Geneva didn't think so. And in any case no amount of heaven would make up for the unhappiness of dying alone the way she had, her body shrunken but her face puffed up like a yellow moon.

And it wouldn't make up for the earlier unhappiness — of getting fucked in stairways for a couple rocks of crack while her daughter waited outside the front door.

Geneva said none of this.

He smiled. 'You've got yourself a real nice place you're staying.'

'It was temporary. I'm not there anymore.'

'You're not? Where're you living?'

'I'm not sure yet.'

She regretted saying this. It gave him, she realized, a foot in the door. And, sure enough, he pushed his way in: 'I'm going to ask my P.O. again if I can move back here. Knowing I've got family to take care of, he might say it's all right.'

'You *don't* have a family here. Not anymore.'

'I know you're mad, baby. But I'll make it up to you. I — '

She flung the book to the floor. 'Six years and nothing. No word. No call. No letter.'

Infuriatingly, tears swelled in her eyes. She wiped them with shaking hands.

He whispered, 'An' *where* would I write? *Where* would I call? I tried steady all those six years to get in touch with you. I'll show you the stack of letters I got, all sent back to me in prison. A hundred of 'em, I'd guess. I tried everything I could think of. I just couldn't find you.'

'Well, thanks for the apology, you know. If it *is* an apology. But I think it's time for you to go.'

'No, baby, let me — '

'Not 'baby,' not 'Genie,' not 'daughter.''

'I'll make it up to you,' he repeated. He wiped his eyes.

She felt absolutely nothing, seeing his sorrow — or whatever it was. Nothing, that is, except anger. 'Leave!'

'But, baby, I — '

'No. Just go away!'

Once more the detective from North Carolina, the expert at guarding people, did his job smoothly and without wavering. He rose and silently but firmly ushered her father into the hallway. He nodded back at the girl, gave her a comforting smile and closed the door behind him, leaving Geneva to herself.

36

While the girl and her father had been upstairs, Rhyme and the others had been going over leads to potential jewelry store heists.

And having no success.

The materials that Fred Dellray had brought them about money-laundering schemes involving jewelry were small-time operations, none of them centered in Midtown. And they had no reports from Interpol or local law enforcement agencies containing anything relevant to the case.

The criminalist was shaking his head in frustration when his phone rang. 'Rhyme here.'

'Lincoln, it's Parker.'

The handwriting expert analyzing the note from Boyd's safe house. Parker Kincaid and Rhyme traded newsbites about health and family. Rhyme learned that Kincaid's live-in partner, FBI agent Margaret Lukas, was fine, as were Parker's children, Stephie and Robby.

Sachs sent her greetings and then Kincaid got down to business. 'I've been working on your letter nonstop since you sent me the scan. I've got a profile of the writer.'

Serious handwriting analysis never seeks to determine personality from the way people form their letters; handwriting itself is relevant only when comparing one document with another, say, when determining forgeries. But that didn't interest Rhyme at the moment. No, what Parker Kincaid was talking about was deducing characteristics of the writer based on the language he used — the 'unusual' phrasing that Rhyme had noted earlier. This could be extremely helpful in identifying suspects. Grammatical and syntactical analysis of the Lindbergh baby ransom note, for instance, gave a perfect profile of the kidnapper, Bruno Hauptmann.

With the enthusiasm he typically felt for his craft, Kincaid continued, 'I found some interesting things. You've got the note handy?'

'It's right in front of us.'

A black girl, fifth floor in this window, 2 October, about 0830. She saw my delivery van when he was parked in a alley behind the Jewelry exchange. Saw enough to guess the plans of mine. Kill her.

Kincaid said, 'To start with, he's foreign born. The awkward syntax and the misspellings tell me that. So does the way he indicates the date — putting the day before the month. And the time is given in the twenty-four-hour clock. That's rare in America.'

The handwriting expert continued, 'Now, another important point: he — '

'Or *she*,' Rhyme interrupted.

'I'm leaning toward male,' Kincaid countered. 'Tell you why in a minute. He uses the gendered pronoun 'he,' referring, it seems, to his van. That's typical of several different foreign languages. But what really narrows it down is the

508

two-member nominal phrase in the genitive construction.'

'The *what?*' Rhyme asked.

'The genitive construction — a way to create the possessive. Your unsub wrote 'my delivery van' at one point.'

Rhyme scanned the note. 'Got it.'

'But later he wrote 'plans of mine.' That makes me think your boy's first language is Arabic.'

'Arabic?'

'I'll say it's a ninety percent likelihood. There's a genitive construction in Arabic called *i.daafah*. The possessive's usually formed by saying, 'The car John.' Meaning, 'The car *of* John.' Or, in your note, the 'plans of mine.' But the rules of Arabic grammar require that only *one* word is used for the thing that's possessed — the 'delivery van' won't work in Arabic; it's a two-word phrase, so he can't use *i.daafah*. He simply says 'my delivery van.' The other clue is the misuse of the indefinite article 'a' in 'a alley.' That's common among Arabic speakers; the language doesn't use indefinite articles, only the definite 'the.'' Kincaid added, 'That's true of Welsh, too, but I don't think this guy's from Cardiff.'

'Good, Parker,' Sachs said. 'Very subtle, but good.'

A faint laugh came from the speakerphone. 'I'll tell you, Amelia, everybody in the business's been doing a lot of boning up on Arabic in the last few years.'

'That's why you think it's a man.'

'How many women Arab perps you see?'

'Not many . . . Anything else?'

'Get me some more samples and I'll compare them if you want.'

'We may take you up on that.' Rhyme thanked Kincaid and they disconnected the call. Rhyme shook his head, staring at the evidence boards. He gave a scoffing laugh.

'What're you thinking, Rhyme?'

'You know what he's up to, don't you?' the criminalist asked in an ominous voice.

Sachs nodded. 'He's not going to *rob* the exchange. He's going to blow it up.'

'Yep.'

Dellray said, 'Sure — those reports we've had, about terrorists goin' after Israeli targets in the area.'

Sachs said, 'The guard across the street from the museum said they get shipments of jewelry every day from Jerusalem . . . Okay, I'll get the exchange evacuated and swept.' She pulled out her cell phone.

Rhyme glanced at the evidence board and said to Sellitto and Cooper, 'Falafel and yogurt . . . and a delivery van. Find out if there are any restaurants around the exchange that serve Middle Eastern food and, if so, who makes deliveries and when. And what kind of van they use.'

Dellray shook his head. 'Half the city eats that stuff. You can get gyros and falafel on every street corner in the city. They . . . ' The agent stopped talking as his eyes met Rhyme's.

'Pushcarts!'

Sellitto said, 'There were a half dozen of them

510

around the museum yesterday.'

'*Perfect* for surveillance,' Rhyme snapped. 'And what a cover. He delivers supplies to them every day, so nobody pays attention to him. I want to know who supplies the street vendors. Move!'

★ ★ ★

According to the board of health, only two companies delivered Middle Eastern food to the pushcarts in the blocks around the jewelry exchange. Ironically, the largest of them was owned by two Jewish brothers with family in Israel and who were active in their temple; they were hardly suspects.

The other company didn't own the carts but sold gyros, kabobs and falafel, along with the condiments and sodas (as well as the heathen but ever-profitable pork hot dogs), to dozens of carts in Midtown. The operation was based out of a restaurant/deli down on Broad Street, whose owners hired a man to make the deliveries around town.

With Dellray and a dozen other agents and cops surrounding them, these owners became extremely — almost tearfully — cooperative. The name of their deliveryman was Bani al-Dahab, and he was a Saudi national, here on a visa long expired. He'd been a professional of some sort in Jeddah and had worked as an engineer for a time in the U.S. but after he went illegal he'd taken what work he could — cooking occasionally and delivering food to pushcarts and other Middle

511

Eastern restaurants around Manhattan and Brooklyn.

The jewelry exchange had been evacuated and swept — no devices were found there — and an emergency vehicle locator was out on al-Dahab's delivery van, which, according to the owners, might be anywhere in the city; the man was free to set his own delivery schedule.

It was at moments like this that Rhyme would have paced, had he been able to. Where the hell is he? Is the man driving around with a van full of explosives at the moment? Maybe he'd given up on the jewelry exchange and was going after a secondary target: a synagogue or an El-Al airlines office.

'Let's get Boyd down here, put some pressure on him,' he snapped. 'I want to know where the hell this guy is!'

It was at that moment that Mel Cooper's phone rang.

Then Sellitto's, followed by Amelia Sachs's.

Finally, the main laboratory phone began to chirp.

The callers were different but the message was virtually the same.

Rhyme's question about the bomber's whereabouts had just been answered.

★ ★ ★

Only the driver died.

Which considering the force of the explosion and the fact that the van was in the intersection of Ninth Avenue and Fifty-fourth, surrounded

512

by other cars, was pretty miraculous.

When the bomb went off, the direction of the blast was mostly upward, through the roof, and out the windows, scattering shrapnel and glass and injuring a score of people, but the main damage was confined to the interior of the E250. The burning van had lurched up on the sidewalk, where it slammed into a light post. A crew from the fire station up the street on Eighth Avenue got the flames out fast and kept the crowd back. As for the driver, there was no point in even trying to save him; the two largest pieces of his remains were separated by several yards.

The Bomb Squad had cleared the scene and the main job of the police now was to wait for the medical examiner tour doctor and the crime scene crew.

'What's that smell?' the detective from Midtown North asked. The tall, balding officer was creeped out by the stink, which he took to be burnt human flesh. The problem was that it smelled good.

One of the detectives from the Bomb Squad laughed at the green-faced detective. 'Gyros.'

'Gear-o, what?' the detective asked, thinking it was short for something — like FUBAR, meaning 'fucked up beyond all recognition.'

'Look.' The Bomb Squad cop held up a chunk of burnt meat in his latex-gloved hands. He smelled it. 'Tasty.'

The Midtown North detective laughed and didn't reveal how close to puking he was.

'It's lamb.'

'It's — '

'The driver was delivering food. That was his job. The back of the van's filled with meat and falafel and shit like that.'

'Oh.' The cop still didn't feel any less nauseous.

It was then that a bright red Camaro SS — one hell of a car — skidded to a stop in the middle of the street, just kissing the yellow police tape. Out climbed a stunning redhead, who looked over the scene, nodding to the detective.

'Hey,' he said.

As the woman detective hooked a headset onto her Motorola and waved to the crime scene bus, just pulling up as well, she sniffed the air, taking several deep breaths. She nodded. 'Haven't run the scene yet,' she said into the microphone, 'but from the smell, Rhyme, I'd say we've got him.'

It was then that the tall, bald detective swallowed and said, 'You know, I'll be right back.' He jogged to a nearby Starbucks, praying he'd make it to the restroom in time.

★ ★ ★

With Detective Bell at her side, Geneva walked into the laboratory portion of Mr. Rhyme's town house, downstairs. She glanced at her father, who looked at her with those big puppy-dog eyes of his.

Damnit. She looked away.

Mr. Rhyme said, 'We've got some news. The man who hired Boyd's dead.'

'Dead? The jewelry store robber?'

514

'Things weren't quite what they seemed,' Mr. Rhyme said. 'We were — well, I was wrong. I was thinking whoever it was wanted to *rob* the jewelry exchange. But, no, he wanted to blow it up.'

'Terrorists?' she asked.

Mr. Rhyme nodded toward a plastic folder that Amelia was holding. Inside was a letter, addressed to *The New York Times*. It said the bombing of the jewelry exchange was yet another step in the holy war against Zionist Israel and its allies. It was the same paper that was used for the note about killing Geneva and the map of West Fifty-fifth Street.

'Who is he?' she asked, trying to remember a van and a Middle Eastern man in the street outside the museum a week or so ago. She couldn't.

'An illegal Saudi national,' Detective Sellitto said. 'Worked for a restaurant downtown. The owners're pretty freaked, of course. They think *we* think they're a cover for al-Qaeda or something.' He chuckled. 'Which they might be. We'll keep checking. But they all come up clean — citizens, been here for years, couple kids in the army, even. I *will* say they're a bunch of very nervous folks at the moment.'

The most important aspect about the bomber, Amelia went on to say, was that this man, Bani al-Dahab, didn't appear to associate with any suspected terrorists. The women he'd dated recently and co-workers said that they didn't know of any times he'd met with people who might be in a terrorist cell, and his mosque was religiously and politically moderate. Amelia had searched his Queens apartment and found no other evidence or connections to other terrorist cells. His phone records were being checked for possible links to other fundamentalists, though.

'We'll keep looking over the evidence,' Mr. Rhyme said, 'but we're ninety-nine percent sure he was working alone. I think it means you're probably safe.'

He wheeled his chair to the evidence table and looked over some bags of burnt metal and plastic. He said to Mr. Cooper, 'Add it to the chart, Mel: Explosive was TOVEX, and we've got pieces of the receiver — the detonator — the casing, wire, a bit of blasting cap. All contained in a UPS box addressed to the jewelry exchange, attention of the director.'

'Why'd it go off early?' Jax Jackson asked.

Mr. Rhyme explained that it was very dangerous to use a radio-controlled bomb in the city because there were so many ambient radio waves — from construction-site detonators, walkie-talkies and a hundred other sources.

Detective Sellitto added, 'Or he may've killed himself. He might've heard that Boyd was arrested or that the jewelry exchange was being searched for a bomb. He must've thought it was only a matter of time until he'd be nabbed.'

Geneva felt uneasy, confused. These people around her were suddenly strangers. The reason they'd come together in the first place no longer existed. As for her father, he was more alien to her than the police. She wanted to be back in her room in the Harlem basement with her books and her plans for the future, college, dreams about Florence and Paris.

But then she realized Amelia was looking at her closely. The policewoman asked, 'What're you going to do now?'

Geneva glanced at her father. What *would* happen? She had a parent, true, but one who was an ex-con, who couldn't even be here in the city. They'd still probably try to put her in a foster home.

Amelia glanced at Lincoln Rhyme. 'Until things get sorted out, why don't we stick with our plan? Have Geneva stay here for a while.'

'Here?' the girl asked.

'Your father's got to get back to Buffalo and take care of things there.'

Not that living with him is an option anyway, Geneva thought. But kept this to herself.

'Excellent idea.' This came from Thom. 'I think that's what we'll do.' His voice was firm. 'You'll stay here.'

'Is that all right with you?' Amelia asked Geneva.

Geneva wasn't sure why they wanted her to stay. She was initially suspicious. But she constantly had to remind herself that, after living alone for so long, suspicion trailed her like a shadow. She thought of another rule about lives like hers: You take your family how you find them.

'Sure,' she said.

* * *

517

Shackled, Thompson Boyd was brought into Rhyme's lab and the two guards deposited him in front of the officers and Rhyme. Geneva was once again upstairs in her room, guarded at the moment by Barbe Lynch.

The criminalist rarely did this, meeting the perpetrators face-to-face. For him, a scientist, the only passion in his job was the game itself, the pursuit, not the physical incarnation of the suspect. He had no desire to gloat over the man or woman he'd captured. Excuses and pleas didn't move him, threats didn't trouble him.

Yet now he wanted to make absolutely certain that Geneva Settle was safe. He wanted to assess her attacker himself.

His face bandaged and bruised from his confrontation with Sachs at the arrest, Boyd looked around the laboratory. The equipment, the charts on the whiteboards.

The wheelchair.

No emotion whatsoever, no flicker of surprise or interest. Not even when he nodded toward Sachs. It was as if he'd forgotten that she'd brained him repeatedly with a rock.

Somebody asked Boyd about it, how'd it feel, bein' in a electric chair. He said it didn't feel like anythin'. It just felt 'kinda numb.' He said that a lot toward the end. He felt numb.

He asked, 'How'd you find me?'

'A couple of things,' Rhyme answered. 'For one, you picked the wrong tarot card to leave as evidence. It put me in mind of executions.'

'The Hanged Man,' Boyd said, nodding.

518

'Right you are: I never thought about that. Just seemed like kind of a spooky one. To lead you off, you know.'

Rhyme continued, 'What got us your name, though, was your habit.'

'Habit?'

'You whistle.'

'I do that. I try not to on the job. But sometimes it slips out. So you talked to . . . '

'Yep, some people in Texas.'

Nodding, Boyd glanced at Rhyme with red, squinting eyes. 'So you knew 'bout Charlie Tucker? That unfortunate excuse for a human being. Making the last days of my people's time on earth miserable. Telling 'em they were going to burn in hell, nonsense talk about Jesus and whatnot.'

My people . . .

Sachs asked, 'Was Bani al-Dahab the only one who hired you?'

He blinked in surprise; it seemed the first true emotion to cross his face. 'How — ?' He fell silent.

'The bomb went off early. Or he killed himself.'

A shake of the head. 'No, he wasn't any suicide bomber. It would've gone off by accident. Fella was careless. Too hotheaded, you know. Didn't do things by the book. He probably armed it too early.'

'How'd you meet him?'

'He called me. Got my name from somebody in prison, Nation of Islam connection.'

So that was it. Rhyme had wondered how a

519

Texas prison guard had hooked up with Islamic terrorists.

'They're crazy,' Boyd said. 'But they have money, those Arab people.'

'And Jon Earle Wilson? He was your bomb maker?'

'Jonny, yes, sir.' He shook his head. 'You know 'bout him too? You people're good, I must say.'

'Where is he?'

'That I don't know. We left messages from pay phones to a voice-mail box. And met in public. Never traded more'n a dozen words.'

'The FBI'll be talking to you about al-Dahab and the bombing. What we want to know about is Geneva. Is there anybody else who'd want to hurt her?'

Boyd shook his head. 'From what he told me, al-Dahab was working alone. I suspect he talked to people over in the Middle East some. But nobody here. He didn't trust anyone.' The Texas drawl came and went, as if he'd been working on losing it.

Sachs said ominously, 'If you're lying, if something happens to her, we can make sure the rest of your life's totally miserable.'

'How?' Boyd asked, genuinely curious, it seemed.

'You killed the librarian, Dr. Barry. You attacked and tried to kill police officers. You could get consecutive lifetimes. And we're looking into the death of a girl yesterday on Canal Street. Somebody pushed her in front of a bus near where you were escaping from Elizabeth Street. We're running your picture past witnesses. You'll go away forever.'

A shrug. 'Doesn't hardly matter.'

'You don't care?' Sachs asked.

'I know you people don't understand me. I don't blame you. But, see, I don't care about prison. I don't care about *anything*. Y'all can't really touch me. I'm dead already. Killing somebody doesn't matter to me, saving a life doesn't matter.' He glanced at Amelia Sachs, who was staring at him. Boyd said, 'I see that look. You're wond'ring what kinda monster is this fella? Well, fact is, y'all made me who I am.'

'We did?' she asked.

'Oh, yes, ma'am . . . You know my profession.'

'Executions control officer,' Rhyme said.

'Yes, sir. Now something I'll tell you 'bout that line of work: You can find the names of every human legally executed in these United States. Which is a lot. And you can find the names of all the governors who waited up till midnight or whenever to commute them if the inclination was there. You can find the names of all the victims the condemned murdered, and much of the time the names of their next of kin. But do you know the one name you won't find?'

He looked at the officers around him. 'Us people who push the button. The executioners. We're forgotten. Ever'body thinks 'bout how capital punishment affects the families of the condemned. Or society. Or the victims' families. Not to mention the man or woman gets put down like a dog in the process. But nobody ever spends a drop of sweat on us executioners.

521

Nobody ever stops and thinks what happens to us.

'Day after day, living with our people — men, women too, course, who're gonna die, getting to know 'em. Talking to 'em. 'Bout everything under the sun. Hearing a black man ask how come is it the white guy who did the exact same crime gets off with life, or maybe even less, but he himself's gonna die? The Mexican swearing he didn't rape and kill that girl. He was just buying beer at 7-Eleven and the police come up and next he knows he's on Death Row. And a year after he's in the ground they do a DNA test and find out they *did* have the wrong man, and he was innocent all along.

'Course, even the guilty ones're human beings too. Living with all of them, day after day. Being decent to them because they're decent to you. Getting to know 'em. And then . . . then you kill 'em. You, all by yourself. With your own hands, pushing the button, throwing the switch . . . It changes you.

'You know what they say? You heard it. 'Dead man walking.' It's supposed to mean the prisoner. But it's really us. The executioners. We're the dead men.'

Sachs muttered, 'But your girlfriend? How could you shoot her?'

He fell silent. For the first time a darkness clouded his face. 'I pondered firing that shot. I'd hoped maybe I'd have this *feeling* that I shouldn't do it. That she meant too much to me. I'd let her be and run, just take my chances. But . . . ' He shook his head. 'Didn't happen. I looked at her and all I felt was numb. And I knew that it'd make sense to shoot her.'

'And if the children had been home and not her?' Sachs gasped. 'You'd've shot one of them to escape?'

He considered this for a moment. 'Well, ma'am, I guess we know *that* would've worked, wouldn't it? You *would've* stopped to save one of the girls 'stead of coming after me. Like my daddy told me: It's only a question of where you put the decimal point.'

The darkness seemed to lift from his face, as if he'd finally received some answer or come to some conclusion in a debate that had been troubling him for a long time.

The Hanged Man . . . The card often foretells a surrendering to experience, ending a struggle, accepting what is.

He glanced at Rhyme. 'Now, you don't mind, I think it's time for me to get back home.'

'Home?'

He looked at them curiously. 'Jail.'

As if, what else would he possibly mean?

★   ★   ★

Father and daughter got off the C train at 135th street and started east, toward Langston Hughes High.

She hadn't wanted him to come but he'd insisted on looking after her — which Mr. Rhyme and Detective Bell had insisted on too. Besides, she reflected, he'd be back in Buffalo by tomorrow and she supposed she could tolerate an hour or two with him.

He nodded back at the subway. 'Used to love to write on C trains. Paint stuck real nice . . . I knew a lot of people'd see it. Did an end-to-end in 1976. It was the Bicentennial that year. Those tall ships were in town. My 'piece was of one of those boats, 'long with the Statue of Liberty.' He laughed. 'The MTA didn't scrub that car for at least a week, I heard. Maybe they were just busy but I like to think somebody liked what I painted and kept it up for longer than normal.'

Geneva grunted. She was thinking that *she* had a story to tell *him*. A block away she could see the construction scaffolding in front of the same building she'd been working on when she'd been fired. How'd her father like to know that her job had been scrubbing graffiti *off* the redeveloped buildings? Maybe she'd even erased some of his. Tempted to tell him. But she didn't.

At the first working pay phone they found on Frederick Douglass Boulevard, Geneva stopped, fished for some change. Her father offered her his cell phone.

'That's okay.'

'Take it.'

She ignored him, dropped the coins in and called Lakeesha, while her father pocketed his cell and wandered to the curb, looking around the neighborhood like a boy in front of the candy section in a bodega.

She turned away as her friend answered. ''Lo?'

'It's all over with, Keesh.' She explained about the jewelry exchange, the bombing.

524

'That what was goin' on? Damn. A terrorist? That some scary shit. But you okay?'

'I'm down. Really.'

Geneva heard another voice, a male one, saying something to her friend, who put her hand over the receiver for a moment. Their muted exchange seemed heated.

'You there, Keesh?'

'Yeah.'

'Who's that?'

'Nobody. Where you at? You not in that basement crib no more, right?'

'I'm still where I told you — with that policeman and his girlfriend. The one in the wheelchair.'

'You there now?'

'No, I'm Uptown. Going to school.'

'Now?'

'Pick up my homework.'

The girl paused. Then: 'Listen, I'ma hook up with you at school. Wanna see you, girl. When you be there?'

Geneva glanced at her father, nearby, hands in his pockets, still surveying the street. She decided she didn't want to mention him to Keesha, or anybody else, just yet.

'Let's make it tomorrow, Keesh. I don't have any time now.'

'Daymn, girl.'

'Really. Better tomorrow.'

'Wha-ever.'

Geneva heard the click of the disconnect. Yet she stayed where she was for some moments, delaying going back to her father.

Finally she joined him and they continued toward the school.

'You know what was up there, three or four blocks?' he asked, pointing north. 'Strivers Row. You ever seen it?'

'No,' she muttered.

'I'll take you up there sometime. Hundred years ago, this land developer fellow, named King, he built these three big apartments and tons of town houses. Hired three of the best architects in the country and told 'em to go to work. Beautiful places. King Model Homes was the real name but they were so expensive and so nice, this's the story, the place was called Strivers Row 'cause you had to *strive* to live there. W. C. Handy lived there for a time. You know him? Father of the blues. Most righteous musician ever lived. I did a 'piece up that way one time. I ever tell you about that? Took me thirty cans to do. Wasn't a throw-up; I spent two days on it. Did a picture of W. C. himself. Photographer from the *Times* shot it and put it in the paper.' He nodded north. 'It was there for — '

She stopped fast. Her hands slapped her hips. 'Enough!'

'Genie?'

'Just stop it. I don't want to hear this.'

'You — '

'I don't care about any of what you're telling me.'

'You're mad at me, honey. Who wouldn't be after everything? Look, I made a mistake,' he said, his voice cracking. 'That was the past. I'm different now. Everything's going to be different.

526

I'll never put anybody ahead of you again, like I did when I was with your moms. You're the one I should've been trying to save — and not by taking that trip to Buffalo.'

'No! You don't get it! It's not about what you did. It's your whole goddamn *world* I don't want any part of. I don't care about Strivers whatever it is, I don't care about the Apollo or the Cotton Club. Or the Harlem Renaissance. I don't *like* Harlem. I hate it here. It's guns and crack and rapes and people getting fiended for a cheap-ass plated bling and drugstore hoops. It's girls, all they care about is extensions and braids. And — '

'And Wall Street's got insider traders and New Jersey's got the mob and Westchester's got trailer parks,' he replied.

She hardly heard him. 'It's boys, all they care about is getting girls in bed. It's ignorant people who don't care how they talk. It's — '

'What's wrong with AAVE?'

She blinked. 'How do you know about that?' He himself had never talked ghetto — his own father had made sure he'd worked hard in school (at least until he dropped out to start the 'career' of defacing city property). But most people who lived here didn't know that the official name for what they spoke was African-American Vernacular English.

'When I was inside,' he explained, 'I got my high school diploma and a year of college.'

She said nothing.

'I mostly studied reading and words. Maybe won't help me get a job but it's what drew me. I always liked books and things, you know that. I'm the one had you reading from jump . . . I studied Standard. But I studied Vernacular too. And I don't see anything wrong with it.'

'You don't speak it,' she pointed out sharply.

'I didn't grow *up* speaking it. I didn't grow up speaking French or Mandingo either.'

'I'm sick of hearing people say, 'Lemme axe you a question.''

Her father shrugged. ''Axe' is just an Old-English version of 'ask.' Royalty used to say it. There're *Bible* translations that talk about 'axing' God for mercy. It's not a black thing, like people say. The combination of saying *s* and *k* next to each other's hard to pronounce. It's easier to transpose. And 'ain't'? Been in the English language since Shakespeare's day.'

She laughed. 'Try getting a job talking Vernacular.'

'Well, what if somebody from France or Russia's trying for that same job? Don't you think the boss'd give them a chance, listen to 'em, see if they'd work hard, were smart, even if they spoke different English? Maybe the problem's that the boss is using somebody's language as a reason *not* to hire him.' He laughed. 'People in New York damn well better be able to speak some Spanish and Chinese in the next few years. Why not Vernacular?'

His logic infuriated her even more.

'I *like* our language, Genie. It sounds natural to me. Makes me feel at home. Look, you've got every right to be mad at me for what I did. But not for who I am or what we came out of. This's

528

home. And you know what you do with your home, don't you? You change what oughta be changed and learn to be proud of what you can't.'

Geneva jammed her eyes closed and lifted her hands to her face. The years and years she dreamed of a parent — not even the luxury of two, but just one person to be there when she came home in the afternoons, to look over her homework, to wake her up in the morning. And when that wasn't going to happen, when she'd finally managed to shore up her life on her own and start working her way out of this godforsaken place, here comes the past to yoke and choke her and drag her back.

'But that's not what I want,' she whispered. 'I want something more than this mess.' She waved her hand around the streets.

'Oh, Geneva, I understand that. All I'm hoping for is maybe we have a couple of nice years here, 'fore you off into the world. Give me a chance to make up for what we did to you, your mother and me. You deserve the world . . . But honey, I gotta say — can you name me one place that's perfect? Where all the streets're paved with gold? Where everybody loves their neighbors?' He laughed and slipped into Vernacular. 'You say it a mess here? Well, damn straight. But where ain't it a mess one way or th'other, baby? Where ain't it?'

He put his arm around her. She stiffened but she didn't otherwise resist. They started for the school.

Lakeesha Scott sat on the bench in Marcus Garvey Park, where she'd been for the past half hour, after she'd come back from her counter job in the restaurant downtown.

She lit another Merit, thinking: There are things we do 'cause we want to and things we do 'cause we gotta. Survival things.

And what she was about now was one of those had-to things.

Why the fuck didn't Geneva say that after all this shit she was booking on out of town and never coming back?

She was going to Detroit or 'Bama?

Sorry, Keesh, we can't see each other anymore. I'm talking forever. Bye.

That way, the whole fucking problem'd be gone for good.

Why, why, why?

And it was worse than that: Gen had to go and tell her exactly where she was going to be for the next few hours. Keesh had no excuse to miss the girl now. Oh, she'd kept up her ghetto patter when they'd been talking a while ago so her friend wouldn't hop to something going down. But now, sitting alone, she sank into sorrow.

Man, I'm feeling bad.

But ain't got no choice here.

Things we do 'cause we gotta . . .

Come on, Keesha said to herself. Got to get over. Let's go. Bring it on . . .

She crushed out her cigarette and left the park, headed west then north on Malcolm X, past church after church. They were everywhere. Mt. Morris Ascension, Bethelite Community, Ephesus Adventist church, Baptist — plenty of those. A mosque or two, a synagogue.

And the stores and shops: Papaya King, a botanica, a tuxedo-rental shop, a check-cashing outlet. She passed a gypsy cab garage, the owner sitting outside, holding his taped-together dispatch radio, the long cord disappearing into the unlit office. He smiled at her pleasantly. How Lakeesha envied them: the reverends in the grimy storefronts under the neon crosses, the carefree men slipping hot dogs into the steamed buns, the fat man on the cheap chair, with his cigarette and his fucked-up microphone.

They ain't betraying nobody, she thought.

They ain't betraying the person was one of their best friends for years.

Snapping her gum, gripping her purse strap hard with her pudgy fingers tipped in black and yellow nails. Ignoring three Dominican boys.

'Psssst.'

She heard 'booty.' She heard 'bitch.'

'Psssssst.'

Keesh reached into her purse and gripped her spring knife. She nearly flicked it open, just to see 'em flinch. She glared but left the long, sharp blade where it was, deciding she'd have a world of trouble when she got to the school. Let it go for now.

'Pssst.'

She moved on, her nervous hands opening a pack of gum. Shoving two fruity pieces into her mouth, Lakeesha struggled to find her angry heart.

Get yourself mad, girl. Think of everything Geneva done to piss you off, think of everything she be that you ain't and never gonna be. The fact the girl was so smart it hurt, that she came to school every single fucking day, that she kept her skinny little white-girl figure without looking like some AIDS ho, that she managed to keep her legs together and told other girls to do the same like some prissy moms.

Acting like she better than us all.

But she wasn't. Geneva Settle was just another kid from a mommy-got-a-habit, daddy-done-run-off family.

She one of us.

Get mad at the fact that she'd look you in the eye and say, 'You can do it, girl, you can do it, you can do it, you can get outa here, you got the world ahead of you.'

Well, no, bitch, sometimes you just *can't* do it. Sometimes it's just too fucking much to bear. You need help to get over. You need somebody with benjamins, somebody watching your back.

And for a moment the anger at Geneva boiled up inside her and she gripped the purse strap even tighter.

But she couldn't hold it. The anger vanished, blew away like it was nothing more than the light brown baby powder she'd sprinkle on her twin cousins' buns when she changed their diapers.

As Lakeesha walked in a daze past Lenox Terrace toward their school, where Geneva Settle would soon be, she realized that she couldn't rely on anger or excuses.

All she could rely on was survival. Sometimes you gotta look out for yourself and take the hand somebody offers you.

Things we do 'cause we gotta . . .

37

At school, Geneva collected her homework and wouldn't you know it, her next language arts assignment was to report on Claude McKay's *Home to Harlem*, the 1928 book that was the first best-selling novel by a black author.

'Can't I have e. e. cummings?' she asked. 'Or John Cheever?'

'It's our African-American sequence, Gen,' her language arts teacher pointed out, smiling.

'Then Frank Yerby,' she bargained. 'Or Octavia Butler.'

'Ah, they're wonderful authors, Gen,' her teacher said, 'but they don't write about Harlem. That's what we're studying in this segment. But I gave you McKay because I thought you'd like him. He's one of the most controversial writers to come out of the Renaissance. McKay took a lot of flak because he looked at the underside of Harlem. He wrote about the primitive aspects of the place. That upset DuBois and a lot of other thinkers at the time. It's right up your alley.'

Maybe her father could help her interpret, she thought cynically, since he loved the neighborhood and its patois so much.

'Try it,' the man offered. 'You might like it.'

Oh, no, I won't, Geneva thought.

Outside the school, she joined her father. They came to the bus stop and both closed their eyes as a swirl of chill, dusty air swept around them.

They'd reached a detente of sorts and she'd agreed to let him take her to a Jamaican restaurant that he'd been dreaming about for the past six years.

'Is it even still there?' she asked coolly.

'Dunno. But we'll find something. Be an adventure.'

'I don't have much time.' She shivered in the cold.

'Where's that bus?' he asked.

Geneva looked across the street and frowned. Oh, no . . . There was Lakeesha. This was *so* her; she hadn't even listened to what Geneva'd said and had come here anyway.

Keesh waved.

'Who's that?' her father asked.

'My girlfriend.'

Lakeesha glanced uncertainly toward her father and then gestured for Gen to cross the street.

What's wrong? The girl's face was smiling but it was clear she had something on her mind. Maybe she was wondering what Geneva was doing with an older man.

'Wait here,' she told her father. And she started toward Lakeesha, who blinked and seemed to take a deep breath. She opened her purse and reached inside.

What's the 411 on *this*? Geneva wondered. She crossed the street and paused at the curb. Keesha hesitated then stepped forward. 'Gen,' she said, her eyes going dark.

Geneva frowned. 'Girl, what's — '

Keesh stopped fast as a car pulled to the curb

past Geneva, who blinked in surprise. Behind the wheel was the school counselor, Mrs. Barton. The woman gestured the student to the car. Geneva hesitated, told Keesh to wait a minute and joined the counselor.

'Hey, Geneva. I just missed you inside.'

'Hi.' The girl was cautious, not sure what the woman knew and didn't about her parents.

'Mr. Rhyme's assistant told me that they caught the man who tried to hurt you. And your parents finally got back.'

'My father.' She pointed. 'That's him right there.'

The counselor regarded the stocky man in the shabby T-shirt and jacket. 'And everything's okay?'

Out of earshot, Lakeesha watched them with a frown. Her expression was even more troubled than before. She'd seemed cheerful on the phone, but now that Geneva thought about it, maybe she'd been fronting. And who was that guy she'd been talking to?

Nobody . . .

I don't think so.

'Geneva?' Mrs. Barton asked. 'You all right?'

She looked back at the counselor. 'Sorry. Yeah, it's fine.'

The woman again studied her father closely and then turned her brown eyes on the girl, who looked away.

'Is there anything you want to tell me?'

'Uhm . . .'

'What's the real story here?'

'I —'

It was one of those situations when the truth was going to come out no matter what. 'Okay, look, Mrs. Barton, I'm sorry. I wasn't completely honest. My father's not a professor. He's been in prison. But he got released.'

'So where *have* you been living?'

'On my own.'

With no trace of judgment in her eyes the woman nodded. 'Your mother?'

'Dead.'

She frowned. 'I'm sorry . . . And is he going to take custody?'

'We haven't really talked about it. Anything he does he has to get it worked out with the court or something.' She said this to buy time. Geneva had half formulated a plan for her father to come back, technically take custody, but she'd continue to live on her own. 'For a few days I'm going to stay with Mr. Rhyme and Amelia, at their place.'

The woman looked once more at her father, who was offering a faint smile toward the pair.

'This's pretty unusual.'

Geneva said defiantly, 'I won't go into a foster home. I won't lose everything I've been working for. I'll run away. I'll — '

'Whoa, slow up.' The counselor smiled. 'I don't think we need to make an issue of anything now. You've been through enough. We'll talk about it in a few days. Where're you going now?'

'To Mr. Rhyme's.'

'I'll give you a ride.'

Geneva gestured her father over. The man

ambled up to the car, and the girl introduced them.

'Nice to meet you, ma'am. And thanks for looking out for Geneva.'

'Come on, get in.'

Geneva looked across the street. Keesh was still there.

She shouted, 'I gotta go. I'll call you.' She mimicked holding a phone to her ear.

Lakeesha nodded uncertainly, withdrew her hand from her purse.

Geneva climbed into the backseat, behind her father. A glance through the back window at Keesh's grim face.

Then Mrs. Barton pulled away from the curb and her father started up with another ridiculous history lesson, rambling on and on, you know I did a 'piece once 'bout the Collyer brothers? Homer and Langley. Lived at 128th and Fifth. They were recluses and the weirdest men ever lived. They were terrified of crime in Harlem and barricaded themselves in their apartment, set up booby traps, never threw a single thing out. One of 'em got crushed under a pile of newspapers he'd stacked up. When they died, police had to cart over a hundred tons of trash out of their place. He asked, 'You ever hear about them?'

The counselor said she thought she had.

'No,' Geneva replied. And thought: Ask me if I care.

★　★　★

Lincoln Rhyme was directing Mel Cooper to organize the evidence that they'd collected from the bombing scene, in between reviewing some of the evidence-analysis reports that had returned.

A federal team, under Dellray's direction, had tracked down Jon Earle Wilson, the man whose fingerprints were on the transistor radio bomb in Boyd's safe house. He'd been collared and a couple of agents were going to bring him over to Rhyme's for interrogation to shore up the case against Thompson Boyd.

It was then that Bell's phone rang. He answered, 'Bell here . . . Luis, what's up?' He cocked his head to listen.

Luis . . .

This would be Martinez, who had been tailing Geneva and her father on foot since they'd left Rhyme's to go to Langston Hughes. They were convinced that Jax, Alonzo Jackson, was her father and no threat to the girl, and that the terrorist had been working alone. But that didn't mean Bell and Rhyme were going to let Geneva go anywhere in the immediate future without protection.

But something was wrong. Rhyme could read it in Bell's eyes. The detective said to Cooper, 'We need a DMV check. Fast.' He jotted a tag number on a Post-it note then hung up, handed the slip of paper to the CS tech.

'What's happening?' Sachs asked.

'Geneva and her father were at the bus stop near the school. A car pulled up. They got inside. Luis wasn't expecting that and couldn't get across the street fast enough to stop them.'

'Car? Who was driving?'

'Heavyset black woman. Way he described her, sounds like it might've been that counselor, Barton.'

Nothing to worry about necessarily, Rhyme reflected. Maybe the woman just saw them at the bus stop and offered them a ride.

Information from the DMV flickered over his screen.

'What do we have, Mel?' Rhyme asked.

Cooper squinted as he read. He typed some more. He looked up, eyes wide through his thick glasses. 'A problem. We have a problem.'

★ ★ ★

Mrs. Barton was heading into south-central Harlem, moving slowly though the early evening traffic. She slowed as they drove past yet another real estate redevelopment project.

Her father shook his head. 'Look at all this.' He nodded at the billboard. 'Developers, banks, architects.' A sour laugh. 'Betcha there's not a single black person running any of 'em.'

Lame, Geneva thought. She wanted to tune him out.

Whining about the past . . .

The counselor glanced at the site and, shrugged. 'You see that a lot around here.' She braked and turned down an alley between one of the old buildings being gutted and a deep excavation site.

In response to her father's questioning glance,

540

Mrs. Barton said, 'Shortcut.'

But her father looked around. 'Shortcut?'

'Just to miss some of the southbound traffic.'

He looked again, squinted. Then spat out, 'Bullshit.'

'Dad!' Geneva cried.

'I know this block. Road's closed off up ahead. They're tearing down some old factory.'

'No,' Mrs. Barton said. 'I just came this way and — '

But her father grabbed the parking brake and pulled up as hard as he could, then spun the wheel to the left. The car skidded into the brick wall with the wrenching sound of metal and plastic grinding into stone.

Grabbing the counselor's arm, the man shouted, 'She's with them, baby. Trying to hurt you! Get out, run!'

'Dad, no, you're crazy! You can't — '

But the confirmation came a moment later as a pistol appeared from the woman's pocket. She aimed it at her father's chest and pulled the trigger. He blinked in shock and jerked back, gripping the wound. 'Oh. Oh, my,' he whispered.

Geneva leapt back as the woman turned the silver gun toward her. Just as it fired, her father swung his fist into the woman's jaw and stunned her. Flame and bits of gunpowder peppered Geneva's face but the bullet missed. It blew the car's rear window into a thousand tiny cubes.

'Run, baby!' her father muttered and slumped against the dashboard.

Get her down, cut her, cut the bitch . . .

Sobbing, Geneva crawled out the shattered back window and fell to the ground. She struggled to her feet and started sprinting down the ramp into the murky demolition site.

38

Alina Frazier — the woman fronting as the counselor Patricia Barton — didn't have the cool of her partner. Thompson Boyd was ice itself. He never got rattled. But Alina had always been emotional. She was furious, cursing, as she scrabbled over the body of Geneva's father and stumbled out into the alley, looking left and right for the girl.

Furious that Boyd was in jail, furious that the girl was getting away.

Breathing deeply, looking up and down the deserted alley. Stalking back and forth. Where could the little bitch — ?

A flash of gray to her right: Geneva was crawling out from behind a scabby blue Dumpster and disappearing deeper into the job site. The woman started off in pursuit, panting. She was large, yes, but also very strong and she moved quickly. You could let prison soften you, or you could let prison turn you into stone. She'd chosen the second.

Frazier'd been a gangsta in the early nineties, the leader of a girl wolf pack roaming Times Square and the Upper East Side, where tourists and residents — who'd be suspicious of a cluster of teen boys — didn't think anything of a handful of boisterous sistas, toting Daffy Dan and Macy's shopping bags. That is, until the knives or guns appeared and the rich bitches lost their cash and jewelry. After stints in juvie she'd gone down big and done time for manslaughter — it should've been murder, but the kid prosecutor had fucked up. After release she'd returned to New York. Here, she'd met Boyd through the guy she was living with, and when Frazier broke up with the claimer, Boyd had called her. At first she thought it was just one of those white-guy-hot-for-a-black-girl things. But when she'd taken up his invitation for coffee, he hadn't come on to her at all. He'd just looked her over with those weird, dead eyes of his and said that it'd be helpful to have a woman work with him on some jobs. Was she interested?

Jobs? she'd asked, thinking drugs, thinking guns, thinking perped TVs.

But he'd explained in a whisper what his line of work was.

She'd blinked.

Then he'd added it could net her upwards of fifty thousand bucks for a few days' work.

A brief pause. Then a grin. 'Damn straight.'

For the Geneva Settle job, though, they were making five times that. This turned out to be a fair price, since it was the hardest kill they'd ever worked. After the hit at the museum yesterday morning hadn't worked out, Boyd had called her and asked for her help (even offering an extra $50,000 if she killed the girl herself). Frazier, always the smartest in her crews, had come up with the idea of fronting as the counselor and had a fake board of education ID made up. She'd started calling public schools in Harlem, asking to speak to any of Geneva Settle's teachers, and had received a dozen variations on, 'She's not enrolled here. Sorry.' Until Langston Hughes High, where some office worker had said that, yes, this was her school. Frazier had then simply put on a cheap business suit, dangled the ID over her imposing chest and strolled into the high school like she owned the place.

There, she'd learned about the girl's mysterious parents, the apartment on 118th Street and — from that Detective Bell and the other cops — about the Central Park West town house and who was guarding Geneva. She'd fed all this information to Boyd to help in planning the kill.

She staked out the girl's apartment near Morningside — until it got too risky because of Geneva's bodyguards. (She'd been caught in the act this afternoon, when a squad car pulled her over near the place, but it turned out the cops hadn't been looking for her.)

Frazier had talked a guard at Langston Hughes into giving her the security video of the school yard, and with that prop, she managed to get inside the crippled man's town house, where she learned yet more information about the girl.

But then Boyd had been nailed — he'd told her all along how good the police were — and now it was up to Alina Frazier to finish the job if she wanted the rest of the fee, $125,000.

Gasping for breath, the big woman now paused thirty feet down a ramp that led to the foundation level of the excavation site. Squinting against a blast of low sun from the west, trying to see where the little bitch had gone. Damn, girl, show yourself.

Then: movement again. Geneva was making her way to the far side of the deserted job site, crawling fast over the ground, using cement mixers, Bobcats and piles of beams and supplies for cover. The girl disappeared behind an oil drum.

Stepping into the shadows for a better view, Frazier aimed at the middle of the drum and fired, hitting the metal with a loud ring.

It seemed to her that dirt danced up into the air just past the container. Had it slammed through the girl too?

But, no, she was up and moving fast to a low wall of rubble — brick, stone, pipes. Just as she vaulted it, Frazier fired again.

The girl tumbled over the other side of the wall with a shrill scream. Something puffed into the air. Dirt and stone dust? Or blood?

Had Frazier hit the girl? She was a good shot — she and her ex-boyfriend, a gunrunner in Newark, had spent hours picking off rats in abandoned buildings on the outskirts of town, trying out his products. She thought she'd been on the mark now. But she couldn't wait long to find out; people would've heard the gunshots. Some'd ignore them, sure, and some'd think the workers were still on the job with heavy equipment. But at least one or two good citizens might be calling 911 just about now.

Well, go see . . .

She started slowly down the truck ramp, making sure she didn't fall; the incline was very steep. But then a car horn began blaring from the alley, behind and above her. It was coming from her car.

Fuck, she thought angrily, the girl's father was still alive.

Frazier hesitated. Then decided: time to get the hell out of here. Finish dad off. Geneva was probably hit and wouldn't survive long. But even if she wasn't wounded, Frazier could track her down later. There'd be plenty of opportunities.

Fucking horn . . . It seemed louder than the gunshot and had to be attracting attention. Worse, it would cover up the sound of any approaching sirens. Frazier climbed to the street level up the dirt ramp, gasping from the effort. But as she got to the car, she frowned, seeing that it was empty. Geneva's father wasn't in the driver's seat, after all. A trail of blood led to a nearby alleyway, where his body lay. Frazier glanced inside her car. That's what'd happened: Before he'd crawled away he'd pulled out the car's jack and wedged it against the horn panel on the steering wheel.

Furious, Frazier yanked it away.

The piercing sound stopped.

She tossed the jack into the backseat and glanced at the man. Was he dead? Well, if not he soon would be. She walked toward him, her gun at her side. Then she paused, frowning . . . How had a man as badly wounded as this poor motherfucker opened the trunk, unscrewed the jack, lugged it to the front seat and rigged it against the wheel?

Frazier started to look around.

And saw a blur to her right, heard the whoosh of air as the tire iron swept down and crashed into her wrist, sending the gun flying and shooting a breathtaking jolt of pain through her body. The big woman screamed and dropped to her knees, lunging for the gun with her left hand. Just as she grabbed it, Geneva swung the iron again and caught the woman in the shoulder with a solid *clonk*. Frazier rolled to the ground, the gun sliding out of her reach. Blinded by the pain and the rage, the woman lunged and tackled the girl before she could swing the rod again. Geneva went down hard, the breath knocked out of her.

The woman turned toward where the pistol lay but, choking and gasping, Geneva crawled forward, grabbed her right arm and bit Frazier's shattered wrist. The pain that could be no worse rose like a shriek through her. Frazier swung her good fist into the girl's face and connected with her jaw. Geneva gave a cry and blinked tears as she rolled, helpless, onto her back. Frazier climbed unsteadily to her feet, cradling her bloody, broken wrist, and kicked the girl in the belly. The teenager began to retch.

Standing unsteadily, Frazier looked for the gun, which was ten feet away. Don't need it, don't want it. The tire iron'd do just fine. Seething with anger, she picked it up and started forward. She looked down at the girl with undiluted hate and lifted the metal rod above her head. Geneva cringed and covered her face with her hands.

Then a voice from behind the big woman shouted, 'No!'

Frazier turned to see that redheaded police-woman from the crippled man's apartment walking slowly forward, her large automatic pistol held in both hands.

Alina Frazier looked down at the revolver nearby.

'I'd like the excuse,' the policewoman said. 'I really would.'

Frazier slumped, tossed the tire iron aside and, feeling faint, dropped into a sitting position. She cradled her shattered hand.

The cop moved close and kicked the pistol and tire iron away, as Geneva rose to her feet and staggered toward a duo of medics who were running forward. The girl directed them toward her father.

Tears of pain in her eyes, Frazier demanded, 'I need a doctor.'

'You'll have to wait in line,' the policewoman muttered and slipped a plastic restraint around her wrists with what, under the circumstances, Frazier decided, was really a pretty gentle touch.

★   ★   ★

'He's in stable condition,' Lon Sellitto announced. He'd fielded the phone call from an officer on duty at Columbia-Presbyterian Hospital. 'He didn't know what that means. But there you have it.'

Rhyme nodded at this news about Jax Jackson. Whatever 'stable' meant, at least the man was alive, for which Rhyme was immensely grateful

— for Geneva's sake.

The girl herself had been treated for contusions and abrasions and released.

It had been a photo finish to save her from Boyd's accomplice. Mel Cooper had run the tags on the car that the girl and her father had gotten into and found it registered to someone named Alina Frazier. A fast check of NCIC and state databases revealed that she had a record: a manslaughter charge in Ohio and two assaults with deadly weapons in New York, as well as a slew of sealed juvie offenses.

Sellitto had put out an Emergency Vehicle Locator, which alerted all law enforcers in the area to look for Frazier's sedan. A traffic enforcement cop had radioed a short time later that the vehicle had been seen near a demolition site in South Harlem. There'd also been a report of shots fired in the vicinity. At Rhyme's town house Amelia Sachs jumped into her Camaro and sped to the scene, where she found Frazier about to beat Geneva to death.

Frazier had been interrogated but was no more cooperative than her accomplice. Rhyme guessed that one had to think long and hard about betraying Thompson Boyd, especially in jail, given the long reach of his prison connections.

Was Geneva finally safe or not? Most likely she was. Two killers under wraps and the main actor blown to pieces. Sachs had searched Alina Frazier's apartment and found nothing except weapons and cash — no information that would suggest there was anyone else who wanted to kill

Geneva Settle. Jon Earle Wilson, the ex-con from New Jersey who'd made the booby trap in Boyd's Queens safe house, was presently en route to Rhyme's, and the criminalist hoped he'd confirm their conclusions. Still, Rhyme and Bell decided to dedicate a uniformed officer in a squad car to protection detail for Geneva.

Now, a computer sounded a friendly chirp and Mel Cooper looked over at the screen. He opened an email. 'Ah, the mystery is solved.'

'Which mystery would that be?' Rhyme said this gruffly. His moods, forever fragile, tended to sour toward the end of a case, when boredom loomed.

' 'Winskinskie.' '

The Indian word on the ring Sachs had found around the finger bone beneath the ruins of Potters' Field tavern.

'And?'

'This's from a professor at the University of Maryland. Aside from the literal translation in the Delaware language, 'Winskinskie' was a title in the Tammany Society.'

'Title?'

'Sort of like a sergeant at arms. Boss Tweed was the Grand Sachem, the big chief. Our boy' — a nod toward the bones and skull Sachs had found in the cistern — 'was the Winskinskie, the doorkeeper.'

'Tammany Hall . . . ' Rhyme nodded as he considered this, letting his mind wander back in time, past this case, into the smoky sepia world of nineteenth-century New York. 'And Tweed hung out in Potters' Field. So he and the

Tammany Hall machine were probably behind setting Charles up.'

He ordered Cooper to add the recent findings to the chart. He then spent some moments looking over the information. He nodded. 'Fascinating.'

Sellitto shrugged. 'The case is over with, Linc. The hitmen, excuse me, hit*people*'ve been collared. The terrorist is dead. Why's something that happened a hundred years ago so fascinating?'

'Nearly a hundred and *forty* years, Lon. Let's be accurate.' He was frowning as he stared intently at the evidence chart, the maps — and the placid face of the Hanged Man. 'And the answer to your question is: You know how much I hate loose ends.'

'Yeah, but what's loose?'

'What's the one thing we've forgotten all about in the heat of battle, if we may tread through a minefield of clichés again, Lon?'

'I give,' Sellitto grunted.

'Charles Singleton's *secret*. Even if it doesn't have anything to do with constitutional law or terrorists, I, at least, am *dying* to know what it was. I think we should find out.'

VAN BOMBING SCENE

- Van registered to Bani al-Dahab (see profile).
- Delivered food to Middle Eastern restaurants and carts.
- Letter taking responsibility for jewelry exchange bombing recovered. Paper matches earlier documents.
- Components of explosive device recovered: residue

of Tovex, wires, battery, radio receiver detonator, portions of container, UPS box.

THOMPSON BOYD'S RESIDENCE AND PRIMARY SAFE HOUSE

- More falafel and yogurt, orange paint trace, as before.
- Cash (fee for job?) $100,000 in new bills. Untraceable. Probably withdrawn in small amounts over time.
- Weapons (guns, billy club, rope) traced to prior crime scenes.
- Acid and cyanide traced to prior crime scenes, no links to manufacturers.
- No cell phone found. Other telephone records not helpful.
- Tools traced to prior crime scenes.
- Letter revealing that G. Settle was targeted because she was a witness to jewelry heist in the planning. More pure carbon — identified as diamond dust trace.
  - Sent to Parker Kincaid in Washington, D.C., for document examination.

- Writer's first language most likely Arabic.
- Improvised explosive device, as part of booby trap. Fingerprints are those of convicted bomb maker Jon Earle Wilson.
  - Located. En route to Rhyme's for interviewing.

POTTERS' FIELD SCENE (1868)

- Tavern in Gallows Heights — located in the Eighties on the upper West Side, mixed neighborhood in the 1860s.
- Potters' Field was possible hangout for Boss Tweed and other corrupt New York politicians.
- Charles came here July 15, 1868.
- Burned down following explosion, presumably just after Charles's visit. To hide his secret?
- Body in basement, man presumably killed by Charles Singleton.
  - Shot in forehead by .36 Navy Colt loaded with .39-caliber ball (type of weapon Charles Singleton owned).
  - Gold coins.

553

- Man was armed with Derringer.
- No identification.
- Had ring with name 'Winskinskie' on it.
  - Means 'doorman' or 'gatekeeper' in Delaware Indian language.
  - Currently searching other meanings.
    - Was title of official in Boss Tweed's Tammany Hall political machine.

PROFILE OF UNSUB 109

- Determined to be Thompson G. Boyd, former executions control officer, from Amarillo, TX.
- Presently in custody.

PROFILE OF PERSON HIRING UNSUB 109

- Bani al-Dahab, Saudi national, in country illegally after visa expired.
- Deceased.
- Search of apartment revealed no other terrorist connections. Presently checking phone records.
- Currently investigating his employers for possible terrorist links.

PROFILE OF UNSUB 109'S ACCOMPLICE

- Determined not to be man originally described, but Alina Frazier, presently in custody.
- Search of apartment revealed weapons and money, nothing else relevant to case.

PROFILE OF CHARLES SINGLETON

- Former slave, ancestor of G. Settle. Married, one son. Given orchard in New York state by master. Worked as teacher, as well. Instrumental in early civil rights movement.
- Charles allegedly committed theft in 1868, the subject of the article in stolen microfiche.
- Reportedly had a secret that could bear on case. Worried that tragedy would result if his secret was revealed.
- Attended meetings in Gallows Heights neighborhood of New York.
  - Involved in some risky activities?
  - Worked with Frederick

Douglass and others in getting the 14th Amendment to the Constitution ratified.

- The crime, as reported in the *Coloreds' Weekly Illustrated*:
  - Charles arrested by Det. William Simms for stealing large sum from Freedmen's Trust in NY. Broke into the trust's safe, witnesses saw him leave shortly after. His tools were found nearby. Most money was recovered. He was sentenced to five years in prison. No information about him after sentencing. Believed to have used his connections with early civil rights leaders to gain access to the trust.

- Charles's correspondence:
  - Letter 1, to wife: Re: Draft Riots in 1863, great anti-black sentiment throughout NY state, lynchings, arson. Risk to property owned by blacks.
  - Letter 2, to wife: Charles at Battle of Appomattox at end of Civil War.
  - Letter 3, to wife: Involved in civil rights movement. Threatened for this work. Troubled by his secret.
  - Letter 4, to wife: Went to Potters' Field with his gun for 'justice.' Results were disastrous. The truth is now hidden in Potters' Field. His secret was what caused all this heartache.

V

THE FREEDMAN'S SECRET

**Friday, October 12,
to Friday, October 26**

39

The fifty-four-year-old white man in a Brooks Brothers suit sat in one of his two Manhattan offices, engaging in an intense debate with himself.

Yes or no?

The question was important, literally a matter of life and death.

Trim, solidly built William Ashberry, Jr., sat back in a creaking chair and looked over the horizon of New Jersey. This office was not as elegant or stylish as the one in lower Manhattan but it was his favorite. The twenty-by-thirty-foot room was in the historic Sanford Mansion on the Upper West Side, owned by the bank of which he was a senior officer.

He pondered: Yes? No?

Ashberry was a financier and entrepreneur of the old school, meaning, for instance, he'd ignored the eagle of the Internet when it soared into the heavens, and hadn't lost a night's sleep when it turned on its masters, except to superficially console clients who hadn't listened to his advice. This refusal to be wooed by fad, combined with solid investing in blue chip companies and, especially, New York City real estate, had made both himself and Sanford Bank and Trust a huge amount of money.

Old school, sure, but only to a point. Oh, he had the lifestyle afforded by a million-plus annual salary, along with the revered bonuses that were the mainstay of Wall Street, several homes, memberships in nice country clubs, pretty, well-educated daughters, and connections with a number of charities that he and his wife were pleased to help out. A private Grumman for his not-infrequent trips overseas was an important perk.

But Ashberry was also atypical of your Forbes-level business executives. Scratch the surface and you'd find pretty much the same tough kid from South Philly, whose father'd been a head-knocking factory worker and whose grandfather'd done some book cooking, and tougher work, for Angelo Bruno — the 'Docile Don' — and later for Phil 'Chicken Man' Testa. Ashberry had run with a tough crowd himself, made money with blades and brains and did some things that could have come back to haunt him in a big way if he hadn't made absolutely sure they were forever buried. But in his early twenties he had the presence of mind to realize that if he kept loan-sharking and busting heads for protection money and hanging out on Dickson and Reed streets in Philly, his only rewards'd be cheese-steak change and a good shot at prison. If he did more or less the same thing in the world of business and hanging out on lower Broadway and the Upper West Side of Manhattan, he'd get fucking rich and have a good shot at Albany or Washington. He might even try to fill Frank Rizzo's shoes. Why not?

So it was law school at night, a real estate license and eventually a job at Sanford Bank

— first on a cash drawer, then moving his way up through the ranks. The money did indeed start coming in, slowly at first, then in a steady stream. He rose fast to be head of the bank's hottest division, the real estate operation, rolling over competitors — both within the bank and outside — with his bare-knuckle approach to business. Then he'd finagled the job as head of the Sanford Foundation, the philanthropic side of the bank, which was, he'd learned, the best way to make political connections.

Another glance at the Jersey horizon, another moment of debate, rubbing his hand compulsively up and down his thigh, solid from his tennis sessions, jogging, golf, yachting. Yes or no?

Life and death . . .

Calculating, one foot forever rooted on South Philly's Seventeenth Street, Bill Ashberry played with the big boys.

Men, for instance, like Thompson Boyd.

Ashberry had gotten the killer's name from an arsonist who'd made the mistake of burning down one of Ashberry's commercial properties — and got caught in the process — some years ago. After Ashberry realized he had to kill Geneva Settle, he'd hired a private eye to track down the paroled burn-man and had paid him $20,000 to put him in touch with a professional killer. The scruffy man (for God's sake, a *mullet*?) had suggested Boyd. Ashberry had been impressed with the choice. Boyd was fucking scary, yes, but not in some over-the-top, ballsy South Philly way. What was scary was that he was so *calm*, so flat. Not a spark of emotion behind his eyes, never spitting out a single 'fuck' or 'prick.'

The banker had explained what he needed and they'd arranged for payment — a quarter million dollars (even that figure hadn't gotten a rise out of Boyd; he seemed more interested — you couldn't say excited — about the prospect of killing a young girl, as if he'd never done that before).

It looked for a time like Boyd would be successful and the girl would die, and all of Ashberry's problems would be over with.

But then, disaster: Boyd and his accomplice, that Frazier woman, were in jail.

Hence, the debate: Yes, no ... Should Ashberry kill Geneva Settle himself?

With his typical approach to business, he considered the risks.

Despite his zombie personality, Boyd had been as sharp as he was frightening. He knew the business of death, knew about investigating crimes too, and how you could use motive to point the police in the wrong direction. He'd come up with several phony motives to mislead the cops. First, an attempted rape, which hadn't worked. The second was more subtle. He'd planted seeds where they'd be sure to grow nowadays: a terrorist connection. He and his accomplice had found some poor raghead who delivered Middle Eastern food to carts and restaurants near the jewelry exchange, the building that was across the street from where Geneva Settle was to be killed. Boyd located the restaurant he worked for and staked out the

562

place, learned which van was his. Boyd and his partner set up a series of clues to make it seem that the Arab loser was a terrorist planning a bombing and that he wanted Geneva dead because she'd seen him planning the attack.

Boyd had gone to the trouble of stealing sheets of scrap office paper from the trash behind the exchange. He'd drawn a map on one sheet and on another written a note about the girl in Arabic-tinted English (an Arabic language website had been helpful there) — to fool the cops. Boyd was going to leave these notes near crime scenes but it'd worked out even better than that; the police found them in Boyd's safe house *before* he'd planted them, which gave more credibility to the terrorism hook. They'd used Middle Eastern food for clues and called in fake terrorist bomb threats to the FBI from pay phones around the area.

Boyd hadn't planned to go any further with the charade than this. But then a goddamn policewoman — that Detective Sachs — showed up right here, at the foundation, to dig through their archives! Ashberry still remembered how he'd struggled to stay calm, making small talk with the beautiful redhead and offering her the run of the stacks. He'd used all his willpower to keep from heading downstairs himself and casually asking her what she was looking into. But there was too great a chance that this would arouse suspicion. He'd agreed to let her take some materials and when he looked over the log after she left, he didn't see anything too troubling.

563

Still, her presence alone at the foundation and the fact she wanted to check out *some* materials told the banker that the cops hadn't caught on to the terrorist motive. Ashberry had immediately called Boyd and told him to make the story more credible. The hitman had bought a working bomb from the arsonist who'd put Ashberry in touch with Boyd. He'd planted the device in the delivery van, along with a ranting letter to the *Times* about Zionists. Boyd was arrested just after that but his partner — that black woman from Harlem — had detonated the bomb, and finally the police got the message: terrorism.

And, since the raghead was dead, they'd pull back the protection on the girl.

This gave Alina Frazier the chance to finish the job.

But the police had outsmarted her too, and she'd been caught.

The big question now was: Did the police believe the threat to the girl was finally gone, with the mastermind dead, and the two professional killers arrested?

He decided they might not be completely convinced, but their defenses would be lowered.

So what was the level of risk if he went ahead?

Minimal, he decided.

Geneva Settle would die.

Now, he only needed an opportunity. Boyd had said she'd moved out of her apartment in West Harlem and was staying someplace else. The only connection Ashberry had was her school.

He rose, left his office and took the ornate

elevator downstairs. Then walked to Broadway and found a phone kiosk. ('Always pay phones, never private landlines. And never, ever mobile phones.' Thank you, Thompson.)

He got a number from Directory Assistance and placed the call.

'Langston Hughes High,' the woman answered.

He glanced at the side of a nearby retail-store delivery truck and said to the receptionist, 'This is Detective Steve Macy with the police department. I need to speak to an administrator.'

A moment later he was put through to an assistant principal.

'How can I help you?' the harried man asked. Ashberry could hear a dozen voices in the background. (The businessman himself had detested every minute he'd spent in school.)

He identified himself again and added, 'I'm following up on an incident that involved one of your students. Geneva Settle?'

'Oh, she was that witness, right?'

'Yep. I need to get some papers to her this afternoon. The district attorney's going to be indicting some of the people involved in the case and we need her signature on a statement. Can I speak to her?'

'Sure. Hold on.' A pause as he asked someone else in the room about the girl's schedule. Ashberry heard something about her being absent. The administrator came back on. 'She's not in school today. She'll be back Monday.'

'Oh, is she at home?'

'Wait, hold on a minute . . . '

Another voice was speaking to the principal,

offering a suggestion.

Please, Ashberry thought . . .

The man came back on the line. 'One of her teachers thinks she's at Columbia this afternoon, working on some project.'

'The university?'

'Yeah. Try a Professor Mathers. I don't have his first name, sorry.'

The administrator sounded preoccupied, but to make sure the man didn't call the police just to check on him, Ashberry said in a dismissing way, 'You know, I'll just call the officers who're guarding her. Thanks.'

'Yeah, so long.'

Ashberry hung up and paused, looking over the busy street. He'd only wanted her address but this might work out better — even though the principal didn't sound surprised when Ashberry mentioned the guards, which meant that somebody might still be protecting her. He'd have to take that fact into account. He called the main Columbia switchboard and learned that Professor Mathers's office hours today were from one to six.

How long would Geneva be there? Ashberry wondered. He hoped it would be for most of the day; he had a lot to do.

* * *

At four-thirty that afternoon, William Ashberry was cruising in his BMW M5 through Harlem, looking around him. He didn't think of the place in racial or cultural terms. He saw it as an

566

opportunity. For him a man's worth was determined by his ability to pay his debts on time — specifically, and from a self-interested point of view — a man's ability to cough up the rent or mortgage on one of the redevelopment projects that Sanford Bank had going on in Harlem. If a borrower was black or Hispanic or white or Asian, if he was a drug dealer or an ad agency executive . . . didn't matter. As long as he wrote that monthly check.

Now, on 125th Street, he passed one of the very buildings his bank was renovating. The graffiti had been scrubbed off, the interior gutted, building materials stacked on the ground floor. The old tenants had been given incentives to relocate. Some reluctant residents had been 'urged' to and had taken the hint. Several new renters had already signed expensive leases, even though the construction wouldn't be completed for six months.

He turned onto a crowded, commercial street, looking at the vendors. Not what he needed. The banker continued on his search — the final task in an afternoon that had been hectic, to say the least. After leaving his office at the Sanford Foundation he'd sped to his weekend house in New Jersey. There he'd unlocked the gun cabinet and removed his double-barreled shotgun. At the workbench in the garage he'd sawed the barrels off, making the gun only about eighteen inches long — a surprisingly hard job, which had cost him a half dozen electric-saw blades. Tossing the discarded barrels into the pond behind the house, the banker had paused, looking around him, reflecting that this deck was the place where his oldest daughter would be getting married next year after she graduated from Vassar.

He'd remained there for a long moment, gazing at the sun breaking on the cold, blue water. Then he'd loaded the shortened gun and placed it and a dozen shells in a cardboard carton, covered them with some old books, newspapers and magazines. He wouldn't need any props better than these; the professor and Geneva weren't going to survive long enough to even look inside the box.

Dressed in a mismatched sports coat and suit, hair slicked back, with drugstore reading glasses — the best disguise he could come up with — Ashberry had then sped across the George Washington Bridge and into Harlem, where he now was, searching for the last prop for the drama.

Ah, there . . .

The banker parked and got out of the car. He walked up to the Nation of Islam street vendor and bought a kufi, an Islamic skullcap, drawing not the least blink of surprise from the man. Ashberry, who took the hat in his gloved hand (thanks again, Thompson), then returned to the car. When no one was looking he bent down and rubbed the hat on the ground beneath a telephone kiosk, where he guessed many people had stood during the past day or so. The hat would pick up some dirt and other evidence — ideally a hair or two — which would give the police even more false leads on the terrorist connection. He rubbed the inside of the hat on the mouthpiece of the phone to pick up saliva and sweat for DNA samples. Slipping the hat into the box with the gun and magazines and books, he climbed back into the car and drove to Morningside Heights and onto the Columbia campus.

He now found the old faculty building that housed Mathers's office. The businessman spotted a police car parked in front, an officer sitting in the front seat, looking vigilantly over the street. So she did have a guard.

Well, he could handle it. He'd survived tougher situations than this — on the streets of South Philly and in boardrooms down on Wall Street. Surprise was the best advantage — you could beat overwhelming odds if you did the unexpected.

Continuing along the street, he made a U-turn and parked behind the building, his car well out of sight and aimed toward the highway for a fast escape. He climbed out and looked around. Yes, it could work, he could approach the office from the side, then slip through the front door when the cop was looking elsewhere.

As for getting away . . . there was a back door to the building. Two ground-level windows too. If the cop ran for the building the minute he heard the shots, Ashberry could shoot him from one of the front windows. In any case he should have enough time to drop the kufi as evidence and get to his car before any other police arrived.

He found a pay phone. He called the school's main switchboard.

'Columbia University,' a voice replied.

'Professor Mathers, please.'

'One moment.'

A black-inflected voice answered, 'Hello?'

'Professor Mathers?'

'That's right.'

In the persona of Steve Macy again, Ashberry explained that he was an author from Philadelphia, doing research at the Lehman Library — the Columbia facility devoted to social science and journalism (the Sanford Foundation had given a lot of money to libraries and schools like this one. Ashberry had attended benefits there; he could describe it if he had to). He then said that one of the librarians had heard Mathers had been looking into nineteenth-century New York history, particularly the Reconstruction era. Was that right?

The professor gave a surprised laugh. 'I am, as a matter of fact. It's not for me, actually. I'm helping out a high school student. She's with me right now.'

Thank God. The girl was still there. I can get it all over with now, get on with my life.

Ashberry said that he'd brought quite a lot of material up from Philly. Would he and this student be interested in taking a look?

The professor said they definitely would, thanked him then asked what would be a convenient time to come by.

When he was seventeen Billy Ashberry had held a box cutter against the thigh of an elderly shopkeeper and reminded him that the man's protection payments were past due. The razor was going to cut one inch for every day the

570

payment was late unless he paid up instantly. His voice had been as calm then as it was now, saying to Mathers, 'I'm leaving tonight but I could drop by now. You can make copies if you want. You have a Xerox machine?'

'I do, yes.'

'I'll be there in a few minutes.'

They hung up. Ashberry reached into the box and clicked the safety button on the shotgun to the off position. Then he hefted the carton and started toward the building, through a swirl of autumn leaves spun in tiny cyclones by the cold breeze.

40

'Professor?'

'You're Steve Macy?' The dowdy professor, sporting a bow tie and tweed jacket, was sitting behind piles of papers covering his desk.

He smiled. 'Yes, sir.'

'I'm Richard Mathers. This is Geneva Settle.'

A short teenage girl, her skin as dark as the professor's, glanced at him and nodded. Then she looked eagerly at the box he carted. She was so young. Could he really kill her?

Then an image of his daughter's wedding on the dock of his summer house flashed through his mind, followed by a series of fast thoughts: the Mercedes AMG his wife wanted, his membership at the Augusta golf course, the dinner plans he had this evening at L'Etoile, to which *The New York Times* had just given three stars.

Those images answered his question.

Ashberry set the box on the floor. No cops inside, he noticed with relief. He shook Mathers's hand. And thought: Fuck, they can lift fingerprints from flesh. After the shootings he'd have to take the time to wipe off the man's palms. (He remembered what Thompson Boyd had told him: When it came to death, you did everything by the book, or you walked away from the job.)

Ashberry smiled at the girl. Didn't shake her

hand. He looked around the office, judging angles.

'Sorry for the mess,' Mathers said.

'Mine isn't any better,' he said with a faint laugh. The room was filled with books, magazines and stacks of photocopies. On the wall were a number of diplomas. Mathers was, it turned out, not a history but a law professor. And a well-known one, apparently. Ashberry was looking at a photo of the professor with Bill Clinton and another with former mayor Giuliani.

As he saw these photos, the remorse raised its head again but it was really nothing more than a faint blip on the screen by now. Ashberry was comfortable with the fact that he was in the room with two dead people.

They chatted for a few minutes, with Ashberry talking in vague terms about schools and libraries in Philadelphia, avoiding any direct comments about what he was looking into. He stayed on the offensive, asking the professor, 'What exactly're *you* researching?'

Mathers deferred to Geneva, who explained that they were trying to find out about her ancestor, Charles Singleton, a former slave. 'It was pretty weird,' she said. 'The police thought that there was this connection between him and some crimes, ones that just happened. That turned out to be pretty wack, I mean, it was wrong. But we're all curious about what happened to him. Nobody seems to know.'

'Let's take a look at what you've got,' Mathers said, clearing a spot on a low table in front of his desk. 'I'll get another chair.'

This is it, Ashberry thought. His heart began pounding fast. He then recalled the razor knife slipping into the shopkeeper's flesh, cutting two inches for the two days of missed juice, Ashberry hardly hearing the man's screams.

Recalled all the years of backbreaking work to get to where he was today.

Recalled Thompson Boyd's dead eyes.

He was instantly calm.

As soon as Mathers stepped into the hallway, the banker glanced out the window. The policeman was still in the car, a good fifty feet away, and the building was so solid he might not even hear the gunshots. With the desk between himself and Geneva, he bent down, shuffling through the papers. He gripped the shotgun.

'Did you find any pictures?' Geneva asked. 'I'd really like to find more about what the neighborhood looked like back then.'

'I have a few, I think.'

Mathers was returning. 'Coffee?' he called from the hallway.

'No, thanks.'

Ashberry turned to the door.

Now!

He started to rise, pulling the gun from the box, keeping it below Geneva's eye level.

Aiming at the doorway, finger around the trigger.

But something was wrong. Mathers wasn't appearing.

It was then that Ashberry felt something metallic touch his ear.

'William Ashberry, you're under arrest. I have a weapon.' It was the girl's voice, though a very different sound, an adult voice. 'Set that breakdown on the desk. Slow.'

Ashberry froze. 'But — '

'The shotgun. Set it down.' The girl nudged his head with the pistol. 'I'm a police officer. And I will use my firearm.'

Oh, Lord, no . . . It was all a trap!

'Listen up, now, you do what she's telling you.' This was the professor — though, of course, it wasn't Mathers at all. He was a stand-in too, a cop who was pretending to be the professor. He glanced sideways. The man had come back into the office through a side door. From his neck dangled an FBI identification card. He too held a pistol. How the hell had they gotten onto him? Ashberry wondered in disgust.

'An' don' move that muzzle so much's a skinny little millimeter. We all together on that?'

'I'm not going to tell you again,' the girl said in a calm voice. 'Do it now.'

Still he didn't move.

Ashberry thought of his grandfather, the mobster, he thought of the screaming shop-keeper, he thought of his daughter's wedding.

What would Thompson Boyd do?

Play it by the book and give up.

No fucking way. Ashberry dropped into a crouch and spun around, lightning fast, lifting the gun.

Somebody shouted, 'Don't!'

The last word he ever heard.

41

'Quite a view,' Thom said.

Lincoln Rhyme glanced out the window at the Hudson River, the rock cliffs of the Palisades on the opposite shore and the distant hills of New Jersey. Maybe Pennsylvania too. He turned away immediately, the expression on his face explaining that panoramic views, like people's pointing them out, bored him senseless.

They were in the Sanford Foundation office of the late William Ashberry atop the Hiram Sanford Mansion on West Eighty-second Street. Wall Street was still digesting the news of the man's death and his involvement in a series of crimes over the past few days. Not that the financial community had ground to a halt; compared with, say, the betrayals visited on shareholders and employees by executives of Enron and Global Crossing, the death of a crooked executive of a *profitable* company didn't make compelling news.

Amelia Sachs had already searched the office and removed evidence linking Ashberry to Boyd and taped off certain parts of the room. This meeting was in a cleared area, which happened to feature stained-glass windows and rosewood paneling.

Sitting beside Rhyme and Thom were Geneva Settle and attorney Wesley Goades. Rhyme was amused that there'd been a few moments when he'd actually suspected Goades of complicity in the case — owing to his suddenly materializing in Rhyme's apartment, looking for Geneva, and the Fourteenth Amendment aspect of the intrigue; the lawyer would've had a strong motive to make certain that nothing jeopardized an important weapon for civil libertarians. Rhyme had also wondered if the man's loyalty to his former insurance company employers had led him to betray Geneva.

But Rhyme hadn't shared his suspicion of the lawyer and thus no apologies were in order. After Rhyme and Sachs had discovered that the case had taken an unexpected turn, the criminalist had suggested that Goades be retained for what was coming next. Geneva Settle, of course, was all in favor of hiring him.

Across the marble coffee table from them were Gregory Hanson, the president of Sanford Bank and Trust, his assistant, Stella Turner, and the senior partner at Sanford's law firm, a trim mid-forties attorney named Anthony Cole. They exuded a collective unease, which, Rhyme assumed, would've arisen late yesterday when he'd called Hanson to propose a meeting to discuss the 'Ashberry matter.'

Hanson had agreed but added both quickly and wearily that he was as shocked as anyone about the man's death in the shootout at Columbia University several days before. He knew nothing about it — or about any jewelry store robbery or terrorist attack — except what he'd read in the news. What exactly did Rhyme and the police want?

Rhyme had offered standard cop-ese: 'Just the answers to a few routine questions.'

Now, pleasantries disposed of, Hanson asked, 'Could you tell us what this is about?'

Rhyme got right to the point: He explained that William Ashberry had hired Thompson Boyd, a professional killer, to murder Geneva Settle.

Three horrified glances at the slim young girl in front of them. She looked back at each of them calmly.

Continuing, the criminalist added that Ashberry felt it was vital that nobody know the reason he wanted her dead so he and Boyd had set up several fake motives for the girl's death. Originally the kill was supposed to look like a rape. Rhyme, though, had seen through that immediately, and as they continued to search for the killer he and the team had found what appeared to be the real reason for the murder: that Geneva could identify a terrorist planning an attack.

'But there were some problems with that: The bomber's death should've ended any need to kill Geneva. But it didn't. Boyd's partner tried again. What was going on? We tracked down the man who sold the bomb to Boyd, an arsonist in New Jersey. The FBI arrested him. We linked some bills in his possession to Boyd's safe house. That made him an accomplice to murder and he copped a plea. He told us that he put Ashberry and Boyd together and — '

'This terrorist thing, though,' the bank's lawyer said skeptically, with a sour laugh. 'Bill

Ashberry and terrorists? It — '

'Getting there,' Rhyme said, equally sour. Maybe more so. He continued his explanation: The bomb maker's statement wasn't enough for a warrant to arrest Ashberry. So Rhyme and Sellitto decided they needed to flush him out. They placed an officer at Geneva's high school, a man pretending to be an assistant principal. Anyone calling to ask about Geneva would be told that she was at Columbia with a professor in the law school. The real professor agreed to let them use not only his name but his office as well. Fred Dellray and Jonette Monroe, the undercover gangsta girl from Geneva's high school, were more than happy to play the roles of the professor and student. They'd done a fast but thorough job setting up the sting, even having some fake Photoshop pictures made up of Dellray with Bill Clinton and Rudy Giuliani, to make sure Ashberry didn't tip to the scam and bolt.

Rhyme now explained these events to Hanson and Cole, adding the details about the attempted murder in Mathers's office.

He shook his head. 'I should've guessed the perp had some connections to a bank. He'd been able to withdraw large amounts of cash and doctor the reporting statements. But' — Rhyme nodded to the lawyer — 'what the hell was he up to? I understand that Episcopalians aren't really a breeding ground for fundamentalist terrorism.'

No one smiled. Rhyme thought, bankers, lawyers — no sense of humor. He continued, 'So I went back to the evidence and noticed something that bothered me: There was no radio transmitter to detonate the bomb. It should've been in the wreckage of the van, but it wasn't.

'Why not? One conclusion was that Boyd and his partner had planted the bomb and kept the transmitter themselves to kill the Arab delivery-man as a diversion to keep us from finding the real motive for killing Geneva.'

'Okay,' Hanson said. 'The real motive. What was it?'

'Had to do some thinking about that. I thought at first maybe Geneva had seen some tenants being evicted illegally when she was scrubbing graffiti off old buildings for a developer. But I looked into where that'd happened and found that Sanford Bank wasn't involved in those buildings. So, where did that leave us? I could only come back to what we'd originally thought . . . '

He explained about the old *Coloreds' Weekly Illustrated* that Boyd had stolen. 'I'd forgotten that somebody had been tracking down the magazine *before* Geneva supposedly saw the van and terrorist. I think what happened was that Ashberry stumbled on that article when the Sanford Foundation renovated its archives last month. And he did some more research and found something real troubling, something that could ruin his life. He got rid of the foundation's copy and decided he had to destroy all the copies of the magazine. Over the past few weeks he found most of them — but there was one left in the area: The librarian at the African-American museum in Midtown was getting their copy from storage and must've told Ashberry that, coincidentally, there was a girl who was interested in the same issue. Ashberry knew he had to destroy the article and kill Geneva, along with the librarian, because he could connect them.'

'But I still don't understand *why*,' Cole, the lawyer, said. His sourness had blossomed into full-fledged irritation.

Rhyme explained the final piece of the puzzle: He related the story of Charles Singleton, the farm he'd been given by his master and the Freedmen's Trust robbery — and the fact that the former slave had a secret. '*That* was the answer to why Charles was set up in 1868. And it's the answer to why Ashberry had to kill Geneva.'

'Secret?' Stella, the assistant, asked.

'Oh, yes. I finally figured out what it was. I remembered something that Geneva's father had told me. He said that Charles taught at an African free school near his home and that he sold cider to workers building boats up the road.' Rhyme shook his head. 'I made a careless assumption. We heard that his farm was in New York state . . . which it was. Except that it wasn't *upstate*, like we were thinking.'

'No? Where was it?' Hanson asked.

'Easy to figure out,' he continued, 'if you keep in mind there were working farms here in the city until the late eighteen hundreds.'

'You mean his farm was in Manhattan?' Stella asked.

'Not only,' Rhyme said, allowing himself the colloquialism. 'It was right underneath this building.'

42

'We found a drawing of Gallows Heights in the 1800s that shows three or four big, tree-filled estates. One of them covered this and the surrounding blocks. Across the road from it was an African free school. Could that've been his school? And on the Hudson River' — Rhyme glanced out the window — 'right about there, at Eighty-first Street, was a dry dock and shipyard. Could the workers there have been the ones Charles sold cider to?

'But was the estate his? There was one simple way to find out. Thom checked the Manhattan recorder's office and found the record of a deed from Charles's master to Charles. Yep, it was his. Then everything else fell into place. All the references we found to meetings in Gallows Heights — with politicians and civil rights leaders? It was *Charles*'s house they were meeting in. *That* was his secret — that he owned fifteen acres of prime land in Manhattan.'

'But why was it a secret?' Hanson asked.

'Oh, he didn't dare tell anyone he was the owner. He wanted to, of course. That's what he was so tormented about: He was proud that he owned a big farm in the city. He believed he could be a model for other former slaves. Show them that they could be treated as whole men, respected. That they could own land and work it, be members of the community. But he'd seen draft riots, the lynchings of blacks, the arson. So he and his wife pretended to be caretakers. He was afraid that somebody would find out that a former slave owned a large plot of choice property and destroy it. Or, more likely, steal it from him.'

'Which,' Geneva said, 'is exactly what happened.'

Rhyme continued, 'When Charles was convicted all his property was confiscated — including the farm — and sold . . . Now, that's a nice *theory*: setting up someone with false charges to steal his property. But was there any proof? A tall order a hundred and forty years later — talk about cold cases . . . Well, there *was* some evidence. The Exeter Strongbow safes — the type that Charles allegedly broke into at the Freedmen's Trust — they were made in England so I called a friend at Scotland Yard. He talked to a forensic locksmith, who said it'd be impossible to break into a nineteenth-century Exeter safe with only a hammer and chisel, which is what they found at the scene. Even steam-powered drills of that era would take three or four hours — and the article about the theft said that Charles was inside the trust for only twenty minutes.

'Next conclusion: Somebody else robbed the place, planted some of Charles's tools at the scene and then bribed a witness to lie about him. I think that the actual thief was a man we found buried in the basement of the Potters' Field tavern.' He explained about the Winskinskie ring and the man who'd worn it — that he was an officer in the corrupt Tammany Hall political machine.

'He was one of Boss Tweed's cronies. And another one was William Simms, the detective who arrested Charles. Simms was later indicted for graft and planting false evidence on suspects. Simms, the Winskinskie man, and the judge and prosecutor engineered Charles's conviction. And they kept the money from the trust that wasn't recovered.

'So, we've established Charles owned a huge estate in Gallows Heights and he was set up so somebody could steal it.' His eyebrow rose. 'The next logical question? The big one?'

No takers.

'Obviously: Who the hell was the *perp*?' Rhyme snapped. 'Who robbed Charles? Well, given that the motive was to steal his farm, all I had to do was find out who took title to the land.'

'Who was it?' Hanson asked, troubled but seemingly caught up in the historical drama.

The assistant smoothed her skirt and suggested, 'Boss Tweed?'

'No. It was a colleague of his. A man who was seen regularly at the Potters' Field tavern, along with some of the other notorious figures back then — Jim Fisk, Jay Gould and Detective Simms.' A glance at each of the people across the table. 'His name was Hiram Sanford.'

The woman blinked. After a moment she said, 'The founder of our bank.'

'The one and only.'

584

'This is ridiculous,' said Cole, the attorney. 'How could he do that? He was one of the pillars of New York society.'

'Just like William Ashberry?' the criminalist asked sarcastically. 'The business world wasn't really any different then than it is now. Lots of financial speculation — one of Charles's letters quoted the New York *Tribune* referring to the 'bursting bubbles' on Wall Street. Railroads were the Internet companies of the 1800s. Their stocks were overvalued and crashed. Sanford probably lost his fortune when that happened and Tweed agreed to bail him out. But, being Tweed, he naturally wanted to use somebody else's money to do it. So the two of them set up Charles, and Sanford bought the orchard at a rigged auction for a fraction of its value. He tore down Charles's house and built his mansion on it, where we're sitting right now.' A nod out the window toward the blocks nearby. 'And then he and his heirs developed the land or sold it off little by little.'

'Didn't Charles claim he was innocent, tell them what happened?' Hanson asked.

Rhyme scoffed, 'A former slave against the anti-black Tammany Hall Democratic machine? How successful would *that* have been? Besides, he'd killed the man in the tavern.'

'So he was a murderer,' the attorney, Cole, pointed out quickly.

'Of course not,' Rhyme snapped. 'He needed the Winskinskie man alive — to prove his innocence. The death was self-defense. But Charles had no choice but to hide the body and cover up the shooting. If they'd found out, he'd be hanged.'

Hanson shook his head. 'Only there's one thing that doesn't make any sense: Why would what Hiram Sanford did way back then affect Bill Ashberry? Granted it's bad PR — a bank founder stealing a former slave's property? That'd be an ugly ten minutes on the nightly news. But frankly there *are* spin doctors who can handle that sort of thing. It's not worth killing somebody for.'

'Ah.' Rhyme nodded. 'Very good question . . . We've done a little research. Ashberry was in charge of your real estate division, right?'

'That's right.'

'And if it were to go under he'd lose his job and most of his fortune?'

'I suppose so. But why would it go under? It's our most profitable unit.'

Rhyme looked at Wesley Goades. 'You're up.'

The lawyer glanced briefly at the people across the table, then down again. The man simply could not hold eye contact. Nor was he given to Rhyme's pointed explanations — and occasional digressions. He said simply, 'We're here to inform you that Ms. Settle intends to file a lawsuit against your bank seeking restitution for her loss.'

Hanson frowned and looked at Cole, who gave them a sympathetic look. 'On the facts that you've given me, making a tortious claim against the bank for infliction of emotional distress probably wouldn't get very far. See, the problem is that Mr. Ashberry was acting on his own, not

586

as a bank officer. We're not responsible for his actions.' A glance toward Goades, which may or may not have been condescending. 'As your fine counsel here will tell you.'

Hanson added quickly to Geneva, 'But, we're very sympathetic to what you went through.' Stella Turner nodded. They seemed to mean this sincerely. 'We'll make it up to you.' He offered a smile. 'I think you'll find we can be pretty generous.'

His lawyer added what he had to: 'Within reason.'

Rhyme regarded the bank president closely. Gregory Hanson seemed nice enough. Boyishly fifties, an easy smile. Probably one of those natural-born businessmen — the sort who was a decent boss and family man, did his job competently, worked long hours for the share-holders, flew coach on the company dime, remembered his employees' birthdays.

The criminalist almost felt bad about what was coming next.

Wesley Goades, however, exhibited no remorse whatsoever as he said, 'Mr. Hanson, the loss we're talking about isn't your corporate officer's attempted *murder* of Ms. Settle — which is how *we* phrase the act — not 'emotional distress.' No, her suit is on behalf of Charles Singleton's heirs, to recover the property stolen by Hiram Sanford, as well as monetary damages — '

'Wait,' the president whispered, giving a faint laugh.

' — damages equal to the rents and profits that your bank has made from that property from the date the court transferred title.' He consulted a piece of paper. 'That'd be August 4, 1868. The money'll be placed in a trust for the benefit of all of Mr. Singleton's descendants, with distribution to be supervised by the court. We don't have the actual figure yet.' Finally Goades looked up and held Hanson's eye. 'But we're ballparking it conservatively at around nine hundred and seventy million dollars.'

43

'*That's* what William Ashberry was willing to kill for,' Rhyme explained. 'To keep the theft of Charles's property a secret. If anybody found out and his heirs made a claim, it would be the end of the real estate division and might even drive the entire Sanford Bank into bankruptcy.'

'Oh, well, now, this's absurd,' the lawyer across the table from them blustered. The two legal opponents were equally tall and skinny, though Cole had a better tan. Rhyme suspected that Wesley Goades didn't get out on tennis courts or golf courses very often. 'Look around you. The blocks're developed! Every square inch is built on.'

'We have no claim to the construction,' Goades said, as if this were clear. 'We only want title to the land, and the rents that've been paid with respect to it.'

'For a hundred and forty *years*?'

'It's not *our* problem that that's when Sanford robbed Charles.'

'But most of the land's been sold off,' Hanson said. 'The bank only owns the two apartment buildings on this block and this mansion.'

'Well, naturally we'll be instituting an accounting action to trace the proceeds of the property your bank illegally sold.'

'But we've been disposing of parcels for over a hundred years.'

Goades spoke to the tabletop. 'I'll say again: *your* problem, not ours.'

'No,' Cole snapped. 'Forget it.'

'Ms. Settle is actually being quite restrained in her damage claim. There's a good argument to be made for the fact that without her ancestor's property, your bank would have gone under altogether in the eighteen sixties and that she's entitled to *all* of your worldwide earnings. But we're not seeking that. She doesn't want the present shareholders of the bank to suffer too much.'

'Damn generous,' the lawyer muttered.

'It was her decision. I was in favor of closing you down.'

Cole leaned forward. 'Listen, why don't you take a reality pill here? You have no case. For one thing, the statute of limitations has run. You'll be kicked out of court on motion.'

'Have you ever noticed,' Rhyme asked, unable to resist, 'how people always lead with their weakest argument? . . . Sorry, forgive the footnote.'

'As for the statute,' Goades said, 'we can make a solid argument that it's been tolled and we're entitled to bring the suit under principles of equity.'

The lawyer had explained to Rhyme that in some cases the time limit on bringing a lawsuit could be 'tolled' — extended — if the defendant covers up a crime so that the victims don't know it occurred, or when they aren't able to sue, like when the courts and prosecutors were acting in collusion with the wrongdoer, which had happened in the Singleton case. Goades reiterated this now.

'But whatever Hiram Sanford did,' the other lawyer pointed out, 'it had nothing to do with my client — the present bank.'

'We've traced ownership of the bank all the way back to the original Hiram Sanford Bank and Trust Limited, which was the entity that took title to the Singleton farm. Sanford used the bank as a cover. Unfortunately . . . for you, that is.' Goades said this as cheerfully as an unsmiling man could.

Cole wasn't giving up. 'Well, what proof do you have that the property would've been passed down through the family? This Charles Singleton could've sold it for five hundred dollars in 1870 and squandered the money away.'

'We have evidence that he intended to keep the farm in his family.' Rhyme turned to Geneva. 'What did Charles say?'

The girl didn't need to look at any notes. 'In a letter to his wife he told her he never wanted to sell the farm. He said, 'I wish the land to pass intact to our son and his issue; professions and trades ebb and flow, the financial markets are fickle, but the earth is God's great constant — and our farm will ultimately bring to our family respectability in the eyes of those who do not respect us now. It will be our children's salvation, and that of the generations that will follow.''

Enjoying his role as cheerleader, Rhyme said, 'Just think of how a jury'll react to *that*. Not a dry eye.'

Cole leaned forward angrily toward Goades. 'Oh, I know what's going on here. You're making it sound like she's a victim. But this's just blackmail. Like all the rest of the slavery reparations bullshit, right? I'm sorry Charles Singleton was a slave. I'm sorry he or his father, or whoever, was brought here against his will.' Cole waved his arm, as if shooing away a bee, and glanced at Geneva. 'Well, young lady, that was a long, long time ago. My great-grandfather died of black lung. You don't see me suing West Virginia Coal and Shale, looking for some easy money. You people have to get over it. Just get on with your lives. If you spent as much time — '

'Hold up,' Hanson snapped. Both he and his assistant glared at the lawyer.

Cole licked his lips and then sat back. 'I'm sorry. I didn't mean it the way it sounded. I said 'you people' but I didn't mean . . . ' He was looking at Wesley Goades.

But it was Geneva who spoke. 'Mr. Cole, I feel the same way. Like, I really believe in what Frederick Douglass said. 'People might not get all they work for in this world, but they must certainly work for all they get.' I don't want any easy money.'

The lawyer eyed her uncertainly. He looked down after a moment. Geneva did not. She continued, 'You know, I've been talking to my father about Charles. I found out some things about him. Like, his grandfather was kidnapped by slavers and taken away from his family in Yorubaland and sent to Virginia. Charles's father died when he was forty-two because his master thought it'd be cheaper to buy a new, younger slave than to treat him for pneumonia. I found out that Charles's mother was sold to a plantation in Georgia when Charles was twelve and he never saw her again. But, you know what?' she asked calmly. 'I'm not asking for a penny because of *those* things. No. It's real simple. Something Charles loved was taken away from him. And I'll do whatever I have to to make sure the thief pays for that.'

Cole murmured another apology but his legal genes wouldn't let him abdicate his client's cause. He glanced at Hanson then continued, 'I appreciate what you're saying and we'll offer a settlement based on Mr. Ashberry's actions. But as for the claim to the property? We can't go there. We don't even know that you have legal standing to bring the suit. What proof do you have that you're really Charles Singleton's descendant?'

Lincoln Rhyme eased his finger across the touchpad and steered his chair imposingly close to the table. 'Isn't it about time somebody here asked why *I* tagged along?'

Silence.

'I don't get out very much, as you can imagine. So what do you think brought me all these long blocks west?'

'Lincoln,' chided Thom.

'All right, all right, I'll get to the point. Exhibit A.'

'What exhibit?' Cole asked.

'I'm being facetious. The letter.' He glanced at Geneva. She opened her own backpack and took out a folder. She slipped a photocopy onto the desk.

The Sanford side of the table looked it over.

'One of Singleton's letters?' Hanson asked.

'Nice handwriting,' Rhyme observed. 'That was important back then. Not like nowadays, all this typing and careless jotting . . . All right, sorry — no more digressions. Here's the point: I had a colleague, fellow named Parker Kincaid, down in D.C., compare that handwriting to all the existing samples of Charles Singleton's exemplars, including legal documents in archives down in Virginia. Parker's former FBI — he's the handwriting expert the experts go to when they have a questioned document. He's executed an affidavit stating that this's identical to the known samples of Singleton's handwriting.'

'Okay,' Cole conceded, 'it's his letter. So?'

'Geneva,' Rhyme said, 'what does Charles say?'

She nodded at the letter and recited, again from memory, ''And yet the source of my tears — the stains you see on this paper, my darling, — are not from pain but from regret for the misery. I have visited upon us.''

'The original letter contains several stains,' Rhyme explained. 'We analyzed them and found lysozyme, lipocalin and lactoferrin — proteins, if you're interested — and assorted enzymes, lipids and metabolites. Those, and water, of course, make up human tears . . . By the way, did you know that the composition of tears differs significantly depending on whether they were shed in pain or because of emotion? These tears'

— a nod toward the document — 'were shed in emotion. I can prove that. I suspect the jury will find that fact moving too.'

Cole sighed. 'You've run a DNA test on the stain and it matches Ms. Settle's DNA.'

Rhyme shrugged and muttered the byword for today: 'Obviously.'

Hanson looked at Cole, whose eyes slipped back and forth between the letter and his notes. The president said to Geneva, 'A million dollars. I'll write you a check right now for a million dollars, if you and your guardian sign a liability waiver.'

Goades said coolly, 'Ms. Settle insists on seeking restitution in the amount of the actual damages — monies that all of Charles Singleton's heirs will share in, not just herself.' He leveled another gaze at the bank president. 'I'm sure you weren't suggesting that your payment would be for her alone, an incentive, maybe, to neglect to inform her relatives about what happened.'

'No, no, of course not,' Hanson said quickly. 'Let me talk to our board. We'll come up with a settlement figure.'

Goades gathered up the papers and stuffed them into his knapsack. 'I'm filing the complaint in two weeks. If you want to discuss voluntarily creating a trust fund for the claimants, you can call me here.' He slid a card across the desk.

When they were at the door the bank's attorney, Cole, said, 'Geneva, wait, please. Look, I'm sorry about what I said before. Truly. It was . . . inappropriate. I honestly feel bad for what happened to you and to your ancestor. And I *do* have your interest in mind here. Just remember that a settlement would be far and away the best thing for you and your relatives. Let your lawyer tell you how tough a trial like this would be, how long it could take, how expensive.' He smiled. 'Trust me. We *are* on your side here.'

Geneva looked him over. Her reply was: 'The battles're the same as they've always been. It's just harder to recognize the enemy.' She turned and continued out the door.

The attorney clearly had no idea what she meant.

Which, Rhyme supposed, more or less proved her point.

44

Early Wednesday, the autumn air cold and clear as fresh ice.

Geneva had just visited her father at Columbia-Presbyterian Hospital and was on her way to Langston Hughes High. She'd finished the paper on *Home to Harlem*. It turned out not to be such a bad book (though she'd still rather have written about Octavia Butler; *damn*, that woman could write!) and she was pretty pleased with her report.

What was especially phat, though, was that Geneva'd written it on a word processor, one of the Toshibas in Mr. Rhyme's lab, which Thom had showed her how to use. At school the few computers that worked were so overbooked that you couldn't get more than fifteen minutes of time on one, let alone use it to write a whole paper. And to find facts or research all she had to do was 'minimize' WordPerfect and call up the Internet. A miracle. What would've otherwise taken her two days to write, she finished in mere hours.

Crossing the street, she aimed for the shortcut through the school yard of PS 288 elementary school, which took a few minutes off the trip from the Eighth Avenue train station to Langston Hughes. The chain-link fence around the school yard cast a gridded shadow on the bleached-gray asphalt. The slim girl slipped

597

easily through the gap in the gate, which had long ago been wedged open wide enough for a teenage boy and a basketball to pass through. The hour was early, the yard deserted.

She was ten feet across the grounds when she heard a voice calling from the other side of the fence.

'Girlfriend, yo!'

She stopped.

Lakeesha stood on the sidewalk, decked out in tight green stretch pants, a long orange blouse, taut over her boobs, book bag dangling, bling and braids glistening in the sun. Her face had the same somber expression as when Geneva'd seen her last week when that wack bitch Frazier tried to kill her and her father. 'Hey, girl, where've you been?'

Keesh looked doubtfully at the gap in the chain link; she'd never fit. 'C'mon here.'

'Meet me at school.'

'Naw. Wanna talk just us.'

Geneva debated. Her friend's face told her this was important. She slipped out through the gate and walked up to the big girl. They fell into a slow walk, side by side.

'Where've you been, Keesh?' Geneva frowned. 'You cut class?'

'Ain't feelin' good.'

'Monthlies?'

'Naw, not that. My moms sent a note.' Lakeesha looked around. 'Who that old dude you with th'other day?'

She opened her mouth to lie and instead said, 'My father.'

'No!'

'Word,' Geneva said.

'He be livin' in Chicago, or somethin', you tellin' me.'

'My moms lied. He was in the system. He got released a couple months ago, came to find me.'

'Where he at now?'

'In the hospital. He got hurt.'

'He down?'

'Yeah. He'll be okay.'

'And him and you? You phat?'

'Maybe. Hardly know him.'

'Damn, him showin' up — musta been freaky.'

'You got that right, girl.'

Finally the big girl slowed. Then stopped. Geneva looked at her friend's evasive eyes and watched her hand disappearing into her purse, gripping something inside.

A hesitation.

'What?' Geneva asked.

'Here,' the girl whispered fast, lifting her hand and thrusting it forward. In her fingers, which ended in black-and-white-checkered acrylic nails, was a silver necklace, a heart on the end of a chain.

'That's — ' Geneva began

'What you give me last month, fo' my birthday.'

'You're giving it back?'

'I can't keep it, Gen. You be needin' benjamins anyway. You can hock it.'

'Don't be wack, girl. Not like it came from Tiffany's.'

Tears were welling in the big girl's eyes, the

599

prettiest part of her face. Her hand lowered. 'I be movin' next week.'

'Moving? Where?'

'BK.'

'Brooklyn? Your whole family? The twins?'

'They ain' goin'. None of the family be goin'.' The girl's eyes swept the sidewalk.

'What's this all about, Keesh?'

'I'ma tell you somethin' that happen.'

'I'm not in the mood for drama, girl,' Geneva snapped. 'What're you talking about?'

'Kevin,' Lakeesha continued in a soft voice.

'Kevin Cheaney?'

Keesh nodded. 'I'm sorry, girl. Me and him, we in love. He got this place he moving to. I'ma go with him.'

Geneva, silent for a moment. Then: 'Was he the one you were talking to when I called last week?'

She nodded. 'Listen, I didn't want it to happen but it jus' did. You gotta understand. We got this thing, him and me. It ain't like nothin' I never felt. I know you wanta be with him. You talkin' 'bout him all the time, lookin' him over ever' day. You so happy that time he walk you home. I know all that and still I done move in on you. Oh, girl, I been worried steady, thinkin' 'bout tellin' you.'

Geneva felt a chill in her soul, but it had nothing to do with her crush on Kevin, which had vanished the instant he showed his true self in math class. She asked, 'You're pregnant, aren't you?'

Wasn't feeling good . . .

Keesh lowered her head and stared at the dangling necklace.

Geneva closed her eyes for a moment. Then she asked, 'How far down?'

'Two months.'

'Hook yourself up with a doctor. We'll go to the clinic, you and me. I'll — '

Her friend frowned. 'Why I do that? It ain't like I laid no baby on him. He say he use protection if I say so but he really *want* to have a baby with me. He say it be like part of both of us.'

'It was a line, Keesh. He's working you.'

Her friend glared. 'Oh, that cold.'

'No, that's *word*, girl. He's been fronting. He's working some angle.' Geneva wondered what he wanted from her. It wouldn't be grades, not in Keesha's case. Probably money. Everybody in school knew she worked hard at her two jobs and saved what she earned. Her parents had income too. Her moms'd worked for the Postal Service for years and her father had a job at CBS and another one nights at the Sheraton Hotel. Her brother worked, as well. Kevin'd have an eye on the whole family's benjamins.

'You loan him any money?' Geneva asked.

Her friend looked down. Said nothing. Meaning yes.

'We had a deal, you and me. We were going to graduate, go to college.'

Lakeesha wiped tears from her round face with her round hand. 'Oh, Gen, you a trip. What planet you be livin' on? We talk, you and me, 'bout college and fancy jobs but fo' me, it just

601

talk. You write yo' papers like they nothin' and take yo' tests and you be number one at ever'thing. You know I ain't like that.'

'You were going to be the successful one, with your business. Remember, girl? I'll be a poor professor somewhere, eating tuna out of a can and having Cheerios for dinner. You're the one going to kick ass. What about your store? Your TV show? Your club?'

Keesh shook her head, her braids dangling. 'Shit, girl, that just claimin'. I ain't goin' nowhere. Best I can hope for is what I doin' now — servin' up salads and burgers at T.G.I. Friday's. Or doing braids and extensions till they go outa style. Which you ask me'll be all of six months.'

Geneva gave a weak smile. 'We always said 'fros'd be coming back in.'

Keesha laughed. 'Word. All you need fo' them is a pick and spray; ain't no need fo' no fresh artist like me.' She twined her own blonde extensions around her finger then lowered her hands, her smile fading. 'By myself, I'll end up a played-out old bag. Only way I'ma get over is with a man.'

'Now who's talking trash 'bout herself, girl? Kevin's been feeding you crap. You never used to talk this way.'

'He take care of me. He be lookin' steady for work. An' he promise he help me take care of the baby. He different. He not like them other boys he hang with.'

'Yes, he is. You *can't* give up, Keesh. Don't do it! Stay in school at least. You really want a baby,

602

fine, but stay in school. You can — '

'You ain't my moms, girl,' Keesh snapped. 'I know what I'm about.' Anger flashed in the girl's eyes — all the more heartbreaking because it was the very same fury that had filled the girl's round face when she stepped up to protect Geneva from the Delano or St. Nicholas project girls moving on her in the street.

Get her down, cut her, cut the bitch . . .

Then Keesh added softly, 'What it is, girl, he sayin' I can't hang with you no more.'

'You can't — '

'Kevin say you treat him bad at school.'

'Treated him bad?' A cold laugh. 'He wanted me to help him cheat. I said no.'

'I told him it was fucked up, what he was sayin', me and you being so tight and ever'thing. But he wouldn't listen. He say I can't see you none.'

'So you're choosing him,' Geneva said.

'I ain't *got* no choice.' The big girl looked down. 'I can't take no present from you. Here.' She thrust the necklace into Geneva's hand and released it fast, as if she were letting go of a hot pan. It fell to the filthy sidewalk.

'Don't do it, Keesh. Please!'

Geneva reached for the girl but her fingers closed on nothing but cool air.

45

Ten days after the meeting with Sanford Bank President Gregory Hanson and his lawyer, Lincoln Rhyme was having a phone conversation with Ron Pulaski, the young rookie, who was on medical leave but expected to return to duty in a month or so. His memory was coming back and he was helping them shore up the case against Thompson Boyd.

'So you going to a Halloween party?' Pulaski asked. Then paused and added a quick 'Or whatever.' The last two words probably were meant to counteract any faux pas created by suggesting that a quadriplegic might attend parties.

But Rhyme put him at ease by saying, 'I am, as a matter of fact. I'm going as Glenn Cunningham.'

Sachs stifled a laugh.

'Really?' the rookie asked. 'Uhm, who's that exactly?'

'Why don't you look it up, Patrolman.'

'Yes, sir. I will.'

Rhyme disconnected and looked over the main evidence board, on the top of which was taped the twelfth card in the tarot deck, The Hanged Man.

He was gazing at the card when the doorbell rang.

Lon Sellitto, probably. He was due soon from

a therapy session. He'd stopped rubbing the phantom bloodstain and practicing his Billy the Kid quick draw — which nobody'd yet explained to Rhyme. He'd tried to ask Sachs about it but she couldn't, or wouldn't, say much. Which was fine. Sometimes, Lincoln Rhyme firmly believed, you just didn't need to know all the details.

But his visitor at the moment, it turned out, wasn't the rumpled detective.

Rhyme glanced into the doorway and saw Geneva Settle standing there, listing against her book bag. 'Welcome,' he said.

Sachs too said hello, pulling off the safety glasses she'd been wearing as she filled out chain-of-custody cards for blood samples she'd collected at a homicide crime scene that morning.

Wesley Goades had all the paperwork ready to file in the lawsuit against Sanford Bank and reported to Geneva that she could expect a realistic offer from Hanson by Monday. If not, the legal cruise missile had warned his opponents that he would file suit the next day. A press conference would accompany the event (Goades's opinion was that the bad publicity would last considerably longer than an 'ugly ten minutes').

Rhyme looked the girl over. Unseasonably warm weather made gangsta sweats and stocking caps impractical so she was in blue jeans and a sleeveless T-shirt with *Guess!* in glittery letters across the chest. She'd gained a little weight, her hair was longer. She even had some makeup on

(Rhyme had wondered what was in the bag that Thom had mysteriously slipped her the other day). The girl looked good.

Geneva's life had achieved a certain stability. Jax Jackson had been released from the hospital and was undergoing physical therapy. Thanks to some prodding by Sellitto, the man had been officially transferred to the care and feeding of the New York City parole authorities. Geneva was living in his minuscule apartment in Harlem, an arrangement that was not as dire as she'd anticipated (the girl had confessed this not to Rhyme or Roland Bell but to Thom — who'd become a mother hen to the girl and invited her to the town house regularly, to give her cooking lessons, watch TV and argue books and politics, none of which Rhyme had any interest in). As soon as they could afford a bigger place, she and her father were going to have Aunt Lilly move in with them.

The girl had given up her job slinging McHash and was now employed after school by Wesley Goades as a legal researcher and gofer. She was also helping him set up the Charles Singleton Trust, which would disburse the settlement money to the freedman's heirs. Geneva's interest in fleeing the city at the earliest opportunity for a life in London or Rome hadn't flagged, but the cases that Rhyme overheard her passionately talking about all seemed to involve Harlem residents who'd been discriminated against because they were black, Latino, Islamic, women or poor.

Geneva was also engaged in some project she

referred to as 'saving her girlfriend,' which she didn't go into with him either; her advisor for this particular endeavor seemed to be Amelia Sachs.

'I wanted to show you something.' The girl held up a piece of yellowing paper containing several paragraphs of handwriting that Rhyme immediately recognized as Charles Singleton's.

'Another letter?' Sachs asked.

Geneva nodded. She was handling the paper very carefully.

'Aunt Lilly heard from that relative of ours in Madison. He sent us a few things he found in his basement. A bookmark of Charles's, a pair of his glasses. And a dozen letters. This is the one I wanted to show you.' With beaming eyes, Geneva added, 'It was written in 1875, *after* he got out of prison.'

'Let's see it,' Rhyme said.

Sachs mounted it on the scanner and a moment later the image appeared on several computer monitors around the lab. Sachs stepped next to Rhyme, put her arm around his shoulder. They looked at the screen.

My most darling Violet:
I trust you have been enjoying your sister's company, and that Joshua and Elizabeth are pleased to spend time with their cousins. That Frederick — who was only nine when I saw him last, — is as tall as his father is a fact I find hard to grasp.
All is well at our cottage, I am pleased to report. James and I cut ice on the shore of

607

the river all morning and stocked the ice-house, then covered the blocks in saw-dust. We then traveled some two miles north through substantial snow to view the orchard that is offered for sale. The price is dear but I believe the seller will respond favorably to my counter-offer. He was clearly in doubt about selling to a Negro but when I revealed that I could pay him in greenbacks and would not need to offer a note, his concerns appeared to vanish.

Hard cash is a great equalizer.

Were you not as moved as I to read that yesterday our country enacted a Civil Rights Act? Did you see the particulars? The law guarantees to everyone of any color equal enjoyment of all inns, public conveyances, theaters and the like. What a momentous day for our Cause! This is the very legislation about which I corresponded with Charles Sumner and Benjamin Butler at length last year, and I believe that some of my ideas made their way into this important docu-ment.

As you can well imagine, this news gave me cause for reflection, thinking back to those terrible events of seven years past, being robbed of our orchard in Gallows Heights and jailed in pitiful conditions.

And yet now, reflecting upon this news from Washington, D.C., as I sit before the fire in our cottage, I feel that those terrible events are from a different world entirely. In much the same way as those hours of bloody combat in the War or the hard years of forced servitude in Virginia are forever present but — somehow, — as removed as the muddled images from an ill-remembered nightmare.

Perhaps within our hearts is a single repository for both despair and hope, and filling that space with one drives out all but the most shadowy memory of the other. And tonight I am filled only with hope.

You will recall that, for years I vowed that I would do whatever I might to cast off the stigma of being regarded as a three-fifths man. When I consider the looks I still receive, because of my color, and the actions of others toward me and our people, I think I am not yet regarded as completely whole. But I would venture to say that we have progressed to the point where I am viewed as a nine-tenths man (James laughed heartily when I told him this over supper tonight), and I continue to have faith that we will come to be seen as whole within our lifetimes, or in Joshua's and Elizabeth's, at least.

Now, my dearest, I must say goodnight to you and prepare a lesson for my students tomorrow.

Sweet dreams to you and our children, my darling. I live for your return.

Your faithful Charles
Croton on the Hudson,
March 2, 1875

Rhyme said, 'It sounds like Douglass and the others forgave him for the robbery. Or decided to believe that he didn't do it.'

Sachs asked, 'What was that law he was talking about?'

'The Civil Rights Act of 1875,' Geneva said. 'It prohibited racial discrimination by hotels, restaurants, trains, theaters — any public place.' The girl shook her head. 'It didn't last, though. The Supreme Court struck it down in the 1880s as unconstitutional. There wasn't a single piece of federal civil rights legislation enacted after that for over fifty years.'

Sachs mused, 'I wonder if Charles lived long enough to hear it was struck down. He wouldn't've liked that.'

Shrugging, Geneva replied, 'I don't think it would've mattered. He'd think of it as just a temporary setback.'

'The hope pushing out the pain,' Rhyme said.

'That's word,' Geneva said. Then she looked at her battered Swatch. 'I've got to get back to work. That Wesley Goades . . . I've gotta say, the man is wack. He never smiles, never looks at you . . . And, come on, you *can* trim a beard sometimes, you know.'

★ ★ ★

Lying in bed that night, the room dark, Rhyme and Sachs were watching the moon, a crescent so thin that, by rights, it should have been cold white but through some malady of atmosphere was as golden as the sun.

610

Sometimes, at moments like this, they talked, sometimes not. Tonight they were silent.

There was a slight movement on the ledge outside the window — from the peregrine falcons that nested there. A male and female and two fledglings. Occasionally a visitor to Rhyme's would look at the nest and ask if they had names.

'We have a deal,' he'd mutter. 'They don't name me. I don't name them. It works.'

A falcon's head rose and looked sideways, cutting through their view of the moon. The bird's movement and profile suggested, for some reason, wisdom. Danger, too — adult peregrines have no natural predators and attack their prey from above at speeds up to 170 miles an hour. But now the bird hunkered down benignly and went still. The creatures were diurnal and slept at night.

'Thinking?' Sachs asked.

'Let's go hear some music tomorrow. There's a matinee, or whatever you call an afternoon concert, at Lincoln Center.'

'Who's playing?'

'The Beatles, I think. Or Elton John and Maria Callas doing duets. I don't care. I really just want to embarrass people by wheeling toward them . . . My point is that it doesn't matter who's playing. I want to get out. That doesn't happen very often, you know.'

'I know.' Sachs leaned up and kissed him. 'Sure, let's.'

He twisted his head and touched his lips to her hair. She settled down against him. Rhyme closed his fingers around her hand and squeezed hard.

She squeezed back.

'You know what we could do?' Sachs asked, a hint of conspiracy in her voice. 'Let's sneak in some wine and lunch. Pâté and cheese. French bread.'

'You can buy food there. I remember that. But the scotch is terrible. And it costs a fortune. What we could do is — '

'Rhyme!' Sachs sat straight up in bed, gasping.

'What's wrong?' he asked.

'What did you just do?'

'I'm agreeing that we smuggle some food into — '

'Don't play around.' Sachs was fumbling for the light, clicked it on. In her black silk boxers and gray T-shirt, hair askew and eyes wide, she looked like a college girl who'd just remembered she had an exam at eight tomorrow morning.

Rhyme squinted as he looked at the light. 'That's awfully bright. Is it necessary?'

She was staring down at the bed.

'Your . . . your hand. You moved it!'

'I guess I did.'

'Your right hand! You've never had any movement in your right hand.'

'Funny, isn't it?'

'You've been putting off the test, but you've known all along you could do that?'

'I *didn't* know I could. Until now. I wasn't going to try — I was afraid it wouldn't work. So I was going to give up all the exercise, just stop worrying about it.' He shrugged. 'But I changed my mind. I wanted to give it a shot. But just us, no machines or doctors around.'

Not by myself, he added, though silently.

'And you didn't tell me!' She slapped him on the arm.

'I *didn't* feel that.'

They laughed.

'It's amazing, Rhyme,' she whispered and hugged him hard. 'You did it. You really did it.'

'I'll try it again.' Rhyme looked at Sachs, then at his hand.

He paused a moment, then sent a burst of energy from his mind streaking through the nerves to his right hand. Each finger twitched a little. And then, as ungainly as a newborn colt, his hand swiveled across a two-inch Grand Canyon of blanket and seated itself firmly against Sachs's wrist. He closed his thumb and index finger around it.

Tears in her eyes, she laughed with delight.

'How 'bout that,' he said.

'So you'll keep up with the exercises?'

He nodded.

'We'll set up the test with Dr. Sherman?' she asked.

'I suppose we could. Unless something else comes up. Been a busy time lately.'

'We'll set up the test,' she said firmly.

She shut the light out and lay close to him. Which he could sense, though not feel.

In silence, Rhyme stared at the ceiling. Just as Sachs's breathing stilled, he frowned, aware of an odd sensation trickling through his chest, where there ought to be none. At first he thought it was phantom. Then, alarmed, he wondered if it was perhaps the start of an attack of dysreflexia, or worse. But he realized that, no, this was something else entirely, something not rooted in nerve or muscle or organ. A scientist always, he analyzed the sensation empirically and noted that it was similar to what he'd felt watching Geneva Settle face down the bank's attorney. Similar too to when he was reading about Charles Singleton's mission to find justice at the Potters' Field tavern that terrible night in July so many years ago, or about his passion for civil rights.

Then, suddenly, Rhyme understood what he was feeling: It was simple pride. Just like he'd been proud of Geneva and of her ancestor, he was proud of his own accomplishment. By tackling his exercises and then tonight testing himself, Lincoln Rhyme had confronted the terrifying, the impossible. Whether he'd regained any movement or not was irrelevant; the sensation came from what he *had* undeniably achieved: wholeness, the same wholeness that Charles had written of. He realized that nothing else — not politicians or fellow citizens or your haywire body — could make you a three-fifths man; it was solely your decision to view yourself as a complete or partial person and to live your life accordingly.

All things considered, he supposed, this understanding was as inconsequential as the slight movement he'd regained in his hand. But that didn't matter. He thought of his profession: How a tiny flake of paint leads to a car that leads to a parking lot where a faint footprint leads to a doorway that reveals a fiber from a discarded coat with a fingerprint on the sleeve button — the one surface that the perp forgot to wipe clean.

The next day a tactical team knocks on his door.

And justice is served, a victim saved, a family reunited. All thanks to a minuscule bit of paint.

Small victories — that's what Dr. Sherman had said. Small victories . . . Sometimes they're all you can hope for, Lincoln Rhyme reflected, as he felt sleep closing in.

But sometimes they're all you need.

Author's Note

Authors are only as good as the friends and fellow professionals around them, and I'm extremely fortunate to be surrounded by a truly wonderful ensemble: Will and Tina Anderson, Alex Bonham, Louise Burke, Robby Burroughs, Britt Carlson, Jane Davis, Julie Reece Deaver, Jamie Hodder-Williams, John Gilstrap, Cathy Gleason, Carolyn Mays, Emma Longhurst, Diana Mackay, Tara Parsons, Carolyn Reidy, David Rosenthal, Marysue Rucci, Deborah Schneider, Vivienne Schuster, Brigitte Smith and Kevin Smith.

Special thanks, as always, to Madelyn Warcholik.

For those readers browsing through guide books in hopes of taking a walking tour of Gallows Heights, you can stop searching. While my depiction of life in nineteenth-century Manhattan is otherwise accurate and there were indeed a number of such villages on the Upper West Side that ultimately were swallowed up by the city's urban sprawl, Gallows Heights and the nefarious doings I describe there are solely creations of my imagination. The eerie name served my purpose, and I figured that Boss Tweed and his cronies at Tammany Hall wouldn't mind if I laid a few more crimes at their feet. After all, as Thompson Boyd would say, 'It's only a question of where you put the decimal point.'

We do hope that you have enjoyed reading this large print book.

Did you know that all of our titles are available for purchase?

We publish a wide range of high quality large print books including:
Romances, Mysteries, Classics
General Fiction
Non Fiction and Westerns

Special interest titles available in large print are:
The Little Oxford Dictionary
Music Book
Song Book
Hymn Book
Service Book

Also available from us courtesy of Oxford University Press:
Young Readers' Dictionary
(large print edition)
Young Readers' Thesaurus
(large print edition)

For further information or a free brochure, please contact us at:
Ulverscroft Large Print Books Ltd.,
The Green, Bradgate Road, Anstey,
Leicester, LE7 7FU, England.
Tel: (00 44) 0116 236 4325
Fax: (00 44) 0116 234 0205

Other titles published by
The House of Ulverscroft:

GARDEN OF BEASTS

Jeffery Deaver

Paul Schumann is a mobster hitman known equally for his brilliant tactics and for taking only 'righteous' jobs. When a hit goes wrong and Schumann is nabbed, he's offered a stark choice. He can travel to Berlin and kill the man behind Hitler's rearmament scheme, and walk free forever, or be sent to the electric chair. The instant Paul sets foot in Berlin his mission goes awry. For forty-eight hours, as the city prepares for the coming Olympics, Schumann stalks Reinhardt Ernst, while a dogged criminal police officer and the entire Third Reich apparatus search frantically for the American. It's a cat-and-mouse chase, with Schumann both cat and mouse, and a man who thinks he has nothing to lose . . .

THE VANISHED MAN

Jeffery Deaver

A killer flees the scene of a homicide at a prestigious Manhattan music school and locks himself in a classroom. Within minutes, the police have him surrounded. Then a scream rings out, followed by a gunshot. The police break down the door. The room is empty. Forensic criminologist Lincoln Rhyme and his partner and lover Amelia Sachs are brought in to help with the investigation. For the quadriplegic Rhyme, it means relying on his ambitious protegee to ferret out a master illusionist, who baits them with increasingly diabolical murders. As the fatalities rise, Rhyme and Sachs must prevent a terrifying act of vengeance that could become the greatest vanishing act of all.

THE STONE MONKEY

Jeffery Deaver

Recruited to help the US Government perform the nearly impossible, Lincoln Rhyme and his partner and lover, Amelia Sachs, manage to track down a cargo ship carrying two dozen illegal Chinese immigrants, as well as the notorious human smuggler and killer known as the Ghost. But when the Ghost's capture goes disastrously wrong, Lincoln and Amelia find themselves in a race against time — to stop the Ghost before he can track down and murder the two surviving families who have vanished deep into the labyrinthine world of New York City's Chinese community . . .

THE EMPTY CHAIR

Jeffery Deaver

When criminalist Lincoln Rhyme travels to a world-famous spinal cord injuries center in North Carolina for some experimental surgery, he hopes that the operation will give him slightly more movement. He knows that it may kill him. But before he has a chance to undergo surgery, Rhyme and his asssistant Amelia are drafted in by the local police department to use their forensic skills to help find two women kidnapped by a psychotic young man known locally as the Insect Boy. A cat and mouse game through the abandoned swamps of North Carolina is to have more devastating consequences than either Lincoln or Amelia can anticipate.